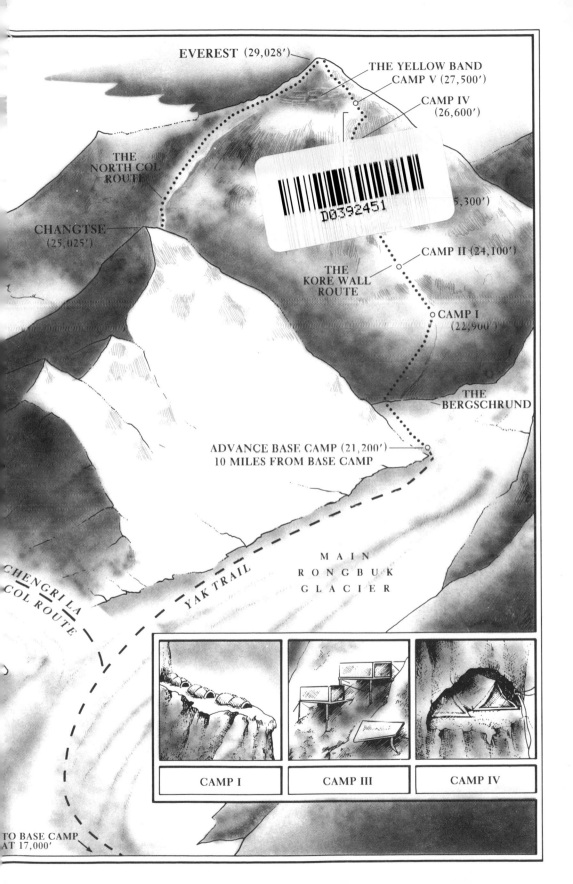

THE
Ascent

ALSO BY JEFF LONG

Duel of Eagles: The Mexican and U.S. Fight for the Alamo

Outlaw: The Story of Claude Dallas

Angels of Light

The
Ascent

A NOVEL

Jeff Long

William Morrow and Company, Inc.
New York

Library of Congress Cataloging-in-Publication Data

Long, Jeff.
    The ascent : a novel / by Jeff Long.
      p.   cm.
    ISBN 0-688-10888-1
    I. Title.
    PS3562.O4943A93   1992
    813'.54—dc20   91-48059
                                 CIP

Printed in the United States of America

First Edition

1 2 3 4 5 6 7 8 9 10

BOOK DESIGN BY J. PONSIGLIONE

To Barbara

ACKNOWLEDGMENTS

ONE WRITES THE way one solos upon a mountain, alone and yet not at all alone. I owe *The Ascent* to many people, among them Cliff Watts, Charles Clark, Michael Wiedman, and Kurt Papenfus, all physicians, all climbers. Over the years, David Breashears, Brian Blessed, Fritz Stammberger, Arnold Larcher, Matija Malezic, and Geof Childs have shared their ropes and wings with me in the Himalayas. I give special thanks to John Paul Davidson and all the members of the BBC crew of *Galahad of Everest,* and to Jim Whittaker of the 1990 International Peace Climb. Thanks also to Craig Blockwick, James Landis, Gwen Edelman, Verne and Marion Read, Rodney Korich, Jerry Cecil, and, as always, my parents for their support, and to Jeff Lowe, Mary Kay Brewster, Annie Whitehouse, Karen Fellerhoff, and Brot Coburn for their extraordinary tales. Elizabeth Crook, Steve Harrigan, Doe Coover, Pam Novotny, and Rex Hauck helped raise me from the abysses of my own making.

I will remember forever Jeanne Bernkopf, who showed me that language is spirit, and spirit, the rope with which we all inch higher. In the human rights arena, the following people and organizations provided guidance and inspiration: Michelle Bohanna, John Ackerly, Tenzin Tethong, Lisa Keary, Marcia

Calkowski, Rinchen Dharlo, Woody Leonhard, Spenser Havlick, Steve Pomerance, Matt Applebaum, Leslie Durgin, Buzz Burrell, Chela Kunasz, the International Campaign for Tibet, the Office of Tibet, the U.S.-Tibet Committee, and the Lawyers for Tibet. I am especially grateful to Cindy Carlisle and Michael Weis for their vision and tenacity. Finally, without my editor Elisa Petrini's magic these pages would be nothing but stone.

AUTHOR'S NOTE

THE KORE WALL Route is an imaginary monster, drawn in bits from the south and west faces of Makalu and glued to the north face of Everest. Himalayan veterans will also note my fiddling with certain geographical features of the region, for example the "loss" of the second road exit from the Rongbuk Valley, the blending of Shekar Dzong with the Rongbuk Monastery, and the movement of Chengri La from some twenty miles to the east. I hope these liberties won't ruin the mountain's realities.

This story is fictional, but the tragedy of Tibet is not. China's illegal occupation of Tibet constitutes one of the great crimes against humanity in this century. Having killed off one sixth of the Tibetan population over the past forty years, the People's Republic of China continues to systematically plunder and destroy the Tibetan culture, religion and environment. What was once Shangri La, however imperfect, is now a graveyard and gulag garrisoned by Chinese troops and overrun by 7.5 million Chinese colonists. A century ago, Native-Americans of the Wild West were conquered with similar violence fueled by similar ideals of racial supremacy. However, a century ago, there was no such sanctuary as the Universal Declaration of Human Rights. The twenty-first century may yet see Tibet restored to its sovereign status.

THE
Ascent

PROLOGUE—1974

FROM FAR NORTH, a breeze rushed and the forest creaked in a wave. The rescue men waited in the frozen white of their car beams, acid from too much coffee, souring among the pines. Abe had never felt cold like this. He tried warming himself with the memory of their midnight breakfast in a truck stop—the fake maple syrup, the bacon, the men's jokes to a waitress with yellow teeth—but then another breeze came through.

It had been an all-night drive to reach this dead end in the heart of Wyoming. Sometime around one the Jimi Hendrix on their airwave had surrendered to honky-tonk and then near four the cowboy ballads had fallen into dark mountain static. The road had quit at dawn and the forest had swallowed them whole and now here they were, kicking about a wild goose chase. If the dead or wounded—the lost—in fact existed, there was no evidence, none, no car, certainly no tracks, not with this fresh dusting of snow.

None of them were big men really. And yet they mustered like unshaven giants—at least to Abe's eye—stomping the snow with lug-soled boots and snorting great streams of white frost through their nostrils. They scared him, though for the most part that was because he had finally, at the age of almost eighteen, succeeded in scaring himself. For as long as he could remember, Abe had wanted to climb mountains. The trouble was he was no mountain man, just an east Texas oil patch brat, a college freshman who'd never climbed in his life except through the pages of *National Geographic* and adventure books.

A ghost of white powder cast loose from the boughs to ride the air in ripples. Snow splashed Abe in the face, then went on. Once more he was left facing the forest in a cupful of men, a watchful boy with a long blade of a face and brass wire-rims and a squared-off homecut. He was wearing immaculate white-on-white winter camouflage purchased with hurried guesswork yesterday afternoon at Boulder's army surplus store. The rest of the men were dressed in real clothes: wool and down mostly, most of it patched up and greasy from use.

Abe could tell they weren't yet finished hanging their jokes on him. It was hard saying what stung more, the justice of their mockery or the mockery itself. He didn't blame them. He looked ridiculous. He didn't belong here, that was sure. But then again, they were all outsiders. Dawn had broken an hour ago with a bright but steely winter sun. And so their engines were kept running and their headlights were on and they were pretending to get illumination and heat from the man-made beams. To some extent, they were all making believe.

At long last their wait ended. "Got him," a voice among them shouted, and the pack of men thronged the shortwave set. It was a Fish and Game pilot calling in. He'd been scouring the peaks since first light and had, he announced, just sighted one of the accident victims.

The rescue leader spoke up, a gruff, meticulous sort with a stained moustache and a white helmet stenciled with ROCKY MOUNTAIN RESCUE. "Ask him can he sweep for the other victim," he said to the radio man. "Tell him there's got to be two. Nobody climbs alone. Not in this kind of backcountry. Not in winter."

But the leader was fishing. In fact, they had no facts. No names, no locations, no missing person reports. Nothing but a drunk elk poacher's phone call about a climbing accident on a mountain in Wyoming.

The pilot answered from far off. He refused. The weather had turned and he couldn't stay. There was only the one victim. He'd looked. He approximated his coordinates for their map finding.

"Ask him the man's condition," said the leader.

"Oh, he's down there," came the thinning voice. "He's alive all right. Flopping around on the high glacier."

"Damn it," snapped the leader. "Is the man hanging on a face? Is he wandering? Is he tore up? What's his condition?"

"Wait till you see this one," the pilot said. "In all my days . . ." Their reception tore to rags.

"Repeat, over."

The voice resurfaced, small and halt. ". . . like a gutshot angel," they heard. That was it, just enough to frown at and shrug away.

"Screw that," someone said.

"Well, whoever he is, let's go save him," said the leader, and they broke the huddle to go saddle on their gear.

In all the mass of hardware and meds they off-loaded from the trucks and jeeps, there was not one single item Abe knew how to use or even handle. Abe recalculated his foolishness. He was a liability, not a savior, and his bluff was getting called. But he couldn't bring himself to confess.

He had joined up, gambling the rescue team would teach him the ropes, literally, as time passed. Afraid they would judge him too young, or his unchipped fingernails or bayou accent would expose him as a flatlander, he had entered the rescue office shyly and with his hands in his pockets. When they asked if he had experience, Abe had said yes, though carefully, keeping the *sir* off his yes, and dropping the names of some mountains in Patagonia which he figured to be safely obscure. Only two days later—yesterday afternoon—they'd phoned him in urgent need of dumb backs and strong legs. And now he could not share that this was the first snow he'd ever seen and the coldest sun he'd ever woken to. This was his first mountain.

They set out through the trees, shortcutting along a frozen river. The water was animal beneath its sturdy shell. Abe could hear it surging under the ice. Its serpentine motion came up through his boots. Here and there the river ice had exploded from the cold and its wounds showed turquoise and green.

Christmas was near and so they were undermanned, meaning everyone was overloaded. Some carried hundred-meter coils of goldline rope and homemade brake plates, others hauled the medicines and splints and the team's sole, precious Stokes litter, a crude thing made of welded airplane tubing and chicken wire.

Abe stayed alive to the other men's cues, to how they breathed and how they set their feet and leaned into their pack straps and to how they just plain managed. With every step he was reminded all over again of his hubris, for he'd loaded his pack himself, hastily and without any order, and now something was stabbing his kidneys and the bags of saline solution kept rocking him off-balance. Each boot step chastised him. He didn't belong, he didn't belong.

The sun died at noon in a gangrene sky. Shortly after, they broke the treeline, but their first clear view of the coppery mountains was undermined by dark storm clouds looming north and west. Even Abe could tell the advancing storm was going to be a killer, the fabled sort that freezes range cattle to glass and detonates tree sap, leveling whole forests.

The line of men struck north across a big plateau scoured bare to the dirt. The wind sliced low, attacking them with a fury that Abe tried not to take personally. In a matter of minutes his glasses were pitted by the high-speed sand. If not for the ballast on his back, the wind would have sent him tumbling down the mountainside.

Midway across the plateau they startled a herd of skeletal deer grazing among the stones. "They oughtn't be up here," one rescuer observed. "It's strange." The deer clattered off with the wind.

The cold day drew on. The air thinned and people quit talking altogether. They hunched like orphans beneath the overcast. Wind bleated against the rocks, a maddened sound.

As it turned out, none of the team had ever visited this region. For budgetary reasons, Wyoming was far beyond their normal range of operations. Abe was secretly gratified that the group seemed as lost as he felt. When the leader unfolded their USGS topo to match its lines with the geological chaos around them, the wind ripped his map in two and then ripped the halves from his hands. After that the group tightened ranks. The mountains took on a new sharpness against the ugly sky.

Nearing the coordinates given them by the pilot, the team reached a natural doorway that suddenly opened onto a hidden cirque of higher peaks. Despite the poisoned sunlight, it was a spectacular sight in there. To Abe it looked like a vast granite chalice inlaid with ice and snow. On every side glacial panels swept up to enormous stone towers girdling the heights. All around, men muttered their awe, and Abe thought this must be how it was to discover a new land.

And then they saw the climber.

"He's alive," someone said, glassing the distance with a pair of pocket binoculars. "There's one alive."

Abe couldn't see what they were talking about until a neighbor handed him a camera with a telephoto lens and pointed.

Perhaps a half-mile distant and a thousand feet higher, a lone figure was kneeling upon the glacial apron, unaware that rescue had arrived. His head was bare, black hair whipping in the wind. He swept one arm up and out to the storm and Abe could see him shouting soundlessly.

"That poor bastard," the man with the binoculars declared to the group, "he's talking to the mountain."

"Say again."

"I swear it. Look yourself."

Abe breathed out and steadied the telephoto lens. The mountain dwarfed the tiny figure and Abe tried not to blink, afraid of losing this solitary human to all that alien expanse.

The climber repeated his motion, the arm raised high, palm out. Abe realized that he was seeing desperation or surrender or maybe outright madness.

After a minute, the climber bent forward and Abe noticed the hole in front of his knees. It was a dark circle in the snow and the climber was speaking to it as if sharing secrets with an open tomb.

"He's praying," Abe murmured, though not so anyone could hear. But that's what he was seeing, Abe knew it instinctively. Abe was shaken, and quickly handed the camera and telephoto lens back to its owner.

"Well if he's got a buddy, I don't see him," the man with the binoculars pronounced. "One's better than none, folks. Let's go snatch him before this front hammers us in."

They hurried. Another twenty minutes of hard march over loose stone brought them to the base of the glacier. Abe edged over and stood on the ice, feeling through his boot soles for the glacier's antiquity. He'd never seen a glacier before, but knew from his readings that this plate of snow and ice had been squatting in the shadows ever since the last ice age.

The rescuers opened the big coils of rope and strapped on their scratched red-and-white helmets and their cold steel crampons. Abe watched them closely and covertly. Between bursts of wind, they heard a distant howling. It didn't sound human, but neither did it sound animal. *A gutshot angel*, Abe remembered.

With a hunger that startled him, Abe wanted to get up close to the blood. It was imperative that nothing keep him from that fallen climber. Something profound was awaiting them up there. He could tell by the way these hardened men had turned somber and frightened. Whatever it was, Abe wanted to see the sight raw, not after they had packaged it and brought it down in a litter. It was an old hunger, a simple one. Abe wanted to lose his innocence.

They set off up the glacier, three to a rope, alert for crevasses. Abe was alive to the new sensations. They stepped across a two-foot-wide crack in the field. It cut left and right across the glacier. As he straddled the crevasse, Abe filled his lungs, trying to taste the mountain's deep, ancient breath.

One of the rescuers pointed at skid tracks leading up the glacier. It reminded Abe of an animal's blood trail. "There's his fall line," the man said. "How'd he live through that?"

Abe stared at the rearing stone and ice, but it was a cipher to him. Standing here in the pit of this basin, it struck him that ascent was less an escape from the abyss than the creation of it. He peered at the heights. A girdle of hanging snow ringed the upper rim. It was an avalanche about to happen. The thought gave new urgency to his step.

As they drew near, Abe heard more distinctly the climber yelling and calling to himself. Closer still, and the climber heard them and he turned his shaggy head. Abe was surprised. The climber was a boy, no older than himself.

But even from twenty yards away, the young climber's eyes were too bright and his clothes were rags, what was left of them, and on his knees in that limbo of gray light Abe thought he looked more like the Lazarus of his grandmother's worn leather King James than a mere teenager in the wilderness.

The rescuers slowed their mechanical pace, intimidated by the strange sight. His jacket was gone and his sweater half off. Now Abe saw that the boy had pulled the clothing away himself. He had started to bare himself to the wilderness.

"You're okay now," someone offered to the climber. But

there was no trust in the climber's look, no welcome, certainly no relief. He didn't speak.

Abe saw that his white T-shirt was soaked in blood and that his left shoulder bulged with a dislocation. His left hand clutched a short ice axe, and with the blood on its silver pick, the axe looked like a medieval weapon.

The rescuers formed a wide circle around the young climber as if they had brought something dangerous to bay. His black hair hung clotted with snow and he had wolf eyes, blue and timid, and he'd been weeping.

"Hey there." Someone's cold voice. "We got you now."

"You want to lay down that axe there?" another rescuer tried. His voice was too loud, and it struck Abe, they were afraid of this boy.

The way the climber stared through them, Abe felt like a ghost. The boy didn't lay down his axe. Its handle lay loose in his gloved hand, a green wrist strap in place. Abe guessed the axe was responsible for the long, seeping gash in his opposite arm.

While the climber knelt in their center—mute now, seeming deaf, too—they discussed him, diagnosing his wounds and trying to understand what had made him so empty and menacing. But to Abe's ear, they were simply diagnosing their own fear.

"What do you think?" one of the rescuers asked another. "Hypothermia?"

"Maybe concussed. Probably. I don't see a helmet."

"One way or the other, he's about as gone as they get."

"Well what we need's his second," the leader got on with it. "Where's your second at, boy?"

Getting no answer, the leader turned away. "Joe," he said, "take some men and hunt around. There's got to be a body somewhere. Maybe it hung up higher on a rock or what have you." The one named Joe patted three men on their helmets and they started up.

The two men by Abe's side continued their evaluation. "I don't see frostbite. A puncture wound on the right thigh, though. And look at the inside of his hand. It's cut to the bone."

At last they noticed the rope tied to his waist harness. It was a beautiful blue rope with red hatching and it led directly into the hole. Abe saw the pink blood marks in the snow and recognized that the climber had stripped his hand raw pulling on the rope.

"Now we'll just take it from here, son," said a man with brushy sideburns. He edged close and gently reached for the blue rope. With a howl, the boy reacted, swinging his axe in a wild arc. He missed goring the rescuer by an inch.

And then they heard a voice.

Dreamlike, it called from far away. It could have come from another valley or from the top of the mountains. Or the bottom of a crevasse. "Daniel?" it said.

"Oh dear God," one of the rescuers breathed.

The leader whistled loud and sharp, and uphill Joe and the others came to a halt. "Down here," the leader shouted. "We found the other one."

"Daniel?" someone said. "Is that your name, Daniel?"

The boy looked at them with a mask of pure horror.

"Daniel," the rescuer pressed him. "Is that your buddy down there?"

Daniel squeezed his eyes shut and tipped back his head. His lips curled back from his teeth and he opened his throat to the sky. What came out was a terrible wrenching groan, something from a nightmare. Then his rib cage spasmed with huge, hoarse sobs.

Abe's mouth fell open at the climber's pain.

While the climber did his weeping, two of the rescuers rushed him from behind and took away his axe. They were gentle, but he was strong and they ended up jostling his disjointed shoulder and he screamed.

"Daniel," the tiny voice called out from the crevasse.

This time they heard it more distinctly and it nearly caved in Abe's heart. Someone among the rescuers whispered "no." Except for that there was silence for a minute. Even the mourning climber fell mute.

"Are you all right?" asked the voice.

It was a woman down there.

"What the hell?" someone demanded.

Now their pity hardened. Abe saw them grow blunt. Astounded. Their gentleness was gone.

"You brought a girl up here?"

The climber turned his eyes away from them and stared blankly at the hole in the snow.

"All right, boys." The leader finally rallied them. "That storm's not going away. Let's do our job."

It was one thing to disarm the boy, they discovered, something else to separate him from his blue rope. He didn't want to relinquish that bond with the voice from below. He held on to the rope with his good hand, the one with the mutilated palm. But once they had tied it off to an ice screw and cut the blue knot, Daniel gave up and seemed to go somewhere else in his mind.

He knelt there, unbudging, as if his legs were bound to the very mountain. In a sense, they were. They learned this for themselves when they lifted Daniel and laid him flat on the snow and ran their hands up and down his body. Both of his knees were shattered, both femurs fractured. Daniel seemed not to care. He seemed dead within his own body.

Abe stood back as the team frantically raced against the storm. Over where they'd laid the boy, two men labored at piecing the halves of the litter together and several arranged ropes for the carry out. Two more knelt over Daniel, fitting his legs with air splints from the Vietnam War and taping his arm across his chest. They weren't exactly rough, but they weren't gentle either. They didn't try to reduce the shoulder, just stuck him with a hit of morphine.

Abe was staggered by the dire scene, by the blood and unhinged bones and the dark clouds and the voice in the hole. Several men set to work with the blue rope.

"We're the rescue, miss," one called down into the crevasse. If she said anything in return, no one heard it, not with the wind mounting and the frenzied shouting and the clank of gear. A man hauled out long hanks of blue rope until it came taut. They tugged on the line experimentally.

"She's down there probably seventy, eighty feet," guessed the man with the hanks of blue rope in his hand.

"Get her the hell out," the leader called over. "And be quick."

Abe went over to help. Bending to take up the blue rope, he noticed it was smeared with gore, what had once been Daniel's flesh and blood. For the next five minutes he and the other men yanked and hauled on the rope, but it was fixed in place.

"You budge, miss?" the man with sideburns shouted down the crevasse. Abe put his head directly over the hole. A few feet below the surface, the ice showed dark green. Below that was blackness and Abe turned his eyes away quickly, as if the darkness were obscene.

"Nothing," said the little voice in the hole.

Abe was surprised by how clear the voice rose to him once his head was right over it. It slid up the glass walls, distinct and free of echoes, counterpointing the building storm.

They pulled again, and this time Abe thought there was progress, but it was only the rope's natural stretch. "How about that?" shouted Sideburns.

"No," said the voice.

They tried again, this time with a complicated winch system of slings and ropes and customized equipment. When that produced no results they tried a different configuration of parts and pulled again. Again it didn't work. She was jammed.

"How about it Ted?" Sideburns asked a small man.

"I'll try," said Ted. While a third man cut away the snow fringing the hole, Ted shucked his jacket, then his sweater and shirts. He tied another rope around his waist and had them lower him down the crevasse. No matter how he shimmied, though, the ice walls were too tight. He got only about five feet down into the darkness and finally called for them to pull him out. He shook his head no and dressed again.

"What on earth possessed him?" Sideburns said, glaring over at Daniel. "Now look at what it is."

"He should have known a whole lot better," someone agreed. "I wonder how old she was." Past tense. Abe cut him a side glance, but already he was trooping off, and Sideburns and the others were walking after him. Abe dumbly followed them, then realized that they were indeed abandoning the effort. He halted.

"You want me to keep trying?" he said.

The men kept walking. "She's jammed," one pronounced.

"I can start digging," Abe offered hopefully.

No one bothered answering him.

Abe saw how useless he was to them, illiterate in their universe of glaciers and mountain storms and green ice. Their very language—of brake plates and 'biners and front pointing and all the rest of it—excluded him. He felt stupid and vulnerable and put himself to work picking up whatever litter didn't blow away.

"You," Abe heard. The team leader had spotted him off by himself. "Come over here."

Abe approached. The leader handed him a small notebook and a pencil.

"I want you to go over and talk to that girl in the crevasse. Get her name, hometown, a phone number, you know, next-of-kin kind of stuff. Don't panic her. Keep her spirits up until we get things figured out. Can you do that?"

Abe nodded his head. He walked over to the black hole and knelt down in the imprints left from Daniel's knees. He peered into the darkness and licked his lips, suddenly shy.

He couldn't see this woman trapped below the surface, and she couldn't see him. All they had were words, and Abe wondered if words could be enough. He felt like a child talking to a blind person. Before he could speak, however, the woman spoke to him.

"Hey," the voice called up from the darkness. "Is everybody gone?" She didn't ask, Is anybody there? It struck Abe that she had no expectations. None. And yet she sounded calm and with no begrudging.

"No." Abe cleared his throat. "I'm here."

"Is Daniel going to be okay?"

Abe flinched at the question. Whose was this voice that put another person's welfare before her own? But at the same time, Abe felt relief. He reckoned that whoever it was down there had to be comfortable and secure, otherwise she would have sounded hysterical. Such calmness had to have a reason. Maybe she'd landed on some soft snow down inside, or simply bounced to a stop on the end of the rope. Abe's spirits picked up. Everything was going to be okay.

"Yes. He's fine," Abe answered. "What's your name?"

"Diana."

She didn't ask for his name, but Abe told her anyway. He couldn't think of anything else to say, then remembered what the leader wanted. "Where are you from?" he asked.

She said, Rock Springs.

He asked for her phone number. She gave it, but warily. When he asked her address, she suddenly seemed to lose interest in his interrogation.

"Is that the wind, Abe?" Her voice was weary and yet alive with instincts. She knew there was a storm building.

Abe lifted his face to the cold gale. They were racing both the storm and nightfall now. Any minute now, the others would come over and figure out how to pull this lonely woman out of the crevasse and they could all leave the mountain and go home.

"We'll get you out," Abe said. "Don't worry." His words sounded little as they fluttered down the hole, mere feathers. The woman didn't waste breath returning the brave assurance and Abe felt rebuked.

"Are you hurt?" Abe asked.

"I don't know." Her voice got small. "Are you going to get me out?"

"Of course. That's why we came."

"Please," she whispered.

Abe tried to understand what that might mean.

"Is there anything you want? Maybe I can lower something." Abe was thinking of food or water.

"A light, please."

Abe goggled at the simplicity of it. He tried to summon an image of being trapped down there, but nothing came. He couldn't visualize lying caught in the glassy bowels of the earth. "Yes," he said. "I'll try."

Abe stood and approached one of the rescuers, who eyed the hole in the snow before parting with his headlamp. He seemed reluctant or maybe just sad, and his attitude irritated Abe. On his return to the crevasse, Abe borrowed one of their coils of goldline rope.

"I have a light," Abe yelled down the crevasse. He felt more useful now. He was this woman's sole link to the surface. Once they rescued her, she would recognize Abe by his voice and embrace him. She would hold him tight and weep her thanks into his shoulder.

Lying on his belly, Abe flicked the headlamp on, stretched his arm and head into the hole and shined it down. He had thought to find the climber sitting far below at the bottom of a rounded well shaft. Instead the crevasse presented crystal lips no wider than a man's rib cage.

To his right and left, the crevasse stretched off into dark, terrifying rifts. Except for this accidental hole, the crevasse was covered over with snow, perfectly concealed from above. Forty feet down, the icy walls curved underneath where Abe was lying. The blue rope led down and under and disappeared from sight.

"Can you see the light?" Abe shouted.

"No," she said. "It's dark here."

Abe was glad to extract his arm and head from that awful hole and return to the surface. Even those few seconds had threatened to rob his self-possession.

While Abe talked and asked questions, he tried lowering the headlamp on the goldline rope. But the braids were new and stiff and the curve of the walls blocked passage at the forty-foot level. Abe pulled the headlamp back out.

"Can you catch it?"

"I can try."

"I'll keep the light on so you can see it coming."

Abe reached as deep as he could before letting the headlamp go. Its light ricocheted from the deeper walls, then blinked out. Abe thought the headlamp had broken in the drop. Then he heard the voice.

"Ah God," she groaned.

"Did you get it?" Abe had expected joy. She had been delivered from darkness. But as the silence accumulated, Abe realized that with the light had come the truth, and now the woman could judge her awful predicament.

"What do you see?"

There was no reply. Abe hung his head into the hole and waited but all he heard was the wind outside. The storm was ripe. He looked up at the darkening sky, then over at the rescuers bustling around the litter. They had snugged Daniel into a sleeping bag and strapped him into the litter. Some of the men were putting their packs on and they looked close to leaving. Now the team could devote all of its energies to extracting Diana.

The team leader walked over to Abe and sternly crooked his finger to draw him away from the hole. Abe pushed up to kneeling. "All right," said the leader. "We're going down now. We'll need every hand. Go saddle up."

Abe was sure he had misunderstood. "Her name is Diana," he explained. "She has a light now."

The leader exhaled unhappily. "You didn't do her any favor."

Abe didn't know what to say. "She'll be fine," he finally blustered.

"I'm glad you think so. Anyway, we're shorthanded. If we can get the litter down before this storm . . . hell, if we can get the litter down period, we'll be lucky."

Abe persisted. "We can dig her out."

"Dig her out?" The leader's eyes glazed over. "She's deep. Way too deep. That kid had no right bringing her to this."

"But if we all pull . . ."

"Look, Tex . . ." And suddenly Abe knew they knew him. He had fooled no one. "Down at the bottom, a crevasse thins into a V. You fall far enough, hard enough, and you get wedged down there. After a while your body heat melts you down tighter. Every minute that girl's alive, every breath, she's working down deeper."

"But we're not leaving her down there."

"We'll come back."

"When?"

The leader paused. His crow's-feet pinched into a fan. "When we can."

"But we have to save her." For the first time, Abe noticed how the rest of the team was shunning the hole.

"We can't, not with things how they are. Maybe later, after she starves some more, loses some of her tissue mass, maybe then. But I doubt it."

Abe shook his head—against this directive, against his vision of a human being pinned in an envelope of clear ice, broken and freezing and blind and yet still aware, still full of her own history and future. She had probably eaten a breakfast yesterday much like they had last night, had probably walked on the same river ice and spooked the same herd of starving deer and crossed this same glacier. And now they were condemning her to infinite darkness.

"Look," said the leader. The icy tails of his gray moustache waggled. "Sometimes this is how it goes. You do a triage. You figure the odds. You save the ones you can save. And you leave the ones you can't. Now it's going to be a long carry out of here. We're leaving. I want you to go saddle up. I'll go tell that girl the news."

"No," said Abe. "I'll tell her." He had the right to the last word. He had touched this blue rope. He had given this woman light and whatever terrible sights that attended.

The leader made a few thoughtful stabs at the hard snow with his ice axe, then he walked off without saying more. The rescuers at the litter had turned their backs to Abe and the hole.

Abe checked his watch, then shook it. Only twenty-five minutes had elapsed since their arrival. Surely hours had passed. He couldn't fathom what was unfolding all around him. They hoisted the litter like a coffin, three men to a side, one standing back and feeding out a safety rope in case they slipped.

The wind sucked at Abe's face, then slapped him. The first snowflakes rattled against the shell of his new white windjacket. The storm was cracking wide open. Their little motions and hopes could do nothing to hold the sky together any longer. The rescue was over, at least for the woman inside this mountain. Abe lay down by the hole to tell her so.

"Hello?" Abe called down.

There was no reply. Abe could feel the blackness down there surrounding that solitary light.

"We have to carry Daniel down," he called into the hole. "We're shorthanded, so all of us have to go. But we'll come back." He added, "I promise." Immediately Abe wished the words away. They had already broken one promise. They had come to save the survivors or carry bodies out, and they were only doing half the job. More promises could only mean more betrayal to this trapped woman.

There was still no answer, and Abe started to push away from the crevasse. Then Diana spoke.

"You're not leaving me?"

Abe shook his head no, but the word wouldn't come.

"You promised," she screamed. Then, quickly, as if chiding herself, she said, "no," and again, more firmly, "no."

"They're shorthanded . . ." Abe started again.

"It was my fault," she said. Her words came to Abe low and awkward with the cadence of a last testament. In her weariness or delirium, Abe heard something far worse than acceptance. It was a tone of surrender similar to what her rescuers were using. "Tell Daniel that. Can you hear me, Abe?"

Abe lowered his head deeper into the hole. "Yes."

Now her voice gained strength. "It was me that fell and

pulled us down. It was me. Tell him. I'm sorry. I'm sorry for what happened to him. I'm sorry for what happened to me. I know Daniel and he'll take this on. Tell him not to."

Abe wanted to protest that the fall had been bad luck and was not a matter for contrition. But maybe that was how Diana had decided to make her peace with it. "Okay," Abe said. "I'll tell him that."

"Now I want you to tell me something, Abe."

"Yes."

"How old are you?"

"Eighteen." For some reason, Abe felt compelled to add the full truth of it. "Almost."

She took a long minute. "I thought something like that," she said. And now Abe saw how they'd used him with this woman. They'd used him to buffer the horror and to interrogate her. And they'd used him for this death sentence.

"Well, Abe," she started, then fell silent. After a moment, she finished. "There's no blame on you either. Remember that."

Abe's throat clenched at that. She was forgiving him, too. He searched for something to say. At last he thought to ask her age.

"Twenty," she said. "Almost."

"You know, I can wait some more," Abe offered. "I don't mind." Until he spoke it out loud, the thought hadn't occurred to him. He could spend an hour here, then race down to catch the others who would be moving slow with the bulky litter. And if he could spend an hour, why not two?

Diana didn't give him a chance. "Is that wind bringing a storm?" she asked.

"The storm's here," Abe said.

"Then get out of here." There was courage in her voice, but hysteria, too. Then she screamed his name. She invoked it. "Abe," she cried.

She needed him to stay. At least until they freed her, this woman wanted Abe with her whole heart. That was more than he'd ever known with a woman.

"I'm here," he replied. "I'm not leaving."

By staying Abe would make himself hostage to his own promise. By staying he would force the rescue team to return and acknowledge the life in this pit of ice. Elated by his decision,

Abe clambered to his feet. He caught up with the leader as the litter team trudged downslope.

"I'm staying with her," Abe announced.

The leader wasted no words. His broad face darkened. He took one step closer and shoved Abe hard in the chest, knocking him to the snow. "You damn cowboy," he said. "I don't take threats."

Abe wasn't hurt by the blow, only surprised.

"It's no threat," Abe said. But it was, clearly. And now he saw that he threatened their tranquility. They had already reconciled themselves to their forsaking the woman. The rescuers were good and decent men, that went without saying. But by staying, Abe seemed to expose them as something less or different or just more complicated.

"Get your pack. Or leave it, I don't care. But get your ass down this mountain. I don't want you on this mountain. I don't want you on this team," the leader yelled over the wind. "You don't know anything."

Without that last insult, Abe might have obeyed.

One of the rescuers, an older man with bad knees, came gimping up to see what the disturbance was about. "The cherry thinks he's staying," the leader said to the older man. "He thinks he's going to save the day."

Now Abe was angry. "You didn't leave her food or water. You didn't even talk to her."

"That's because she's already dead."

"But she's not."

The older man took a minute to study Abe's earnest face. There was no friendliness in his look, but no hostility either. He was measuring Abe the way he would a mountainside or an approaching storm or any other obstacle. "Leave that poor girl alone," he counseled Abe. "There's not a thing we can do now except let her go. Have some mercy."

Abe heard the logic there, but he had decided. "No sir," he said.

"Listen to me. All you'll do is torment her. With food and water, she could drag on for days. Don't do that to her."

"That's not the point," Abe said. "If it was me . . ."

"If it was you, you'd pray to God I had a gun to finish you quick."

Abe shrugged. He was afraid to argue because he knew they were probably right. But he was staying.

"I admire your chivalry," the older man said, and Abe blushed because the man was talking about naïveté. "Just the same, you'll put everybody at risk all over again, and all to rescue you. Not her. She's gone. Now come on with us."

"No sir."

"Damn it," the leader blew. "You see?"

"I don't want to leave her either," the older man said. "If you ask me, it ought to be that one over there"—he jerked a thumb at the litter—"who's stuck in the hole. As far as I'm concerned, he as good as killed that girl. All the same, it's her who stays and him that gets saved."

"There's no right or wrong in the mountains," the leader added. "There's just whatever happens."

"What's your name?" the older man asked.

"Abe Burns."

"Well, Abe, if we were down in the World, I'd have you tied up. But we don't have the manpower to carry you out. So that's no good. All we can do is rely on you to do what's right."

"Yes sir," Abe said. "I'm trying."

"Quit your jacking off," the leader shouted. "We got an avalanche overhead and a storm and a hurt man. And no time for you to get a hard-on for a dead woman."

Abe didn't hesitate. He knocked the leader backward onto his pack and would have kicked him, too, except he had on crampons and the teeth would have cut the man.

"Jesus," the older man hissed at the leader, "Jesus." Then he turned to Abe. "You know, you can't save her."

"I don't care," Abe admitted.

"Then why?"

Abe didn't answer. He couldn't.

The older man looked around at the peaks. "Have it your way," he said. "I just wish you wouldn't do this to yourself."

"It's your funeral," the leader cursed Abe, struggling to his feet. He pointed at the hole. "She's already had hers."

The older man shouted the litter crew to a halt two hundred yards down the glacier and Abe trailed him down. The team set down the wounded man, who was delirious with the morphine and warmth. The rescuers all went through their packs, donating food and an extra sleeping bag and a bivouac tent and a little kerosene stove for melting water. They did it quickly, with little respect for Abe but no discourtesy. They thought him a fool, that was plain, but no one said it out loud. They simply left him their surplus. To a man, the rescuers were sullen. Clearly they did not relish carrying Daniel down at the expense of the woman in the crevasse. But the decision had been made. One went so far as to wish Abe well. Then they were gone.

Abe trudged back up the slope with the supplies. In all, their charity weighed about twenty pounds, and suddenly that seemed very little against the dark mass of storm and twilight.

Abe lay the things beside the crevasse and assembled the bivouac tent as best he could before the wind blew everything away or the snow buried it or he got too cold. He set the tent door inches from the mouth of the crevasse, which made for an awkward entrance. But it would facilitate communication, and that was the whole point. Once inside the tiny tent and burrowed into the sleeping bag, Abe felt like he was the one trapped. Only then did he call down into the hole and tell Diana what he'd done.

The woman didn't answer. Not a whisper issued up from the crevasse.

"Diana?" he called. Abe had prepared himself for resistance, which was why he'd waited to set camp before announcing his presence. Her silence confused him.

"Well, I'm here," Abe said.

Hours passed. The storm swallowed them alive. What light remained was scooped away by the wind.

Abe fell asleep and began dreaming he'd fallen into the crevasse. He couldn't move his arms or legs and it was hard to breathe except in shallow birdlike bursts. He woke from the dream to find himself smothering in complete darkness. The tent had collapsed beneath a heavy mantle of snow and his limbs were lodged tight inside the cocoon of the sleeping bag.

It took all Abe's strength to jackknife his body up and down and punch the tent and himself free of the snow. Frenzied with claustrophobia, he managed to claw open the door. There he lay with his bare head extending into the blizzard, gulping huge, searing lungfuls of air and snowflakes, overjoyed to find himself free of the dream, even if not the mountain.

It was only then that he heard singing. The song was eerie

and distant and sounded like nothing human, and Abe guessed
the wind was playing through the high towers. That or some
animal had been driven up from the forest. Or spirits were on
the loose.

Abe listened harder. Between the howl of wind and the
hiss of corn snow guttering off his tent wall, he found a rhythm
and a tune and a sunniness to it. It was a Beach Boys song.

Even as he listened, Abe felt the storm layering him with
snow all over again. He shook the tent hard but carefully, for
after all his snaking around there was no telling where the
crevasse lay now. Rooting through the folds of the tent, Abe
found a flashlight and shined it outside. He was horrified and
at the same time enchanted by how the falling snow actually
devoured his light. The beam reached a few feet beyond his
little nylon cave, then vanished.

It took him several minutes to locate the crevasse. The hole
had closed to a small circle, as if sealing its catch away from the
world for good. Still lying inside his sleeping bag and tent, Abe
edged closer. The singing became more distinct, but that only
made it more alien because Diana wasn't singing real words,
only jibberish.

Now Abe found the ice axe they had left him. In thrashing
around, he'd landed on top of the axe. The pick had slashed
his sleeping bag and down feathers had spilled everywhere.
There was blood on the metal head, and for a bad moment Abe
thought he'd cut himself and was too cold to feel the wound.
Then he realized this was Daniel's axe and Daniel's blood.

Reaching his arm outside, Abe poked at the edges of the
hole to widen it. He began chopping, methodically cutting away
at the snow even though the debris poured down the crevasse,
adding to Diana's misery. "I'm sorry," he shouted to her, "I'm
sorry." It was for himself that Abe cut at the snow. He needed
to keep open this doorway to the underworld. He was afraid to
lose contact, quite certain that without Diana's company, he
would never make it through this ordeal.

When Abe had finally cut down to the blue rope and gained
proof of his companion, he rested. He slept. When his eyes
opened again, it was day, but it might as well have been night
still. The storm was raging more fiercely than before. Abe
couldn't see anything outside the tent and he couldn't see anything inside it, either, without the flashlight.

Abe turned to rebuilding his tent. Section by section, he propped the walls up with the broken poles and taught himself to rustle the fabric every few minutes to shed the snow. And all the while, he listened to Diana's mindless singing.

"You're going to make it," Abe shouted down the crevasse. He found some cheese and a chunk of wet bread and a plastic bottle of mostly frozen water. "You want some food?" he yelled.

Diana made no answer. She just sang on and on.

While Abe ate and drank, he listened. It was essentially the same tune over and over. The words weren't real words. They were sounds to mark a path. Locked in place, Diana was circling around and around. Soon the vortex would suck her into its deepest part. Abe knew he was listening to the sound of death.

Finally Abe joined in the singing. He'd heard this song many times before, but he couldn't remember what the words were either. With the woman's same abandon, Abe threw his voice out into the void all around them.

After a while Diana seemed to notice the extra voice. Somewhere in her benighted skull, Abe's singing freed Diana to depart from the song and actually talk. She began to emit bursts of story. Abe labored to hear what she had to say. It was a freewheeling autobiography, woven together from memories and fictions and pleas for her mother's comfort. It made Abe weep sometimes, and other times just bored him.

The stormy day passed. Night moved in again.

As the darkness stretched out and Abe drifted into delirious catnaps, it was hard to tell what was real anymore. He grew colder and a little crazy himself, and it was hard to know what was even spoken. Much of what Abe heard he may have imagined. Diana may or may not have been a college student with a bad job and a drafty trailer-home and allegiance to some crazy woman. She seemed to have three brothers named John and Wes and Blake, which Abe began to suspect because those were his own uncles' names. Her talk about mountains was probably real, because she described spring wildflowers Abe had never heard of. She wanted to climb Everest someday, though that might as easily have been Abe's overlay. Abe gave up trying to keep the woman—or himself—lucid with questions or dialogue.

Abe finally concluded that the name of her dogged savior was completely lost to her, for she'd quit saying his name altogether. He accepted that she had ceased to understand he was lying on the surface above or even that she was caged inside the mountain. Abe's presence had not loaned one ounce of dignity to her long and ugly dying, and he resigned himself to anonymity. It was then, during a lull in the gale, that she cried out.

"I love you," she yelled.

Abe knew she meant someone else, yet all he could think to reply was the same. "I love you," he shouted into the crevasse, and so she wouldn't think it was just her own echo, he added, "Diana." Her name sank down the hole, a pebble dropped into the ocean.

But something happened. A single word came drifting back up the hole. "Abe," she spoke.

The storm and the waiting went on for a very long time. Abe's watch had come off in his struggles, so he had no idea how much time passed, only that he and his invisible lover were both losing their faculties and blurring their memories and mixing in the same dream.

At one point Abe turned his palms up and noticed that he'd rope-burned the pads down to the white gristle. He didn't remember doing that, but the snow was pink with blood around the blue rope, and the pink was fresh.

In the end, there was silence.

Dawn never broke, but an exhausted light did finally seep into the sky. Overnight, Abe had taken ill from the water or maybe from the storm itself and the cold and the sounds, and his tent had collapsed again. He was very cold and thirsty and tired. But the storm had passed. The wind had quit. He flapped open the tent door. The crevasse had pinched nearly shut. Nothing more could be done.

"Hello," he called into the crevasse. The word emerged as blue frost.

There was no answer. No more song, no more jibberish. Maybe she was still alive, just mute now, eyes wide, a zombie pinned in its crypt for the rest of time.

Abe shook loose from the snow and wormed out of the tent. The night and day and night had bled him of his strength. It took his full concentration just to stand up. His parka was soaked and frozen. His feet were dead blocks.

He faced the crevasse, which had puckered shut again. The hole was only a few inches across now. The blue rope was buried deep again. The earth was sealing over. "Good-bye," Abe croaked. He said it to a memory, to the place itself. He said it to a deep part of himself.

Without another thought, Abe abandoned the tent and the torn sleeping bag and his pack, which had blown away anyway. The water bottle was frozen solid and useless. The thought of food turned his stomach. He simply backed away from the hole and faced downhill and let gravity herd him off the glacier.

Abe stumbled and kicked and plowed his way out of the high cirque and across the plateau, which was now scalloped with drifts like a hard, white sea.

He descended into the forest.

The path they had taken up the frozen river was buried under two and three feet of snow, but he was patient. Every time he seemed lost, Abe stopped and listened for the water running through its deep veins. He followed that song, humming to himself.

It took all day. Not once did Abe sit down, because then he would have lain back and disappeared into the dream. He reached the trailhead at dusk and started down the road into night.

Abe kept moving simply because he could. There was no other reason. Survival was the furthest thing from his mind. Night came on.

The path turned black. The forest walled him in, squeezing him tight. After some time Abe couldn't be sure his legs were still moving. He felt motionless and suspended.

Just before dawn on the next morning a single bright light appeared like a hole in the darkness. It was a big truck with one broken headlight and it was filled with rescuers. While the engine idled, Abe stood transfixed by the hard white light. One by one the rescuers emerged to touch him.

When they laid him down, it was tentatively, not quite certain of his reality. They had been on their way to retrieve Abe or Abe's body from the cirque. They dressed the wounds in his hands and started on IV and zipped him into a sleeping bag in the back of the truck and started the long road back to Boulder. The roof rocked back and forth.

Two rescuers sat beside Abe to monitor his vital signs and pour him full of soup and coffee and herbal tea, whatever hot liquids the group could muster. Abe's voice was nearly gone from dehydration and the raw cold and his singing, so they

filled his silence answering questions they thought he might
have asked.

Daniel was in intensive care, they said. He had gotten very
agitated at the hospital and kept repeating the woman's name
until a nurse explained that someone had stayed at the crevasse.
After that he'd dropped into deep sleep. He had multiple fractures, but the doctors said Daniel would recover.

"That's the good news," said the man pumping up a blood
pressure cuff on Abe's arm. "The bad news is the girl. She was
a dropout from the university at Laramie. She moved back to
Rock Springs to take care of her sick mom, Alzheimer's or
something. Anyway, that's where she hooked up with this fella
and he got her into the climbing."

"She was getting good. But nowhere close to good enough
for that wall," the second rescuer said. "I guess the boyfriend's
some local legend. First ascents all around here. That's what this
was supposed to be. A new route. New wall. New mountain."

"Some wedding present," the first man said.

"Yeah, that, too. They were supposed to get married. In
the spring."

Abe could tell they found their information poignant and
moving. But he was confused.

The two rescuers exchanged a glance.

"She's not still alive up there?" one asked in a low voice.

Abe looked from one to the other with blank eyes, wondering if he'd done something wrong.

"Who?" he whispered timidly.

CHRISTMAS EVE—1991

ABE REACHED HOME bloodstained and bone weary, with the song of sirens still screaming in his ear. Two back-to-back twenty-four-hour shifts had left him so empty it took a full minute just to recognize the living room as his own. He needed some serious downtime, a bed, even just a flat spot on the floor so long as it was out of the way and dry and warm and quiet. But he knew there was no way.

This was the afternoon of Christmas Eve and Jamie had charged him with making his special sour cream enchiladas for the dinner party that night and there were still gifts to wrap and the faucet to fix. Abe found some orange juice in the refrigerator and the aspirin in the cupboard. He wondered why. Why fix it. He'd promised her a long time ago, but the faucet was really the least of their worries anymore. Besides, drop by drop, the slow leak had come to provide a clockwork to their discontent. Like an old man, he had grown used to hearing it in the middle of their cold nights.

Abe pulled out his toolbox from under the stairs and rummaged for a pair of vise grips. He rattled the eighteen-cent washer inside its little white bag, then went up to the bathroom.

By the time Jamie returned from work, the faucet would be silent. She probably wouldn't even notice.

Abe's pager started beeping.

Abe sighed. He laid down the wrench. It had been too much to hope for that the street would be done with him. Even without this snow in the air and glare ice on the highways, there was something about the holiday season that always invited extra chaos. More car accidents, more cardiac arrests, more domestic violence and suicide attempts. More loneliness. More need. More overtime. So much for Christmas Eve. Jamie would say nothing when he told her. She would simply turn away and busy herself with the salad or eggnog or something else. Anymore that's how they managed together.

Abe straightened and stretched and there in the mirror, move for move, the cannibal rose up into the electric light. Long ago, twelve years next May, back when he'd first become a paramedic, Abe had seen the cannibal inhabiting his universe of ambulance crews and emergency room staff and cops and firemen. Since calling it burnout only half described the living deadness, the offtime wags had cooked up the cannibal, this voracious eater of the heart. Abe had sworn to leave the pain business before it got to him, but here he was, thirty-five years old and still riding shotgun for Boulder Ambulance and packaging disasters for Rocky Mountain Rescue. And the cannibal had caught him.

He knew, because of late his work had turned into a sort of cheap pornography, less for its voyeurism than for its repetition and the predictability of his responses. When his pager went off, when the siren turned on, when he smelled the blood, Abe could almost stand back and watch his body react—patching and splinting and injecting the afflicted. Jamie saw it in him, too, though on another level. "You don't love me," she pitied him. "You don't know how to love anymore."

Abe turned off the pager and called in.

"You ever hear of some guy named Peter Jorgens?" asked the dispatcher.

Abe hadn't.

"He's called about you twice today. A pretty pushy guy. He's in some kind of major sweat. Says there's no time for reference letters. Some kind of emergency. He makes me hook whoever's closest to the phone and he pumps them for your rep, your experience, all that."

"Med school," Abe said. Like the faucet, that was something else he was finally getting around to. Of the four schools he'd applied to, two still seemed interested. He wondered which school Peter Jorgens would be with and what kind of war stories the other medics had probably fed the man, not that Abe was worried. He had a good reputation. Better than good. He'd seen some of the references people gave him and they were good. They called him their best, with over a dozen years of experience in both the city and the mountains. Rock, snow or ice, day or night, he was an all-weather, all-terrain, one-man scoop. Someone had stenciled ST. BERNARD on Abe's locker at work. Underneath someone else had taped a piece of movie poster: *Terminator*. A lot of death, as well as life, had passed through Abe's hands in the last dozen years.

"He just called again," said the dispatcher. "Says he needs you to contact him. And not tomorrow. Tonight. Right now."

All Abe could guess was that one of the schools had accepted him and wanted to give him the word before Christmas closed their offices. What would Jamie say? he wondered. Probably not much, they were so wounded by each other. Once upon a time, he'd thought they would celebrate just such a moment. But those days were gone.

Abe placed the call to an area code he didn't recognize.

A game-show voice answered, female. "U.S.U.S. Expeditions," she singsonged. "Merry Christmas."

Abe's anticipation fell to pieces. U.S.U.S. Expeditions? This was no med school. They were peddling something, American flags or adventure-travel tours or what? Worse, they were peddling on his one night off and after snooping on him at work.

"May I help you?" the woman said.

Tired, his temper short, Abe nearly hung up. On second thought he decided to confront their trespass.

"Yes." He made his voice flat and statutory, a lawyer's trick. He wanted their full attention, their fear of litigation or at least a promise to stay out of his life. "I want you to tell Peter Jorgens . . ."

"Oh, wait," she interrupted. "Pete just walked in the door. You can talk to him directly. May I ask who's calling?"

Abe gave his name. He checked his clock. Thirty seconds. That's all this got.

"Burns?" a hearty man boomed. "Abraham Burns? Do I have an offer for you."

"Yeah, well I started to tell your secretary . . ."

"Wife," Jorgens said, "that was my wife. She didn't tell you yet, did she? I want to be the one."

The clock showed forty seconds gone. Abe meant to register at least one profanity before hanging up on the man. "Listen," Abe tried again.

"Are you sitting down? It's the kind of thing that makes strong men weak," Jorgens barreled on. "Even a bull like you."

Abe said "piss off" and hung up. He got as far as the hallway before the phone rang. It was Jorgens.

"At least hear me out," the man said.

"Whatever you're selling . . ."

"No, no." Desperation came over the phone line. "This isn't for contributions. Our war chest is full. We're totally solvent. We're going. And we want you to go with us. We need you."

Abe was more mystified than annoyed by the man's persistence. This had to be the worst sales pitch in history. "Hurry up," Abe growled.

"You're the one," Jorgens said. "Your buddy Corder said so."

The name Corder tickled his memory, but not enough. Abe decided to finish this.

"Look, mister," he told Jorgens. "It's Christmas Eve, and you're not making any sense." Sometimes that worked on the Gomers, the get-out-of-my-emergency-room riffraff destined for detox. A single moment of definition sometimes provided them a floor to stand on. The screamers would shut up. The wild men would calm down. But it only seemed to inspire Jorgens.

"You've heard of us," he declared. "The U.S. Ultimate Summit Expedition? The Nordwand '92 team? That's us. We're in the latest Rolex commercial."

"Rolex commercial?"

"The one with the ice climber, the backdrop . . ."

Abe's amusement expired. "Time's up," he said. "Don't call here again."

"Wait," Jorgens shouted. He sounded shocked. "Everest. I'm talking about Everest."

It worked, that single word.

"Everest?" Abe breathed.

Now they started over again.

"My God." Jorgens sounded chastened. "I thought we'd lost you before we even had you." Abe could tell Jorgens was the nasty sort who believed in jumping out at people to test their reflexes. Maybe next time he'd remember this backfire.

"I better start from square one," Jorgens said. "You've really never heard of us?"

They were a team of Americans going to the Tibetan side of Mount Everest. Three days ago, their physician had fallen on a training climb and rebroken an old rugby ankle. Almost on the eve of its departure for Asia, the U.S. Ultimate Summit Expedition, a.k.a. Everest Nordwand 1992, was suddenly without medical backup. No major expedition could afford to go without a doctor, not to a country as remote as Tibet. But time was short. Their departure date was early February. A burst of phone calls had failed to produce a single physician in all of North America willing to climb to five miles high, commit to a hundred-day absence, and leave in five weeks.

"I've hunted hard these last three days. Days and nights," Jorgens said. "I've been calling hospitals all across the country. I even hired a computer search of med students and physician assistants and paramedics. And it all comes down to you."

"You need a doctor," Abe observed. "An M.D. Not a paramedic." He was too realistic about mountain medicine to be modest. Whoever they took along would have to be a walking hospital, capable of tackling everything from tropical parasites to compound fractures.

"We've got you," Jorgens said.

"I've never been to the Himalayas." As much as he wanted to shout *Yes, I'm your man,* these things had to be said. If they were going to disqualify him, he wanted it to be now, not halfway up a mountainside. Not even next week. If there was any chance they would extinguish this dream, he wanted it over with. "And you're weak on ice experience," Jorgens said. "Don't worry, I've asked. But you can lead 5.11 on rock, which is solid, not hot. Then again, I'm not looking for any more ninja, Mr. Burns. All we need is a good bones man who can make house calls to eight thousand meters. That's you."

"What about the mountain?"

Jorgens filled him in. Over the last ten years, three different teams had attempted the route, a vertical chimera of rock and ice known as the Kore Wall. It was known among mountaineers as a severe creation—9,000 vertical feet from top to bottom—that approached the summit straight on, a direct or *direttisima* up the right center of the vast North Face. The first try back in 1984 had been all British, with the exception of one American climber. After pioneering to 27,000 feet and surmounting most of the geological barriers, they'd gotten mauled and surrendered. In '89, half of a New Zealand expedition had vanished on the upper reaches in a storm. And last spring, two Japanese and a Sherpa had been killed by an avalanche.

"So it's the Kore Wall three, climbers zip," Jorgens finished. "She's had a lot of suitors. But we own her cherry."

Abe didn't trust the overstatement.

"What about other lines?" Abe asked. He was already trying to visualize alternate retreat routes for injured climbers, because that would be his job. But Jorgens took his question to imply second-choice lines for ascent.

"Not interested," Jorgens said. "There's three other routes on the north side, but they've all been done, especially the North Col. Frankly our team's too damn good to be pulling a repeat. It's the Kore Wall or bust."

Like most climbers, Abe had dreamed of Everest, tired and exaggerated as it was. The mountain had handled too many people to deserve coveting, yet no one could erase the memory of her glorious virginity. He'd wanted to go to the big mountain for so long that the very idea had come to defeat him. But the Kore Wall?

"Four of our team's already in Kathmandu," Jorgens said. "The rest of us leave in thirty-four days. That's five weeks minus a day," Jorgens said. "Can you handle that?"

"I could try," Abe said.

"Is that the broader affirmative then? You can appreciate my need to know. Are you with us, son?"

Abe knew ex-military when he heard it. Emergency work abounded with it: cops, medicos, firemen. He had nothing against hierarchies and their jargon, but life was too short to spend three or four months at high altitude fighting cabin fever with a commander in chief. Jorgens was handing him Everest on a silver platter, and Abe wanted it. But some inner radar told Abe that if he didn't back this man off right now, even just a little, then he might as well not go. And so, though he meant yes, Abe said maybe.

"I'll have to call you back," Abe said, For extra weight, and just to prick Jorgens's chauvinism, he added, "My wife gets final say." Then he hung up.

Jamie wasn't his wife, but Abe figured "girlfriend" would never carry enough weight with a man like Jorgens. He'd once asked Jamie to marry him, but the institution hadn't worn too well with her. She'd already been married once, too young and to the wrong man. She had borne a baby boy. Her husband had disappeared with the child. Jamie had fallen into emptiness.

Abe had met her a few years after that tragedy. It seemed like a long time ago. The first time she told him her story, Abe had determined never to speak to her again. He had enough doubts about why he did what he did for a living without taking on a victim for a lover. But she had eyes like black magnets. And Abe found himself in love.

It was one of those hospital hookups, the ambulance cowboy and the angel of mercy. She was an R.N. up in maternity, slender and quiet as a flower. Between his reserve and hers, it was a marvel they'd ever gotten beyond hello. On the day they started living together in his Victorian townhouse with the skylight over the bed, they'd made a house rule: No shoptalk. She wouldn't talk about birth. He wouldn't talk about death. As it turned out, all their problems lay in between.

Over the years, Abe had watched other professional samaritans grow to distrust their own charity. With Jamie he tried to be careful to keep the kindness of rescue out of the kindness of love, only to discover she was beyond rescue anyway.

Every night he helped her bury the lost child all over again. Every morning he helped dig up her hopes for the new day. She had a habit of sleeping curled in a fetal ball and sometimes crying in her sleep. It was not the best life.

They had grown apart. Abe blamed her losses. She blamed him. "You never let me smile," she accused him. He wondered if that could be true. He wanted her happiness and had said so. But that left him uncertain about what it was he wanted for himself. Life with the drama stripped out and the siren turned down, that much for sure. Life without the noise, without the losses. Part of him believed she had worn him out.

Jamie got home from the hospital at 5:30, out of sorts over a new boss and rumors of a pay cut. Abe gave her a few minutes to sit on the couch and unwind. Then he broke the news about the Ultimate Summit invitation. She took it well.

"I'd be gone a hundred days, maybe more," Abe said.

"You really want this, don't you?" She was decent about subduing her relief. This was probably the good-bye they'd been waiting for. There were no tears and she didn't say leave. She said go. "You need this."

Abe was grateful for her dispassion. On a sudden impulse, he wanted to convey to her just how important the mountain was to him.

"I can still remember, I was seven years old when the first Americans to climb Everest came to the White House. JFK was there in the Rose Garden and he welcomed them like they were astronauts. I saw it in the papers and my mother cut the photo of it out and taped it to the refrigerator door."

Abe paused and looked at Jamie to see if she cared about any of this. She was wiggling her toes and winnowing her black hair with long fingers. Her interest seemed more than polite.

"That photo stayed up on the refrigerator all week long, eye-level, and for a whole week I imagined what it must be like up there. And then my father came home. You know, rig work, one week on, one off."

Now Jamie spoke, perhaps to abbreviate his tale. "And your dad took you on his knee and he said, 'Someday, Abe, someday.'"

"No," Abe said. It was his father who had first traced constellations for Abe, flat on their backs pointing between the fireflies, and taught him how to build a fire, how to whittle and read a compass. But all of that had stopped when his father lost part of one hand to a wellhead accident. After that he'd quit sharing the stars. "No. He took the photo off the refrigerator door."

When he was done, she said, "I feel sad, Abe."

Abe swallowed. "I haven't said yes, yet," he said.

"No," she said. "That's not what I mean. It's just, I can remember when you used to talk like this. Excited. Alive."

Thinking she wanted to hear more, Abe went on. "I would bring you a fossil," he said. He told her about how climbers would fill their pockets with the sea fossils that riddled the summit rock band. They had jewelers make the fossils into earrings and pendants for gifts.

"You need to go," she said. "Now I've said it twice. You should go and climb your mountain. Is there something else you want me to say?"

"I'm afraid of losing you," Abe said. He didn't mean to be that blunt. They had so many reasons to separate, but had never had the hate or anger to do it with. How strange that a cold faraway chunk of stone was going to give logic to their parting. He felt close to tears and at the same time freed.

Jamie didn't reply that she was afraid of losing him. Instead she said, "I'm afraid of you losing me, too, Abe. But your staying won't change that. As for your going? I don't know. Or maybe I do know." She stopped. "Do we have to do this tonight?"

That was the closest she'd ever come to telling him her truth, that through their three years together it was she who had protected him. Abe heard what Jamie meant and it startled him because he'd never seen himself as someone needing protection.

"Call the man back," Jamie urged. She leaned forward and kissed him. "And smile. I'm happy for you."

"I have to go get an onion at the store," Abe remembered. "A red onion." He was stalling. He wanted more time to think.

"I'll go to the store," Jamie said. She seemed to have thought about things enough. "You make your call."

Abe gave it another half-hour before calling Seattle. By then Jorgens had recovered his gruff poise. He sounded disgruntled that the team's new medic didn't gush thanks, but Abe didn't see this as a favor. It was a job, and if it was an opportunity, too, then it was going to be an earned one. Jorgens said, "Welcome on board."

"Tell me what needs doing," Abe said.

"Do you have a fax machine?"

Abe didn't.

"First thing, day after tomorrow, go rent one. You've got some catching up to do."

Abe didn't waste time being thrilled. He marked five weeks on his calendar and got on with it. He had to get immunized against eight different diseases, obtain a passport, read and memorize thirty-seven monographs and books on high altitude medicine, buy a small fortune of personal gear, and train for the most extreme route on the highest mountain on earth.

Abe had developed a habit of tidiness in approaching new terrain, and that included the names of things. He'd always assumed Kore was Japanese or Chinese or Tibetan for north. It sounded Oriental, and the Japanese had spent a number of lives trying to climb the route in '90. Finally, most big mountain routes were named prosaically for their geographic features: the North Face, the West Ridge, and so on. But he was wrong. In an article about the New Zealand attempt three years ago, he found the briefest of etymologies. Kore was another name for Persephone. Kidnapped by Pluto and taken into cold darkness to become the queen of Hades, the goddess was permitted to surface into the sunshine six months of the year. It was an apt name for a north-facing wall that saw the light of day only with the approach of spring. According to the article, a climber on the initial British expedition had baptized the route.

Near the end of his thirty-four-day whirlwind, Abe received a two-pound package. Compiled by the expedition's former physician, it contained detailed medical histories of all the members. Abe was just leaving to grab a quick few miles of trail running on Mount Sanitas, but when the package came he bagged the run, kicked off his shoes, and put on a pot of coffee. This would be his first look at the people whose health and lives were his mission.

Inside the package were ten manila file folders with a passport photo paperclipped to the inner flap of each. Abe cleared a corner of his kitchen table and stacked the files where they wouldn't fall. One by one, Abe drew these people to him, matching their pictures with their names and telephone voices—the few he'd spoken to—and trying to read from their eyes and dimples and haircuts what kind of spirits moved their cages of bone and flesh. He stared at their photos and tried to guess how they would laugh and cry, or if they would. Then he lifted their skin aside and peered at the machinery, translating their medical histories into makeshift biographies, finding here and there broken bones, a missing thyroid gland, three abortions, a heart with murmurs, a case of diabetes, and the secretly mentioned venereal diseases.

You are my flock, Abe thought in his kitchen. Their mortality was abundant. Beneath their muscles and tanned squints and high-flying grins and their dreams like wings, these eagles were human, and they would need him.

There was only one surprise in that stack of folders, really. It came in the next-to-last file. Abe opened it as he'd opened the others, casually, and he looked at the photo, not even the name.

It was Daniel.

Abe had not seen Daniel since that once upon a time on the glacier seventeen long years ago. He lifted the photo closer, disbelieving. Here was that same black Irish brow, those same Lazarus eyes and the cheekbones and unsmiling laughlines. The boy had grown into a man. His features had gravity now, though the wildness was still evident. The blood was washed from his hair, of course, and life had etched his forehead.

"Corder, D. W.," Abe read aloud from the file, forcing the conviction. He laid the folder open on the stack of others.

For a few minutes, Abe sat stunned by the coincidence, then it caught up with him. He had a connection to this man, so of course they would meet. Now or later, standing in line at a grocery store or walking down a sidewalk or climbing a mountain. The only real surprise was that they had not met before.

Then it caught up with him, what Jorgens had said in their first conversation: *Your buddy Corder said so.* This was Corder then. *You're the one.*

For a time, Abe had liked to believe that he and Daniel had been orphaned by the same event and that they had been bound by the same disappearance. But that had just been his way of not making the event answer for itself, a chore that he'd conveniently heaped onto his other, this twin, Daniel.

After a while, Abe had dismantled that imagined fraternity. For one thing, it was bizarre. And for another, Abe had held the hands of too many patients who in their fear and pain had raved with his own confusion about the falling rock or the car or the bullet or the cancer, whatever it was, to believe death had any value.

They had talked to a ghost, he and Daniel, but that didn't mean they had to be haunted for the rest of time. For his part, Abe had finally made himself be done with it all. After recovering from his own ordeal, Abe had avoided revisiting that fateful range in Wyoming, never even learning the name of Daniel's mountain. Abe had closed the whole thing off. He had sealed the voice in the crevasse beneath seventeen years of daily happenstance.

Yet here was Daniel again. He wondered why the man should remember him now, so many years later. Was this expedition some sort of payback? Or was Daniel perhaps still haunted, still needing rescue? Or just curious about that girl's long ending?

Almost as if he were invading his own privacy, Abe picked up the folder.

Daniel's medical record read like a masochist's ode to the wilderness. Their former physician had listed Daniel's injuries in careful reverse chronology, like a résumé, which made it easy for Abe to construct Daniel's story. Abe skipped through the list at random.

Eight years ago Daniel had elected to have arthroscopic surgery on both knees, one at a time, for cartilage torn by years of humping big loads down big mountains. And the year before, he'd spent three weeks hospitalized for malaria contracted in New Guinea.

Around that same time, surgeons had fused part of his spinal column after he'd fallen and collapsed several vertebrae. There was a note that Daniel would be bringing along a TENS unit, a portable battery-powered device that electrically over-rode chronic, localized pain. Killing two birds with one stone, the surgeons had taken the same occasion to cut the nerves in Daniel's toes to address the pain of his Morton's neuroma. Climbers liked their rock shoes so tight that they sometimes developed hammer toes, similar to the effects of Chinese foot binding. That was back when Daniel still had toes.

In 1984, the records showed, Daniel had spent several months in the hospital getting most of every toe amputated because of frostbite. Abe checked a secondary page in the folder, and there it was, a photocopied report chronicling the long, agonizing fight to save the damaged toes. Abe flipped back to the first page and found what he was looking for. The frostbite had occurred on Everest, in Tibet, on the north side, in 1983.

"You," Abe whispered to the page.

Now he recollected the tale of five Brits and an American

who had been the first to attack the Kore Wall. Just before reaching the summit slopes, they had been struck by a winter storm. No one had died, but the group's horrible retreat had come to be dubbed the Lepers' Parade. The American media had ignored it altogether—they rarely took notice of mountaineering triumphs, much less failures. But among climbers the story had spread. In fighting their way down the valley to a Tibetan village each had suffered major frostbite. Each had lost toes, three had lost fingers, and one had lost portions of his lower legs. Afterward, so the story went, all of the climbers had given up climbing, all except one. Now Abe knew. Daniel was that one.

Sobered—a little sickened, even—Abe stored the nugget of history away and finished studying Daniel's long list of injuries and disease. The severity of pain and debilitation ebbed and flowed on the page, and Abe had to remind himself that this was the profile of one man, not an entire ward.

The previous year Daniel had undergone surgery for another problem common to high standard rock climbers, tendinitis in his elbows. The doctors had split the tendons in both arms, cleared out the scar tissue, and transferred the ulna nerve from its normal groove to across the elbow. Abe could picture the half-moon scars Daniel would be carrying on his inner arms.

There had been double pneumonia in '84, tropical parasites in '82 and '79, the anterior reconstruction of his left shoulder in '83, rabies shots for a dog bite in Rawalpindi, Pakistan, in '80, and a spiral fracture of the right tibia in '77.

The list went on. It was grotesque. In the context of a normal sport, Daniel's relentless suffering and compulsion would have depressed Abe. But this fascinated him. Here was the sort of obsession he'd always associated with Himalayan ascent, and it was written in flesh and blood. The other members might have the same passion, but only here did Abe see proof of a heart and mind whipped by demons. Now he knew who it was on that British expedition who had named their route for a woman locked away in the underworld.

THE BEGINNING—1992

ABE WOKE AT dawn on the border of Tibet, flat on his back beneath a truck axle. After a late start from Kathmandu, they had reached the border too late for crossing, so the climbers had slept where they could, on one of the big Indian Tata trucks or under them. Hauling himself out by one of the worn black tires, Abe squinted up and around at this borderland in the light of day.

He had come prepared for a landscape of collision, a place where two continental plates were warring for dominance. What he hadn't prepared for was this: a single bridge wedged at the base of an emerald green gorge, half a mile deep. On either side, monkeys barked in the trees and thousand-foot waterfalls threaded walls thick with rhododendron and pine.

They had spent six days in Kathmandu, speedy with jet lag, racing to finish stocking the expedition with food from the local bazaar and with secondhand mountain gear from the trek shops and from other expeditions. With his partner Gus, Daniel had already headed north into Tibet to weed through the red tape and choose a site for their base camp at Everest. Abe was

53

glad for that. For the time being it was enough to get acquainted with these strangers and this new land.

From their moment of landing, Abe had been enchanted. Kathmandu was a vortex of centuries swirling upon themselves. Electric lines threaded among thirteen-tiered temples. Honda motorcycles wove between ambling sacred cows. Ancient stone gods peeked out of brick walls or peered up from holes in the asphalt. There was a layering of time here that sucked at Abe's spirit, and at every turn he felt himself pulled deeper and harder into Asia.

Yesterday they had mounted a jitney bus and the Tata trucks and the city had given way to countryside and the countryside to mountains. The green and red hills with their sleepy cattle and terraced fields had slipped by. The Kathmandu highway had turned into this mean dirt strip hugging a white river.

High in the distance, in a scoop of morning sunlight, a Tibetan village lay carved into the stone and clouds. Down here the air was warm and sticky and crowded with nasal childlike songs from a shopkeeper's radio. Every breath tasted like truck fuel and last night's rice and lentils. But up there, high overhead in Tibet, it looked chilly and remote and peaceful.

Someone came up behind Abe and pointed at the distant floating village. It was Jorgens, Abe could tell by the hand— square and veined like a miner's, with latticed, weather-beaten skin—and because only Jorgens had the ease to go around slapping backs or propping his arm on shoulders. Most of the climbers were still stalking wary circles around one another, snuffling for aggression or dominance like pack wolves. In a fit of bonhomie at the Kathmandu airport, Jorgens had even called them "kids," exposing his wish that they be one big family. Abe canted his head enough to catch the cropped monastic tonsure and the clunky horn-rims that ex-marines seemed to favor. "Breakfast," Jorgens grunted, and then he was gone, rousting climbers from their nooks and crannies by the roadside.

Abe looked around him as the group rose up from the ground. There were leaves in their hair and bags beneath their eyes. The ones who had slept under the trucks sported oil stains, and now Abe found a greasy stripe on his own jacket. Half of them limped from old sports injuries or tendinitis sustained in training for this expedition. They did not inspire confidence as a collection of world-class athletes coiled to strike the highest mountain.

Their Chinese permit listed them as members of the U.S. Ultimate Summit Expedition to the North Face of Qomolangma —or Everest. But one of the climbers—probably Robby with his mouth or Thomas, in another fit of forlorn criticism—had dubbed them the Yeti, and it stuck. Composed of fifteen testicles, four breasts, and "nine too many brains," they were indeed a creature fit for the mountains. Including airfare, gear, food, permit fees and bribes, it was costing over a half million dollars to stitch together this monster. Its life expectancy was a hundred days, though just now, after a single night in the open, the team looked mostly dead.

They limped and shrugged across the Friendship Bridge that spanned the border. All their gear had to be off-loaded here and then loaded onto Chinese government trucks hired at exorbitant rates. And because a section of road to town was in poor repair, the bus chartered to bring up the climbers had been canceled. They would have to walk for their breakfast.

On the far side of the bridge, four People's Liberation Army soldiers awaited the expedition, their pea-green uniform jackets unbuttoned and their cheeks chapped the color of radishes. They stared without amusement as several climbers capered back and forth across the international line for each other's cameras.

At the end of an hour of hiking, the string of hungry climbers reached the village, walking past shacks made of radiant blond pinewood saturated with dew. A waterfall sluiced beneath the roadway and rocketed out into free space, springing hundreds of feet into the depths. They came to a concrete arch marking the customs entry point and overhead a huge fire-red Chinese flag billowed in the mountain air. Abe took a deep lungful of the dream.

Big Tibetan half-breeds with gold teeth and white cotton gloves drove them up out of the gorge and onto the high plateau where they connected with a new Old Silk Road, a two-lane bulldozed road that extended from China all the way to Pakistan. To Abe, the ancient trade route promised riches and forgotten cities. But around every bend it delivered only more mountains and more emptiness.

"A war road," Carlos Crowell called it. He and Abe were riding side by side atop a canvas tarp in the bed of one truck. Along this road, Carlos said, the People's Republic kept Tibet garrisoned with occupation troops and stocked with everything from rice to nuclear weapons. Along this road, back to China, flowed commune crops and minerals and what was left of Tibet's forests.

"They've stripped her clean," Carlos said. Even stating the facts depressed Carlos, who felt he had a special connection to Tibet, and indeed most of the Third World. This was his fourth time here.

Whippet-thin, Carlos was an ex–Peace Corps hand who had served in Rwanda a decade ago, then drifted on to become a part-time dharma bum and entrepreneur. He knew just enough Asian slang to keep everyone wondering how much he really did know. Part of his uniform was the fresh set of red *puja* threads on his wrist from a blessing he'd arranged for himself back in Kathmandu. At his throat hung a turquoise cylinder from his New Age import-export shop in Eugene, and his wispy ponytail was pulled back to show two tiny gold earrings.

Most of the other climbers tended to treat Carlos's colorful spiels about the holocaust that China had unleashed upon Tibet as ghost stories rather than real history. The stories were fabulous and gruesome and no one paid much attention except for Jorgens, who had instructed Carlos to zip his yap once they crossed the border. "A million-plus Tibetans snuffed since 1959," Carlos regaled Abe as they motored along. "That's one out of every six people here starved, shot, bayoneted, burned, crucified or beaten to death with iron bars. Manifest Destiny, Han-style." His claims were horrific, but the land seemed too barren and empty to support such bloodshed. Certainly there were no bodies heaped along the roadside. For the sake of keeping up his end of the conversation, Abe said so.

"Oh, there's killing fields here. They stretch for acres. Miles. I haven't found them yet, but I'm looking, man. Mountains of skulls with a single bullet hole through the buttside of each."

They managed to ride in silence for a while, then Carlos leaned close. "I shouldn't ever have come back here," he said.

Abe had no idea what he meant, but it sounded circular

and self-absorbed the way Carlos liked to be. "Back to Tibet?" Abe asked.

"Everest," Carlos said. "Here we go again. Renting the mountain from a regime that doesn't even own it. Paying lip service to butchers."

"But all we're doing is climbing," Abe said.

"Yeah, yeah. I've heard that one. All the world's a playground for us climbers. The thing is, every time one of us comes and climbs here, we kiss the Chinese ass."

"Well, I guess I don't know about that."

"That's okay. You're ignorant," Carlos said, but it wasn't meant as an insult. "You don't know what it's like here. I do."

"Ignorance is bliss," Abe lamely offered.

Carlos shook his head bitterly. "Maybe so. But one thing's sure. Knowledge is complicity."

For the rest of the day, their convoy of three army surplus trucks spewed huge roostertails of dust across the land. The plateau was barren. The land lay as flat as a Wyoming oil range—except to the south. All along the right-hand horizon lay the Himalayas, abrupt and enormous. Unlike the Nepalese side of the chain with its foothills and forests and paddies, there was no preface to these eruptions. Abe couldn't get over that. There was nothing intermediate between the extremes.

Human beings—even animals or vegetation—were practically an event. At one point, Carlos thrust his arm out. "Would you look at that," he said.

Three horsemen were riding past, dour and fierce-looking. Two wore Aussie-style cowboy hats, the third a fur cap. One carried a rifle with a twin-pronged stand made of long animal horns.

"Khambas," Carlos said. "Once upon a time the CIA trained a bunch of those dudes as guerrillas."

Abe waited. Even when he was serious, Carlos seemed to be pulling your leg.

"No, no, it's true, man. They used to fly guys like them to the Rocky Mountains, an old army camp in Colorado. Taught them, armed them, had them running ops across the Nepal border. They'd blow up roads, attack convoys or outposts. But you know how that goes. After a while the Agency pulled the plug. The spooks call these kind of guys Dixie cups. Use once, throw away."

The horsemen had long braids bound with chile-red twine. None of the three wasted so much as a look at the truck convoy. Abe reached for his camera, but already they were gone.

They reached a cold little village called Shekar at five and drove straight to a concrete hostel provided by the Chinese Mountaineering Association. The village stood at 11,000 feet. Their Chinese liaison officer—their keeper while they were in-country—met them with a smile. "There's one of the butchers," Carlos muttered. "We belong to him now."

Wearing a crisp yellow windbreaker with ULTIMATE SUMMIT on the back and along one arm, the L.O. was easy to recognize. "Welcome to my country," he greeted them. His name was Li Deng and he was tall and well educated, a Han apparatchik from Beijing, maybe thirty-five years old. He spoke superb British English and occupied some high rank in the Chinese Mountaineering Association, a government bureau. With his brand-new clean pump-up basketball shoes and hundred-dollar Revo sunglasses—all expedition issue—he didn't look very Marxist or genocidal.

There was no heat in the rooms and what illumination there was came from a bulb dangling by exposed wires. An industrial-strength quilt covered Abe's bed. All the rooms lacked to be jail cells were metal bars. The CMA was charging over a hundred dollars per climber for the lodging, but no one complained because that was the price of climbing in Tibet.

Abe stood at the window. The truckyard was losing its daylight and Abe shivered, unprepared for the teeth of this highland cold. Tonight's roommate was Robby, a spidery carpenter with an old two-tone crewcut gone to seed. He was flopped out atop his quilt, prattling on about about how he'd stayed in this same miserable hostel in '87 on his way to another mountain, Shisha Pangma. He ranked staying here alongside giving blood—he had a needle phobia—and swimming in the ocean—sharks.

In the window's reflection, Abe could see Robby sitting on his bed. The lightbulb cast his eyes into shadowy sockets and there was no mirth on his lips. His Great Plains inflection blunted any intended humor, another misfire. He seemed trapped in his own monologue.

Abe had a headache and didn't feel like conversation, and it was too early in the expedition to be telling Robby to pipe down, so he stood there and tuned out, watching the truckyard. A scarred black mongrel was creeping beyond stone's throw of a pack of ragged children. Further out, the notorious Tibetan wind skirled dust clouds that blotted out the middle distance, but not the distant Himalayas.

Abe pressed his fingertips against the dusty Chinese glass and pondered the ghostly scenery. There was mystery out there and he welcomed it. Absentmindedly he started tracing a silhouette of the mountains on the cold glass. A moment later Abe noticed the idle sketch under his finger and stopped immediately. It looked, for all the world, like the lifeline on an EEG readout. He lifted away his finger before the line went flat on the far horizon, then chided himself for being superstitious.

It was a forgivable primitivism. They were already beginning to starve for oxygen. Abe could sense it. From the medical literature he'd steeped himself in, Abe felt well versed in the effects of high altitude. Even so he was surprised to see the faint blue coloration underneath his fingernails already.

From here on out, they would be living in a constant state of hypoxia, or oxygen starvation. In fact there was just as much oxygen in the air—21 percent—here and on the top of Everest as at sea level. What varied was the ambient pressure needed to force the oxygen from the lungs into the bloodstream. So they would have to breathe more air. Their bodies would produce more red blood cells to carry the oxygen. Their blood would thicken almost to syrup, forcing their hearts to labor harder. Even the youngest and fittest climbers would soon run an increased risk of heart failure. The margins of normal health would wither away. And above 22,000 feet or so, their bodies would slowly begin dying.

Out of his crash course in high-altitude physiology, Abe had derived one bit of poetry. It turned out that even among people with a genetic tolerance for high altitude, people like the Sherpas or Peruvian miners, life inside the womb was, in effect, close to a sea-level existence. Newborns had to acclimatize like mountaineers. Mountaineers had to adapt like newborns. For all its jagged contours, the world at high altitudes presented a level playing field.

Abe tried to identify some of the far peaks, but without luck. Over the years, he had memorized the contours of Everest and Lhotse and Makalu and Cho Oyu and others without stop-

ping to think that all the pictures showed the range from the
Nepal side. Here in Tibet, the profiles were not only reversed,
but distorted.

When Abe asked which were which, Robby said, "Forget it.
We're on the backside of the moon now. Our labels don't count
here." But then he joined Abe at the window and pointed out
different mountains and gave their names. Even with Robby's
help, though, the range didn't become any more familiar to
Abe, and that just made it seem more alien.

"And that there's the Big E," Robby said, pointing at a
small, triangular bump to the south.

"Sorry?" He wasn't paying attention.

"You know, like E Sharp, Big White," Robby jived. "Chomolungma, Mother Goddess. The Hill."

Abe nodded: Everest. It looked very small from here.

"I wish we were there already," Robby said. "Daniel's been
out there a week now, nothing to do but smell the roses and do
the hang with old Gus. But then luck's his middle name."

"Daniel?" Abe said. "I never thought of him as lucky. Just
the opposite." Abe had made a pact with himself not to preface
his meeting with Daniel with expedition gossip. But here it was
getting handed to him and it was hard to turn away.

"Not lucky? Come on."

Abe kept it general. "Don't get me wrong," he said. "I don't
know Daniel. But the man's lost his toes. He's broken bones.
Taken bad falls. And he's tried Everest how many times now,
and never made the top." And seen his young fiancée eaten
alive by a mountain, Abe almost added. So far as he could tell,
no one on the expedition knew about the nightmare that bound
Daniel and Abe.

"Yeah," Robby agreed, "but he's alive." His eyebrows
jumped electrically.

"That's something," Abe conceded.

"I'd trade him anyday. You know what he does for a
living?"

Abe didn't.

"He's a crash dummy. A technical adviser to manufacturers
of climbing equipment. He has to try out all the new toys. He
has to climb full-time. And not on scruffy little backyard cliffs
either. You know how car companies like to name their cars
after power animals? Mustang, Cougar, Stingray, right? Well

it's Daniel's job to do power climbs. He gets sent around the world to all the best faces on all the best mountains. All expenses paid. Free air, free gear, free food. And everywhere he goes, Gus goes too, and she is something. All in all, Doc, I'd trade a few toes to be in Abe's shoes."

For dinner they had gray, rubbery dumplings in the cavernous dining hall built to feed a Western tourist trade that never happened, especially after martial law. The hall was unheated and it leaked the cold wind. Everyone was feeling the altitude, so dinner was brief. Jorgens spoke of their need to buy Chinese stamps for the expedition's five hundred postcards, to be signed by all the members and sent from base camp to contributors at ten dollars apiece, the standard scheme for raising money. Stump, their wide-bodied co-leader, promised to score the stamps in the morning. Then everyone scraped their chairs back from the table to go off to bed, but Li intercepted them to offer a toast.

Li explained that he'd never climbed in his life nor been to Tibet before, but he enjoyed Americans and he enjoyed the outdoors. "The natural world is like an unfinished poem," he told them. "It needs care and labor before it reaches completeness. You Americans understand this because of your frontier days. Tibet is our Old West, you see. And so, from one frontiersman to another, I say let us write a grand poem of friendship and adventure upon our mountain."

"Give me a break," Carlos rumbled at the end of the table. He started to stand and leave, but Stump caught at his jacket.

"Shut it," Stump commanded. Carlos paused and blinked, then sat back down.

"To friendship, to the mountain." Jorgens seconded Li's toast, and everyone but Carlos drank a few tablespoons of scotch from their dirty teacups.

Back in the room, just before hoisting the quilt up around his shoulders, Abe peered out the window. The moon was up and the Himalayas were stretched long and white in the moonlight like a vast, shearing coral reef.

Abe rode the last few hours to Everest on the front seat of the front truck in their convoy, squeezed beside Jorgens, who couldn't seem to stop remembering old mountain stories, all of them long and involved and about himself. They were inoffensive tales, mostly designed to excuse his age, which was fifty-four, and Abe didn't begrudge that.

Abruptly, with a suddenness that bounced Abe against the door, the truck turned left off the road. This was the start of what became a long grinding crawl up the Pang La, a 16,000-foot pass bridging the Tibetan plateau and the deeper range. They were only forty miles from Everest now, but according to Jorgens, it was going to be a tortuous forty miles of bad roads and wild scenery. "The Pang La's our doorway to Everest. All ye who enter, know your soul," he joshed.

For the next two hours, the road switched back and forth past shields of gleaming black granite. Here and there the road evaporated altogether under fresh slide scars only to reappear again. Not a hint of vegetation graced the bleak stony land. It was still winter here. Hour after hour, they saw no animals, no people, no houses. No justification for this strange highway.

"The world's highest dead end," Jorgens declared over the whine of downshifted gears. "The PLA hand-constructed it in 1960. They're very proud of it. They need to get a three-hundred-man expedition in to Everest. So they cut this road in. And they climbed their mountain."

It was hard to tell which Jorgens respected more, the Chinese road or their climb. Abe wondered if Jorgens had heard Carlos's theory, that the Chinese had merely claimed the summit in 1960 in order to cement their occupation of Tibet. It was a claim that remained dubious, since the Chinese had supposedly summited in the dark when photography was impossible. Further Carlos held that this road had been built with slave labor.

For the sake of argument, and because Jorgens was in such a garrulous mood, Abe challenged him. "I've heard the story told a little different," he said. "That it was Tibetans who built this road, and with a gun at their head."

The deep dimples in Jorgens's beard vanished. He shot a look at their driver, who spoke pidgin Mandarin and pidgin Hindi and even pidgin Japanese, but, judging by his blank look, no English at all. Then he turned a stern look upon Abe.

"You had a chat with Mr. Crowell, I take it."

"We rode together," Abe said. "It was an education."

"Half an education," Jorgens qualified it. "There's always two sides to a story."

Abe almost spread his hands as if to disown his own remark. He hadn't meant to trigger a confrontation. At the same time, he didn't appreciate being lectured. Jorgens went on.

"Take the story of this road, for instance. It took a long time to build this road," he said. "You may not believe this, but the Tibetan workers would stop after every shovelful to pick the earthworms out of the dirt. Can you imagine? Every shovelful, stop to save an earthworm's life. Talk about benighted. It drove the Chinese nuts."

Jorgens stared out at the blank countryside. "What a country. What a sorry ass-backward excuse for a country. People going around day and night mumbling prayers, worshiping stones, prostrating themselves. Frankly I think the Chinese did these Tibetans a favor. At least these people can see a hint of the twentieth century now."

Abe noticed that Jorgens hadn't disputed the charge of slave labor. At best he'd put a happy face on it. "Sounds to me like Tibet didn't really need the twentieth century," Abe said.

"Tibet." Jorgens spit the word. "You have to understand something about this place, then you'll understand Mr. Crowell's fixation on it. Tibet was called the forbidden kingdom for a reason. People like us were kept out. But even when we're let in, we're still out. We're all strangers here. And that's why people like Mr. Crowell feel so at home here—because nobody knows Tibet, and so we can all imagine it is whatever we want."

After that, they rode in silence.

At the top of the Pang La, Jorgens breathed a long whistle. "My God," he said. "Would you look at this."

It was indeed a sight. The Himalayan range lay spread before them, a tonnage of angles and sunlight. Jorgens signaled their driver to stop. The driver scowled and tapped his wristwatch. Jorgens waved him to a halt anyway.

A second truck pulled up and Li disembarked. Bundled in cherry-colored expedition parkas, Thomas and Robby and J. J. Packard rose up from their nest atop the boxes stacked in back. They moved slowly, cold and stiff. But their teeth gleamed in huge grins and they were excited to be getting so close to the mountain.

A third truck arrived, and more people joined them. Cameras snapped and whirred. Not a cloud adulterated the blue

sky. The air was still. They were twenty miles or more from
Everest, but with the humidity content near zero, there was no
haze and it looked close enough to touch.

Even though Daniel and Gus were missing, Jorgens decided it was time for "the Picture"—the official "before" shot
which, months later, would go with the "after" shot in their slide
shows to prove how Everest was about to ravage them. He called
one of their Sherpas over to round out the group. They put on
their best face, eight mountaineers radiant in their shorts or
jeans or Lycra tights, bellies taut, teeth white. But while Abe
steadied his bulky old Pentax on a tripod, they flexed anyway.

The most obvious as usual was J. J. Packard, who whipped
off his sweatshirt to display thick lats like a peacock in rut. He
came advertised as a magnificent summit animal, capable of
squatting a quarter-ton of iron draped across his neck, but Abe
wondered. His exhibitionism and dirty blond dreadlocks aside,
J.J.'s sheer bulk seemed more likely to gobble up his oxygen
capacity and leave him far behind, and Abe was curious to see
how it would go.

Next to the giant, like spidery twins, Robby Powell "sucked
cheek" in Revo sunglasses and his buddy Thomas Case postured
with a dour, foreboding frown. Both were wearing the expedition T-shirts that Robby had compared, unkindly—it was Jorgens's design—to a cheap supermarket tabloid. The logo
showed an ice climber peering into the neon orange cosmic
reaches. The title ULTIMATE SUMMIT: EVEREST NORDWAND galloped across the chest. Under that, in hot purple ink, the shirt
bragged, "Getting High the Hard Way!"

Kelly, their beauty queen, just cocked her head and the sun
poured gold on her Viking locks. Though she was embarrassed
by her flat chest and regularly joked that her butt looked like
hams waiting to happen, Kelly was the ultimate tits-and-ass
show to ever play Everest. A schoolteacher in real life, she had
consented to model on the expedition. On her crystal blue eyes
alone, magazines and cosmetic companies had paid the Ultimate
Summit $150,000. A pantyhose company had kicked in $80,000
for rights to her legs, providing darker shades to hide the scars.
Her hair had gone for another $35,000 to a shampoo maker,
and her skin had fetched still more from a tanning lotion manu-
facturer. The rest of their money had come through more
conventional expedition schemes such as T-shirt sales, a book

contract—null and void if they failed the summit, unless there was a death—ten-dollar "Postcards from the Edge," a wristwatch endorsement, and some last-minute corporate checkkiting that involved the venture's nonprofit status and the future profits from Jorgen's Chinese permit for Everest the following year. Abe didn't understand it all, nor did he waste much time inquiring.

Nima Tenzing, the top kick of their climbing Sherpas, looked as grave as a nineteenth-century chieftain facing the lens of history. Centuries ago, the Sherpas had migrated from their native Tibet into the high valleys south of Everest in Nepal. They'd been "discovered" in the 1930s by Western mountaineers in need of cheap labor on Everest, becoming famous as "tigers of the snow" who functioned as high altitude Gunga Dins, capable of carrying enormous loads by day and cheerfully delivering cups of tea each morning at dawn to their sunburned sahibs.

Back in Kathmandu, Abe had met a worn-out old Sherpa missing most of the fingers on one hand. What it had brought to mind was not tales of Himalayan heroism but the memory of his own father, maimed in service to an oil company that soon after fired and forgot him. In Nepal, tourism was the number one industry, and with their good humor and charming English and their appetite for Western fashion, these Sherpas were less tigers than safari porters who were usually the first to get eaten by the mountain. Just prior to the first successful ascent of Everest in 1953, Tenzing Norgay and the team's other Sherpas had been stuck in a converted stable without a toilet while Hillary and his comrades enjoyed the British embassy building. From then on, the Sherpas had known their place in the scheme of things.

Glen "Stump" Wilson, the co-leader, anchored their center. An arbitrator and construction litigation attorney, Stump was built from the waist down like a pro fullback. His enormous thighs were offset by what he termed "the littlest man," a genuinely small penis and a lone descended gonad which Abe had seen for himself while probing for a hernia in Kathmandu. He had climbed on Everest twice before, and both times seen expeditions flame out because of personality disputes. "That's not going to happen this time," he'd warned them, and left it at that.

To the far left stood Peter Jorgens, beaming in his salt-
and-pepper beard. With his crisp widow's peak and sunbaked
crow's-feet, Jorgens looked every inch the Hollywood alpinist.
In fact he was an accountant who had somehow ascended to
the presidency of the American Alpine Club. Abe had heard
that Jorgens dreamed of becoming secretary of the interior
someday, and that this expedition was meant to be a stepping-
stone to Washington. Some of the other climbers considered it
funny, and sad, too, that Jorgens had already ordered a set of
vanity plates reading "29,028"—the height of Everest—for his
family Jeep.

While Abe got his tripod legs screwed tight and attached
his camera, the team stood around wisecracking and catcalling
at Everest, so many apes hooting at the moon. They were in
high spirits and Abe thought it fine and promising for them to
be thumbing their noses at the monster. It meant they were
ready or thought they were, and sometimes that was the same
thing.

He panned his viewfinder across the bunch, smiling to himself. Each and every one of them was dedicated to his reputation, though in reality they all were essentially anonymous
figments of their own imaginations. They hadn't come here to
buy a name by dying on the mountain; rather they'd come to
emulate those who had, miming the hard-core giants with their
brilliant teeth and their posturing in the wind.

Abe was finally ready and called to the climbers to take
their places again. Kelly moved panther-soft, her black Lycra
rippling like midnight, and J.J. squeezed some more veins to
the surface, and the truck drivers gaped. Abe focused and was
about to trigger the self-timer and jump in line, when suddenly,
without warning, a puff of air—the softest of breezes—brushed
their faces.

Someone groaned. It was a bad news groan and everyone
turned to look at the jagged horizon behind them.

A tiny comma of a white cloud had appeared in the sky.
The cloud was nothing more than a mare's tail—altocirrus at
35,000 feet—and it drifted silkily. It hung up there like white
ink on a cobalt canvas, a beautiful Zen master stroke.

But the little cloud was a warning and every climber there
understood, all except Abe, who didn't know this mountain's
traits.

"Damn," J.J. whispered, as if he were just now realizing a mistake.

A moment or two passed. And then the mountain sprang to life. Everest's curt left edge released a ghostly plume.

"Snow?" Abe asked quietly.

Carlos shook his head. "Water vapor," he said. "The Indian air mass is hot. And when it hits the cold mountain, zap. Smoke." He checked his watch, synchronizing with the pattern. Abe did the same. It was not quite two, Beijing time.

"That's not the monsoon, is it?" Abe asked.

"That?" Carlos said. "That's just Everest. She likes to send up a flag in the afternoons. Don't worry, Doc. The monsoon's still three months off. You'll know when it comes. That's when we close the works and get the hell out of Dodge."

Before their eyes, the white plume turned into a long ragged flag reaching east.

"It's probably one-ten, maybe one-twenty miles per hour up top there," J.J. said. "That's major air, man. Hurricane force."

The white flag might as well have been black. It signified no quarter, nullifying the climbers' coltish good humor. Abe took his cue from their spoiled bravado. He stowed his grin like everyone else. Weather was everything on an Everest climb. But Abe was handicapped, because they were half the planet removed from any skies he could reliably read. All the same he meant to learn the patterns fast.

"That's that," Stump called out with the enthusiasm of a man heading off for his own execution. "Let's knock off then and get on with the show."

They turned their backs on the Hill. Everyone returned to the trucks.

The convoy moved down off the pass toward the floor of the Rongbuk Valley, heading due south for Everest. As they wove back and forth down the steep, miles-long pass, or *la*, Everest disappeared from view. After a half-hour, the Pang La flattened out and the road jogged left and right through canyon walls. Soon the pass vanished behind them, and their entrance and exit to the outside world was just a memory.

There was a whole other world in here. If Shekar was poor, then the settlements in the Rongbuk Valley were desperate. Poverty lay everywhere—in the soil, in the adobe dwellings, in the children's astonishing nudity beneath the cold wind. Here and there, little clusters of stone and adobe dwellings popped up like southwestern pueblos. Some of the buildings were white-washed, some were banded white and orange. The flat rooftops were ringed with sticks of firewood that must have been brought from far away, for there was not a tree in sight.

The people didn't smile from their rock-strewn fields at the passing truckloads of climbers. They glared, then went on with their tilling. Jorgens seemed not to register their bleak circumstances. Instead he waved heartily at the brown land. "When we leave in June," he said, "these fields will be green. The ewes will be dropping their lambs. This road will be cut by dozens of irrigation ditches. You'll see. It'll be pretty as a picture."

There were more ruins—old stone fortresses and monasteries and desolate villages. The convoy crossed dry irrigation ditches, then a wide riverbed. In the summertime, Jorgens promised, it would carry runoff "as thick and white as sperm" from the Rongbuk Glacier at the base of Everest. Now it held only a blue thread of water.

More hours passed and the sun stayed dangling on the southern rim. Having descended into a valley, they now began to climb out again. The road turned menacing with deep gullies and big gutting scree. Abe kept expecting their tires to blow out or the oil pan to get disemboweled. Patches of ice waited in the shadows and on switchbacks. The truck nearly high-centered on one rutted patch, then skidded on another. They crept along at five kilometers per hour. For some reason, Abe had never imagined a truck engine could still function at 17,000 feet. Theirs did.

The truck rounded a hillock of glacier debris. To the right and left, satellite peaks couched a long, perfectly flush moraine. And then, from out of nowhere, Everest leapt up before them. It seemed close, but that was the optics of high altitude and it was still miles away. The trucks crept along toward where the valley floor quit and became mountainside.

"There," Jorgens pointed for their driver. At the same time Abe saw it too, a tiny bubble of color. A moment later, the bubble became a green tent and Abe caught sight of two minia-ture figures. One figure approached them. As they closed on him, the man grew larger.

Though his head was bound with a red-checkered *kaffiyeh*

and he looked more like an Afghani rebel than a climber, and his eyes were covered with sunglasses, Abe somehow recognized the man. It was Daniel, of course. He walked with wide, rolling strides, but Abe could see the hitch in his one leg—that would be the spiral fracture; and the exaggerated agility would be the amputated toes and scoped knees. He was baked to copper by two weeks of Tibetan sun, and even with the daylight failing in this deep valley his grin was an act of magnificent anarchy.

"Daniel," Abe said aloud, greeting his own history.

Jorgens craned forward and squinted through his black horn-rims at the figure, then at Abe. "Good eyes," he said.

Daniel waved the load truck to a pause and pulled up to Abe's open window. "Hey, Jorgens," he said, and reached through the window and across Abe to shake hands. It struck Abe that he'd never heard Daniel actually speak, only howl. His voice rasped slightly, the edge of bronchitis or a windpipe raw from the cold. "I was starting to think we'd have to climb without you."

Abe looked at the paltry encampment in the distance and its other sticklike inhabitant, then up at the huge mountain, and concluded Daniel was making a joke. But Jorgens didn't snort his amusement and Daniel kept on grinning, and Abe wasn't so sure after all.

Jorgens canted his head toward Abe. "You two have met," he said to Daniel.

Daniel backed off to get Abe in focus. He studied Abe's face for an intent minute, then stuck his open right hand through the window to him. "Once upon a time," he said, and it struck Abe that Daniel had never really seen him before. Abe's would have been just one more face in a circle of pain.

"It was a long time ago." Abe wasn't offended.

"Abraham Burns," Daniel said, half to himself.

"I take it this is your pick for Base Camp," Jorgens interrupted.

Daniel slung his face toward the distance. "Looks like hell, doesn't it. But if we camp over that way, the wind kills us. And over the other way, we get no sun. Gus and me, we've spent the last week trying all the sites out. So here it is, as good as it gets."

"Let's do it then. Show us where. We've got everything to do before night drops on us."

Daniel arced down off the running board, loped ahead of the truck, and then swept his hands in a big half-acre half-moon on the ground.

The convoy circled on his geometry and came to a halt. The driver of Abe and Jorgens's truck switched off the ignition. The cab fell silent.

"Home sweet home," Jorgens pronounced.

Abe tried hard not to gawk. On the one hand, it looked the way it was supposed to look, just as India had smelled the way India should smell when he'd first stepped off the plane. But it was different, too.

Maybe he should have known better, but Abe had imagined their group would land on Everest's soil like astronauts—or migrant workers—carrying with them everything necessary for life where there was no life. Food, shelter, literature, even oxygen: all of it imported. And like astronauts—or Okies—they would arrive bearing hopes and dreams, most forcefully the dream of virgin territory, of a fresh start, of frontier. But what Abe saw through the cracked windshield destroyed all such sentiment and he was shocked.

At first glance, it looked like the aftermath of a gigantic New Year's Eve party with confetti thrown across the whole landscape. Then Abe saw that it was trash, years and years of trash. Like jackals, the wind had raided the garbage dumps of past expeditions and cast debris across the entire moraine. Pieces of paper and plastic clung stubbornly to rocks, hundreds of pink and blue and yellow entrails.

That wasn't the worst of it, either. Abe opened the door and hopped nimbly to the ground and landed, literally, in shit, in the dried feces of their mountaineering ancestors. And now Abe saw that in every direction, human and yak dung lay coiled and dropped in random piles, each one mummified by the sun.

Wasteland, Abe thought, and immediately filed the pun for his slide shows. But the filth and desolation kept on hitting at his mind. It was so unexpected.

Daniel breezed past, hustling to get the trucks unloaded and camp set up. "Welcome to paradise," he said without a trace of irony.

None of the other climbers seemed fazed. If anything, the trash lent a festive spirit to the place and people seemed energized by the emptiness of this Himalayan clearing. Abe looked around, groping to get his bearings. When he finally did move, he moved slowly. He wasn't the only one. In contrast to the Sherpas, most of the climbers looked clumsy and crippled by the altitude.

Everest was actually ten miles distant, but from here on they were on foot. Though the valley floor was as flat as a billiard table, the climb began here.

In between them and Everest stood a satellite mountain called Changtse which blocked the lower five thousand feet of their route from view. But above Changtse's dark, blunt massif, Everest was projecting brilliant white light. The sight only exaggerated the squalor of Base Camp, for the valley had fallen into shadow. It would be daytime up there for hours to come, while down in the valley, the climbers were already layering on sweaters and parkas for night.

Eager to depart before the sun was altogether gone, the truck drivers pitched in. They hastily unroped the tarps and clambered on top of the gear and started tossing it from the trucks into a mountain of jumbled boxes, packs, and utensils.

Standing atop one of the truck cabs, Jorgens was shouting, "System it, people, system it," for he'd painstakingly tapped together a computerized blueprint for the supply dump and spent extra money for color-coded boxes.

But as the sun sank lower and the wind blew harder, Jorgens's dream of a system completely disintegrated. The drivers were rough and indifferent to their loads. They kicked and pitched and shoved at the gear and the climbers simply tried to keep up with them. The pile of gear grew taller and more hectic. Everyone worked with a gasping determination. No one relished spending their first night at Everest in the open.

As Abe labored, he felt oddly desperate. He had thought they would arrive on this island and carefully inhabit it, and instead they had crashed upon its rocky shores and were now frantically salvaging their gear before the ships sank altogether.

"Goddamn it, get the system, people," Jorgens bellowed helplessly. He spotted one of the Sherpas. "Norbu, tell these damn drivers, system it."

"Yes sir," Norbu said, and turned away, having no idea what Jorgens meant, or if he did, no intention of doing it.

Alpenglow radiated orange and pink off the highest tips of the surrounding peaks. But down in the valley it was dark.

The darker it got, the harder people drove themselves, frantic to make a shelter against the night and make this refuge habitable.

First one truck, then all of them disgorged their contents and bolted for the Pang La. Abe watched the trucks' headlights cast crazy patterns in the dusk. Finally, like spiders retracting their white silk, the trucks and their cobweb of lights were gone and the climbers had Everest to themselves. They were alone. To Abe's surprise, his heart felt heavy. Not since his father's death a few years ago had Abe felt so profoundly abandoned. It wasn't logical, but there it was.

They secured the gear as best they could, but soon it got too dark for them to be useful. The climbers and Sherpas gathered at Krishna Rai's food box and stood around in the wind and stars and shared a twenty-pound block of cheddar cheese and three cans of tuna mixed with ice crystals. No one could coax the Indian kerosene stoves into firing, and so there was no boiled water for tea or for brushing their teeth. Daniel and his companions shared what little water they had, but it wasn't much more than a swallow apiece.

Everyone economized on the dialogue. But when they did speak Abe could hear their low mood. This was their first night at the grand destination and the entire team was now together for the first time. The evening should have been filled with joy and excitement and camaraderie. Instead the climbers were about to drag off to bed thirsty and exhausted and hungover from the thin air. Abe could tell he wasn't alone in already feeling flatass defeated. He figured the only thing to do was go sleep it off.

But then something happened that strangely lifted their spirits. A meteor shower suddenly emerged in the sky above Everest.

"Look," someone said, and they all turned to see the extraordinary thing, this bunched strafing surge of lights.

The meteors appeared like wild parrots, a whole flock of colors slashing through the night. They sprang through the blackness in silence.

"Is it real?" someone marveled. There were dozens of flashing meteors, then a hundred and maybe more. Abe had seen comets and falling stars before, but never in such abundance as this, and never so incisive and brilliant and obtainable. He felt sure they would slug straight into the mountain.

"It's not the Perseids," Carlos pronounced for their benefit. Abe had already been treated to his theories on the universe. "They come in August. But I don't know what else it could be, not this bright and not this many and at this season. I don't know."

The shower went on and on. Abe forgot his thirstiness and fatigue and the cold wind. Everyone did. They all just stared at the extraordinary fireworks.

People remarked aloud as the green and red and white lines materialized from deep space and stung downward toward their Hill. The general tone was awe. Stump was so entranced that he forgot to instruct Robby and Tom to catch the stars on film. After a few minutes, Abe could hear the Sherpas muttering darkly in their own language, and he felt them shifting around and realized they were afraid.

"So beautiful," Kelly was murmuring.

Then Nima spoke. "This thing, very, very bad," he pronounced to the group.

"I don't think so, Nima," someone consoled him. "It's just meteors."

"It is scientific," the Chinese liaison officer Li explained, and by his tone Abe could make out his impatience with the Sherpa's fear.

But by Nima's silence, Abe could tell science had little place in this outland.

TEN DAYS STRAIGHT the climbers looked north toward the Pang La, praying for their yak caravan to materialize, marking their calendars, waiting. Every day the skies were swept so bare that Abe imagined he could see the stars at high noon. It was so still in the mornings he could actually hear tiny icicles melting, their droplets chiming like bells. The weather was perfect. But the yaks didn't come.

"Our valley is a gigantic prison cell," Abe wrote in his growing letter to Jamie. "Barren. Tedious. There is no life here. Time has stopped. Everything occurs in enormous proportions—the blue sky, the mountainsides, the Rongbuk Glacier. I've never known such vastness. It humbles me. The closest things to human scale in this outsized land are the tiny fluorescent red and blue and green lichen that freckle the rocks. The lichens and us—we share this dead place. I can almost hear my hair growing."

Base Camp was up and running. Tents were pitched, walls taut, latrines dug. The heap of gear had been sorted and re-sorted. The climbers were ready to climb.

There were two ways to attack a mountain of this size and height. The simplest, by far the most dangerous, was the so-called alpine ascent, which pitted two to four climbers against the clock as they made a single-minded dash for the summit. Using this strategy, the climbers would continue progressively higher, taking their camp and supplies with them. When someone pulled off an alpine ascent in the Himalayas, it was treated as a brilliant theft, a jewel stolen from under the dragon's nose. The problem was risk. Stripped for speed and isolated high on their mountain, an alpine team depended on perfect conditions, perfect teamwork and perfect health. One mistake, one stormy day, and it was all over, you froze to glass where you lay. Everyone agreed that an alpine attempt on a route as complicated and vast as the Kore Wall would have been insane.

The more tried and true strategy, the one the Ultimate Summit Expedition had been built around, was the old-fashioned siege. This called for methodically setting permanent camps at successive heights and linking each to its neighbors with thousands of feet of "fixed" safety rope. In contrast to the blitzkrieg motion of an alpine ascent, siege climbers shuttled up and down repeatedly, stocking the highest, newest camps—what climbers called "building the logistics pyramid"—and acclimatizing slowly. The rule of thumb for siege ascents was "climb high, sleep low," the idea being that you climbed high and slept low at progressively higher elevations.

From his childhood reading through the mountaineering classics about the first ascents of Annapurna and Nanga Parbat, the early British assaults on the north side of Everest and their first conquest of Everest on its southern side, Abe knew the concepts behind laying siege to a mountain. What he lacked was the mindset. Robby clued him in one afternoon.

With every word, the garrulous man made it clear they were at war. He described the upper camps as firebases, with all the rough-and-ready charm of temporary defenses injected deep into enemy territory. Every camp would depend on its lower neighbor for support and reinforcement. None was designed for long-term occupation on the Hill. The very highest camp would be placed and stocked for one-day guerrilla strikes on the summit.

"On summit day, you go for quick penetration," Robby preached. "Quick up, quick down."

Abe listened, rapt. Climbing in the Himalayas was like climbing nowhere else in the world. It had a language all its own, a risk and a mindset, and Robby—and all the others—

brimmed with it. The very language of ascent abounded with war terms: siege tactics, assault, base camp, supply lines, logistics, planting camps, pushing the line, retreat, victory, conquest, and planting the flag. Abe was getting a clear sense that one brought to Everest a lifetime of battle plans, of occupied landscapes—high ground, always the high ground—and of risks, blood, and wet socks on cold nights. Taken altogether, it was a kind of high-speed imperialism, the rise and fall of a dynasty within a few months. The idea behind their occupation was less to inhabit a land than to enter into history.

But without the yaks, they couldn't even begin to climb.

Through the Chinese Mountaineering Association, a caravan of sixty yaks—each able to carry seventy pounds—had been contracted to ferry gear up to Advance Base Camp. With them the expedition would move two solid tons of rope, shelter, food, oxygen and film equipment up to 21,700 feet in the span of two days. Without them, the climbers would simply waste their strength humping loads. Worse, they would waste their time. Using a laptop computer, Jorgens estimated it would take sixty-three good-weather days for the climbers to pack the gear in and begin climbing . . . and by then the monsoon would be looming and they would fail.

And so they waited. They sat and tinkered with gear. They read novels and snacked on popcorn and grumbled. "It's like being an animal in a zoo," J.J. complained. "Every time I look up there, it's watching us." It was true. All morning long the mountain taunted them with its silence and light. At sunset it smothered them in shadows. Whenever they turned around, Everest was there.

Ten miles shy of their grail, the climbers stewed. Li Deng quit showing the glum Americans his dog-eared, rubber-stamped CMA contract with the yakherders. He quit making promises or inventing excuses or cursing the "minority nationals," as he called the Tibetans. He even quit playing chess games with the climbers, and that had been his one pleasure.

April approached. Jorgens soured. Everything seemed to rankle him. From what wags were calling their "yak gap" to the manner in which they pitched their tents, nothing pleased him. He had visualized setting camp in something like an iron cross, with straight lines and right angles that would speak to their souls and declare that here in this netherland, under the hand of man, lay order. But the only tent sites available were on patches of soft tundra which projected above the rocky floor like small islands. This archipelago of tundra patches rambled here and there, and as a result Base Camp resembled less a cross than a mutilated starfish with arms cast out in every direction.

Every morning Jorgens was freshly assaulted by the camp's chaos. Every morning he scowled and cursed and his displeasure would orbit his head in a puff of frost. It got so that every morning Robby or Carlos or J.J., each to needle or fawn or just find out, would ask, "What's wrong, Captain?" or "Problem, Boss?", and Jorgens would glare at them, then wheel around and walk off into the distance to take his morning relief, a tiny figure squatting on the immense valley floor with his bare ass turned impudently to the sun.

Along one of these starfish arms, on a yellowed tundra patch, Abe set up his big "hospital" tent, a peach-colored dome with an eight-foot ceiling. His site was remote enough from the mess tent for him to suppose there wouldn't be any neighbors, which suited him fine. But he got neighbors anyway, and that suited him fine, too, because who he got were the women and Daniel.

Daniel and Gus set up their dome to one side. Farther out, in a direct line between Abe's front door and the morning sun, Kelly pitched her own tent. Abe knew he was lucky. But he didn't appreciate the other climbers' envy until one drowsy afternoon when Thomas paid a visit.

He came into Abe's big tent the way everyone did, without announcing himself or asking. The hospital—and Abe's services, for that matter—were considered public property, like the mess tent and Krishna's cooking. It wasn't unusual for people to enter Abe's tent at strange hours in search of drugs or surgical tape or just some company. For all his love of privacy, Abe was actually enjoying his lack of it. He'd heard how some expedition doctors could be completely ignored for months at a time by fanatical climbers who considered their diagnoses bad omens. So far, this bunch was having no trouble assimilating their shaman, and Abe had found the impromptu visits a chance to try to figure out what—if anything—made these Himalayan climbers different from ordinary humanity.

Abe was lying on a ground pad flipping through his big *Principles of Internal Medicine* when Thomas entered. "Hey,

Doc," he said, "you got any good stuff for a headache?" Even before Abe could answer, Thomas was on his knees in front of a box that had been pawed through by others. Judging from the looks of it, the climbers seemed to know Abe's medicine cabinet better than he did. Abe went back to his book.

"Talk about a room with a view," Thomas said. He was looking out the door at Kelly's tent. "Your neighborhood's a lot cozier than mine."

"Lady luck," Abe joked.

"Lady luck," Thomas muttered to himself. "You know," he said more loudly, "you better watch out for that one."

It was a warning, Abe could hear its tone, and it took him off-guard. "What's that?" he said.

Thomas rummaged idly through the supplies. "I'm talking about her."

"Kelly?"

"Call it the fruit of a bad harvest," Thomas said. "I'm just suggesting you want to watch your headset with her around, Doc." Thomas tapped his skull. "She'll dial the tune on you. Before you know it, you're on her program."

Abe didn't know how to respond. He was still sorting out the group's braided strands. Some of these people had climbed together before. All seemed to have heard of one another. They shared a powerful, interwoven history, all except Abe, who was new to it.

"You two were on the South Col, weren't you?" Abe seemed to recall that connection, a failed attempt a year ago on the classic route up Everest's sunny side. "You climbed with Kelly?"

"Carried Kelly is more like it," Thomas snapped. His reaction made Abe suddenly cautious. There was something raw here, and he wasn't sure he wanted to be an audience to it.

"She cost me my summit," Thomas added darkly. He had lean-cut pilgrim jowls, good for deep dimples when he was smiling, which was seldom.

He looked over at Abe. "Don't get me wrong, Doc. I'm a consenting adult. I should have known better. But she has a way, you know. Like a witch."

Abe decided to make light of it and snorted. "A witch?" The man was obviously talking about love, or maybe just fornication. It didn't escape him that Kelly had placed her tent far from Thomas's. Abe didn't even try to guess at the meanings.

"Yeah," Thomas said. "You'll see. A woman like that can wreck an expedition. She needs a man. That's how she works it, on the backs and heads of men."

"Well, it won't be me," Abe said. "I'm already carrying around a broken heart." That wasn't exactly true. It was just something to say. In spite of himself, Abe felt a touch of championship toward his solitary blond neighbor. She was pleasant, a welcome contrast any day to Thomas's sour moods.

"Tell me," he asked. "I thought you were a taken man." They had all been treated to Thomas's photos of the woman he was going to marry upon his return to the States.

"I am," Thomas replied.

"So what's the beef?"

"We're not in the World anymore, Doc. We're on expedition now. And that's my advice."

This could only get worse, Abe decided. "Find your medicine?" he asked. End of conversation.

"Screw it," Thomas said. "Don't listen." He stood up and left.

As a matter of principle, some climbers had a fierce aversion to women on big mountains, reasoning that Fay Wray never belonged in the jungle in the first place and had only accomplished getting a natural-born climber killed off in the end. Women couldn't hack it, lacked mountain sense, and threw an expedition's clockwork off. Abe had seen the same logic work among firemen and Colorado miners, and he passed Thomas off as one more dinosaur.

But while the man was wrong, he was also right, for the very sight of Kelly was starting to do something to Abe's heart. At night, Kelly's lithe silhouette trembled against her tent fabric as she readied for sleep, and in the morning she emerged to unfold her beauty like an angel in the clear dawn light.

She was a fraction of an inch shy of six feet tall, half of it blond hair, the other half Hollywood legs laced with childlike scars and bruises. Abe had heard how Kelly treated her masterpiece body with dreamy recklessness, and each time he saw the scars, it struck him as a sort of vandalism. But that was just how Kelly proceeded through life, bumping and tearing and scraping her way up climbs, through brush, and across the lava fields and coral reefs and hot asphalt of countless triathlons.

Abe had seen the advertising shots of Kelly and heard the

stories about how she sometimes played to her appearance, donning slit skirts and painting her nails with fuck-me glitter. But, like a snake shedding its skin, she would plunge into the wilderness all over again where her nails would be broken, her hair tangled with pine needles, her arms and legs bruised and torn.

Their other woman, Gabriella Gustafson—Gus, as she preferred it in her clipped British Columbian manner—lived with Daniel on the opposite side of the hospital, and she was a different concoction. Abe thought of her as night, in part for the color of her cropped hair, but more because Kelly so completely inhabited what he thought of as day.

Gus was all business, Kelly all play. Gus had the green eyes and carved cheekbones of a Highlander princess, but a stern homely slash for lips, and she was notorious for her hair-trigger readiness to compete at the top levels, what was known as "punching out the guys." Her résumé as a hard-core mountaineer included some of the wildest routes in North America. She and Daniel had once pioneered a new line in the Karakoram range of Pakistan, and two separate parties had suffered casualties trying to repeat it. Abe had heard of Gus, though always in terms of her machinelike strength and endurance. No one gossiped about her being a girl climber or a husband hunter or a black widow. She was a climber—a climber's climber, and she belonged to Daniel, or Daniel belonged to her, Abe couldn't quite tell how it was, not until their first night of the full moon.

It was after dinner. The afternoon winds had died early, giving them a respite from the cold. Their garden thermometer, tied to a ski pole beside the mess tent, was registering a relatively balmy 10 degrees Fahrenheit. In the distance, Everest hovered like the ghost of an Egyptian pyramid, triangular and alabaster and remote. No need for his headlamp. When he entered his tent it was in darkness. It took a moment to see that someone was already there.

Stripped to the waist and bent over in the semidarkness, the climber was busily scrubbing his face with one of the hundreds of surgical wipes Abe had made available. The moon was cutting the tent's interior into black and silver tatters, and that made it impossible to tell who the person was. He studied the bare glittering back, sorting through the possibilities, and decided it was probably Robby.

Zebra-striped with moonlight, he had one of those precision-built climber's bodies, 95 percent fat-free. Flaring latissimus dorsi joined at the spine in tightly knit striations. An ugly lightning-shaped scar scuttered off one trapezoid and across the big rib cage. And a tattoo of some kind peeked insolently above the elastic waistband of his surfer pants. His physicality was branded sharply. He belonged to the wilderness.

"It's a warm night," Abe greeted the climber.

"Doc?" the climber answered, straightening up and turning around.

It wasn't Robby. It wasn't even a man. It was Gus.

Abe didn't know what startled him more, her quicksilver nipples or the corrugation on her stomach or her indifference to his shock. Indeed her attitude seemed to dare him.

Gus made no attempt to hide her nakedness. She just stood there, her white eyes locked on Abe's. He felt paralyzed by Gus's metamorphosis from man to woman. Her red hair was bunched up beneath a baseball cap. Abe saw that now. And her skin was gleaming.

"I was just washing up," she said. Warshing hoop.

"I didn't know you were here," Abe said. "I'll step out."

"Why? It's your tent," Gus dryly observed.

So it was. She was telling him to stay.

Abe passed his eyes down her body. He did it quickly, trying to disguise it as an afterthought. She had a bodybuilder's pectoral ridgeline, and to the sides stood her breasts, almost supernaturally round.

Gus was watching his eyes. She was letting him look. For a moment, a vain instant, Abe thought she was trying to seduce him. In a way she was.

"I know about you," she said, then started to towel herself off. "Daniel told me." Still facing him, she took her sweet time with the towel, but the eroticism was gone. If it was his attention—or confusion—Gus had wanted, she had it.

"What did Daniel say?"

"No big secrets. I've known about his dead Diana ever since I met him. And I've known as much about you as Daniel has, which is next to nothing. You did the deathwatch with his girlfriend. Your name is Abe. That's all we knew."

All? Abe wondered. He wanted that to be all they knew. He wanted the past to be done.

"So you buried her," Gus said. She reached for an undershirt and pulled it over her head. For all her seriousness, she could not help but luxuriate in her cleanness. The shirt slid across her bare skin.

"You could say that."

"Yeah," she said. "Anyway, I have a favor to ask."

Abe felt oddly exposed. This stranger had just washed her body in front of him as if his desire were irrelevant. Something close to contempt laced her attitude, and that threw Abe because he'd done nothing to deserve it. Not if she knew nothing.

"What do you want?" Abe asked.

"Between you and me, okay?"

"Fine." Was that her reason for presenting her nakedness then, to create a precedent of secrecy between the two of them?

"Good," she said. "I know this is the very beginning of the climb. But I want you to stay away from Daniel. And I'll keep him away from you."

Abe gawked at her with a mute farmboy look. First Thomas had warned him away from Kelly. Now Gus was taking her turn. Maybe they were freezing him out.

"Nothing personal, Abe. But you have no right to him, no more right than you had to her. Okay? So I'm asking you, just stay away."

Abe took a half step backward, speechless. "Gus . . ." he finally said, but nothing more came to mind. It was she who had no right here, not he. She had to be kidding.

"I know Daniel," Gus explained. "He's not like the rest of us. He can't afford memories, not that one anyway."

Abe recovered enough to be stung and then angry. "But that's between him and me," he said. Gus had nothing to do with that long past matter. It was he who had lived all these years with the voice in the crevasse, and it was Daniel whose girlfriend had furnished the voice. Together they had sealed the dead girl in ice. Then it occurred to him that Gus might be jealous. She could be jealous of Abe's connection across time with Daniel, he considered. Or jealous of a dead girl. But he didn't say so. It was too juvenile.

"I don't understand," he said.

"You could kill him with all that shit." Gus's white eyes flared in the darkness. "I mean it. There's something about this wall. And you. Of all people, he gets you invited. I don't know

what he's thinking. But I do know this. If he can just make it
past the Kore Wall, everything's going to smooth out for him."

Abe saw the sense she'd made out of the same coincidences
he'd already noticed. But he didn't agree with her. "Once the
monkey finds your back," he said, "things don't ever smooth
out."

"He wants peace, Abe. Is that so bad?"

"So do I. So do you. Who doesn't."

As quickly as she'd flared, Gus grew soft again. "I want to
get old," she said very simply. "And I want Daniel with me."

"Gus," he started to say.

Abruptly she was gone out into the blinding full moon. Abe
was left standing in the big dome tent by himself, smelling her
smell. She had seen his desire and turned it back into itself,
forming a circle for him. In the middle lay his emptiness, a
surprise. The memory of Gus's silver flesh stayed with him for
hours. Her demand stayed with him longer. But the more he
thought about it, the less he agreed. They had come to climb,
not act out old history. And besides, as Thomas had put it, they
were all consenting adults.

And still the yaks did not come.

Day after day, Abe preoccupied himself. He arranged his
library of medical texts in a line on one side of his tent. His
medicines and equipment were assigned boxes neatly labeled
with a Magic Marker. One morning, he moved everything out
of his tent and took it down, then spent an hour smoothing out
the ground and put the tent back up again and returned his
possessions to their previous order. He stacked rocks on the
south side as a windbreak. Next day he took the break apart
and stacked it differently. His chin was shaved to a smooth
polish. He washed his white socks three times in as many days.
He even recorded the laundry dates in his journal.

On March 25, someone killed Kelly's potted geranium.
Back in her fall quarter at the high school she taught in, Kelly's
students had cooked up a theory that plant life would add
oxygen to their beloved teacher's Base Camp tent. Kelly didn't
believe it herself, but nevertheless she'd gone ahead and bought
the stoutest green geranium Kathmandu had to offer. She had
carried it past glaring Chinese border guards who suspected
the plant for no other reason than because a Western woman

with yellow hair happened to be carrying it. She had guarded it from hungry goats and curious Tibetans and—ultimately—from Jorgens, who one night groused that the plant was a childish affectation and that they had come to Everest to climb, not garden.

Like a canary in a coal mine, the wilting plant clearly evidenced the effects of their environment, losing color and leaves by the day. It was dying anyway. But someone helped it along one morning by reaching into Kelly's tent and setting it out beneath the sun. By noon it had shriveled to a crisp. Gus caught Kelly weeping over the small vandalism and tongue-lashed her for showing weakness in this camp full of men. Stump heard Gus and told her to ease up, and that led to more hard words.

"This is no good," Robby said to Abe later on. "You can't park combat troops in a box like this or they turn mean. You watch what I say, there's going to be blood soon."

Abe filed the prediction with all of Robby's other predictions. The carpenter was best at forecasting dumplings and blue sky, things that were inevitable. Mostly he just registered hot air.

The yaks still didn't come.

Camp turned into a pressure cooker. The climbers fretted and muttered and sometimes bellowed, but always in the privacy of their tents or on short day hikes around the valley. People grew afraid of their own frustration and meals became largely silent with a sprinkling of small talk. The group's morale spiraled downward. Abe could see it in his dwindling supply of Percodan, amphetamines and morphine, the recreational drugs, to which some climbers freely helped themselves in the hospital. Abe didn't stop them—they were getting his surplus—but he did note their despair.

And then the sky came tumbling down, or almost did. It was the middle of the day on March 28, though Abe was starting to slip on which day of the week it was anymore. They were gathered at what was called the Tomb, a squat stone hut some hundred yards out from camp on top of a small hill.

When George Mallory disappeared near the summit in 1924, his comrades had stacked a primitive monument atop the hill. Over the years, expeditions had borrowed flat stones from the monument for windbreaks and to make this ten-by-ten-foot hut with its doorway aimed at Everest. Now the only thing left of the monument was the hut, and there was little left of that. The tops of the walls were falling in and there was no roof.

Jorgens had talked about making the Tomb their latrine, declaring that the women should have privacy, a building with walls, not just a hole in the ground. But it was Gus, a woman, who got mad and told him no. "It wouldn't be proper," she said. Jorgens scoffed and said everything and nothing was proper up here on Everest. And Gus replied how that was the point, it was up to them to decide what was right and what wasn't, and shitting in a hut made of monument stones wasn't right. It would be like shitting into a grave.

The climbers liked to gather here and lounge about, some reading bad horror and techno-military novels and comic books, others snoozing with their feet jutting out the hut door or fiddling with climbing gear or sipping Sherpa tea.

Behind a rock, Thomas was puffing short, breathless blues riffs on one of his harmonicas. Jorgens and Robby were taking their crack at trying to fix their seven Korean-made walkie-talkies. Without the handsets there would be no communication between camps on the mountain. But that was providing they ever got on the mountain.

Stump was dabbing at his latest watercolor of the Hill, continually thwarted by the cold and dryness. Every time he had it right, the paint would freeze and when it thawed his image became something completely different.

Krishna Rai, their lilliputian cook, had propped the expedition boom box outside the mess tent and Cowboy Junkies music was drifting between sunbeams. Today was Abe's day with the stack of Ultimate Summit postcards, and he still had two or three hundred cards left to sign.

It was about then J.J. erupted.

"Hey," he suddenly shouted, and Abe's pen halted. The harmonica died in the background. Stump lowered his paintbrush. A dozen heads swiveled to see what J.J.'s hormones had jumped at this time.

It was Li. The liaison officer was striding by on his way back from the mess tent with a refill of Swiss chocolate coffee, a luxury fast becoming a personal addiction. Li had no inkling he was J.J.'s target, and so, concentrating on his full mug and the bumpy terrain, he just kept on walking.

"Hey you," J.J. shouted again. He was standing in shorts and thongs and the noon sun filleted his physique into gleaming lines and plates. "Where's those yaks, man."

Li slowed. He looked up, surprised. "Mr. Packard?" He blinked.

"We had promises," J.J. said more softly. Now was his turn to be surprised, for he hadn't meant to make a complicated declaration, only to bark once or twice and shake some rust off. But he had begun.

"We paid for those yaks. We paid the Chinese government. In American dollars. In full."

"J.J.," Jorgens growled up from his spot on the ground. But he didn't move and J.J. ignored him.

"You owe us yaks, man. I didn't quit my job and leave my kid and come six thousand miles around the world to get had by the People's Republic."

"Had?" wondered Li, who was just starting to get the gist of this harangue.

"Hell yes, had. Like, ripped off."

The L.O. looked around at the crop of uplifted faces. Some of the Sherpas had come over and curious climbers were appearing from their tents. Abe watched, fascinated by the brewing ugliness. There was a sense of mob excitement here. Abe felt it himself, the allure of an August lynching. Li's face hardened by degrees, in direct proportion to the crowd's growing interest.

"The yaks will come," Li said. "I have told you this."

"There are no yaks," J.J. shot back. "It's all make-believe."

Li blushed. "The yaks will come."

That was when Daniel stepped from out of nowhere and faced J.J. He was wearing baggy blue jeans and a baggy gray shirt, and though he had Abe's same height and his forearms looked like feeder cables in some sort of power tool, Daniel looked thin against the giant. "Enough," Daniel said.

"Stay out," J.J. snarled.

"You're out of line," Daniel said. "I'm telling you—politely—just stand down."

J.J. looked up at the sky for an instant. Something like anguish flashed across his face and Abe could tell that J.J. wished he'd never started this, not with Daniel in on it now. But the event had taken on its own momentum and J.J. had to play it out.

"Out of line?" he said, twisting to address the circle of onlookers. The veins were standing in his neck and biceps. "We got no yaks. Our good weather's wasting. We're getting fat. And all the L.O. does is drink fancy coffee and make up lies. And I'm out of line?"

Abe felt himself nodding his head in agreement. They had come to climb, not feed and sleep and listen to the boom box. J.J.'s anger was his anger, too. It was all of theirs, and it was genuine.

But then J.J. made a mistake. He ran out of things to say, you could tell. His face went blank for a full minute. Then he slapped his bare thighs and shrugged his big shoulders, and ad-libbed his idea of a finale. "Well anyway," he sighed to the gathering, "what do you expect from a gook?"

Later Abe would allow that Li probably never heard the slur, because Abe wasn't sure he'd heard it himself. As it was, the word was barely a syllable before Daniel's fist was plowing a tight furrow across J.J.'s face.

J.J. dropped hard. His legs crumpled like a killed steer's. He hit the ground so fast that gouts of blood were still flying when his head slapped the earth. A moment later Abe felt a warm raindrop on his face and when he touched it, his fingertip showed red.

Instantly the fight was over. Without a single word, the climbers and Sherpas turned away from the nasty spectacle, each returning to their distractions, everyone but Abe and Daniel, who shook his hand as if he'd just barked it on a tree. Li moved on with his mugful of chocolate coffee, stepping very carefully around the giant's body. Stump went back to his painting. J.J. lay in the dirt.

It took a minute for J.J. to even moan, and by then Abe was kneeling over him, doing his damage control. There was blood on the rocks, on J.J.'s face, on Abe's new Nikes. His chief concern was J.J.'s teeth, because any dentistry would have to be derived from a book. To his relief, Daniel's fist had opened a simple gash over the right eye, and that was only a matter of thread and a tube of Neosporin.

Jorgens stood up and came over. He nested his fists on his hips and blew air through his sharp beard.

"I didn't mean it that hard," Daniel spoke down at J.J.'s stunned form.

"Well I'm glad you didn't mean it any harder, then," Jorgens approved. Abe had seen Jorgens's scared look while J.J. was hectoring the L.O., but the look was different now. Jorgens was excited and relieved both, charged by Daniel's power and relieved that the mutiny was over. Abe could tell it in the man's eyes and by the rural fatalism in his voice.

"I can't have him fouling this climb, that's all," Daniel explained.

"Hell, no," Jorgens agreed.

Abe kept his head down. He couldn't believe the violence, first the shout, then the raving, then the fist. And the indifference, he saw it from the corner of his eye, indifference all around the Tomb.

But more, Abe couldn't believe that Daniel had decided so quickly, though that wasn't it either. No, it wasn't so much the quickness of Daniel's act that overwhelmed Abe but the completeness of it. Daniel's fist had completed the thing so fully that in itself it didn't admit right or wrong. The fist was just something that had happened, like the yaks not showing up or like the sun going down.

"Hell yes, you were right," Jorgens said. "That was close. One more word, and we would have been packing for home. But you stopped it. Hell yes, you were right. And J.J. was wrong."

"No," said Daniel, "he was right too. Li owes us the damn yaks."

Jorgens's head snapped back, not much different from taking a blow to the jaw. In a panic, he cast around for Li, but Li had left, toting off his Swiss chocolate coffee.

J.J. was beginning to recover his senses. He was shaking his head, tossing blood drops right and left and lifting his eyebrows and declaring, "Gaw, man. Gaw."

Daniel looked down at J.J. and said, "Damn it." Slowly, with a pained hitch, Daniel knelt down and rested one hand on J.J.'s shoulder.

J.J. focused on Daniel's face. His eyes cleared. He smiled. "Daniel," he said. "Are we okay, Daniel?"

And suddenly Abe knew this had been a mutiny and everything would be different from now on. The outfit had a new leader.

* * *

As if the demons ruling this Himalayan niche had decided
the blood offering was enough, the mountain finally opened to
them. That very same afternoon, the climbers' destiny broke
free of the valley.

Abe was facing north and he was the first to see them in
the far distance, huge dark birds swinging back and forth
through the empty sky like albatrosses following a fleet of galle-
ons. One minute the northward view was nothing but rocks and
flat valley floor and the next there were these birds, and then,
even as he looked, a mass of dark, lumbering figures appeared
at the far mouth of the valley.

"Look," he said.

"The yaks," someone shouted, "they're here."

Everyone came out from their tents to watch the yaks arrive. It took almost two hours. The herd came slowly, and from
the distance Abe heard a guttural blat and sharp cracking. The
blat was easy to place, it was a shout, a grotesque human shout.
As for the sharp cracking noise, Abe decided it was the snapping
of whips. Closer still, he saw it was the sound of stone on bone.
The yakherders steered their animals by throwing rocks at one
or the other side of their horns.

All through camp, the climbers were whooping like cow-
boys on Saturday night. Abe grabbed his old Pentax camera
and a telephoto lens and hustled through camp for a closer
vantage. He saw Li near the mess tent doorway and paused, a
friendly gesture. The Chinese official was wearing a look of
vindicated authority and Abe allowed that he deserved it. He
hoped Li wouldn't carry it too far, however, because it would
only make him enemies among these climbers.

The braying shouts and cracking of rocks against horn
grew more distinct, and now Abe heard the big black ravens
calling from above the herd. "Now you will see," Li said, "the
Tibetans are barbarians."

Abe had to agree. Through his telephoto lens, the herders
and their animals resembled nothing short of a Gothic invasion.
They moved stolidly, like a storm cloud. The yakkies' faces were
black from the sun and their thick layers of clothing were so
filthy they had the color of the earth. Some of the men had
removed one arm from their jackets, nomad-style, baring a

white shoulder. Some wore long black braids, others Mao caps and ancient mountaineering goggles.

They loomed closer in the lens and Abe heard the primitive ringing of yak bells, all pitched differently, and he saw that some of the men wore pants made of thick leather, others of Chinese quilting. Some were barefoot, others walked in ragged tennis shoes or hide wrappings.

"The edge of the world is here," Li commented.

Abe didn't answer. It was easy to see these yakherders the way Li saw them, as children of the wilderness, the real wilderness, even a brood of the darkness. If there was a Chinese Rome, it was Li's Beijing, and here he was, a functionary faced with the hairy underbelly of his empire. From within the safe walls of his bureau, order must have seemed automatic. But out here, the blue sky and these gutting mountains and strange, dark natives wrecked the order.

"We must be careful," Li said, "we must guard against the . . ." he searched, "the danger."

Abe had never seen a yak before, and he was a little disappointed by how small they were. What few wild yaks remained in Tibet were said to be prehistorically enormous. These domestic versions were a comedown, standing midway between a St. Bernard and an American dairy cow. They had the wild aspect of Texas longhorns, but none of the menace. They were shy animals that spooked easily, and so the climbers quit their joyous cheering. There were fifty or sixty of them, some blond or tawny, some black. Their hair hung shaggy.

The herders and their herd entered Base Camp and immediately it became their camp, too. Now Abe saw why the yak and human dung had been so intermixed on the ground. The Tibetans pitched their open-sided tents among the climbers' tents and their beasts milled everywhere, bells chiming, grazing on straw.

From the midst of the yak mass, someone hallowed Abe. He searched the throng for the voice. It took him a minute to spot Daniel, who was taller than the Tibetans and white with a pronounced limp and dressed in Western gear. But something about him tricked Abe's eye and he was hard to distinguish from the nomads.

"Heads up," Daniel called over the backs of milling yaks.

"Tie down everything you've got. These yakkies are pirates." He was wearing what Abe termed the Nordwand grin. Something about the North Face—just this promise of it, these yaks that would bring them to its base—had unleashed an epidemic of toothy hellbent smile. Every climber had it. Abe could feel it stretching his own face.

"I wasn't sure they'd come," Abe said.

"These guys? They'd come even if they weren't invited. We're like the circus, the mall and the bank all wrapped up in one. We provide the entertainment and put on a feed and pay them to watch all at the same time." In the distance, Gus was watching them talk. When Abe nodded to her, she turned away.

"You knew they'd show up?"

"That's the easy part. The question with these guys is always when. The trick is understanding that Tibet's on the Mexican time plan. Around here you have to be ready for lots and lots of *mañana*."

"So now the climb begins," Abe said.

"Abe," said Daniel, and he suddenly sounded cold sober, "the climb began a long time before we ever got here. But you know that."

Abe glanced at him quickly. The words were cryptic, the smile was not. But Daniel had no intention of explaining himself. Already he was looking away, reveling in the chaos with his cocked white grin.

A sharp light, a dark voice, someone's hand—Abe's sleep blew to pieces.

"Doctor, sir." It was a Sherpa crouching at the far bright end of a headlamp. His voice was solemn, not so different from the wind.

"Nima," Abe registered. Something was wrong. Someone was ill. He knew this ugly rousing and blinding light and voices soft and solemn. They needed him.

"One man," the Sherpa said. "Very sick."

"Now?" Abe pleaded. He was so warm in his cocoon of goose down and the night was so cold. He resented it a little that Nima had just woken him from a shoreline of white sand and bare flesh and lime green tequila. Abe squinted and shielded his eyes. He had a headache and craved glacier water.

"This man very sick," Nima repeated. "Please you coming

now." There was demand behind his calm. The calm was Sherpa, the demand was not, not to a white employer. Abe paid more attention.

"Bring him here then."

"Not possible, sir."

"I'll look at him. But I want to do it here. All my equipment is here." There was some truth to that. Mostly he didn't want to go out into the wind.

Nima was adamant. "Not possible."

"What's wrong with him?"

"Very, very sick." Berry, berry sick. "Maybe dying now. This way, sir." He was pointing away from camp, but at this hour there was nothing that way except night and more night. Still Nima was not the sort to cry wolf.

"Yes, okay." Abe heaved himself to sitting. There was never a dignified way to rise from sleeping on the ground, and he felt doubly awkward under the beam of Nima's light. He dressed quickly, then thought to check the time. It was three-thirty.

Abe rooted through the open boxes lining his tent wall and located some of the basics. He stuffed a stethoscope, a BP cuff, and a penlight into his parka pocket, then laid out some medicines on the sleeping bag. A bottle of injectible lidocaine and a 3-cc syringe for local anesthesia, plus a few packs of silk and needles. A number 15 scalpel. Scissors. A Betadine scrub brush. Gloves. Bandages. Cipro for general infection, though that was expensive and not so plentiful. Percodan for pain. Benadryl for inflammation. He glanced through the mechanisms and chemicals and, satisfied, tossed it all into his little daypack. He trailed Nima out into the cold blackness.

Abe splashed white light through the silent camp, then swung it outward in Nima's direction. There was only darkness. Almost until they reached Mallory's Tomb, Abe could not figure out where he was being led.

Now he saw that someone—the Sherpas or the herders—had lashed old tent fabric on top of the listing walls for a roof. Yesterday the hut had been an empty shell. The raggedy improvement actually made the building appear less habitable and more inconspicuous. By the light of Abe's headlamp, the hut had achieved a look of eerie corruption befitting its nickname.

At the hut door, Abe paused and silently wished for a mug of hot tea and hoped this was blood or bones, not some disease.

He was good with trauma. With trauma, the problem was often obvious, and better yet, it usually responded to touch. It healed and you could see it heal. But with disease, the body hid its problems. It impeached whatever you thought you knew and made you suffer for the suffering.

Abe took a deep breath and slipped through the ripped tentage posing as a front door. He was unprepared for the primitive scene. The hut was lit with two headlamps hung from pegs in the wall. Thick incense choked the air and it was impossible to see how many people were crowded inside. Their eyes glowed white in the gloom.

The patient was lying in an expedition sleeping bag on top of three or four brand-new air pads, a luxury even Jorgens would not have allowed himself. The Sherpas had obviously donated their own gear to this man's comfort, which was extraordinary because Abe had seen no love lost between the Sherpas and the yakkies. Nima roughly ordered the herders to make room, and they scuttled backward.

The patient was a young man, probably still in his teens, and his hair was cropped close. Underneath a layer of grime and blue wood smoke, the boy's face was handsome, more round than long, and yet slighter than most of the Tibetan faces Abe had seen. Under his dark sepia pigmentation, the boy's big Mongolian cheeks were flushed and rosy. He was unconscious and his respiration was labored, yet he looked healthy enough, even robust. Abe hadn't noticed the boy among the yakkies and concluded he'd arrived in the night, maybe herding strays.

"Hold my light," Abe told Nima.

He knelt in the cold dirt. Overhead, the nylon ceiling rustled in the wind. The incense drifted like fog, gray and aquatic. Everything in the room had an aspect of slippery illusion. Abe peeled back the edge of the sleeping bag.

Then Nima moved the light or the fog shifted and suddenly the left side of the man's face leapt into view. It was completely different from the healthy face of a moment before. From his lips to left ear, the jaw was contused, purplish and swollen, a fighter's mask. Very obviously the boy had been beaten. Abe had heard how violent these Tibetans got when they drank, but if this was the result of a brawl, then it was an old one. The bruises were too mature, days old, maybe older.

Abe made a mental note to check for facial fractures and

loose teeth, then moved on. Vitals first, he told himself. Then head to toe. Keep in order.

The boy's throat was hot under Abe's fingertips, the pulse fast and thready. His blood pressure was high, but then everyone was running high BPs because of the altitude. Abe pressed back the eyelids. The pupils looked unequal, one blown, one pinpoint. That could mean an epidural hematoma: arterial bleeding within the cranium. This far from a hospital that would spell certain death. Abe leaned in closer to the boy, determined to prove himself wrong.

He ran his fingers around the back of the boy's skull, searching for lumps or blood. The boy's hair was stubbly in Abe's palms. He handled the skull carefully, almost sacramentally. No matter how many times he held a victim's head, it never ceased to astonish him that a lifetime of memories and thoughts could weigh so little, and yet at the same time that a mere two handfuls of bone and water could weigh so much.

With an epidural hematoma, most patients died within eight hours. And yet the discoloration on this man's jaw—which might coincide with any possible skull fracture—looked a week or more old. There were no goose eggs. No blood or fluid in his ears.

What then, Abe silently demanded. Head injury or not? And then Nima moved the light again and suddenly the pupils evened out. Now they looked equal in size. Abe was baffled but relieved. He moved south from the troublesome head.

"Let's see what else," he said to Nima. Together they unzipped the sleeping bag and exposed the boy to view. He was dressed in yak skins and a pair of quilted pants. Abe smelled old vomit and there were bloodstains on his shirt. Whoever had laid him here hadn't gotten around to removing the Chinese sneakers from his wide feet. Abe opened the hide jacket and lifted up the bloody shirt. And halted.

In the first instant Abe thought it was measles. A dozen or more circular wounds splashed across the boy's barrel chest, each the size of a pencil eraser. But they were grouped—oddly—around his nipples. Abe revised his guess. The pustules might be the infected bites of some large parasite. Then he reverted to disease theory and conjectured it might be some sort of Asian plague. That could explain the fever and coma. But it might not.

Mystified, Abe looked up at Nima. "What happened to this boy?" he asked.

Nima shrugged helplessly.

"He was beaten," Abe said, and clenched his fist for illustration.

"Yes sir."

"Who did this?" Abe asked. Then he amended his question. "When?"

"This man, very good man," the Sherpa said.

All right, Abe thought. Let's talk about the man. "Who is he? Where's he come from?"

Nima shook his open palm in the air to show uncertainty. "I don't know, sir. Some guy."

"Is he a yakherder?" Abe tried.

"Yes." Nima's eyes shifted away. "Yok hoda." Nima knew more than he was saying. Abe didn't know why, nor did he ask. That was a different pursuit.

"Did this happen on the trail?"

"Yes."

"What happened, Nima?"

"I don't know, sir."

"Nima, please . . ."

Nima thought about it. "Not possible."

"You can't tell me? Or you don't know?"

"Yes sir."

Abe sighed. "Ask his friends, Nima."

Nima barked a question at the yakkies, then turned back to Abe. "They say, this man falling down. Shaking, shaking. I don't know."

There was the suggestion of malaria again, but Abe discounted it. He would have to look it up later in the big *Physician's Desk Reference* in his tent, but this just didn't seem like malaria.

"Anything else?"

"No sir."

Abe glanced up and around at the stark white eyes glowing in the smoke and gloom. The shadows were too thick to show the stone walls and their dark faces were invisible. But their eyes leapt out of the murkiness, peering and cryptic. Their curiosity went beyond the ordinary voyeurism that attends any accident. These yakkies had awe and fear written on them—it showed in their multitude at this early hour and it sounded in their hushed murmurs and repetitious mumbles. Prayers, Abe decided. Some of them were praying, and praying hard, nonstop. But why? He looked down at his patient, and all he saw was "some guy," a creature like himself except for the strange markings and hot delirium.

"Nima," he started again, then gave it up. Abe admonished himself. It wasn't up to Nima to provide answers. It was up to him, Abraham, their pretend-physician, to solve the greater mystery of why this man lay unconscious and stretched out on the ground. Always before, Abe had known his patients would move into the care of men and women who knew more than he did and had technology he didn't. Once he packaged and delivered them to the emergency room, his patients disappeared, and he could quit thinking about them. But there was no other place for this Tibetan boy to go, and no higher authority than Abe himself.

At the same time it touched him, Abe was also annoyed that these yakkies—indeed, all of the men and women now gathered in the lap of this mountain—needed him, or might need him, which was the same thing. He was not their answer to pain and sickness, risk and death. He was just one more of them, a wanderer bearing his own question mark.

They called him Doc for their own peace of mind and because they thought it would flatter him, but Abe was embarrassed because he knew real physicians considered his type wannabees and shake-and-bake messiahs. He was good at what he did, but a paramedic is never a doctor, only at best the cowboy who first reaches the car wreck or cardiac arrest or climbing victim and lays on the hands and manipulates the horror and fear. Abe had saved people. He had been saving them most of his adult life, sometimes even bringing them back from clinical death. But he no longer trusted his motives, because at bottom what he did fed upon human beings at their most vulnerable. He was needed by people who could not help but need him.

Abe had thought these thoughts too often to let them distract him. They came to him as second nature, and he handled them with the same ease as he now handled the boy's limp arms, palpating for fractures. He had a talent for treating his doubts as background noise and getting done what needed doing.

He moved quickly, feeling for broken ribs, for deformities along the lower spine, for pelvic fractures. The light shifted again, this time revealing yellowish bruises on the boy's belly. But there were no distended areas, no unusual lumps or masses, not to Abe's touch.

The rule was to assume spinal injuries with an unconscious patient. He hoped the story of this boy collapsing on the trail was true, because anyone with cord injuries might just as well die as be evacuated back across the Pang La and the corrugated Tibetan roads.

Gently Abe pulled off the boy's shoes—he had no socks— and scratched his bare soles with a pebble off the floor. To Abe's relief, each foot twitched. Abe got a distal pulse behind each Achilles tendon and that meant there was circulation, more good news.

Abe ran his hands down the bones of each leg, hip to toe: no gross fractures, no dislocations. Then, with Nima's help, he slid off the Tibetan's quilted pants. His first glance showed nothing out of the ordinary, but then the light—or shadows— revealed more damage and once again he was scowling in puzzlement.

The flesh of both lower legs was ripped and torn and con- tused. Some of the wounds appeared to have a pattern, some overlaid other wounds. His legs were like a canvas of bad paints. Some of the marks were fresh and dark blue. Others showed green or yellow, a month old. The overall effect was gruesome.

The yakherders against the wall muttered at the sight. Nima reacted, too. Abe could feel the Sherpa withdrawing into himself. Nima still knelt beside him and held the light. But his poise was gone, replaced by shock or fear or loathing. Some- thing. For whatever reason, his sense of command had drained off. Curiously, Abe felt himself gaining strength from Nima's unnerving.

Abe took the light and bent close to the mysterious trauma on the boy's legs. He pried open some of the lacerations for a cursory look and prodded at the terrible bruises, investigating the clues. Abe had rescued—and when they were beyond res- cue, had bodybagged—climbers who had fallen from great heights and gotten torn and shredded by their descent. Some of this boy's tissue injuries were consistent with that, a bad tangle with old-fashioned gravity.

But some of these wounds were different.

"Damn," Abe swore and pulled away, shocked.

His reaction alarmed Nima, who said, "Sir? Sir?"

"These are animal bites."

"No sir." Nima categorically rejected the notion. "Not possible."

Abe didn't know what kind of animal, but he definitely recognized the puncture wounds and lacerations.

"What's going on here?" Abe demanded. This was no ordinary camp accident. He tried to piece together the injuries. Had the boy fallen off the trail and lain unconscious while animals chewed at him? Or had animals attacked and driven him off some cliff? Stranger things had happened.

"Very bad," Nima murmured. "Very bad." Nima rocked back on his heels. He wouldn't meet Abe's eyes.

Abe felt defeated, completely lost, like a traveler who wakes up in a dark forest. Abe wanted a story to go with these wounds, as if that would somehow locate him in this wilderness. But that was just laziness speaking. It was up to him to create the story with a diagnosis. Wound by wound, he had to put in order this poor body.

Abe sighed. He was about to begin at the top again, with the boy's head, when suddenly the body stiffened under his hands. The muscles seized and shuddered and the boy gave an inhuman cry as if to answer all of Abe's questions.

Naked to the world, the body released its momentary tension, then spasmed again, and the boy commenced to jerk and moan, gripped in the throes of a violent grand mal seizure. Abe had seen epileptic fits before and knew what was happening. But the yakherders were terrified by the monstrous sight, this human pinned and writhing upon the cold dirt. Shouting, they scrambled backward against the wall and those by the door darted out into the black wind.

Abe didn't hesitate. Still on his knees, he swept away the loose rocks and slid the bunched sleeping bag under the boy's skull to prevent his braining himself. All the while, the boy's hard fists and elbows flailed against Abe. Even though unconscious, he seemed to be doing battle with some terrible enemy.

Abe hunched against the blows, but a sudden flurry caught him square in the face and he shouted with pain and surprise. Blood flew from his nose and then another blow caught him and knocked him flat. The safest thing seemed to be to lie close to the epileptic and cover his head, so he huddled against the body and gritted his teeth and felt the frozen earth against his cheek.

Finally someone thought to grab hold of Abe's ankles and pull him free of the violence. It was Nima, and he propped him against the stone wall. There Abe panted and pinched the blood from his nose and waited out the convulsions. The boy went on twitching and fighting his demons in that ill-lit little hovel.

And then, abruptly, the boy went still. His possession simply ceased. His silence and immobility were doubly blunt against the wild moments before. Abe stayed lying against the wall in case there were any neural aftershocks. One pummeling was enough.

All around him, Nima and the yakherders were staring at the still, heaped body, mumbling and praying. They were horrified. But Abe was not.

He was relieved. He was cheered even. At least he knew now what was wrong. The boy was an epileptic. Somewhere out there in the terra incognita called Tibet, this boy had suffered a seizure and fallen and been set upon by animals. Nothing more. Now Abe knew. Beyond sewing the torn flesh and treating the infection, there was little Abe could do about that. The boy had his own mountain to climb. It was that simple, after all.

With the same patient manner he unraveled knots, Abe worked on the boy's wounds one by one. He started an IV to rehydrate the feverish boy and asked Nima to recruit one of the herders to keep the bag of saline solution warm with his body, but Nima chose to do it himself. While the bag was warming, Abe injected an ampule of D-50, pure dextrose, through the IV needle. It was an old paramedic trick to revive the unconscious. With diabetics it worked instantly. With this boy it didn't work at all. Abe went ahead and connected the saline bag.

Finally Abe was able to seal the boy's bruised and torn and bandaged body back into the warm sleeping bag. He knelt back on his heels and rested his hands on his thighs. Abe had felt this helpless before, but never so hopeful at the same time. Still the margins of chance were thin in this harsh borderland. Undiluted, destiny was more likely to turn out here as it was meant to.

When Abe emerged from the hut, dawn was just seeping down the western slopes. It had been hours since he'd disappeared into the hut's smoke and gloom and now the sun was softly peeling away the frost.

The valley's blue air turned clear and a tiny flock of dawn quail gabbled and tuttered. The yaks lay on their curled legs, crunching cud, drowsy.

In the distance, on the far side of camp, the liaison officer had risen, as was usual, to perform his morning t'ai chi. With slow, fluid sweeps of his hands, Li stalked his invisible opponents and defeated them. His motions were more beautiful this morning than Abe remembered.

And up the valley to the south stood Everest. Its jagged right-hand edge was lit golden and the mountain was still, not a breath of wind stirring its snows

THEIR CALM WAS broken.

On the morning of April Fool's Day they cut loose from Base Camp. Abe woke early and lay still, smiling. Watching his tent wall come alive with pure tangerine light, he felt hope. The yak caravan had left yesterday, taking with them two tons of gear and a whole circusful of noise. Only the young herder had remained behind, and though he hadn't regained full consciousness, his delirium and fever were abating, and so was Abe's pessimism. With bed rest and fluids and Western vitamins, the boy would probably recover. Abe had spent an hour instructing Krishna, their cook, on how to tend the patient. Krishna had solemnly promised to be devout in his care.

In this morning's hush it was easy to forget the shock of Daniel's fist on J.J.'s skull and the mutiny against Jorgens's plodding *ancien régime* and the Tibetan boy's horrible seizures. Abe thought to himself, Today has promise, today is new. It was the kind of thing he used to tell Jamie every morning before they slipped from bed and dressed. She had liked to hear it. He had liked to say it.

Abe hooked on his wire-rims and opened his sleeping bag and piece by piece dressed with the clothing he kept warm every night for this very moment every morning. On his way to the mess tent, he paid a a visit to the expedition's water skull.

It was a sheep skull nestled into a rocky crevice by the glacier pond which provided their water. It was still possessed of a good portion of its flesh, meaning it was in a state of slow decay. The grisly head lay rotting within inches of their drinking water, and Li had made several complaints, citing the People's Republic's campaign against rats, flies and other germ carriers. But the skull served as a sort of Tibetan mousetrap for bad spirits, and supposedly kept the water pure on a supernatural level. And since Krishna Rai boiled all their potable water, hepatitis or cholera or any other plague nesting in the head was rendered more unlikely than demon possession. Despite Li's fussiness, the skull stayed in place.

Abe had come to enjoy waking early and sitting here in wait for the sunshine. It was quiet and primeval and satisfied his streak of pantheism. But this morning he didn't linger. The camp was alive. Krishna made farewell omelets with the last of their eggs and talked about how he would miss them while they were on the mountain. Li wagged his finger at the little cook and told him in English, "Now you will be alone with me and I will teach you how to play chess," and Krishna laughed even though he didn't like Li.

At the end of breakfast, Stump said, "Let's do it to it," with the enthusiasm of an original thought. Outside the mess tent, Robby and Carlos started singing the *Rawhide* theme, lashing the cold dirt with hanks of loose sling.

They loaded their packs and hefted them for weight, then added or subtracted things and closed the packs and slung them on. In the coming week, some of the yakherders were scheduled to make a second trip up with any mountain supplies still remaining in the dump. By the middle of April it was projected that the next camp, Advance Base Camp, would be self-sufficient. The climbers kept their loads light for the trail and so Abe did too—a sleeping bag, some food, and his streamlined jump kit, his trauma box for mishaps along the trail. On second thought he went ahead and stuck a twelve-pound cylinder of oxygen in his pack just in case someone crashed.

It was going to take three days to trek up to their next camp, four days for the yaks. It was only ten miles away, but the altitude was going to slow them. If all went well, the climbers would arrive at Advance Base Camp—ABC—on the same day their gear did. Some of them would immediately return to Base Camp to recover from the altitude and to escort the final yak carry back up. Others would get ABC up and running. Still others would begin climbing toward the next camp. The siege was now begun.

In bunches, the climbers left camp and aimed for the throat of the Rongbuk Glacier, a huge body of ice left behind by the last ice age. On maps, the glacier resembled a white octopus with its tentacles flung out among all the surrounding valleys. Abe set off with the last wave. Li stood by the trail and wished them good luck.

Five minutes out of Base Camp, Abe turned around to take a photo of their comfortable little tent city, but it was already gone. When he looked back up at Everest, it, too, had disappeared, blocked from view by Changtse, the satellite peak.

Single file on the trail, the climbers were swallowed whole by a maze of looming mud walls and loose stone and deep, icy corridors. Once again Abe had no idea where they were going or what to expect. Li was right, they truly had come to the edge of the world.

It would have been hard to get lost on that twisting path, at least on the first part of it, for dozens of expeditions had been here before them, and the trail was clearly imprinted. Where the tracks disappeared on long, jumbled fields of scree, they simply had to follow heaps of old frozen yak dung. But even with the sun out and the air warm, it seemed to Abe that a careless soul could wander forever in this labyrinth, and he was glad to have Daniel leading them.

At a prominent fork in the glacier, they found a huge, thirty-foot arrow made of piled rocks. It pointed left.

"Mallory and his bunch went that way," Daniel said. The Brit's body had never been found, and the mountaineering community was still divided over whether he had summited.

"It takes you to the North Col," Daniel said. That was what climbers called the "trade route" up the north side. It was by far the easiest climb up Everest's north side, and for that reason was the most often repeated. With huge sums of money and oftentimes national prestige at stake, most expeditions to Ever-

est opted for a sure summit rather than a new or more difficult
route. Part of Abe wished they were heading left for the North
Col's well-known terrain and relative safety.

"That's also the trail you take to the Chengri La," Daniel
added. Chengri Pass, which James Hilton had turned into the
fictitious Shangri-La in his *Lost Horizon,* crossed south into Nepal
at a height of 18,000 feet. Over that *la,* Daniel and his Lepers'
Parade had escaped during the '84 debacle.

"We go this way," Daniel pointed, and they turned right
into the shadows, moving quietly, as if giants had built this stone
arrow and might still be lurking nearby.

The trail roller-coastered up and down, mostly up. For
some reason a sense of vertigo kept sneaking up on him. From
minute to minute, he couldn't shake the sense of being out of
control. Usually he only felt this way on steep rock, and yet it
was plain to see that both his feet were planted on flat ground.
Abe tried to reason with his fears. Finally he just accepted that
he was going to have to live with them.

The climbers gained elevation. A day passed, then two,
then three. In between they suffered two long, cramped nights
of too many people sharing too few tents. Despite the bitter
cold, Abe ended up sleeping outside under the stars both nights.

Their pace slowed, and so did their thoughts, or at least
Abe's did. He tried to remember Jamie's face, but to his dull
alarm it eluded him. The more he tried, the less he remembered. Before it was too late and she was altogether erased from
memory, Abe decided to quit searching for her and instead
concentrated on Carlos's heels in front of him, plodding, mindless.

"Eventually we'll acclimatize," Robby told Abe. "This will
seem just like sea level." Abe listened to Robby's words but
watched his lips. They were bright blue, a symptom of the
hypoxia all of them were enduring. As their bodies cued to the
altitude, some of the blue would return to pink, but Abe
doubted 20,000 feet could ever feel like sea level.

Their third morning on the trail, the climbers penetrated
a long bank of penitentes, or seracs. These were tall pinnacles
of ice that had been sharpened to a point by the sun. Some had
warped into grotesque shapes. Others had collapsed. One had
toppled and speared the earth.

Abe looked around, startled by the unnatural quiet in this

place. He knew what these penitentes were but had never seen them up close like this. Abe rubbernecked until Gus came up behind and nudged him onward.

If ever nature had erected a sign to warn away man, the penitentes were it. It was like an evil forest in there. The thirty-foot fingers of turquoise ice were utterly beautiful and seductive, but they were also deadly and looked it.

Here and there, big boulders sat five and ten feet above the ground, balanced atop thin sun-carved columns of ice like huge petrified mushrooms. "I feel like Alice in Wonderland," Abe said to Gus.

Gus glanced at him sharply and hushed him with a finger. "This place is booby-trapped," she whispered, and pointed at the hair-trigger stones and penitentes. "If one of those bastards collapses, it could bring the whole place down." There was no way to tiptoe with a fifty-pound pack on, but Abe did his best to walk more gingerly.

Soon they came upon a horribly twisted animal dangling from an ice wall. Half of it lay outside the ice, the other half still frozen into the blue glass. Birds had pecked away the eyes, and the elements had stripped much of the rest down to bone.

"Road kill," Gus whispered, poking at the hide and bones with her ski pole.

It had long matted hair and thick joints, and the ice and wind and sunlight had rendered it almost shapeless. Though it looked like the thawing remains of a mastodon, Abe knew it was a yak.

"Is that one of ours?" he whispered. Gus shook her head no.

"Did a rock fall on it?"

"Nah," whispered Gus. She opened her pocketknife and stepped closer to the thing. "If a rock fell on it, the yakkies would have butchered it for the meat. This poor thing probably fell down a crevasse, probably during some expedition. Now the glacier's just getting around to belching it up. Everest does that a lot, turning out its dead."

Gus reached forward and grabbed one of the horns and wrenched the animal's head up. With her free hand, she snaked her knife under the neck and sawed away with the blade. After a minute, a fist-sized cup of metal fell out of the filthy hair and hit the ground with a clank.

Gus picked the bell up. She let the clapper strike the metal cup once, gently. The solitary note trembled through the glass forest. "For my collection," she said, stuffing one of her gloves inside to muffle the clapper.

Abe was glad when they finally reached the end of that hour-long bed of crystal thorns and stone mushrooms. The rest of the group was waiting for them on a clearing, lounging against their packs or stretching sore shoulder muscles. J.J. was reading one of Robby's old Silver Surfer comics, and the Sherpas were sharing some *tsampa,* or roasted barley, with Daniel. When Abe and Gus appeared, the climbers all got to their feet and started loading up.

Only then did Abe realize that the group had divided itself into pairs and trios to pass through the penitentes, one team at a time. Nobody had told them to do it, they'd just split up and staggered their own ranks so that if there had been an accident among the penitentes, there would have been a minimum of victims and a maximum of rescuers. Abe's confidence in the group soared.

They headed higher up a series of glacial steppes, holding close to a wall of blue and white ice. Another two hours ground away and the natural terracing grew steeper. Here and there they had to grab at outcrops to clamber higher. The party slowed to a crawl, gasping and resting their hands on their knees.

"I must be getting old," Kelly said. Abe remembered she was just thirty. Her hair hung in long golden rags, partly braided.

"Twenty-one thou," Stump consoled her, referring to the altitude.

"Twenty-one seven," J.J. corrected him. He looked jolly and warm and primitive in a big fur Khampa cap he'd bought from a nomad in Shekar. His black eye was buried behind glacier glasses. "We're getting up there."

"No excuses," Robby threw in, gasping along with the others. "You *are* getting old, Kelly. Especially for a woman." Kelly delighted in having her beauty deflated, but no one else was particularly amused. They were too tired.

"It's only a little more," Daniel told them. As if to confirm him, some of the yak caravan appeared, wending its way back down to Base Camp. Unburdened of their loads and with gravity helping them along, the yaks and their herders were practically running downhill. Their rapid descent made Abe feel that much slower.

Soon the afternoon winds began. The trail's corridor funneled blasts straight down into their faces. Without breaking stride, Abe zipped his jacket closed to the throat and fished some thin polypro gloves from a pocket. They wound through the convolutions.

Abruptly, as if bobbing to the sea's surface after a deep dive, they emerged onto a flat mesa, perhaps an acre wide.

And suddenly the whole earth just halted. And so did Abe.

With no warning, the gigantic gleaming body of Everest was rearing up in front of them. They had lost sight of it for three days and now it jutted one and a half miles above them, stabbing into the jetstream. Its curtains of afternoon light hung before them like a dream.

At first the mountain distracted all attention from ABC, which lay in shadow at the back of the mesa. The mesa was butted snugly against a soaring rock wall, and the wall had shed copious piles of limestone down onto it. Including Daniel's pioneering attempt six years ago, theirs was the fourth expedition to make camp on top of the rubble.

Low-slung and mean, the camp had the lean, breathless look of a battlefield headquarters. In effect, ABC robbed Base Camp of its function. From here on most of the assault would be supplied and coordinated from ABC. Earlier expeditions had piled rocks into semicircular walls to cut the wind, and the faster moving Sherpas had erected tents in steps among the rubble, one above the other. Someone—probably Nima, trying to make them feel comfortable—had attached one of their twelve-inch American flags for the summit to a bamboo wand and wedged it among the rock. Bright blue and yellow tarps covered a small stockpile of food and equipment, and yaks and herders were wandering around.

The closer Abe got, the uglier the camp appeared. It seemed to squat in the shadows beneath the rearing prow of white and black stone. Above ABC the mountain didn't get just steep, it got vertical. This close, Abe couldn't see the top of the stone wall and all of the mountain's other features vanished. He knew the wall was just one more piece of the puzzle, though from here the Kore Wall seemed to stretch all the way to the sky. Had he been the first to arrive here—had he been Daniel ten years ago—he would have pronounced the route inconceivable and turned around.

Nima and Sonam were laboring among the rock, heaving chunks atop new walls, building new spaces for more tents. Sonam nudged his sirdar, or boss, and pointed at Abe, and Nima descended goatlike from the rubble to greet him.

"Oh, hello, sir." Except for his bright Gore-Tex climbing uniform, Nima might have been one of the yakherders. His cheekbones stood like fists, and his short city-cut had grown wild and the black hair was below his ears.

"You are coming onto the mountain now," Nima said. He was smiling.

"Yes, here I am," Abe acknowledged. He was feeling nauseous and hitched his pack higher on his shoulders, mostly for effect. He wanted to sit down. No, that wasn't true, he wanted to lie down.

Nima wanted to talk. "The mountain is very strong."

"Yes, very impressive."

Nima finally got around to his question. "This yakherder in Base is all better now?"

Abe had forgotten all about the Tibetan boy. For a brief few days, he'd even forgotten he was the team's archangel and had thought of himself as simply one of the climbers. To an extent that Abe could not help but appreciate—for it let him be something other than a doctor—they had begun replacing science with superstition. Some had taken to refusing all medicine, relying instead on their crystals and vitamins and herbs. Others had become alchemists, mixing cocktails of Halcion for sleep with Diamox for respiration with codeine for coughing and aspirin for thinning their blood. And J.J., of course, had his steroids. There was no thwarting them, so Abe didn't try. There was no escaping duty, though.

"Nothing's changed, Nima. I checked him before I left Base Camp." He didn't want to raise any false hopes by explaining the subtle improvements. And besides, his nausea was crawling up.

"But medicine, sir."

Abe belched and swallowed. He wanted to be irritated, but that required too much vigor. He had mounted to almost 22,000 feet on the mountain of his dreams, and his only welcome was to be pestered about an epileptic yakkie in a coma? "I did what I could," he said.

"Yes, sir," Nima said.

Next to one of the empty tents, Abe backed against a rock and nestled down his pack with a bovine groan. He unharnessed himself from the shoulder straps and waistband and slumped forward, breathing deep. One of the other Sherpas brought over a cup of tea and just the fumes helped restore him. He drank and felt better.

ABC was a bleak place made all the bleaker because it lay in the very palm of the mountain. Night was coming on and alpenglow had turned Everest into a vast crimson spike. Its plume of red snow reached out for the plunging sun. Abe noticed that everyone else seemed to be ignoring the mountain with a business-as-usual nonchalance. He was alone in relishing the spectacle.

Everest didn't just overshadow ABC, it towered above. It utterly dominated the land. Time and space had frozen tight here. The earth had stopped. As in Ptolemy's scheme, the sun seemed to orbit this point. Here was the center.

From the outset Abe had imagined that this expedition was going to be a great collective memory, one that he and his comrades would each harken back to in their old age. Forever after, it would warm them on cold days, strengthen them, give them an epic poetry to tell their grandchildren. Back in Boulder, Abe had lain awake beside Jamie at night and stared up through the skylight, telling himself stories about how he was going to climb a great mountain. But now, faced with actually ascending into this pure light, his only thought was "how absurd."

"Doc?" Kelly was standing beside him, hunched beneath her big blue pack. For the first time, Abe noticed a monarch butterfly she had embroidered onto the side pocket, an iridescent creature that would have died within minutes up here. He wondered what the yakherders thought of it, if they even associated it with reality.

"Is that your tent, Doc?"

Abe looked around at the other tents, already filling with people. "Yeah, I guess," he said.

"You got a bunkie?"

Was this the beginning of what Thomas had warned him against? Abe hesitated, less out of loyalty to Jamie than disappointment. Kelly obviously thought him safe to share quarters with, and part of him didn't want to seem too safe to her. Even with her hair greasy and eyes bloodshot from the sunscreen and sweat and her lips blistered, the sight of Kelly took his breath away. It invaded what was left of his dwindling memories of Jamie. It was difficult enough to remember what Jamie looked like without waking to this other woman, this strange, harrowed beauty. But the truth was, he did want to wake to her.

"It's just me," he said.

"What would you think if we hooked up?" she asked. "I think we're the last two not paired off. And this is the last of the tents." She seemed to think he might say no.

"I'd like that," Abe said.

He reined it all in—the libido, the fantasies, the disbelief at his good fortune. In itself, the prospect of a tentmate cheered him. He had grown tired of being alone at Base, even with the traffic of visitors in and out of his tent. Kelly would be good company, he sensed, and she could teach him things about the mountain. If things worked out, they might even team up for some climbing and carrying. Abe had noticed most of the climbers already matched up, and it was starting to look like he and Kelly were the ugly ducklings. Thomas was looking at them from an uphill tent, but when Abe stared back, he ducked away.

Quickly, because it was turning cold now, they set up house together. Kelly crawled inside first. One at a time, Abe handed her the basics, staying outside while she laid out their pads and sleeping bags, then hung a small propane cookstove by wires from the ceiling. Elsewhere, other climbers were going through the same ritual, bracing for night. One by one, they climbed into their tents and zipped up.

While Kelly worked in the tent, Abe watched Sonam, a Sherpa with gap teeth and the slow gait of a sumo wrestler, chop pieces of ice from the bare glacier with his ice axe. Like some burly Yankee peddler, he loaded the pieces into a burlap sack and carried the ice around from tent to tent, leaving a pile of chips for each to use.

As Sonam approached, Abe could hear him mumbling prayers under his breath. He dumped some chips by Abe and Kelly's door and looked up and said, "Docta sob, docta sob."

"Thank you," the doctor sahib said.

"Oh ho," Sonam droned on, and returned to his prayers and ice delivery.

Abe was the last to get out of the wind. He took one last look at the mountain overhead, then scooted into the doorway, feet last. He removed his shoes and clapped off the limestone gravel and zipped the door shut. He was alone with one of the most beautiful women on earth, but suddenly it didn't matter. There were more important things than desire. Warmth and food and plain company easily outweighed other inspirations.

Kelly had already fired up their little hanging cookstove and started a potful of ice melting for hot chocolate. Until the team's second mess tent arrived with the next yak train, the only communal meals the group was likely to share would be outside on sunny days. For the time being, each pair of climbers cooked for itself. Over the next two hours, Abe and Kelly took turns melting ice chips and cooking noodle soup or hot drinks and melting more ice. It was vital that they drink two gallons or more per day. Abe had quickly learned to read his urine, a literacy peculiar to high altitude mountaineering. The darker the urine, the worse your dehydration, and at these heights dehydration was a homicidal maniac. One's bodily fluids vanished into thin air, expired and sweated away at dangerous rates.

It grew dark and cold, but they kept the flame at work under pot after pot of ice melt. It gave them something to do while they talked. Abe learned a little about Kelly's life in Spokane, that she was a biology teacher at a rural high school, that her sisters all had babies, that she had been the youngest, and that her mother had long ago despaired of her climbing adventures.

"It surprised me that you teach," Abe said. "They told me you were a model." He was thinking specifically of the hundreds of thousands of dollars in endorsement money she'd brought in to the expedition.

"No way." Kelly laughed self-consciously. "It's one thing to hang clothes on a beat-up blonde in the outdoors. As long as you keep the camera at a distance, I'm okay. But for studio work, you have to be gorgeous. No wrinkles. No scars. No way. Not me."

"But you must get a percentage of the endorsement money," Abe said.

"Of course not," Kelly said. "I'm a climber, not a model." She wasn't just shocked. She was angry.

Abe saw he'd touched a nerve. "I didn't mean to pry," he said, and made himself busy with the stove.

Kelly was frowning, figuring something out. "It's okay," she said. "I just can't fight everybody all of the time."

"I don't know what that means."

"This Barbie-doll crap. People act like I don't have any credentials. Like I'm here for the photo ops but not for the climb."

Abe didn't deny it. It was true. He'd heard the others talking. Until now it hadn't occurred to him that Kelly might object to her role. "Actually that sounds familiar," he said. "They brought me along to doctor. But I came to climb, too. And I'm having my doubts whether they'll ever let me."

Kelly weighed his sincerity and was satisfied. "That's what I mean," she said. "I know I'm not the greatest climber in the world. I'm not a Daniel, say. But then no one else is Daniel either. We all brought our weaknesses here."

Now seemed the time for Abe to sketch some of his own past, and as an act of faith—to whom he couldn't say—he mentioned Jamie.

"I didn't know her name," Kelly said. "But I knew you were married. Jorgens told me."

Abe was quick to deny it. He had indeed said that to Jorgens, but only to gain some sort of advantage that was lost to him just now. "But I'm not," he told Kelly. "Not really."

Kelly looked at him. "Right," she said. She'd heard that one before.

Abe started to elaborate. Kelly cut him off.

"I've been here before, you know. At the foot of the Hill with three months to go. A woman in a tent with a man I've never met. And every time before I've thought, this time it's going to happen. But every time it's been a bust."

She was talking about Thomas, Abe realized. Thomas or others. Or perhaps she meant only the summit.

Abe decided he was better off talking about her dreams of the summit than of Thomas. "How high have you gotten?" he asked.

"To the South Col," she answered. Besides designating the easy route on Everest Nepal-side, the South Col was also a feature, a broad dip in the ridge between Everest and another of its satellite peaks, Lhotse. Situated at over 26,000 feet, the col provided a virtual meadow for climbers to camp in before making their final leap upward.

"So close," Abe said. "Was there a storm?" That was mountaineering diplomacy talking. One put questions about failure delicately, and storms were a favorite scapegoat.

"No," Kelly said. "I don't know what you've been told. But there was no storm."

Abe didn't press.

"This might sound bizarre," she said, "but I once thought love might have something to do with it." And still she didn't say Thomas's name. "I was wrong. Wrong up here anyway. Up here it only breeds distraction. It gets in the way." She glanced at Abe, and he saw the plea in her eyes. "That's not what love should be," she finished softly.

Abe studied the callouses on his open palms. There was little left to add. As unsettling as he found her candor, he was also grateful for it. Everything was in the open now. At least they wouldn't be wasting their time or their dignity or their hearts on a distraction.

"I didn't mean to go on," she apologized. But of course she'd meant to. She was hunting for a partner, not a sackmate. This was a test.

Abe tried to think of the right reply, trusting her confusion more than Thomas's bitterness. And he wanted to climb with her.

"You're right," he said. "That does sound bizarre. Love. It's not a word I ever thought to hear at twenty-one thousand feet on Everest. Not with so much mountain ahead of us."

He let it go at that, and so did she. In their silence, Abe could hear snatches of conversation as climbers familiarized themselves with one another.

"You know, I've looked at the photo a hundred times," Kelly said. On to a new topic. "But now we're here and I still can't figure out the line." No one else had admitted as much, though Abe had suspected he wasn't alone in feeling intimidated by this great unknown. It was good to hear that underneath the cocky self-assurance they all affected, at least one other climber had some fears, too.

"I thought it was me," Abe said. "I thought I was getting stupid." He said it by way of trade, his anxiety for hers.

"Then we're all getting stupid together," Kelly said. "I mean, you tell me . . ." and she suddenly flipped onto her stomach and rummaged through a stuff sack. She extracted a stubby pencil, a spiral notebook, and one of their Ultimate Summit postcards with a color picture of the North Face. "Look at this," she said, and stabbed her pencil at the photo. "What's up here? And how do you get past this?"

For the next two hours they lay side by side like newlyweds talking about the future and making plans. Zipped chastely into their separate sleeping bags, they kept their hips and shoulders pressed together, hungry for the extra warmth. They talked on and on, Abe with his headlamp lit, Kelly pumping out pictures and maps with her pencil. To an extent it worked. Even between the two of them, they couldn't decide how Daniel had deciphered this route. But at least they managed to reduce the monster towering above them to a paper cartoon, something both could manage in their minds.

"What are our chances then?" Abe asked her.

"Are you kidding?" Kelly nudged him with her hip and her teeth flashed in their ball of light. "You don't have that one figured out yet, Doc?"

Abe snapped off the headlamp and closed his eyes. Kelly's bravado comforted him more than he cared to admit. Maybe the Hill wasn't such an alien place after all. It had been conquered before. It could be conquered again.

But around midnight, the moon burned a hole in Abe's sleep and his eyes came wide open. He lay still and listened to the night.

He heard a woman breathing softly beside him, her warm back against his, and he liked that it was Kelly there. In a nearby tent someone was hacking away with a dry cough. A stiff breeze was beating their camp, but, oddly, he could even hear people rustling in their sleeping bags fifty feet away. It still amazed Abe how acoustically transparent tents could be, like tonight with every tent a bubble of sound connected to all its neighbors.

Even in a high wind, Abe had discovered he could hear his neighbors whispering. They may as well have been a tribe of Neanderthals piled one against another in a cave.

But what Abe was really listening for was not human at all. And now he heard it again, the glacier, beneath his pillow of spare clothing.

Hundreds of feet thick, the ice was alive and moving. He could hear it popping and groaning and cracking. And suddenly his vertigo returned and the very earth seemed to drop out from under him.

Abe had once read that in the Dark Ages, peasants used to believe it meant certain death to sleep upon a glacier. Now, listening to the dragons stirring within the mountain, Abe came close to whispering a prayer. But for the life of him, he couldn't remember a single one.

Long Before The morning sun could reach around Everest's north-facing architecture and unearth ABC, Abe left Kelly's warmth to go chop ice for breakfast. He was the first up, or thought so until he found Daniel alone, perched upon a boulder. The man was hunkered down upslope with a big expedition sleeping bag draped across his shoulders, and he was facing the mountain. He might have been a gargoyle frozen in place. His hair lay heavy with human grease, long and black upon the bag's cherry-red Gore-Tex.

At Abe's approach, Daniel twisted. His eyes were glittering in a mask of sunbaked cheekbones and black whiskers and the pale skin of his goggles mark. He looked wild, but not because of the burnt flesh or unwashed hair or gleaming eyes which marked them all by this point. Rather it was his grin. The white teeth in that dark mask showed a joy so savage it made Abe cold.

"Here it is," Daniel said. He turned back to relish the wall, his horseshoe jawline thrusting out at the great North Face, and Abe stood beside him.

The North Face was astounding. Where its lines had been washed out by shadow and light yesterday afternoon, this morning Abe could see the route's features in clean, blue detail. ABC

sat so close to its base that the mountain was foreshortened and
looked squashed. The upper reaches beetled out. Gullies and
ridges seemed warped out of their actual shape. The summit
was barely visible as an insignificant bump. All the parts of it
stood assembled just so, and now Abe could see a logic to the
route that made Daniel's climb a little more imaginable, almost
accessible.

"This beauty . . ." Daniel started to say with faraway re-
membrance, but he faded off.

"I didn't know it would be so elegant," Abe remarked, and
he meant it. For all its brute, compacted massiveness, the line
had a delicacy and straightness that would appeal to any
climber, even a newcomer like Abe. Now, with the route
stretched full above him, Abe could see that Daniel's *direttisima*
was more direct, and ingenious, than any he'd ever seen. Abe
stood quietly by the monster's author, marveling at Daniel's
hubris.

It was almost as if Daniel had laid down a giant ruler in the
middle of all this geological anarchy and drawn a path of absolute simplicity. Not that simplicity meant ease or safety. To the
contrary, the Kore Wall was going to demand extraordinary
risk. From top to bottom, the 8,000-foot wall was exposed to
weather and rockfall, and there was no exit onto easier ridges
should they run into trouble.

Daniel spoke again, his voice darker. "This fucker. . . ."

He rustled under his crisp Gore-Tex shroud and looked
around at Abe. For an instant—no longer—Abe saw a face
from long ago, a look of utter blank panic or worse, a look of
terrible surrender. Then Daniel drew a deep breath and brought
himself back from the depths, and Abe drew a breath too.

"I can't believe I'm here."

"Me either." Abe meant himself.

But Daniel was lost in his soliloquy. He snorted, shook his
head. "I'll tell you one thing," he said. "It's not for the love of
it. No way. I hate this fucker."

Abe digested that. "Bad attitude," he finally joked, at a loss
otherwise.

It was just the right thing to say. Daniel was delighted. He
grinned more fiercely. "Ain't it though."

They ate breakfast, then gathered by the jumbled heap of

supplies, eager to climb. Out came the ice screws and snow pickets and pitons of every shape, and "Friends," the spring-loaded cams that looked so high-tech that James Bond had employed one in a recent movie, and the deadmen, stacks of aluminum anchors. In one linked silvery bunch lay their carabiners, or snap links, the all-purpose safety pins that would channel ropes, complete belay anchors, connect harnesses, hold hardware, brake rappels, and give a dumb extra hand with a 1,200-pound grip whenever an extra hand was needed. Abe knew his way around most of this sharpened, customized, taped, initialed, store-bought and homemade weaponry, even the two battery-powered hand drills someone had brought for drilling bolts, a rock climber's touch. What was unfamiliar to him he hefted and fiddled with and figured out on his own.

Sporting his black eye still and a huge grin, J.J. got them in the mood when he reached deep into the pile and extracted a 300-foot coil of orange rope and held it over his head, whooping, "Firepower."

Three days passed before Abe got his turn to go up. In teams of two, the climbers fanned upward. They took new territory, inflicting their calculations upon the mountain, pinning their camps to the rock and snow and ice. Each team rotated to the high point to push it higher, then retreated to ABC to rest and make room for fresh troops. Forsaking the tactics which alpinists normally employed in almost every other range on earth, the Ultimate Summit proceeded carefully and slowly. These were the Greater Himalayas. Were Everest located at lower elevations, they could have made a concerted push to the top in a single week.

They had entered the so-called deathzone, where big mountains tend to wreck the delicate mechanisms of human physiology. Nothing lived up here for long except lichen and a rare breed of spider with antifreeze glycerine for blood.

Up and down, up and down: When they weren't leading they were humping loads. On any given day there were four to eight climbers occupying different levels of the mountain. With the yaks unable to go any higher, they became their own beasts of burden. Daniel's strategy called for five camps above ABC, each to be stocked with progressively smaller quantities of food and cooking fuel. The upper camps—those above

26,000 feet, if they got that far—would get bottled oxygen. Ounce by ounce, every thread, every crumb, had to be carried on their backs.

At last Abe moved up. Because they were sharing a tent and wanted to try climbing together, he and Kelly got teamed. That meant they were supposed to keep track of one another, and to share "hill rats," or mountain food, which were broken into two-man-day packets, and to climb as a pair. Today the two of them were scheduled to reach Camp One, which one team had helped supply yesterday, and which another team was using to sleep in while pressing the ascent to what would become Camp Two. Tomorrow they would take the sharp end—the high point of the rope—to lead toward Two. Maybe they would reach it, though Abe had no idea where Two was supposed to be located or exactly what to do when they reached it. He was depending on Kelly to know how to configure and erect a Himalayan camp from scratch. A few yards beyond the border of ABC, the rocky detritus gave way to pure glacier. The north bowl swept up toward the bergschrund—that fetal tear which separates a mountain from its glacier—and then steepened.

Blowing wreaths of frost in the chill blue air, the two climbers clamped on their crampons. Somebody had landed a batch of twenty pairs of a brand called Foot Fangs, and Abe's were factory fresh, sharp enough to draw blood. He clapped shut the heel mount with his palm and tugged the ankle strap good and tight and stamped once against the snow. This was his first time in crampons on the mountain, and it felt a little like mounting a horse, this stout bonding of foot to steel to ice.

They plied the glacial plain, navigating by instinct mostly. The wind had covered over yesterday's tracks with snow the texture of sand grains. It was obvious where they were going— to the fractured schrund a mile away—but between here and there lay an obstacle course of crevasses, false promises and wrong turns. Parts of the labyrinth were marked with bamboo wands brought up from Nepal and tipped with red duct tape. Most of the way lay unwritten, though. Kelly said "no problem" and surged ahead.

They moved from one crevasse to the next, zigzagging back and forth in pursuit of marker wands. In between they methodically probed for crevasses, Kelly with her ice axe, Abe with a ski pole. Overnight some of the bamboo wands had tipped over or simply been ingested by the crevasses. Abe noticed that the bamboo—still green when they'd unloaded it from the trucks—had dried to a dead gray, every hint of water sucked out by the mountain.

Most of the crevasses were easy to step across or hop over. Several were too wide for that and so snow bridges had been hunted out and tested for human weight, carefully, and then marked and roped for safety. These required long detours to reach.

One crevasse gaped so wide it seemed impassable. But after a half-hour of walking along its lower flank, they came to a battered aluminum extension ladder with Japanese script along one side. Daniel had salvaged it from the garbage dump at ABC and with Gus and Nima's help had carefully laid it flat across the twenty-foot gap and staked it in place. Abe took an immediate dislike to the ladder. He was tempted to crawl across it, but with a pack on it would have been even more awkward. Besides that, Kelly had just walked it with robotic ease, clanking metallically. With each step, his crampon teeth threatened to slide or catch on the metal rungs. At the halfway point, the bottomless crevasse seemed to howl up at Abe. He scuttled across the rest of the span like a stick figure on fire.

Kelly turned out to be better acclimated, but Abe managed to keep up. Their pace was relatively quick—one step, one breath. Higher, the ratio would widen radically, Abe knew, four or five lungfuls per step. Their crampon teeth squeaked on the ice bed.

After two hours, Kelly paused and pointed up. Through his glacier glasses, Abe saw pink and green sunrays suddenly flare over the northeast shoulder of Everest. It turned into a wild jagged corona and he heard the mountain stretch itself. Its joints creaked underneath his boots as the glacier settled. Snowbeds rustled. A distant green avalanche sloughed loose, beautiful and deadly.

"No problem," said Kelly. "We're still ahead of the warm." Once the sun hit, the upper mountain would begin its daily thaw and send rocks and ice and maybe worse rattling down. Abe was not looking forward to that deadly rain.

They moved off again. A gust of wind brushed across the glacier. Spindrift flowered up from underfoot and for thirty seconds or so a ground blizzard whistled at knee level. Because of its curvature, the immense northern bowl spawned dervishes. Slender ice tornadoes tap-danced here and there. One crawled partway up the wall before gravity pulled it back down. Then the wind stopped. The snow settled. The dervishes died. It was still again.

More time passed. Overhead the wall of stone and ice grew enormous, but remained untouchable. Somewhere at its base lay Camp One. Since Abe had no idea where, time ceased to matter. They would get there when they got there.

Finally they reached the bergschrund. Here was the start of the technical climbing and it was announced by the first rope. It was a thick snake of polypropylene, once white, now gray. Fixed ropes like this one would allow them to carry heavy loads in safety, giving them a handrail for guidance and support. As the angle grew more radical, they would be hanging from the ropes. In addition to aiding their ascent, the ropes were an insurance policy. If—when—the weather turned ugly, the ropes would allow them to bail out in a hurry, rappeling down the ropes at ten times the speed they'd gone up them.

Abe didn't recognize the gray rope as any of their stock and he guessed it had been plundered from somewhere else on the mountain, maybe from the old pile Nima had uncovered in ABC. Abe wasn't in the habit of using a rope he didn't know. Wind and ultraviolet rays could age a rope in a matter of weeks, and there was no telling how long this one had been getting whipped and fried at the roof of the world. But since Kelly didn't hesitate to clip onto it, Abe didn't either. So much depended on sheer faith up here.

They attached themselves to the rope with jumars, mechanical jaws that ratcheted upward, but caught downward. Abe slid his jumar high on the rope, and when he came to the four-foot-wide slash that was the bergschrund, he stopped beside Kelly. She was peering into the deep chasm at her boot tips.

"You see it down there?" she said. "That must be from Daniel's first go at the Hill."

The huge block of ice they stood upon was calving from the slope, and deep in the turquoise cleft Abe saw the taut green rope she was talking about. It stretched from one wall to the other and looked like the final thread holding two naturally opposed forces together.

"How'd it get so far down?" Abe asked. It had been six

years since Daniel's last visit here, yet the rope seemed centuries deep.

Kelly shrugged and turned her attention uphill. "Yeti," she said. The abominable snowman. Things happened on mountains that couldn't be explained and humans weren't very good at letting that be. They needed dragons or gremlins. Or yeti.

One at a time they took off their packs and leapt for the far side of the bergschrund. Abe's Foot Fangs bit into the snow with a jolting halt. They were on the mountain itself now, behind enemy lines.

The gray rope ended a hundred meters higher in a mass of knots that disappeared into the snow and ice. Abe knew that somewhere under the surface an aluminum plate called a deadman was locked in place, anchoring the rope. But to the naked eye, it looked like the rope had been sucked into a devouring mouth. The mountain was alive, no doubt about it.

They unclipped from the gray rope and clipped onto the next one, a section of weathered blue nine-millimeter Perlon. This wasn't Ultimate Summit stock either, and Abe realized the team was saving its new rope for more severe terrain. The line of fixed old ropes went on and on like that to the top of the slope, jointed together with bits and pieces of used nylon. Using the rope as an occasional handline, he slid his jumar along just ahead of him. The slope steepened. More and more he had to haul against the rope and kick his feet against snow that had been annealed by the sun and wind. One short 65-degree required the front points of his crampons.

Kelly was kind, pacing their ascent to Abe's first time at these altitudes. She didn't remark at his gasping, merely stopping each time he bent over his high knee to rest. He felt ill and exhilarated at the same time. Part of him reveled in the height and spectacle. Part of him just wanted to quit moving and lie down for a nap. Try as he might, the ambivalence—the charged current between misery and magic—wouldn't switch off. Twice he noticed colorful stains in the snow alongside the ropes, and realized it was old vomit where others had found it tough going, too.

Camp One lay cupped at the tip of a knife ridge. Three bright yellow tents stood in a lengthwise string, end to end, and it was the most precarious site Abe had ever seen. At its widest point, the ridge was only five feet across, scarcely wide enough to hold a tent. On either side, the ridge plummeted a thousand feet. The outermost tent had part of its back wall hanging over the edge.

"Not too shabby," Kelly said, checking her watch. It was only two o'clock—real time, not Beijing time, they'd given that up upon reaching ABC—but their workday was done. She was sitting in the doorway of one tent, dangling a foot over the edge.

Far below, the immense northern bowl with its crevasses and snowy expanses had become a cup full of lines and white spaces. ABC was tiny, just a spray of colored freckles. If anyone was moving among the tents, they were too small to see. The sun was wheeling around the northwestern crest, cutting the bowl into dark and light halves. Even as he watched, the sunlight gave up some of its territory, and the halves were no longer halves.

Abe bit down on his vertigo and smiled weakly. He'd slept on ledges and in hammocks on big walls in Yosemite, but never on a ridge jutting this thinly into space. The placement looked insane, but Abe knew he should appreciate its logic. Very simply, sitting on this ridge, the camp was out of reach of avalanches and rockfall. In the long term, his dread of heights always simmered into a healthy fear. It was the short term that was so rough. He tried reasoning it away.

They had lost the earth. They had thrown it down beneath their feet. Like monks they were giving up their place in the world and becoming anonymous. Unlike monks, they were striking pacts with their individual demons, honing a radical arrogance and rising upon their whims.

Abe forced himself to stare into the abyss. See it, he told himself. Make it yours. Sometimes that worked for him, incorporating the physical void into the center of his soul. Today it didn't. He just felt sicker.

Since looking down was a wash, Abe looked up. A line of ropes led into a dark icy gully and the gully led vertically into the unknown. Tomorrow and tomorrow and tomorrow, Abe thought. The higher they rose, the deeper the abyss.

He'd always thought that a moment like this—a moment of crystalline reckoning—would be glorious and Zen-like. His mouth would drop open and his eyes would see a million miles and he would think, So this is what it is. Instead Abe carefully knelt by the edge and gripped the rope tight. Positioned just so, he took the liberty of emptying his stomach a thousand feet into the deep.

Another week passed. Each morning the climbers wrapped themselves in Gore-Tex and polypropylene armor. They donned their helmets and goggles and glittering crampons, took up their sharp ice axes, draped ropes like ammunition bandoliers across their chests. They locked and loaded into their harnesses and onto their ropes and humped their backpacks with the grim pluck of grunts on patrol, infiltrating the mountain in tiny platoons, probing it for weak points, relentless.

Some days the mountain just sat there like a titan's still life, not a color moving on the hot blinding canvas. Then again there were days of rage, everything torn to rags if you could see the Hill at all, the mountain reassembling its arsenal, shifting its defenses, readying for a kill. The mountain changed, but the climbers were just as metamorphic. Abe could see it.

The fat was vanishing from their bodies, stripped out by the rigors of their journey. They were turning to bone and gristle. Abe could see it on warm mornings when the camp-bound stripped down to their T-shirts. Their muscles had thinned out and their arms were ropy with veins. Their hands had taken on the horny, banged-up look of roughnecks' hands. The pads were cut and fissures spread like drying mud and simple scrapes ulcerated. Their fingernails had quit growing or were just continually chipped and worn down. Every cuticle was split and bleeding as if their fingers were rejecting the very nails, spitting them loose.

Abe tried in vain to remember what they'd looked like before. Like Himalayan deities, their skin had turned blue, the higher they climbed the lusher the blue. And their urine had turned the color of blood because the glacier melt was loaded with so much raw iron and minerals. At supper, pieces of fried skin fell from their faces into their food. Their eyes had grown huge and hungry behind their goggles and glacier glasses. The mountain had spawned a pack of maniacs, it seemed, zealots. The mountain will fall, Abe thought. To people like these it will fall. And he was one of them.

Slowly, in bits and pieces, they were gaining on the beast. They prosecuted their ascent by inches, cannibalizing the remains of earlier expeditions to feed their upward journey. Their "yak gap" had put them behind schedule, but through brute risk they were beginning to make up for it. By the end of two weeks of brilliant route-finding, most of it accomplished by Daniel and Gus, the climb was almost back on track. Morale rose high, but so, curiously, did the group's anxiety. Every one of them was feeling overextended, and no one could quite explain it, not for a climb that was going so well.

"We're like casualties waiting to happen," Robby said. "You'll see. The machine will start to break down. Then it all becomes a matter of forward momentum, how far can we go before we stop."

The breakdown started soon.

Carlos had arrived with chronic tendinitis in both ankles, and to compensate had taped them tight like a Super Bowl halfback's. That stabilized the ankle but cut the blood supply to his feet, causing some minor frost nip on his toes. Abe prescribed warm socks and nixed the tape. Two days later Carlos stumbled and wrenched his left ankle, and Jorgens sent him down to Base Camp to recuperate.

On April 14, Robby and J.J. got food poisoning at Camp Two. They'd been pinned in their tents for two days as a cold front moved through, and neither man was known for his fastidiousness. While the storm buffeted them, they did what everyone else was doing on the mountain. They lay low, slept, BSed, and cooked. The water for cooking came from melted snow. The snow came from outside the tent. Robby and J.J. didn't bother reaching very far outside their tent, and ended up ingesting their own feces. Their violent bout of vomiting and diarrhea had abated by the time the storm lifted, but each man was left seriously dehydrated. Since the combination of dehydration and altitude sickness could be deadly, Abe sent them down to Base Camp to rest.

Abe had read about winter-long science expeditions to Antarctica which became disease-free while in isolation. After sharing each other's flus and colds in the first month, everyone's immune system adjusted and the incidence of viral infections plummeted. Only with the introduction of a new arrival was the stasis violated. In theory, Abe knew the Ultimate Summit Expedition could become disease-free also. But the reality was that time was against them and they weren't a truly isolated population anyway. The yakherders had exposed them to a host of Asian viruses that were still waylaying the climbers a month later.

For a while everyone suffered sore throats and packed sinuses. Some went on to develop the infamous high altitude cough, a persistent, wracking hack. Stump got the worst of it. A few days after chipping his front tooth on a frozen chocolate bar at Camp Three, he descended to ABC doubled over with "cough fracture." It was not unheard of for Himalayan climbers to break their own ribs in coughing fits. Abe examined Stump's beer keg of a rib cage and said the "fracture" was probably not a break, but that he'd definitely separated some ribs. He put Stump on Cipro, an all-inclusive antibiotic, and sent him down to Base Camp to recover.

About the time Carlos returned to ABC from his convalescence at Base, limping gamely, Thomas keeled over with a high fever, chills and wet rales. Abe was carrying up to Camp Two at the time. When Jorgens brought the news up at four in the afternoon—they still had no radio contact—Abe immediately descended to ABC. From Jorgens's description, Abe guessed Thomas had developed HAPE, or high altitude pulmonary edema, a frequent killer at these heights. An indirect result of dehydration, HAPE had a terrible irony: It drowned its victims in their own fluids.

Abe reached ABC at eight o'clock that night. Daniel was already there, sitting beside the patient. He seemed much too relaxed under the circumstances. Thomas had glazed eyes and cold perspiration, and Abe could hear the bubbly sound of wet rales even without his stethoscope. Thomas coughed and colored sputum spattered the front of his sleeping bag.

"HAPE," Abe said. "We better send one of the Sherpas down to Base for the bag." The Gamow "bag" was a portable pressure chamber made of plastic. You put the patient inside, pumped it full of air, and basically dropped him to 12,000 feet elevation in a matter of minutes. It had saved many lives in the past few years.

"You're right and you're wrong," Daniel said. "We definitely ought to get the bag up here. But there's no hurry. This isn't HAPE."

"Of course it is. Look at him. He's got all the symptoms. Rales, the sputum."

"Almost, not quite," Daniel said. He was kind in his contradicting. "I would have thought the same if I hadn't seen it before. With HAPE there's no fever. And look at the color of this stuff." He tore a page from a magazine and scooped some of the sputum up. "See? It's rusty. Not pink. Pink's HAPE."

"Pneumonia," Abe said. And it was. The good news was that the pneumonia sounded confined to the left lower lobe, and lobar pneumonia responded well to antibiotics. Thomas would recover quickly, provided he went down to Base Camp.

"We're starting to look like a ghost town up here," Abe said. "And we're not even halfway."

"I don't hear the fat lady yet." Daniel smiled.

On April 17, Pemba Sange fell down a crevasse above ABC during a routine carry. Thirty feet down, the Sherpa landed on a false floor of snow. Happily the floor held and he was safely extricated, but two days later two other Sherpas came down with severe headaches, which Jorgens insisted was "Himalayan AWOL." After accidents or a death, he said, hypochondria sometimes ran rampant among climbers or Sherpas or both.

"Treat them like they're real patients," Jorgens advised. "Give them aspirin. Inject them with vitamins, whatever it takes. Just get them on their feet. They'll get over it. That or we pack them off to Base for the duration with no pay. We can't have slackers up here. They'll kill our morale and eat us out of supplies." He instructed Abe to stay down for the day and play doctor with them.

In fact, the two Sherpas were really sick. Abe found them in their tent suffering fevers and severe diarrhea and mildly disoriented. One of them had even started up the glacier with a fifty-pound load before surrendering to his illness. No slacking here. Winging it once again, Abe put the two on a five-day course of Cipro and told them to go down to Base Camp when they felt strong enough.

The accidents and near misses left them all jumpy and fitful. They were stretching their limits up here, and there was a growing sense that they were going to need something more, some extra auspices. Otherwise the mountain was going to take a victim.

When help arrived, it came from an unexpected quarter. It was the third week of April and Abe was crossing the last of the crevasses in the north bowl, descending from yet another tedious load hump, when he chanced to spy a kite floating in the thermals above ABC. It was a box kite, the color of lemons and pomegranates, and someone had nursed it a good two hundred feet into the air. There was no great mystery who the someone had to be. Robby had brought three kites from the States, hoping to stage a calendar photo of kites flying against the Himalayan backdrop. So far he'd been too busy climbing or being sick to attempt more than one launch, and on that occasion the winds had been too fierce. Today, apparently, he'd achieved takeoff.

With its tropical colors and alien weightlessness, the kite practically shouted its presence, and judging by its height, it must have been up there for quite some time. But it was only now that Abe happened to take notice. The rest of his way to camp, he rode on its swoops and Promethean trembling, enchanted by its coltish delicacy. Every moment the string seemed ready to snap, taxed by the wind, and the sky's blueness alone looked enough to crush the toy.

At the edge of camp, Abe sat down on a rock to shuck his crampons, and Thomas came up. He was swearing by a full recovery, but Abe could tell the man was still weak. "You got a visitor," Thomas said.

"You're kidding," Abe said.

"Nope," Thomas said. "Showed up this morning."

For one crazy instant, Abe imagined that Jamie had somehow made her way to Everest and trekked the long trail up to ABC. Just as quickly he dismissed the thought. Even if Jamie had been the type, there were too many twists and turns in this adventure, too many borders. He decided his visitor had to be Li Deng, in the role of a patient or a bureaucrat or just in search of company. If so, he was definitely unwelcome. The last person they needed up here was a liaison officer badgering them about rules and deadlines and watching over them. They had a hundred days for this climb, but counting them out bean by bean wasn't going to get them any higher.

"Hey," said J.J., who had just come straggling down off the glacier. Others were coming down behind him. "Isn't that your idiot?" The story had gotten around about Abe and his epileptic yakherder.

It was indeed the Tibetan boy. He was standing in mid-camp with the spool of kite string in both hands, wearing a

clean expedition T-shirt and quilted pants and dirty animal
skins.

Three of the Sherpas were sitting on rocks, offering jokes
and helpful comments while they watched him pilot the kite.
Pemba's near brush in the crevasse had sobered the Sherpas,
but the kite, or its handler, seemed to have returned them to
their usual animation. Nima caught sight of Abe and immediately stood up and said something to the Tibetan.

"Well look at who's here," Stump said, kicking off his crampons. "It's Abe's little stray. I thought he'd disappeared."

Abe saw the boy turn to view the growing knot of climbers
and a wide, bucktoothed smile splayed across his broad face.
He had the look of a child with all the time in the world. He
bent and lodged the kite spool under some rocks, then made a
slow beeline toward the climbers. Nima trailed after him.

Abe's fatigue fell away. The last he'd seen him, the boy was
a write-off. Now he'd recovered enough to walk ten miles and
fly a beautiful kite in the lap of the Mother Goddess. There was
something so simple and wonderful about it that Abe smiled
right back. After a dozen years of emergency work, he'd seen his
fair share of so-called miracles, but never so poetically rendered.

The boy walked haltingly, with a left-sided palsy, and it was
plain to see that he'd suffered neurological damage somewhere
along the line. Once again Abe wondered about a head injury
that might have predated or even caused the epileptic seizures.
He wanted to take another look and ask some questions now
that the patient could answer for himself.

As the boy struggled across the gray and white debris,
the climbers talked baldly about him. "What a gimp," J.J. said,
astonished. "How'd he ever make it up here?"

Robby sauntered over in moonboots and a pair of purple
polypro pants. He looked like a rodeo clown with fuzzy chaps
and two cameras slung around his neck. "Can you believe it?"
He beamed. He turned to photo-frame the kite between his
fingers.

"Will wonders never cease," Stump cracked. "You finally
got it up."

"Look at it," Robby said. "I'll tell you what, though. This
Tibetan kid definitely missed his calling. He's born to fly. He
could have been an aviator the way he works the wind. You

should have seen the way he sent my kite up, just kind of opened his hand and it took its place."

"These Asians, man, they love their kites," Carlos said. "Down in Kathmandu, they get so excited with their stringwork, they'll forget where they are and run right off of five-story rooftops."

"Maybe that's what happened to this guy," J.J. suggested.

"Or a yak stampede," Gus said.

They made a few more jokes. The boy continued laboring across the loose rocks toward them. The afternoon's late rays cut him out from the shadows, making him hard to look at for his radiance.

"You didn't tell us he was a *tulku*," Daniel said to Abe. He had one hand shading his eyes and was squinting at the boy.

Abe had never heard the word. He faked it. "Yeah, one more yakherder."

"A *tulku*?" Carlos said. He pulled his goggles off and looked more closely. "Jeez, Daniel. You're right." He was excited and hushed in the same breath. "He's no yakherder. Look at that round face, and those pointy elf ears sticking out. And the eyes. And look at the Sherpas, man, they're blown away. They look like disciples waiting for the body and blood. Nah, nah, this guy's beaucoup holy, you can tell. Doc, you saved a *tulku*."

"What the hell's a tulkoo?" J.J. asked.

Carlos sighed and tried again. J.J. thrived on reiteration, though even on the second and third explanations there was no guarantee he'd get it. "*Tulkus* are holy men. They're like a monk and a prophet all rolled into one. And they can tell the future."

"Yeah," Daniel joshed, "and *tulkus* can fly, too. And they fight demons."

Carlos grew cautious. "That's what they say."

"All I know is I thought he was a dead man," Abe said.

"Oh, they can do that, too," Gus threw in. But whereas Daniel had been gently teasing, she meant to sting. Gus had her virtues, but suffering credulous dharma junkies was not one of them. She'd been through Asia too many times to get snookered by the smoke and mirrors of local religions. Ascent was her dogma. "These *tulkus* can think their body temperature up or down. They can quit breathing and fake death," she lectured facetiously. "They can even pick a precise moment to die and then just check out, snuff themselves with a prayer, and catch the next cycle on the merry-go-round."

The Tibetan boy limped closer. His affliction became more graphic and they quit talking about him. Chances were he couldn't understand a word of English, but he was a thin frail reed among these sturdy climbers and he was their guest. Above all his smile was the real McCoy. He looked positively overjoyed to have them down off the mountain safe and sound. Despite themselves, the climbers seemed to warm to him.

To everyone's surprise, since it was presumably Abe he'd come to see, the boy walked directly to Daniel.

Nima was embarrassed for the boy and stepped up beside him and laughed off the mistake. "This man is thinking you save him."

"Me?" Daniel was startled. "No. Him." He clapped Abe's shoulder. "Here's your archangel. Not me."

Switching to Tibetan, Nima corrected the record. The boy's smile didn't falter, though a slight confusion clouded his brow. It was apparent he thought Nima was wrong. He continued studying Daniel's blue eyes with some cryptic recognition, and Daniel looked strangely off-balance. Then the boy twisted to face Abe. His smile broadened, if that was possible, and Abe beamed back.

"Ask him how he feels," Abe told Nima.

Nima didn't bother to ask. "All better, sir. You see."

"I don't think so, Nima. He looks very weak. He should be at Base Camp eating lots of food and sleeping. This altitude is very bad for him. You should tell him that."

But Nima was a Sherpa. High altitude was a fact of life and this Tibetan holy man was here, so how could it be bad. "This man is coming now to see you, Doctor. Coming now eight days."

From the back of the gathering, out of nowhere, Jorgens's voice crashed their little party. "The boy thinks he's going to stay here for another week? Not a chance."

Nima didn't understand and his expression said so. But he seemed to realize Jorgens wasn't addressing the issue of hospitality. This was gringo politics, Abe saw it clearly. Still reeling from the shift in leadership, Jorgens was out to score some points. The beauty of this issue was that he had logistics on his side.

"Tell him he can't stay, Nima," Jorgens said. "We don't have the food for an extra mouth, and he doesn't have a permit to be up here. You know the rules. The yakkies come up. The yakkies go down. One night here, that's it. More than that, he needs a Chinese permit, understand?"

Somebody said, "Chill out, man."

Jorgens flushed. In the old days, before the mutiny, he would have cut the offender down. Now he was reduced to trying to build a coalition. "We can't afford trouble with the liaison officer," he clarified, straining for a civil tone. "That's the bottom line."

"That's not what Nima meant, though," Abe said. He turned to the Sherpa. "Eight days. Are you saying it took this boy eight days to walk here from Base Camp?"

"Yes sir. Eight days maybe, maybe more. Many days, walking, saying the prayers, slowly, slowly."

One of the climbers whistled. "Eights days from Base. He must have been crawling."

"The dude must like you, Doc," J.J. said.

"He had a debt," Daniel stated. To him, anyway, it made perfect sense.

"Tell him I'm glad to see him," Abe said to Nima.

Like a minister of the court, Nima didn't bother his prince with the small talk. Speaking for the boy, Nima replied, "He is very glad to see you, sir."

"But Nima, ask him. Why did he come so far?"

"To give the *puja*, sir. We need the *puja*." Nima's delivery was emphatic. Obviously he thought they needed the *puja*, too. That was some kind of ritual. Abe had never seen one.

"He's right," Carlos said. "We've been running on empty ever since we got here. We should never have left Base without a *puja*."

Immediately Jorgens went on the attack. His exasperation was tinged with the weariness of a schoolmaster at the end of a very long semester. "There are sensitive issues here, people. I keep telling you, when in Rome we have to do as the . . ."

"This is Tibet," Carlos overrode him. "And this is Everest. And we need a *puja*. You go climbing in these hills without a *puja*, you're asking for trouble. We're damn lucky to have a monk who can do one."

"A *tulku*," J.J. added.

Jorgens weighed the vote with a quick scan. "Fine, have your ritual," he said. "But keep it up here at ABC. I don't want word one of this getting down to Li. It's one thing for Li to think we're hosting a dumb, hurt yakherder. I don't want to test him on a monk. Li's got his rules. Got it? Silence on the monk. Silence on the *puja*."

Abe found it touching and a little childlike that hard-core mountaineers could be in such a state over a good luck cere- mony. He figured they couldn't really take this *puja* business seriously. But when he looked around, there was satisfaction on people's faces, a quiet relief that had been missing since their arrival. Even Gus seemed more at ease.

The climbers disbanded and crunched off through the limestone rubble to their tents, leaving Abe behind with Nima and the boy. Overhead the North Face burned with a tea rose alpenglow.

"One more thing, Nima. Tell him I want to examine him before he leaves. Let's just make sure he's good and healed." In truth it was in the role of a skeptic that Abe wanted to look the boy over. He couldn't fathom a recovery so complete, especially at these heights. Maybe *tulkus* really did have magical powers.

"Okay," Nima said. "When, sir? Now?"

Abe hesitated. He was tired. "Yes, okay," he decided, "now."

On their way to an empty tent, they passed Daniel peeling off his super-gaiters. The monk slowed his jerky pace for an- other look and came to a halt. Daniel glanced up, startled by the boy's quizzical gawk.

"You sure you two haven't met?" Abe asked. "Maybe on your last expedition."

"Doubtful. He would have been ten or eleven years old." Once again Daniel seemed nonplussed.

"Maybe he saw you on your trek out." Abe didn't say "Lep- ers' Parade." He'd never mentioned it before, uncertain how Daniel preferred his history. But what a sight that must have been to the Himalayan villagers, five monstrously ravaged hu- man beings straggling down from the outlands, feet and hands frozen black. A sight no young boy would have easily forgotten.

"Doubtful." Now, behind Daniel's bemusement, Abe saw the look of a hunted animal. Daniel was afraid of this boy and his eerie recognition. He was afraid of the past. Abe shifted the topic.

"I still can't believe he came just to say thanks." The thought of a boy with nothing more to do on this desolate plateau than set off into the deep wilds to randomly bless a bunch of strangers made Abe feel lonely for him.

"I like him," Daniel said. The boy had lifted Daniel's ice axe and was testing the point's edge on his thumb. "He's got real sand. We ought to make him a climber." With a sudden sweep of his arm, Daniel seated his black and orange Baltimore Orioles baseball cap on the monk's head. It was sweat-stained and much too big, but the gift could have been gold. The boy's eyes widened and he grunted, "wah."

"What's his name?"

Abe blinked. He'd never thought to ask. Unconscious, the boy hadn't needed one.

"His name is Wangdu," Nima said.

Daniel tried it out. "Wangdu." Then he asked, "Where are you guys off to?"

"Final exam," Abe said. "I want to give a last look over. You can tag along if you want."

Daniel pushed against his knees and stood up. His joints crackled and Abe could see the electric painkiller box bulging on his hip. What a bunch we are, Abe thought, lame and halt. Mortals beneath our immortal grasping.

The four of them crowded into the empty dome tent. The smell of unwashed humanity was a given, but another odor was harder to ignore. Abe hadn't noticed it in the open air.

"Nima, ask him to take off that skin jacket and his shirt."

When the boy shed his final layer, the tent filled with a terrible stench of rotting flesh. Abe sat back, stunned.

"He's dead," Daniel murmured. "He looks dead."

He was half right. Under the skins and T-shirt the monk was only half alive. His various wounds had grown worse, much worse. In the light of day—what light was left—his bruises had taken on the vile yellow and gangrenous hues of rotten fruit. The animal bites were leaking a foul sap, and the strange eraser-tip markings around his nipples had putrefied.

"It wasn't like this," Abe said. He placed a bare palm against the boy's suppurating chest and, through the callouses on his hand and fingers, he could feel the infection hot and animate. The monk was being consumed alive.

Abe struck back at his own repulsion. He searched for another emotion and found his anger and started to lash out at Nima. "I thought Krishna was going to care for him. I gave instructions, damn it. I told him . . ."

Nima wasn't even listening, too shocked by what they were all seeing and the foul odor they were breathing. Abe bit the scolding off. He was the doctor, not Krishna, and this wasn't Main Street, USA, where modern medicine was a God-given right and a second language. It was Tibet, on the edge of time. The world was rough and primordial out here. People died of things like wood splinters and chickenpox and broken bones and insect bites.

"Tell him to lie down, Nima. Keep him here. I'll be back with some things. Pills and salve and bandages. I have to clean him. I have to start all over again."

He turned to exit, but Daniel was blocking the doorway, sullen with disgust and curiosity. "Abe, I don't understand this."

"I don't either. But if we can't handle this infection, you're right, he's dead."

Abe returned to find Daniel forcing a dialogue that Nima clearly did not want to be part of. The Sherpa's face was dark and outraged, but so was Daniel's. Everyone seemed angry but the monk, who had lain back in a nest of soft down bedding.

Daniel turned on Abe. "You told me he got hurt in a camp accident."

"I guessed," Abe said. "He was unconscious, and no one knew for sure."

"Oh, they knew." Daniel bitterly spat, but it wasn't a bitterness aimed at Nima. "They just weren't talking."

"But why?"

"They were scared."

Abe persisted. "I don't see why."

"See those holes on his chest?"

"Parasites? Maybe some kind of disease." Abe shrugged. He knew Daniel was setting him up to expose his naïveté or simpleness, and that didn't improve his mood. He had done the best he could in that smoky hut at three in the morning.

"Tell him about those holes," Daniel said to Nima.

Nima frowned at Abe. The mistrust stood heavy and black

in his face. Finally Daniel gave the answer. "Red Pagoda Mountain," he said.

"Pardon me?"

"It's a Chinese cigarette. The army officers like to smoke them."

Abe gaped stupidly. What was being said here?

"These didn't happen on the trail. They're cigarette burns."

"Come on." Abe shut it out.

"And these bruises? And the dog bites?"

Dog bites, Abe thought. That's what the punctures and lacerations were. He kept it simple and organized and manageable.

"Abe, listen to me. These aren't camp wounds. Think about it."

He knew what Daniel was going to say. Daniel said it.

"These are torture wounds, Abe. He got these in a Chinese prison."

"Impossible."

"Why?"

Abe glared at him. "Impossible."

"You hear stories over here. What the Hans are doing to the Tibetans. But it always sounds too much. Like, you know, a million dead? And the torture stories, what they do to these people. Raping nuns with cattle prods, flogging monks to death with iron bars. . . ."

Abe had no idea what Daniel was telling him. He had no idea what to think. He had come to climb a mountain. That was all he knew.

"Nima," Daniel demanded. "Tell what you know."

The Sherpa spoke haltingly, with reluctance. "This man, you know, they put him in the prison. They making very bad things happen to him. He run from there. Now he is going to Nepal side."

"He's escaping?" Abe asked.

"He's trying to," Daniel said. "But the passes are high. He's trapped. He wouldn't stand a chance in his condition. Look at him. No wonder he had to crawl to get this far."

Through his paramedic work, Abe had seen terrible things, things worse than this, bodies torn in two, skinned by windshields, ruptured like soft grapes, ripped and shredded. But in all of that the suffering had never had a purpose, a reasoned cause, never anything like this. What made this unthinkable was that another human being had written the suffering into the boy's flesh, one wound at a time. It was beyond belief. Abe's teeth were gritted and he felt tears of frustration forming in his eyes. This wasn't supposed to be part of the deal. He'd come to see beauty and strength and utopia. He blinked his tears away.

"The yakkies got him as far as Base," Daniel went on, and Abe could tell that Daniel was extrapolating much of this even as he spoke. "And the Sherpas, they don't know what to do with the poor kid except keep it quiet. If the Chinese get wind of this . . ."

"What did he do to them?" Abe asked. He was fighting to accept what lay before him, the proof of evil. He needed more time. Or a good reason. One or the other.

Nima asked the monk, and the monk crossed his wrists, made two fists, thrust them down and lowered his head. Abe needed no help translating. Defiance. Resistance.

"He maked this at the Jokhang," Nima explained.

"The big temple in Lhasa," Daniel added for Abe's benefit.

"Now what?" Abe asked.

"Keep it quiet," Daniel counseled, inventing by the moment. "We've got to keep the L.O. in the dark. As far as he knows, this is just one more yakherder. I think the rest of the members should know what's going on. But Li can't find out."

"Everyone?"

"Everyone. Informed consent. If they don't know, they might say something by accident. And besides, we're all part of it now, and the others have a right to know."

"Even Jorgens?" Abe asked. "He'll kick if he knows we're part of some underground railroad."

"He doesn't have to like it," Daniel decided. "He's part of us, though. We owe him the truth."

"Okay then," Abe said. "Tell them."

"And all you have to do is fix him. He's got to get his strength up or he'll never make it over the pass. If he can't make it over the pass, things will go badly. In these parts, Tibetan families have to buy the bodies back from the Chinese. Going rate is five yuan, the price of a bullet. And I don't think this poor guy's got a family to bury him."

"I'll do what I can."

Daniel placed one hand on Abe's shoulder. "Do your best, Abe. Save the ones you can save. I learned that from you."

But before Abe could add to it, Daniel had lurched out through the dome entrance to go and instruct the others.

Abe suddenly found himself wishing that the boy were unconscious again. Unconscious he had been mute, and mute he had been merely the canvas on which these bruises and cuts and burns had been painted. But the boy was conscious now and his story was no longer a fiction. Abe set himself to changing what dressings had not fallen off and to cleaning the monk's sores and lacerations.

Next morning they had their *puja.*

The Sherpas made little towers of flour paste and put Oreo cookies and hard candy on a platter and brought out a few precious bottles of Star beer packed in from Kathmandu. They started a fire with cedar branches and pine needles that had come from nowhere within a hundred miles. The sweet white smoke lay over ABC as a center post was erected. From this post, four fifty-foot-long streamers of prayer flags were stretched out and anchored in four different directions.

The flags were thin cotton, each dyed a different color and printed with prayers in square Tibetan script. Despite her irreverence about *tulkus* yesterday, even Gus looked pleased and comforted to see the prayer flags get unfurled. While Abe watched, Kelly stood beside him and explained things. She held one of the cotton squares still and showed him a crude horse block-printed among the fresh script.

"They call that a *lung ta.* A wind horse. Every time the wind flaps a flag, the horse carries a prayer to heaven," she told Abe. "They'll keep us safe and sound. All of us."

The Tibetan boy sat on a small carpet by the center post with white smoke wafting through the prayer flags overhead. One of the younger Sherpas, Ang Rita, was a lama initiate back in his home in the Solu Khumbu. He'd either smuggled in the carpet and the prayer flags for his own use, or else bought them from a yakherder. Kelly didn't know which.

The *tulku* chanted and murmured while he turned the narrow pages of an old book. The *puja* had the gravity of a mass but the air of a carnival. Through the entire two hours, the Sherpas and climbers came and went, talking loudly and laughing and taking pictures.

The ceremony had become more than a *puja*, Abe knew. It was a binding together. When Daniel had laid out the monk's sorry tale last night, the climbers had reacted with Abe's same disbelief, then personalized it. Kelly had teared up. Jorgens had objected to jeopardizing "his" climb by harboring a fugitive. Carlos had ranted about the Chinese overlords. In the end they had agreed with Daniel, though. Silence gained them everything. The little *tulku* would have time to heal and finish his escape. The climbers could climb. And Li would be spared doing his duty.

Carlos originally explained to them that their *puja* would address Tara, a goddess associated with compassion. As it developed, the *tulku* chose a different god for his ritual, Mahakala. Carlos passed around a small book on Tibetan culture, and Abe saw the picture of Mahakala. He was intrigued by the monk's selection.

Black and ferocious, the god was a demonic creature with six arms and a rosary of human skulls. He held numerous weapons and his head was surrounded with a halo of flames. He was drinking brains from a skull. Abe tried to square the image with his frail patient. Carlos said it made perfect sense.

"Mahakala—Gompo, to the lay Tibetans—he's the Great Black Lord of Enlightenment," Carlos said. "He's a killer, but also a protector. He defends us against selfishness and slaughters the demons of ignorance. On the Tibetan hit parade of deities, this guy scores in the top three. He's the perfect symbol of killing the self to achieve knowledge. Rebirth out of destruction, all that good stuff. With this dude watching over us, we're double safe, man. It's a good choice. Excellent."

Nima and Sonam distributed *puja* strings, blessed pieces of red twine that were tied loosely around people's wrists or throats. "You keep it on until it rots off," Kelly explained.

"What about Li?" Abe asked. "What if he sees these strings?"

"We'll just say the truth, that these are our lucky charms. Maybe I'll give him one, too."

Abe didn't get a string until the very end.

Closing the long, wooden covers of an old prayer book, the *tulku* got up on unsteady legs and came over and tied a red string around Abe's throat himself.

Abe didn't know the Tibetan word for thank you, and so

he determined to give a present in return. All he could think of was a second stethoscope from his medical kit. But by the time Abe returned from his tent with the stethoscope, the monk was gone.

"Where did he go?" Abe asked Nima.

"I don't know, sir."

They looked for the boy, but he had disappeared.

The prayer flags stayed up, flapping prayers into the blue sky. And the *puja* strings turned dark red from their sweat. Abe figured that he would never see the monk again. He had vanished outward into that idea called Tibet. He wanted for the monk to be more than just a voice and this *puja* string. But that's all that was left.

THE SIEGE TIGHTENED through May.

Camps One and Two had fallen easily, as if the mountain didn't want them anyway. They took Three in a snowstorm up a long gully filled with slag and junk ice; nothing difficult, but it took some fight. Four was next, but first they had to pacify a wild mean narrows dubbed the Shoot, short for the Shooting Gallery. Rocks and loose ice bombed the Shoot at all hours. No one had gotten hurt yet, but people knew that even *puja* strings and prayer flags couldn't hold down the odds for long.

Near the end of April—he'd lost all track of the actual date—Abe headed up the line, this time humping forty pounds of rope, fuel, two sleeping bags, and five "hill rats" or two-man-day packets of high altitude rations that were fast-cooking and easy on the GI tract. The food, gas, and bags were for Three, the rope was for their continuing drive on Four.

The camps were spaced a day apart from each other. Abe felt strong and could have pushed from One to Three in a day, but that kind of leapfrogging was a fast track to exhaustion and edema. He'd noticed how everyone else was saving their physical and mental reserves for the summit bid, and he saw no reason to ruin himself hauling heavy on a milk run. He wanted his crack at the top, too, though the closer D day approached, the more nebulous it became. Some people said a month, most just shook their heads and talked about something else.

Abe arrived in Three alone. Thomas and J.J. had already spent a day and night there. It was midafternoon, maybe 90 degrees Fahrenheit, and the two men were putting the final touches on two rectangular box tents. Thomas's crewcut had gone to seed, but not enough to shield his balding crown, and he had fresh red sunburn on top of old sunburn scabs. He looked like a thermometer ready to explode. J.J. was stripped to his muscle shirt: Gold's Gym. Neither man greeted him. They'd been watching his torturous coming for the last two hours, and by the time of his arrival it seemed like he'd been among them forever.

This was Abe's first visit to Three, and now he saw for himself the problems he'd been hearing about. The camp was an aberration. There was no ice or snow to cut tent platforms into, and the rock lay at a 60-degree angle with no ledges. It would have been a hopeless site except for the multimillion-dollar Japanese expedition of '87. With portable drills, anchor bolts and aircraft tubing, the Japanese had constructed a metal ghetto here, or at least the skeleton of one. The result was four artificial platforms with flat floors and roofs and perpendicular walls. In its heyday, the camp would have accommodated up to twelve climbers.

The wind had shredded the nylon walls of each box tent and falling rock had sheared some of the poles and smashed some of the infrastructure, but in three years Everest hadn't yet managed to shed this evidence of earlier colonists. Now the Ultimate Summit climbers had occupied the camp, cannibalizing platforms that were wrecked to repair and buttress the ones that weren't. It was a vertical shantytown, a sorry-looking place for such a magnificent abyss.

"Where's Kelly at?" J.J. asked. As a rule, the buddy system was inviolate. It was peculiar for Abe to show alone.

"Sick," Abe answered. More and more their language was getting truncated, cut down to monosyllables their lungs could handle. Sometimes their dialogue sounded like single-shot gun-fire.

"At least she's not knocked up," Thomas said. "Let it flow." His thin Yankee lips sealed shut again, no sneer, just the senti-ment. J.J. gave a small shake of his head, less reconciled to the tiresome misogyny than Thomas seemed to think. In a flash, Abe saw a whole lifetime of tiny mundane compromises in J.J., and realized the muscle man wasn't so much stupid as judicious. For the first time since meeting him, Abe didn't feel sorry for J.J.

But Thomas was correct, if impolite. Kelly was having her period and that's why she hadn't made her carry today. By now Kelly's menstrual cycles were common knowledge, and her cramps were notorious. Still it was none of Thomas's business, or ought not be, and Abe almost said so. On the other hand, Abe was learning how every sneeze and hangnail along the route moved up and down to affect the other climbers. A missed carry could throw the logistics off for days.

Abe contained his annoyance. "She'll come," he said. "Tomorrow."

Thomas explored the hollow of one cheek with his tongue and looked off to the north. Behind the bulging grasshopper goggles, his face said, We'll see.

"I'm hungry," J.J. said. He was inhabiting his usual oblivion and Abe was grateful for it. Surprisingly J.J.'s simpleminded cheer, so grating at lower altitudes, had become a definite asset. One didn't want complications up here, and with J.J. you didn't get them.

"How's it going up above?" Abe asked, indicating the Shoot's entrance.

"It's going," Thomas grumbled.

"Daniel won't let go of the lead," J.J. expounded. He seemed pleased. J.J. had entered into a fruitful bondage under Daniel, happy to harness his strength and courage to this mountain, happier still to be serving under Daniel.

Thomas was just the opposite. A general contractor from northern California, he was both older than Daniel and more serious about his chains of command. He seemed to regard Daniel's brilliance in the mountains as an accident, and accidents could go wrong just as easily as they went right.

"I've seen this before," Thomas said. "High altitude kamikazes. You try to keep up with them. But nobody can. A guy like Corder can use up a whole team before people say enough. Slow down. And by then it's too late."

Abe didn't much care for Thomas's certainties and glumness, but the man had climbed on a dozen expeditions and it would be foolish to discount his authority. "So we're going too fast?"

"Too fast?" barked J.J. "Man, we're short. You can about smell the monsoon. We got to go fast. We'll go bust without some pedal to the metal."

"We'll go bust with it," Thomas said. "Another week at Daniel's pace, we'll hit empty. You'll see. Kelly's just the first. He'll waste us all."

Abe started to say that Kelly was having cramps, not bailing on the climb, but that didn't change Thomas's basic point. Then he started to say it was all a matter of degree—to most other people they were all kamikazes up here.

J.J. spoke first, though. "We came to climb." He shrugged heavily. "We're climbing. I want the Hill. Daniel wants the Hill. We're together."

"Together?" Thomas squeezed a pair of pliers around a wire clip. "Corder doesn't care about together. He couldn't care less about you or me. Or even himself. He's a freak. And he scares me."

Just then a slight cloud passed across the sun, instantly reminding them of what was what. The temperature plunged in a 70-degree gulp. Then the cloud passed and they were panting and sweating once more. They quit talking. Soon voices came trickling down from above and the limp orange rope looping across from the Shoot suddenly came alive, jumping and jerking. People were descending. Daniel would be among them.

"We've got to take it on our own terms," Thomas closed. "That's all I'm saying." Then he clammed up, and Abe knew the man was more intimidated by Daniel than by the mountain. Given the mountain's perils, that was a major league fear, and Abe wondered how many others doubted or feared or maybe even loathed Daniel, too.

As the climbers rapped down, the orange rope twitched and curlicued like a dying snake. The voices grew louder and Abe heard the tinkling of hardware on a sling. The climbers sounded close because the Shoot funneled their sounds down, but their descent took a while. Finally Gus appeared, running rope through the brake at her belly.

"Hi guys," she said, and blew a pink bubble of her private stock of Bazooka. She snapped the bubble hard.

Thomas grunted at her and went back to fine-tuning the guy wires holding the Japanese platforms together. J.J. greeted her with a lift of his chin, but then his chin just stayed aloft and J.J.'s mind wandered off in some other direction. The altitude had whittled their attention spans down to thin parentheses.

They had taken to using Swiss Army knives on their hair, at first snipping away with the little folding scissors and finally, impatient, opening the long blade to saw away whole hanks of hair. Under her scratched white helmet Gus's red locks looked spikey and tattered and for some reason it brought to Abe's mind the scar along her back. That in turn reminded him of her beautiful silvery front, her round, round breasts. It seemed long ago, that night in his tent. He dug for some sort of context, trying to remember if it had been warm beneath the moonlight, how her belly had been muscled, if perhaps behind her warning there had not been the slightest of invitations.

But none of that mattered, not at these killing heights. The memory closed itself off. The image of a mysterious moonlit nude vanished. In its place Abe found himself staring dumbly at this wild, primitive female gnawing gum and shaking ropes and now picking at a knot jamming her figure-eight brake. She could have been his sister or his mate or his mother. There was nothing spiritual in the recognition. She was part of his tribe, it was that simple.

Edging out of the Shoot, Gus unclipped from the rope and peered up at activity Abe couldn't see. She shouted up that the rope was free, then picked her way across to the precarious campsite.

Close up, Gus looked cooked and shaggy and beat. Her energy and insouciance were a mascara, Abe saw. They were aging fast up here, and no pretenses of youthful vitality were going to change that.

Gus wasted no time resting. She poked her head through the door of the uppermost box tent. Seeing it empty, she slung her pack in and claimed it for her and Daniel. She got to work firing up a hanging stove to melt ice.

"Jorgens flamed out," she remarked to anyone listening.

Thomas gave Abe the look: I told you so. Daniel's push was too extreme. "Spell it out," he told Gus.

Gus goosed the butane flame hotter. It would take an hour

to melt the ice into water. Even boiling, the water would only be tepid, a function of the loosened air pressure.

"No biggie," Gus said. "Jorgens needs some drink. Then down. All the way to Base. The sooner, the better."

"What happened?" Thomas pressed.

Gus made it short and sweet. "It was a long day. He's an old man. He won't be back up again. It's rough as hell up there."

Abe knew more than the others did. Jorgens had come to him a fortnight ago, complaining about having difficulty urinating. Though it could have been any number of things, the problem sounded like an enlarged prostate to Abe. Jorgens had been crushed by the possibility. "Why don't you just de-nut me while you're at it," he'd told Abe. Then he'd made Abe promise not to tell anyone else, as if Abe wasn't already keeping everyone's secrets.

"How about Carlos?" Carlos had gone up, too. Now Abe remembered.

Gus pointed down, down, down. Down the Hill, away from the front, out of service. "He gave it a go. But you know Carlos. He never belonged high in the first place." Her glib obituary ignored the sprained ankle hobbling Carlos. Then again, they were all impaired to some degree. What it came down to was that Carlos had finally acknowledged his own mortality. And that scared Gus.

"So what I'm hearing is we just lost two guys in a single day?" Thomas said.

Now Gus caught his drift. She cocked her head over. "No problem, Tom. We still got you, right?" She went back to feeding ice chips into the pot.

It took another hour for Carlos and Jorgens to show up. The two were in sorry shape, gray under their blue and sunburn. Jorgens looked dazed and Carlos had no voice left, and each moved with loose, sloppy duck steps. Daniel was shepherding them, keeping a sharp eye on the details: what they clipped and unclipped from the ropes and anchor, how they managed themselves, where they placed their feet. That was good.

Jorgens and Carlos sat where Daniel sat them, hunched and bleak like famine victims. Gus brought them the lukewarm water with Kool-Aid and extra sugar in it. Abe took his cue and checked their pulses and eyes and asked them to count his

fingers. Carlos's helmet was tipped to one side. Jorgens had
been drooling into his beard. Both were in disarray with zippers
unzipped and clothing untucked. It was easy to tell when a
person was falling to pieces in the mountains; they came apart
at the seams.

"You guys ready?" Daniel asked the two. It was kindly but
stern. There was no question that they would continue down
the mountain.

Carlos gave a game thumbs-up. Jorgens set his jaw, revived
enough by the sugar to realize that he was out for the count.
There was bitterness in his eyes, but it wasn't directed at Daniel.
Jorgens was coming to terms with himself.

"You want me to go down with them?" Abe asked Daniel.

Jorgens rejected him instantly. "The day I need a baby-
sitter . . ." He winced and looked off toward the mouth of the
Shoot.

"Just the same," Thomas said. "I'm going down. We can go
together."

The declaration stunned them. Gus paused in her pouring.
J.J. scowled. Even tired old Jorgens snapped his head up in
surprise. Thomas descending wasn't part of the plan.

"You're sick?" said Daniel.

"You could say so." But the way he said it, and his level
stare at Daniel, told them what it was Thomas was sick of. Daniel
had rebelled against Jorgens, now Thomas was rebelling against
Daniel. The dominoes were falling.

Abe raced to calculate the implications. Thomas was slated
to carry in the Shoot tomorrow. By dropping out—even for a
day—he would deprive them of supplies up high and bottle-
neck them down below. It meant that he had eaten hill rats
and used fuel and occupied a space here at Three to do nothing more than fine-tune a couple of tent platforms. It wasn't
good.

Daniel made no attempt to stop him. "Good idea," he told
Thomas over Jorgens and Carlos's heads. There was no sarcasm
or punishment in his voice.

"The hell . . ." Gus protested.

Daniel hushed her. "If the man's sick, we can't use him
anyway."

After more Kool-Aid, Thomas ushered Jorgens and Carlos
down the ropes toward Two. Even moving slowly, it would take

them only a couple hours to descend. The weather was perfect. As they sank from sight, J.J. said, "Bummer for Jorgens. There's no more big mountains in him."

"Tough," Gus said, but her voice was empty. With Kelly's no-show and Thomas's bail, their six-man carry to Four tomorrow was cut to four people.

Daniel said nothing. He just watched the empty depths for a minute, maybe cobbling together a new strategy, maybe just spacing out. Then he got on with things. They worked on the camp for another hour, ratcheting nuts, twisting wires, tightening their grip on the mountain. Daniel prepped a rack of climbing gear, adding some super-light titanium ice screws he'd purchased on a climbing trip to the Caucasus in the Soviet Union.

The sun still had an hour when Daniel and Gus crawled into one of the box tents and Abe and J.J. got into the other. The tents were spacious, the floors flat and comfortable. But when the wind came, the platforms creaked and scratched at the rock. Abe was afraid as he drifted into sleep. He could feel the abyss under his back.

It was still dark and windy when Abe heard a yakherder's blatting call. He wasn't dreaming—there wasn't enough oxygen to dip that low into the REM levels—and yet for a moment he was disoriented and thought their little herder, the monk, might have returned somehow. The yawp sounded again, and this time Abe knew it was Daniel in the other tent, waking them all.

By headlamp, Abe and J.J. readied themselves, dressing while the stove flame roared blue under a pot of ice. It was three o'clock. The mountain would be locked tight at this hour, frozen to its coldest point of the night. Rockfall would be at a minimum. Also, Daniel wanted to land at Four today. They had to ascend some eight hundred feet of rope already fixed in the Shoot before they could finish off the last three hundred feet of climbing. In J.J.'s thick, slurring SoCal, the day promised to be a hump and a half. An early start meant everything.

Abe gave his straps and buckles a final tug. The supergaiters, his helmet, the pack flap and side pockets, his harness—everything got cinched snug.

"I'm on my way," J.J. promised, but he was at best only half ready. He had bad stomach cramps in the morning, and it took him longer than most to gear up. J.J. had cavalierly diagnosed his distress as a side effect of the anabolic steroids he used. Abe thought the problem was more likely aspirin. At these elevations the red cells—the oxygen carriers—multiplied so thickly the blood turned to syrup. The climbers who chewed aspirin to counter the effect usually ended up with ulcers, bad teeth and epic constipation.

"See you there," Abe said, wherever *there* was. He braced for the cold air and unzipped the tent door. The cold lashed him across the eyes and he flinched. Then he got a good look and said, "God." Outside the blackness was perforated with a million stars. There were stars behind the stars, a solid carpet of lights. He looked up and where the carpet ended in a raggedy line, the mountain pronounced its dark domain.

Abe saddled himself. He wanted to keep up with the gang today and had packed for speed, a manageable but still respectable thirty pounds. Holding on to a handline, he picked his way horizontally across forty feet of stone to the base of the Shoot. Gus was already there, similarly burdened.

"Daniel's barfing," she said to excuse her partner's absence.

"J.J.'s sour too," Abe said.

Gus slugged Abe softly on one shoulder. "Then it's you and me, Doc. We'll show these wimps. They can straggle behind." Abe felt warmed by her camaraderie. She had read his apprehension. For weeks people had been talking about the horrors of the Shoot. Now he was about to be exposed to them for the first time.

Gus swept her headlamp back and forth across four ropes lying side by side in the back of the Shoot. There was one rope for each of the expeditions that had entered this corridor.

With one gloved hand, Gus plucked at the orange rope— the Ultimate Summit stock—but let it go and tried a second and a third rope. She seemed to be shopping, though to Abe's mind there was no question, the newest was the best. Then he saw her dilemma. Overnight the ropes had become coated with transparent ice. They were all sheathed with verglas.

"Heads up," Gus said. She took the end of the new orange rope again and swung it out from the wall. Then she cracked it against the stone like a gigantic, ponderous whip. The ice fractured off and maybe twenty pounds of chandelier glass came tinkling down, pattering on Abe's helmet and hunched shoulders.

"Dibs," Gus said, grabbing first place on the rope. She thumbed open the metal jaws of her two jumars and clipped them onto the cleared rope. She slid the uppermost jumar high, then tugged to see if it caught on the downstroke and it did. As the rope iced up, the jumars would slip now and then, but that was a nuisance, not a hazard.

Abe didn't mind going second, even though it meant more work. With Abe beneath Gus, the rope would be weighted and that always made jumaring the ropes—jugging the line—much easier. But going first was a mixed blessing, because if one of these ropes was abraded, it would break under her weight first.

Abe felt a twinge of something, shame perhaps, or guilt. The truth was he appreciated Gus's making herself the guinea pig. He was scared. He knew his nerves would smooth out eventually. Maybe in an hour or two he could take over jugging the lead and spare Gus some of the risk.

Gus finished rigging her stirrups to the jumars, then headed up the line. The rope creaked under her weight. Abe gave her a few bodylengths, then started up behind, walking his stirrups up a foot at a time.

The going was slow. Repeatedly the teeth in their jumars caked with rime and the jaws missed their bite and slipped. Each time one of Abe's jumars fouled, he had to unclip it and thaw the teeth with his warm breath and clip it back on the rope.

At the top of the first ropelength—or pitch—they rested, standing in their stirrups since there were no ledges here. Abe leaned his shoulder against the cold rock. The corridor was only five feet across at this level, and its boxlike sides channeled the wind straight up between their boots.

"One down, six to go," Gus said. Shoulder to shoulder, Abe could smell the coffee on her breath. He checked his watch. It was going on four-thirty. At the rate of a half hour per rope, they could possibly reach the top of their line by eight or nine.

Abe looked between his knees at the ground. Far below, almost a mile beneath his boots, the glacier was giving off a phosphorescent glow. Closer in, a tiny headlamp was bouncing white beams against the corridor's walls and Abe could feel the climber's movement vibrating in the orange rope. Gus whipped the next rope to clear its ice. They continued up.

The Shoot's slick stone turned to panels of ice, green beneath Abe's light. They put on crampons and kicked at the ice, biting it with their front points. The ice squeaked, a comforting noise that told them the ice was plastic this morning, not brittle. Here and there the wall lay bare and their crampon teeth scuttered against the exposed rock and sent out electric sparks, red and blue.

At the top of the second pitch, Abe realized that either his calculations were off or his watch was. It was nearly six. Already an hour and a half had passed. At this rate, it would be late morning before they got to the high point. And by then the sun would have renewed its conspiracy with the mountain. Abe tried not to think of what that was going to mean.

They went on and on. Dawn broke.

Near eleven the sun painted them with hot light. Abe was already sweating under the pack straps, deep in his own animalism. Even if he could have thought in full thoughts, he wouldn't have dared. Ascent hurt too much at these heights. Abe had never had to fight his own body this way. The aches and pains were bad enough. The lassitude was worse. He wanted to obey his instincts. He wanted to go down. But that was unthinkable. He concentrated on brute primary motion. He kept his mind slave-empty.

Abe lost count of the time, of the ropes, of his pain.

The Shoot opened to thirty feet across, and the ice took on the white marbling of snow. The angle eased slightly. Tiny balls of snow—sunballs—loosened in the heat and tumbled in minuscule avalanches that evaporated before they could grow bigger than a fingernail.

"Look," said Daniel.

"Huh?" said Abe. He lifted his head to see, but his helmet hit the high crown of his pack. He shifted the load and cocked his head sideways and indeed, Gus had become Daniel. Somehow, in the hours since dawn, Daniel had moved from last to first on the line of ropes. Abe was startled to the extent his apathy allowed. He hadn't noticed the changing. He couldn't remember passing Gus on the ropes nor Daniel passing him. One thing was certain, Daniel no longer looked sick. His pack looked full and his power was obvious in the way he dominated the ice.

Abe looked off to the right where Daniel was pointing. He blinked. He blinked again.

There was paradise out there. They had climbed so high they could look right around the mountain and into Nepal.

Off in that far distance lay a land of kaleidoscopic peaks. They poked their summits up among a white lather of clouds like a chain of bony, carved islands. Even as Abe watched, wind vacuumed the clouds out from the distant valleys, exposing a topography of light and dark hollows. The sunlight twisted in strange patterns. A razor-sharp feather of snow, at least three thousand feet in length, appeared as a streak of glycerine quicksilver, a divine flourish.

Abe lowered his head to break the spell. He looked at the glacier between his crampon teeth. It was gleaming like a slick reptile down there, vast, coiled dragon's vertebrae. He looked back to the south, enchanted, drawn by the promise.

For months now, he had spent his gaze—his belief—upon Everest alone. But here, this morning with half the Himalayan range unfolded before him, Abe faltered. It hadn't occurred to him that they might see Nepal before reaching the very summit, and he hadn't really expected to reach the summit. This unexpected view brought to mind all that the south represented to him: a diminution of the mountains, a relinquishing of all that was sharp and vertical and lifeless, a backing away from the Hill. Out there, he knew, the mountains gave way to foothills and the foothills of Nepal gave way to India, and India was his doorway. Through her riot of colors and smells and tangled human energy, he had come here. Through Nepal, then India, he would return.

As Abe stood sweating in his black windsuit and glittering crampons with taped jumar handles in each fist and his mouth wide—dumb as an ape and sucking at what little was left of the atmosphere—he could almost see home. For an instant even, he could almost see Jamie, and it was almost enough to remember that she was completely forgotten. Under his helmet, Abe's forehead wrinkled with the nearness of a memory. Behind his goggles, his eyes gained a glimmer, and he blinked.

It was then, when he was most vulnerable, that the mountain commenced fire.

Abe took the day's first hit.

He wasn't listening, so he wasn't ready. There wasn't even time to flinch. One moment he was still, feet splayed on the side points of his crampons, swimming against his riptide of amnesia. The next moment he was hanging limp upon the rope, harness tight, staring straight into the Egypt eye of the sun. His goggles were askew on his face. His ears were ringing. His pack straps were creaking, and it came to him that he was nearly upside down and the pack was dragging the very breath from him.

Just as suddenly, he felt a pair of strong hands hoisting him away from suffocation. The hands would be Daniel, Abe registered. He felt himself hauled upright and shoved face first against the slope. Abe was at a loss. First gravity had him, then Daniel did. He was caught between forces. He tried to fathom what was going on.

"Rock!" Daniel bellowed down the ropes.

Far below, someone passed the word, a tiny voice peeping into the depths. "Rock. Rock."

"A rock?" Abe mumbled. He kicked weakly at the ice, finally getting the front points of his crampons into the ice. Standing up gave him at least a measure of self-control, more so than just lying helpless and suspended on the rope. He pressed his fingers under the left edge of his helmet and held them in front of his eyes. It was a paramedic's habit, not to trust your touch alone. He looked at the wetness on his fingertip, but the sun had seared his vision and he couldn't see if it was sweat or blood. Quite certain he was thinking clearly, Abe tasted for blood, but all he got was the filth off his gloves.

"Rock, ice," Daniel muttered, fussing with Abe's pack, straightening his goggles, "at terminal velocity, it's all the same." Daniel stank the way they all stank. It verged on the smell of oiled leather, and Abe breathed it in with relief. He was alive. Whatever had happened, he was still part of the dream.

The ringing subsided. Abe's vision flooded back in. Daniel was crouched against the wall beside him, one hand holding Abe firmly by the scruff of his pack. He was peering upward for more debris. Abe shook the messiness from his head but it was impossible to tell if he was dazed by the hit against his helmet or by the altitude or just the adrenaline surge. He drew a string of quick breaths and kicked his crampon points in and put his weight back onto his feet.

"I'm okay," he said.

The upper mountain unleashed a second barrage. This time Abe heard the warning sound, a hybrid whistling and buzzing. Abe gasped, horrified to be caught in the open like this.

The rocks—or ice or both—skipped hard against a blunt gray spur overhead, and Abe could hear rocks ricocheting all around with a desolate, predatory humming like hornets make.

"Jeezis." Abe squeezed the oath between gritted teeth. He shut his eyes and dug his head fast against the ice and the plastic clacked on the ice wall. "Jeez," he said again.

The rockfall snicked and screamed on every side. Each flashing bit of debris was hunting along its fall line to gouge them, to break and skin them. Abe knew what contact looked like. He'd seen people opened up by rocks. He'd seen skulls emptied. Once his rescue team had found a climber with a fist of quartz inside his abdominal cavity, no viscera, just that transparent crystal lodged between the pelvic wings.

Something exploded beside him. Abe was showered with slivers of glass. The glass became ice. It melted on his burning face.

Harm's way, Abe thought. There were so many prayers to dodge it, so many words to dread it. And here he was courting his own mutilation, a hero with fouled pants. Yes, he realized. That warm mud in his crotch was his own shit.

Then it was past, at least for the moment.

Abe blew air through his nostrils and unwrapped his grip from the rope. But he still lay flat against the wall, afraid to move, afraid to look down but more afraid to look up. He'd seen that, too, a climber with shards of his crushed glacier glasses jutting from one socket.

Daniel was moving, though, blithe to the dangers, craning backward to scan the upper mountain and survey their people down the Shoot. Abe peeked. A hundred feet down the ropes, Gus was spidering upward once again, and beneath her another hundred feet, J.J. was on one knee.

Daniel exposed his Kmart wristwatch. "Clockwork," he grinned. "Eleven oh-five. The daily wake-up call."

Abe grinned back. He grinned wide. "Good clean fun," he said. He wiped the ice melt off his goggles and rapped a knuckle against his helmet. But for all his bluff pluck, he still lay fast against the wall. Behind his hell-bent grin Abe could feel his sphincter seized up and his pants damp. He was gripped.

He'd known fear before, even been nailed by stray rockfall. But this was different. There was the suddenness of it for one thing, and for another there was Daniel's nonchalance. It informed Abe that rockfall was a commonplace up here, no more extraordinary than the dandruff in their tea and Top Ramen, or the blood on their ragged lips or their fits of delirium.

"You took a hit," Daniel said. He was offering Abe an exit. There was no dishonor in retreat, not for the wounded.

Abe rejected the offer. "I'm good," he said. It hadn't been so bad. No damage done, and they needed him to hump the load. He would go on.

Daniel was pleased. Abe could tell by the way he nodded and the set of his jaw. They were together now. They were brothers. "We're there." Daniel pointed. "Our high point."

Abe saw an outcrop of gray stone fifty feet higher. A mass of coiled rope and parked gear hung from pitons driven into a crack.

"From here it's only another couple hours," Daniel estimated. "I can lead it fast. We'll be okay at Four. It's a cave."

"Yeah," said Abe. Daniel was double-checking his morale. All for one, one for all. The fear had seemed huge and catalyzing and significant, but now Abe buried it deep.

They moved up the rope and nestled beneath the outcrop. It wasn't much of an abutment, but it was enough. They would be protected from rockfall here.

Abe peeked around the corner at the remainder of the Shoot without learning much. The corridor took a bend and there was no sight of Camp Four. There was no more orange rope up there. The Ultimate Summit had not yet made its mark above this stone.

While Abe shook out a coil of new rope and Daniel tightened the wrist loop on his ice axe, another hail of stone and rotten ice came slashing down.

"Rock!" he shouted down the line.

This time Abe had nothing to fear. He hid behind the outcrop and the rockfall whined and hummed past harmlessly. With a curious detachment, he watched first Gus, then J.J. react. Gus balled tight with her armadillo technique. J.J. cumbrously turned his pack upslope to let it take any beating. Everyone had theories on how to survive a rockfall.

The debris skipped left, mostly strafing empty air. Here and there puffs of ice smoke showed where rocks barked the wall. After a minute Gus and J.J. started jumaring again. Abe was impressed with how slow and tiny they appeared, even though they weren't so far below. The mountain had miniaturized them. They looked trivial and expendable.

Daniel started up the Shoot, trailing a rope. Hanging from the rack crossing his chest, his Soviet ice screws tinkled dully. He wasn't carrying much in the way of protection. He didn't need to, he was that good.

The sun continued to plasticize the ice, softening it for Daniel's toe plants—quick, powerful kicks to seat his front points. He flicked the tip of his ice axe into the mountain with the finesse of a switchblade fighter, every motion surgical and understated. Abe had never seen an ice climber operate so economically. Where most climbers hammered at the ice for deep purchase, flailing and overdriving their tools, Daniel seemed content to stroke it, scarcely entering the ice at all.

As Daniel advanced, Abe fed him rope through a brake mechanism. If the leader fell, the second was supposed to catch him. Daniel wasn't the type to fall, however, which freed Abe to gaze at Nepal and stare into the abyss. Time bent around him. From his little perch, ABC was much too small to see and all the other camps were out of sight. He tried guessing where Base might lie along the glacial tendrils, but the Tibetan plateau swallowed his estimations whole. He had the sense of having climbed right out of the world.

After another half hour, Gus reached the outcrop, groping for air like some chemical warrior. While she was bent over, gasping and coughing, Abe clipped her pack off to a runner sling attached to the anchor and helped her from the straps. Gus recovered enough to straighten up.

Down below, J.J. was approaching with amazing torpor. He had the dense, coagulated motions of a deep sea diver. He would slug his way up a few steps, then hang on the rope for minutes at a time, paralyzed by the thin air. Then he would move again. His progress was pained, but Abe felt no pity. He just watched. It was like watching a bug move.

Daniel's rope slid through the brake with little pause. Abe snuck a glance around the outcrop, but Daniel was already out of sight up the corridor.

Another rockfall shelled them. Gus huddled against Abe under the outcrop. J.J. was still two hundred feet down, still exposed. He turned with all the speed of a tortoise. He completed his turn just in time to take a rock square against his pack. It made a pillowy thud and J.J. was promptly plucked from his stance. He swung out from the wall and bounced across the slope. J.J. didn't shout out or scramble for cover. There was no cover. He simply turned his pack upslope and took a second hit and swung again. Then the rockfall was done. He twisted around and resumed his reptilian progress.

"Piece of gum?" Gus asked. Abe nodded yes. He was parched. The sun was unmerciful. What little water he had left in his bottle had to last until they reached Four and could melt more. That could be many hours. Water, water, everywhere, he thought, and leaned against the blazing ice.

Gus gave him a pink chunk of her Bazooka with the exaggerated care wall climbers use to hand things back and forth. It was soft from her body heat. "You owe me," she said.

Abe chewed carefully because his teeth had begun to loosen. Mostly he sucked at the sugar. It revived him from his stupor, then dropped him back into it all over again. He wondered if the chunk of rock or ice had given him a concussion. He felt all the more tired and debilitated seeing Gus's animation. A nap would have been nice.

"You're on," Gus said. Daniel's voice was chirping down at them from the Shoot. Neither could hear what he said but both knew what he meant. It was showtime.

Abe kept his dread mute and worked into the pack straps. He wanted to stay under this outcrop for the rest of his life. He loved this stasis, this bombproof sanctuary, and this piece of wet gum on his sunburned tongue.

"Want me to go?" Gus prodded him. She didn't want to go either.

"Photosynthesis," Abe said, trying to make a joke of his inertia. Gus gaped without comprehending. He clipped his jumars onto Daniel's rope and left the outcrop, ascending with all the speed he could muster. Daniel couldn't safely advance until Abe arrived to belay him and tend his climbing rope. Every minute wasted was another minute Daniel could be investing in their reach for Four. More to the point, every wasted minute exposed Abe to more rockfall. The wall's angle eased slightly. Abe let his quadriceps take the brunt of the toil.

The Shoot curved left. Daniel came in view. Above him the corridor seemed to extend without end. Abe despaired at that. He'd hoped the Shoot was nearly played out. He reached a little ledge and Daniel helped him out of his pack.

"Damn, Abe. You're running heavy."

For the first time all day, Abe was glad he hadn't lightened his load. It was a good respectable carry and it was plain that Daniel appreciated that. For all its brute danger and hard labor, today was going to turn out well after all. No climber can know in advance how well he will perform at high altitude. Abe was performing. He belonged.

Abe had meant to ask how far it was to Four. After Daniel's praise, he didn't. They would get there when they got there. At any rate, Daniel answered without being asked. "See it?" he grunted.

Abe looked. Less than eighty feet overhead stood the mouth of a cave. It opened in the rock like a desert miracle. Only one rope led up to the cave. It looked very old and most of it lay buried within the ice wall. Daniel had already opened a coil of new rope to climb with and fix at the cave entrance. One end was tied to his harness.

"How about that," Abe marveled. His words rasped out, no saliva left. He couldn't remember spitting out the gum, then found it lodged inside his leathery cheek. It might be okay to drink the last of his water now. They were almost there.

The rope Abe had just ascended began jerking. That would be Gus coming up.

"I'll just run this pup out, fast like," Daniel said. He was cranking one of his precious Soviet ice screws into the ice to bolster their belay anchor. The screws were only six inches long, stubby with threads coiling around the exterior of the tube. Inside his beard, he had weariness cut in deep lines beside his mouth. "Ten more minutes and we're home." He started off.

Abe could see the cobalt sky between Daniel's outstretched legs. He was moving quickly, especially for a man nearing 26,400 feet. Among climbers, 8,000 meters marked the border between what was mortal and ordinary and what was something more. Back in Boulder, Abe had been awed at the very prospect of grappling his way into that fabled region. Now that he was here, over twice as high as Mount Olympus, 8,000 meters seemed impoverished, hardly Olympian. Far from anointing them, the mountain had reduced them to virtual idiots, with spit on their faces and shit in their pants and scarcely enough wind in their lungs to complete a full sentence. He tried to remember what treasure he'd come to find. Everest was supposed to have bestowed on him all the sacraments in one, baptizing and confirming and confessing him all at once. But the only blessing he was likely to return home with was a piece of red string tied around his throat by an epileptic in yak skins. So much for glory, he thought, and paid out more rope to Daniel.

Daniel scooted up fifty, then seventy feet. He didn't bother placing any protection. Setting an ice screw took time, and besides the Shoot was laid back now at a relatively comfortable 70-degree angle. For a climber of Daniel's abilities it was next to impossible to fall from such a plane.

Just the same, Daniel fell. In truth he was shoved. Shot. Ambushed by the Yeti.

It was a lone piece—rock or ice, all the same thing. Abe never heard it. He was watching, but all he saw was Daniel suddenly kicked backward into space. He didn't touch the slope for a full ten feet, the shock was that powerful, and when he did it was to glance off and fly another five feet.

Abe was sure he had no more adrenaline left after their long, hot gauntlet of rockfall. But he did and it jolted him with a chemical voltage that bulged his vision and sped his mind and turned his hands into vise grips. He locked down on the rope. He stared hard at the sure death of an alpinist.

Daniel skipped twice more on the ice and by that time he

was halfway down to Abe. There was no time to react really. Abe made a try at pulling in some of the slack rope, but it piled in wild serpentine loops over his arms and shoulders.

Minus the ten or fifteen pounds they had all lost on this expedition, Daniel still weighed a good one-eighty. With the instantaneous wisdom a catastrophe inspires, Abe knew the man would strike him with a gross force approaching a ton or more. Abe's sole hope was to be missed. And to hold on to what was in his hands. And to pray that the anchor would hold, that the world would not let him go.

Daniel neared. Abe could hear his Gore-Tex windsuit hissing on the ice. Then he heard the metal chattering of Daniel's ice axe beating loose against the wall, and a loose ice tool was like a chainsaw amok.

Abe's lips peeled back from his teeth. Now it was clear what he had come so far to face, not the summit but the abyss. It wasn't Daniel's death he was witnessing, but his own.

And then Daniel was past. He sliced within inches, close enough so that one crampon tooth ripped a neat gash down Abe's right arm. He heard the fabric unzip. When the opening burned—when it sluiced a line of blood against the ice—he knew the fabric had been his flesh parting.

But his wound and his pain were beside the point. The anchor could not hold. Not against this kind of momentum. Here was chaos. Here was the world unpiecing itself at a speed beyond all reckoning. All the same at terminal velocity.

Abe wondered if it would seem this fast all the way down. He wondered how deep into the pit he would stay alive. Sometimes people went all the way without losing consciousness. Sometimes they lived for a while, tucked down a crevasse, say. He remembered that Gus was on a rope that was anchored to him. And J.J. was on a rope attached to her. They would all go, tangling into a ball of bloody yarn. The glacier would eat them. In a hundred years someone would find what was left. Abe was sorry for the others. He was sorry for himself.

The loops of rope draped across his arms began vanishing, one by one. He didn't follow Daniel's descent with his eyes. He just stared at the anchor. He counted four ice screws. They had been so close. A drink of water, that's all he'd really wanted. The rope whipped away from his arms. For a moment there was peace.

The peace shattered. Abruptly Abe heard a howling.

It was himself. He was filling the void with a cushion of sound. Here was his precious sacrament then, all he was going to get, last rites.

In that millisecond of acceptance, the rope came taut. Abe's hands flew from their grip. The ice wall sprang into his face, smashing against his helmet. One—then two—then three—ice screws blew free like rivets in a submarine bottoming out.

But the last screw held. For no good reason but the faith that had placed it—Daniel's faith, not his—the titanium ice screw stayed firm.

Abe was saved.

He returned to himself tenuously. He took his time. He trusted nothing. Until he touched it all with his fingertips, piece by piece, he could not take for granted even that single bent ice screw with the mass of ropes and loose screws dangling from it. Even then he hardly dared to trust that he'd survived.

For a space of time, Abe simply drew in perceptions and let his senses sort through them. His goggles were still intact and the light filtered through with the color of new lettuce. The still air was moving now, bringing with it a whiff of the solar winds just beyond their tissue of stratosphere. In the ice dust from the blown anchor holes, Abe could smell time itself, geological afterbirth. He felt the breeze cooling his face, listened to it whistling through the stem of Daniel's good ice screw. His right forearm hurt, but the pain was ritual, bearable. He held the hurt with his left hand. From a great distance, he watched blood running through the sleeve and between fingers that were his.

In that dazed state, Abe sat on his ledge. Head back against the ice, he stared into the blankness of Tibet. He might have dozed.

At some point Daniel appeared. The black-haired ghost rose up along the newest of the ropes, seeming no worse for the wear. Abe knew that couldn't be so, not after such a fall. On second glance, he saw that this figure was moving much slower than the old Daniel. But that was to be expected from a dead man.

"Abe?"

Abe didn't answer. He knew the mountain was playing a trick on him. Starved for oxygen, the human brain freely invented its own fictions, populating the world with angels and demons and other imaginary beings. High altitude climbers often reported a third man on a rope for two. They would talk aloud to their guest. They would cook food for him.

"Are you okay? Look at your arm."

Abe ignored the hallucination.

"It hit you too?"

"No," Abe said. "That was you."

The apparition sat down beside Abe on the little ledge.

"Man. What a ride."

"Now what," Abe said aloud. He didn't mind the company, but he wasn't speaking to it. He was talking to himself, company enough.

"How about one more go?" Daniel asked. "We were so close. And I saw something. Up in the cave. It might be good."

"Sure," said Abe.

"Or we can go down."

"No," Abe decided. "Up. It might be good."

"Can you belay?"

"Of course."

For the next space of time, Abe belayed the ghost. He fed rope out with his good arm.

Gus appeared. She was quite ugly just now, but beautiful too.

"Hi, Gus," Abe said.

"What's this shit?" Gus gasped. Abe followed her gaze. She was staring dismayed at the anchor. It was in near ruins—a lone, bent screw—and she had just trusted her life to it. Abe tried to see it from her perspective. He could have repaired the anchor. At least he could have warned her. He felt a little bad about that. On the other hand he couldn't say if she was any more real than Daniel. How odd, he thought. Even in death, Daniel was somehow their higher standard.

Then Gus noticed the blood heating in a small pool on the glassy ledge. She knelt beside Abe and peered inside his ripped sleeve.

"We have to get you down."

"No. Up," said Abe.

"Where's Daniel at?" she said. "Does he know you're like this?"

"He fell."

"No," Gus determined. "He's okay. Up there. He's in the cave."

From above, Abe heard Daniel's voice. "Abe. You can come on now." Showtime again.

"What happened here?" Gus said.

"It doesn't matter," Abe said.

Daniel's voice moved between them. "Gus. Can he climb?"

"Are you kidding?" Abe could tell she was mystified and angry. He wondered idly how it would be to kiss those torn lips smeared white with zinc oxide. She was his angel. "He has to go down," Gus reiterated.

"It's a thousand feet down," Daniel argued. "Only one pitch up."

"But he's hurt. He's in shock."

Not so bad, Abe thought. In most respects, it was pleasant sitting here at Gus's knees with the planet curving on the north horizon.

"There's a camp here," Daniel said. "It will be dark soon. We're best here."

"I thought I belonged," Abe confided to Gus. "I'm sorry."

"That's all right," Gus said. "Can you stand?"

Abe stood.

"Let me check your jumars. And your harness. And fix this helmet." She was trying to take charge here. Abe could tell she was thinking of many things. "Daniel," she shouted up the wall. "Abe's pack. Can you pull it up on a rope?"

"I don't think so," Daniel answered.

"No problem," Abe said. He reached for his pack, his pack of wonderful heaviness. He had hauled so much so high and there was only this eighty feet more to go.

"Leave that," Gus said. "I'll bring it up. Can you climb?"

Abe made his way up. It was much, much easier without the weight on his back. His wings were freed. He could fly.

Daniel met him at the mouth of the cave. The cave was almost supernaturally perfect for human occupation. The floor was flat, the ceiling was seven feet high, and the walls were spaced wide enough to admit the two tents that were standing side by side. One was a faded peach color, the other was still orange. The cave wasn't very deep, maybe fifteen feet, and it looked like some equipment had been parked in the very rear.

"Maybe you should lie down," Daniel said.

"I'm fine." Abe was enchanted. He had entered another dimension in here. Outside there had been no respite. But here there was an inside to the mountain. There was a sanctuary not only from the rockfall and the crucifying sunlight, but also from the relentless verticality. He took a few prickly steps forward atop his two-inch crampon teeth. The floor was flat. He couldn't get over that. He had forgotten what it was like to stand on a horizontal surface.

"We lucked out," Daniel said. "Look at all this stuff. The Kiwis just left it all."

Both tents were zipped shut, both were intact. Neither had so much as a tear in the fabric or a split in the seams. In contrast to the Ultimate Summit's fancy dome tents, these were old-style triangular structures with guy lines and center poles, the kind that required daily attention or else they collapsed. But years had passed and these tents were standing whole. Their spines were tight, not an inch of sagging, and their walls drummed to Abe's finger tap. They could have been pitched yesterday.

Yellow urine stains to the side of each tent looked fresh. Empty food cans and paper wrappers lay loose in nooks and crannies of the cave, unperturbed by so much as a breeze. Ropes lay piled in limp butterfly coils, ready for use. Behind the tents, in the deepest recesses, heavy oxygen bottles were stacked like firewood, and red stuff sacks contained windpants and sweaters and personal gear—a Led Zeppelin tape, a can of sweet condensed milk, a photo of a woman.

Tucked in this squared-off pocket of stone, the camp was free of the hazards that normally plague Everesters. No falling rock or ice in here, no avalanches, no wind, apparently not even the passage of time. In here the sanctuary was complete.

"Let's sit down," Daniel said.

Abe sat in the open doorway of the faded peach tent. The air pads were still buoyant. Tears of happiness welled up at this luxury of sitting on a thing that was soft in a place that was safe. They were out of danger. Nothing could hurt him anymore.

"Pretty wild out there," Daniel said. He turned from the cave mouth and carefully eased himself to sitting beside Abe in the tent. He grimaced. Abe knew he would. Abe's muscles and joints were stiffening. His arm wound was starting to burn. It was logical that this hallucination would reflect his hurt.

Side by side, Abe sat with his other. They didn't talk. Eventually Gus appeared at the cave entrance, wheezing for air. The outside had gone dark gold. The sun was setting.

Gus pulled down her goggles and cast her fresh green eyes across them. Abe saw that she had carried a double load, tying his pack on top of hers. Without ceremony, she dumped the gear against one cave wall.

"Now what the hell's going on, Daniel," she demanded. She was angry. She didn't like mysteries.

"The mountain whacked me," Daniel said. "I whacked Abe."

Close enough, Abe thought, though his own telling of it would have elaborated on the ferocity of sunbeams upon a rock in ice, the gentle unlocking of noisy fate.

"So fix him," Gus said. "Don't just sit there."

"Gus . . ." Daniel held out his hands with a gesture of helplessness. That was the first Abe saw of the flayed palms. Daniel's hands were laid open and bleeding. They needed help, he and Abe.

Gus didn't hesitate. "All right then," she breathed. There was work to do and no one but her to do it. She set aside her own weariness. Abe saw the tired resolve in her eyes.

Gus started three stoves and cut ice for water with the adze of her axe. She worked on Abe first, stripping off his torn black wind shell and rolling up his sweater sleeve to expose the incision. It was deep. Abe looked in when Gus opened its lips.

"You're the doctor," she told him with a question mark on her face. She had his jump kit spread out on the ground, all his trauma equipment and meds.

Abe was tempted to remark on the brightness of her eyes. That was all that came to mind. She was a masterpiece.

Gus frowned at his staring and said, "You're fucking useless, Abe." But she wasn't angry. Abe was glad for that because he loved her, she was his sister, too, just as Daniel was his brother. She customized a crude, bulky patch job on his arm. It turned red through the white cotton. Abe knew he ought to be concerned, but couldn't figure out why. He had begun to shiver in great spasms.

"Daniel?" Gus pleaded.

Daniel was watching from the side, his back slumped, palms bleeding. He was fading. "There's oxygen," he told Gus.

"No, Daniel. There's not. We didn't bring any." Oxygen usually came up in later loads after more fundamental needs were met, such as food, fuel to make water, and shelter. And today they'd been stripped for speed, carrying mostly ropes and a single night's needs, and that didn't mean toothbrushes. Or air.

"The Kiwis," Daniel said. He was hurting more now. His voice was getting smaller. "Back of the cave. Hook him up."

Gus crawled over Abe to the back and unzipped the rear flap of the tent. A wealth of goods lay stacked in neat piles. The oxygen was in two gleaming rows of upright tanks. Gus manhandled one of the bottles and found a regulator and mask, then zipped the door shut and returned to Abe's side.

When she fitted it to his face, the mask smelled like old food, and then Gus started the flow. Immediately Abe heard the oxygen flooding through the mask. Warmth crept through his limbs, and with it came a blossoming awareness. The afternoon's surreality drifted away like a rare gas. He was bleeding and would have to be sewed. He'd possibly suffered a concussion and should descend. Daniel was hurt and needed examining. And they were all near collapse from the long day. Clearly he had to help. But he was so tired.

Abe lifted the mask away. "What about J.J.?" In all his sorting out the dead, he'd forgotten the living.

"J.J. bailed." Gus's voice had sunk to a slur. "Stashed his load. Rapped away."

So it was just the three of them. Abe wiggled the mask against his face, the slip loops tight, the air bladder snapping rhythmically. His head dipped down toward its pillow, Gus's lap. The wind had ignited outside. But here, inside, there was not a breeze. Just the three of them. Safe.

"I wish we had the radios," Gus murmured, slumping against Abe and Daniel. "They should know. We need them."

Together, heaped against one another, they did the worst thing possible. They let down their guard and fell asleep.

Abe woke with a start, struck by the image of Daniel falling toward him. He threw up his arm and there it was again, the slashing pain. Abe cried out, but his cry was muffled.

He found the face mask wet with his own exhaled breath. Someone had turned on a headlamp, then dropped it to the floor. Its batteries were freezing up and the light was jaundiced. Abe lifted his head. In another setting, under different light, the scene might have been fraternal, even erotic, the three of them lovingly entangled. Beneath this sick yellowish beam, however, they looked like three corpses dumped into a common grave. Daniel lay flopped on one side, arms outstretched to keep the pain in his hands at bay. Gus was slumped against him. The gauntness in their faces carried surrender.

"No," Abe groaned. He forced himself upright. For a full five minutes he just sat, dully pulling at the oxygen in his mask. Then he clawed the mask from his face and leaned toward Daniel.

"Here." He pressed the mask to Daniel's mouth, closing away the bared teeth, the black beard. The mountain had begun to mineralize the climbers, coloring them like stone. Now, before Abe's eyes, Daniel's cheeks took on a flush and the beds of his fingernails washed pink.

"Gus," Abe said. Her eyes barely opened and Abe drew back, unnerved by the oxen dumbness in her gaze. He shook her. "Gus, wake up. We have to wake up." Her eyes glazed over and closed.

Abe's watch said 12:35. Past midnight. He winced at the impossibility of that. The mountain was voracious and they were in its very belly. But where Jonah could afford to wait it out, they could not. By dawn they might never wake again.

Abe unlocked his stiff joints and crawled to the rear of the tent. By the dimming light, he unzipped the door and found two more regulators for oxygen sets. He screwed the pieces together with his good hand and bayonet-mounted the masks and dragged the assembled sets back in. He strapped a mask to Gus's face and one to his own and cranked the flow to its full six liters per minute, not much by paramedic standards but the maximum for these mountaineering regulators. With his portable Gamow bag, Abe could have dropped them to a pressure relative to 12,000 feet elevation in a matter of ten minutes. But that was down below. On oxygen alone, the climbers all descended several thousand feet anyway, a temporary relief.

With everyone "sucking O's," Abe scooted forward to address the water situation. The stoves had burned out while they slept, so he fished out three full cartridges and started new fires. He worked with the slow deliberation of a drunk. The oxygen was sobering, but with the pain in his arm wound and the stiffness in his limbs and his diarrhea and the bronchitis and all his other woes, the high altitude hangover was wracking.

Gus revived before Daniel did. Finally all three of them were sitting upright, hunched close among their piles of sleeping bags and parkas and boots and overpants like sadsack figures in a Beckett play. The wind was roaring past the cave's entrance, but in here the tent walls didn't even ripple. It was as if the mountain had wanted them to slumber undisturbed, on and on.

"We have to get down," Abe said. First it had been Daniel in charge, then Gus. Now it was his turn. He had to manage this emergency. Gus had said it: He was the doctor. He loosened the slip loop around his head and pulled the mask down so that his words were unobstructed.

"We have to go down," he repeated. The altitude had eviscerated them. They had to descend and regroup. They had reached their limit this round.

"We're close." Daniel's words were muffled by his face mask, but his eyes were glittering with summit fever. He was happy. They had pushed far and even if descent was in order, there was still time to come back and break through Everest's glass ceiling. The route's most serious obstacle, the Shoot, was now tamed. They had captured it with their ropes and it was open to passage. From here to the summit was only another 2,500 vertical feet, a matter of one more camp, maybe two, a week or a fortnight, no more, and suddenly it seemed they were very close indeed.

"Close," Abe agreed. "But we have to go down." Descent was imperative. They had wounds to lick. And with Jorgens and Carlos out of the picture, and Thomas on his mutiny, the entire effort had to be reassessed. Even if the team could pull together the numbers for a summit bid, it didn't have the strength just now. Plainly they had to get down to Base Camp, all of them. Only then could they hope to launch the final assault. To continue on in their condition was simply to hand the mountain three victims.

"Yes," Gus said. "Down."

"We'll come back," said Abe.

"Yes," Daniel said.

"Let me see your hands."

Daniel held out his palms. Abe hissed inside his mask. On each hand, the flesh lay peeled open in long flaps. He cleaned the flaps and laid them in place and wrapped each hand with white tape. He used a special pattern favored by boxers and jam crack climbers, thick across the palm, strung between the fingers. Daniel would need all the extra padding possible for the long rappel back to ABC tomorrow.

"Anything else?" Abe asked. He knew there was. Daniel had been favoring his left side ever since arriving at Four.

Daniel removed his jacket and pulled up his sweater and shirts. Wrapped partway around his rib cage stood a livid bruise the size of a watermelon. The rock had bounded between his arms, just missing the abdominal cavity. A little more to the center, the rock might have punched in a whole section of the chest wall: flail chest sternum. At this height a flail chest would have killed him hours ago.

Abe prodded at Daniel's huge rib cage. "Is this tender? Here? Here?" As he probed and interrogated, Abe took stock. A gruesome furrow tracked along Daniel's spine and there were purplish surgery scars on his shoulder and the half-moons where they'd gone after the tendinitis in his elbows. There were other old marks on his arms and hands, and compared to these gouges and furrows and purpled seams, Abe's own climbing scars looked like the hesitation marks of a fake suicide.

"Could be some hairline cracks," he said.

"Probably just bruised," Daniel said.

"You're lucky," Abe said. He closed Daniel's jacket and started to lay an oxygen mask over his mouth, but Daniel took hold of his wrist.

"I wondered about you," he said.

Abe felt his heart sink. At long last, this was it. But why was Daniel choosing to resurrect the past in this midnight storm so far above the earth? Their shared past could easily wait. For that matter, it could go unspoken altogether. Half a lifetime had passed without Abe feeling this need to dredge up the memory. What did it matter. Because it's there? he wryly thought.

Above her mask, Gus was frowning. There was alarm in her eyes, though Abe allowed that could have been a trick of the light. She started to shake her head no.

"I wondered what you'd be like," Daniel said.

"Then you remembered me," Abe said. The words billowed from his mouth, cold layers of frost. He lifted the mask and took a deep draw.

"No. But later they told me. There was a wild kid who stayed through the end."

"That was me."

For a minute neither of them spoke, then Daniel did. "It must have been spooky up there all alone."

There had been a time when Abe had meant to say something like that to Daniel. But Daniel stole the march and now Abe was obliged to answer.

"I wasn't alone," he reminded Daniel.

"They told me you went crazy," Daniel continued. "You quit school. You disappeared."

This wasn't going the way Abe had thought it would. "It wasn't that dramatic," he said. "I had to think, that's all."

"Yeah," Daniel said.

There was no thanks. No explanation. Abe felt outmaneuvered. He had meant to ask Daniel what he'd done with the girl's haunting voice, and maybe this was his answer, that for him there had been no voice or at least no haunting, just a day and a night of prayer and broken knees and then the peace of morphine and a ride out in the litter. But Abe didn't believe it was that simple.

"And I heard about your visit," Daniel said.

Abe looked away.

"You went to her mother's. It took awhile to get it all figured out. But we figured it out. Some kid with wire-rims and a swamp drawl. You." Daniel paused. "In the middle of the night? You terrified her."

"I know." Abe barely heard himself.

"She was already out of her head."

"Yes."

Behind the mask, Abe bit at his torn lips. This was the part that shamed him. All over again he remembered the windblown trailer park outside Rock Springs and near the back a lone trailer with a burned-out lightbulb over a makeshift porch. It had been late spring, a cold Wyoming night with no stars, and right through the aluminum paneling he had heard a dog barking inside and footsteps as she came to the door.

Abe felt old vertigo now, just the way it had been when the old woman's voice had asked who it was through the door. And then the handle had turned and the door had opened. Abe felt himself spinning desperately with no solid footing. He could feel Gus's eyes on him. She had not heard this story yet. Her confusion was becoming wonder, though. She had pulled off her face mask, too. The oxygen had suffused her features with color, highlighting their ravages.

"But why?" Daniel said. He seemed genuinely perplexed. Probably he had been angry about it once, maybe he still was. But right now what Abe heard was pure curiosity.

Indeed, thought Abe. All he'd gotten were more tears and more heartbreak. What more had he thought there was to get? "I wondered, that's all. I was seventeen. I could hear her voice. But I'd never seen her face."

"But why?"

Abe shrugged helplessly.

"We didn't tell her about how long Diana lived," Daniel said. "We didn't tell her for a reason. She didn't know, not until you came along."

"I know." Abe remembered how her eyes had grown wider, but by then it had been too late to stop and he'd told everything. He had put her through the whole tale. She hadn't said stop so he'd made her die all over again with her dead daughter.

"It was bad enough," Daniel murmured.

"I know."

The three of them huddled there for another few minutes while the hanging cookstoves roared with blue flames and the wind thundered past like a waterfall and their words settled as cold vapor onto their worn-out hands.

At last Abe spoke. "I'm sorry," he whispered. Was this why he'd come then? Yet it didn't feel like reason enough.

"Now I know," Daniel whispered back.

Sitting stock-still in the tent crammed with gear and injured humanity, Abe could feel the chaos gathering all around him. Captured by a voice from long ago, he had caused suffering that came from the suffering Daniel had caused, merely by taking a risk. Neither he nor Daniel had ever meant to bring hurt into the world. And yet neither of them could seem to exist without the pain. How strange, thought Abe. How sad.

Then Gus spoke up. "That's all there was to it?" She looked shocked.

"It was enough," Daniel said.

"Enough?" she spat. "But that's nothing."

Daniel was unprepared for her outburst. "What is it you want, Gus?" He glanced at Abe, who was equally baffled.

"You guys," she snorted, indignant. "All this time it's been, like, Jesus, one killed the girl, the other ate her heart. I thought, these two guys, they must have shared a great sin. Or sacrament. Something. Something bigger than this."

She didn't understand, Abe realized. Or maybe she did. She had expected whatever it was that bound Daniel to Abe—and through Abe, to the darker obsession—to be profound. Yet all he and Daniel had revealed was a memory of the aftermath. To Gus, it must have sounded like two old men trading tired gossip.

"It was between Abe and me," Daniel tried to explain. "It had nothing to do with you."

"No?" She was angry now, a feat in this cold tent. "Years now. Years, I've been fighting her ghost for you."

She turned on Abe. "Remember? In the beginning I was afraid of you."

Abe remembered the night in his Base Camp tent, but he wouldn't have termed her warning shot "afraid." Before he could reply, she returned her attention to Daniel.

"I told him to stay away from you. I thought he'd dig her up and bring her back to life. But I was wrong. Abe couldn't have brought her back. Because you never buried her."

Daniel fell silent.

"I live with her. In our house. In our bed. Yes, you talk to her in your sleep, Daniel." She drew at the air for breath. "And now I come onto the mountain and she's here, too. Her name, her ghost. And it has nothing to do with me?"

Gus glared at them both. Then her eyes started to glaze and her flesh darkened with cyanotic blue. Her anger thinned out.

"Look, Gus," Daniel murmured, "I'm sorry."

"Not as sorry as I am."

Peeled back, her anger was pity and love, Abe marveled.

She lifted the mask back to her face. The wind's thunder took over.

Abe twisted away. One of the pots of water was ready. They shared, speechless, and started more ice over the flame. It would go on like that until dawn, Abe knew. They would eat and drink until it was safe to descend. No more sleep. No more words. Not tonight, not in this dangerous place.

AT DAWN, STANDING at the cave mouth in streamers of cold light, Daniel changed his mind. Abe was goosing his harness good and snug around his loins, and Gus was resting on her knees, pacing herself for the long descent back to ABC and from there down to Base for some rest.

"I don't get it," she murmured. "So tired." No mystery there, Abe thought. Even willpower could run out of steam.

Just behind Daniel, their orange line plunged off into the black depths. No rope led upward into the sun, not even old Kiwi or Japanese stock buried under the green ice, because Four was the highest anyone had ever climbed on the Kore Wall. Above this point the route was a blank tablet, just as the entire face had been when Daniel first approached it seven years earlier. Maybe it was that resonance—the tug of terra incognita—which caused Daniel's about-face.

"I'm not going down," he announced to them quietly. "Not quite yet."

After a moment, just as quietly, Gus said, "Say again?"

"Believe me," he said. "I've been here before. And stopped. That was our mistake. One camp more, then we'll be in position. We can rest. And when we come back up, we can take this beast down. One stab. All the way."

"We're tired," Abe said. From here to Five would require fresh cannon fodder to explore the way and build and stock the next camp. One thing Abe could say with absolute certainty. He was scarcely fit to descend, much less climb to 28,000 feet.

"You're not invited," Daniel said. "It's my deal."

"Negative," Gus said. She tried to put some razor in her inflection, but it came out slurred and dull. She couldn't even lift the orange rope to rig her descent and kept fumbling stupidly with simple carabiners. Only yesterday this woman had carried two heavy packs upon her back. Now she seemed feeble. If anything, her debilitation spurred Daniel's resolve.

"Two more days, maybe three," Daniel insisted. "I'll use the gear the Kiwis left us." There was at least 1,800 feet of rope stacked in coils, he explained. He would climb as high as possible each day, extending their reach. Each night he would return to the cave. He could sleep on the Kiwis' bottled oxygen and eat from their cache of freeze-dried food and nuts and even listen to their music. He was adamant.

Abe tried to gauge his recklessness. Daniel wasn't exactly restored to yesterday's strength, but he no longer looked stripped and bloodless either. A night on oxygen appeared to have layered flesh and muscle over his near transparency. His eyes were clear, his strategy complete.

"It makes sense," Abe argued. "But not good sense. Gus is right. You can't push it alone."

Suddenly Abe heard himself. He'd heard words little different from these in the thick of a Wyoming blizzard many years ago. Words hadn't swayed him from his mission then, and words weren't going to convert Daniel now. Abe blinked. He quit arguing. There was nothing to argue.

"At least let me tape your hands again," he said.

Instantly Gus heard Abe's surrender. "Screw you, both of you," she said. She unclipped her rappel device from the rope and sat back against the cave wall and shut her eyes. She was pulling herself together. She was Daniel's archangel and would never leave him, Abe knew. If Daniel went up, she would not go down. There was no point arguing that either.

Daniel had taken the bandages off and the ugly flaps of skin were still weeping. Abe could see meat through one slice.

"I should sew these first," Abe said. He'd hoped to wait

until they got down to ABC or Base, where the wounds could be properly cleaned and the thread wouldn't tear out in manual labor and his fingers wouldn't be half-frozen while he pressed the needle through.

Daniel had his own considerations. "There's not time for that," he said.

"But they can't stay open like this."

"Plastics, Abe, plastics." Daniel grinned his cockeyed grin. It was the first time in many days Abe had seen anyone smile. Instinctively he smiled back.

Mystified, Abe watched Daniel open the top pocket of his pack and fish out a tube of Super Glue. It struck him what was about to happen. "That stuff's toxic," Abe objected.

"Yeah? So's the Hill." Daniel's grin widened. The splits in his lips beaded with blood. With deft robotic efficiency, Daniel squeezed long strings of glue into the gashes on each palm and pulled the flaps shut with careful fingertips. He let the glue set up, holding his hands over the blue stove flame like a welder closing a seam, then flexed his hands in fists to assess the patch job. It was a rock-climber's trick, though Abe had never heard of people gluing more than a finger pad back in place.

For a moment, Abe considered tearing the bloody bandage off his own arm, pouring Super Glue into the slit and continuing up with Daniel. But even at the thought, a chill went through him and he realized that it was this from which Thomas had fled down the mountain. It wasn't Daniel's natural authority up here that had driven Thomas away, nor that this black-haired kamikaze was berserk for ascent. No, what had scared Thomas off was the sudden recognition that he would become willing to die up here, not for this mountain with its pure diamond light and not for his own glory and benediction, but rather for Daniel, for the sake of freeing one soul from its cage. Daniel had led them so high they were nearly out of air and yet he was still aimed at the sun and they were still following. Abe wanted—desperately wanted—to stay with Daniel and climb on. But it was time for him to flee.

"Good luck," Abe said.

"See you down at Base," Daniel said.

"Good-bye," Abe said to Gus. She didn't even open her eyes to glare at him.

Shortly after Abe started down, Daniel sallied up, trailing a rainbow of three colorful nine-millimeter ropes and bearing four more still coiled in his pack. Gus was belaying him from inside the cave, paying out rope as Daniel climbed up. He was bearing almost a thousand feet of rope, upward of eighty pounds. If there had been anyone else to watch, it would have seemed a boast. Alone, the load was nothing more than one man's calculation of himself.

Just before Abe lost sight of him, he saw that the Shoot opened wider and angled back above the cave and that Daniel had quit front-pointing and was walking almost upright on the icy slope. At the rate he was going, Daniel might just do what he'd said: fix all the way to Five and still have time left over to build the camp and descend before he ran out of steam. As usual in matters of this mountain, Daniel was proving himself correct.

The expedition would have a definite advantage with Five set in place. It would give them a high point from which to launch their all-out assault. Providing there were still enough healthy, willing players down at ABC or Base, they could repopulate the mountain all the way to 28,000 feet in a little less than a week of climbing. That would leave just a thousand feet more to go. They still had a chance. The last Abe saw of him, Daniel had come to a halt to pin one of his ropes to the wall with ice screws.

It had taken Abe four hard days to get from ABC to Four. Now, in less than nine hours, he dropped a vertical mile and reached ABC in time for supper. Along the way, every camp was deserted, not a climber in sight. Except for Daniel and Gus high above, the mountain appeared to have been abandoned.

ABC was deserted, too, except for Nima and Chuldum, who had been instructed to guard the camp. Abe couldn't comprehend what there was to guard against—the wind, perhaps, or the beat of sunlight—but that was Jorgens for you. He ran a tight ship even when it was in drydock.

First thing next morning, Abe set off in his trail sneakers alone. The ten miles of trail seemed to fly underfoot. That was his imagination at play. In fact what felt like an effortless tumble into the lower valley was a struggle. His watch told him he was going slower and slower. But the farther he descended, the richer the air became and so he didn't mind. After weeks on end of following the scant vertical tracery of their ascent, this flat trail seemed blatant, a virtual highway. Abe found it hard to believe the trail had once struck him as vague and confounding. The way was so clear down here, so inevitable. His pack was empty, his spirits light, and he wanted to race pell-mell down the rocky lane. It was frustrating to feel so invigorated and yet have such an unsteady step. He lurched on.

All around him, the world assembled itself with details that grew sharper and more lustrous. A chorus of grouse gabbled on the perimeter of sunshine and frost. Big sticks of glacier mud hung beside the trail like temple columns. Insignificant rocks took on an almost sacramental distinctness beneath his Nikes. Part of his awe was plain hunger and fatigue and the richer air, Abe knew. But there was more than that to it. He had heard that monks wake in darkness so as to welcome the order of day. Now, descending from the Kore's dark, slaughtering radiance, he understood. These rocks, this birdsong, the blue sky: They were simple things, but they were everything.

Base Camp sprang out at Abe with its candy-colored domes and bustling industry. He came to a surprised halt and stood still, weaving slightly, taking it all in. He had forgotten how many tents were down here and how level the moraine was and what it was like to hear water flowing loose in a stream.

There was laughter in the air, and an aroma of fresh-baked bread—that would be from Carlos's solar oven—and even the background silence had a lush melody to it. Robby and Stump were rearranging what was left of the supply dump, and J.J. was clowning for the Sherpas, walking around on his hands. From the boom box by the mess tent, Pink Floyd—a high altitude mainstay—was weaving electric notes into the carnival of sights and sounds and smells, and Abe moved stiffly, drawn by the music.

Suddenly he wanted to be among these people. He felt starved for their voices and their touch and their company.

Kelly emerged from a tent swinging her waist-length mane—freshly washed, heavy as white gold—and she was the first to catch sight of Abe. Her face lit with a smile and she came toward him.

"Abe," she greeted, and opened her arms to hug him. "I am so glad to see you." She smelled like coconut shampoo and Ivory soap and like the woman he had gotten used to smelling in their shared tents on the mountains. They had been apart for less than a week, but it felt like a season since he had seen her. She had missed him. He had missed her. He had missed them all. It was good to be down. He was dizzied by how good it felt.

"Kelly?" he rasped.

Her embrace had flesh to it, warmth and substance. She didn't pat him quickly on the back and release him. She held him against her for a long, long minute.

In the span of that embrace, Abe was flooded with so many thoughts that they came to him only as a babble. He wanted to sing his joy and cry at the same time.

"You look so good," Kelly said.

Abe knew that wasn't so. He could feel his lips splitting, literally, in a smile. He tasted blood and knew his face was blistered and skinned and hairy and smeared with old glacier cream. Worse than the ugliness, he stank. There had been no chance to wash in the weeks at ABC and higher, and now he smelled the feces caking his underwear. He was ashamed and yet strangely exhilarated. He had become a child of the Kore Wall, a foul yeti himself. Even so, this golden woman held him.

It struck him. He had survived the mountain. And not just in the minute-to-minute sense of dodging its missiles or making it through another night. He had turned his back on the Hill, and however temporary this respite, it was now only an image against the sky. He was alive.

Abe wanted to tell Kelly some of this, but when he opened his mouth all that came out was his bronchial croak. "Kelly," he said again.

Kelly held him out from her and looked at his eyes. She seemed to have some notion what his wild gleam was all about. Maybe she had suffered this same ecstasy.

"Come on, Abe," she said, and led him by the arm. They went directly to her tent, not to his cold, empty hospital dome. She stripped the pack off his back and made him sit. He felt drunk and couldn't quit grinning. After the mountain's murderous violence, this peace seemed surreal. He could actually sit here without ducking or listening for the crack of avalanches or shivering or sucking at the air for a breath. He could just sit.

Kelly disappeared, then returned with a steaming mug of

tea and bright boxes of crackers and a slab of cheese, and the crackers weren't a ball of mangled wet crumbs and the cheese wasn't frozen to stone. "I told the others you're down," she said. "Jorgens wants to debrief you right away. But I told everyone to stay away."

The sun was warm and not a breeze was stirring. She helped him from his sweater, which was stiff with old blood. "Christ, Abe," she said when the gash in his arm came in view. "Was there some kind of massacre up there?"

"It was . . ." Abe stopped, trying to recall the ordeal.

"I asked Krishna to heat some water," Kelly said. "I'll wash you. Then we'll clean that arm. And there's time to sleep before dinner. Here. I want you to sleep in my tent."

Abe felt tears running down his face.

"Thank you," he creaked.

She reached for his hand and squeezed it. "You're down," Kelly assured him, knowing his disbelief. "It's time to rest."

At dinner that night, Abe related the latest news on their progress to Four. He described Daniel's fall and the bad night at the cave and Daniel and Gus's continuing effort to establish Camp Five. Freshly washed and shaven, wearing a clean white T-shirt with a tequila advertisement on the chest, he sat at the table and felt profound contentment. His arm was throbbing under a bandage that stood brilliant against his bronzed flesh. Kelly had cleaned and stitched it for him, and Abe was getting drowsy from a Percodan he'd taken for the pain. He would sleep well tonight.

With grave courtesy, Krishna served the climbers plates piled high with steaming rice and lentils and Tibetan dumplings. Krishna surveyed the general vicinity to make sure people had the necessary amenities—a spoon, a bottle of ketchup, some Tabasco sauce—then hustled back to stir his pots and start supper for the Sherpas who sat in the corner by Krishna's stoves, warming themselves, waiting politely for the members to finish. Their happy chattering blended into the background noise of the stove roar and the wind whipping a loose cord against the tent.

People reacted to Abe's news as if Daniel had just subdued a dragon and made their valley safe. They were excited and grateful and eager to have him return to their ranks. Even

Jorgens and Thomas were pleased. The summit was within striking distance now. Their long shot was suddenly much shorter. It would be difficult to fail.

"It will be different this time," Stump said. "I've found the bug in our radios. This time we have communications."

"This time we're rested," Robby added.

"Then we're agreed," said Jorgens. "We go for it. Three days," Jorgens said. "Then we go back up. We finish our business."

They had been down for several days already, some for more than a week, and the hiatus showed in their faces. Their concentration camp visage had fattened. The faraway stares, the bony grimaces, even their raggedy, emaciated beards had filled out. The mineral blueness of their flesh had softened and receded, leaving them with the color of life.

"Three days," Thomas seconded.

"And then," someone pronounced, "home."

"Meanwhile," another voice piped up. "I have for you a surprise." It was Li. Bundled to the skull in expedition gear, he stood from his chair at the end of the wicker table. He threw back the cherry-red parka hood and smiled at them, though the kerosene light pulled out the struck hollows and bony edges of his face and it was hard to tell if he was happy or in pain. His parka and Gore-Tex overpants had the crisp spotlessness of a dress uniform and appeared to have suffered little exposure to the elements for which they were intended.

"Good night," he greeted them with a lecturer's formality. He had a starved man's gleam in his eye, and his look of loneliness was almost obscene. Abe had forgotten him completely.

"Tomorrow, for you, my friends and guests, is the viewing of Shangri-La," he said. Abe was shocked by how much Li's accent had thickened over the last nine weeks. His syntax had slipped radically. It was the altitude and the forced hermitage, Abe knew. They were lapsing, all of them.

Li continued with a showman's pitch. "The real Shangri-La, you see."

"The Rongbuk monastery," Carlos blurted aloud.

"Yes, Mr. Crowell." Li beamed. "Sixty years ago, Mr. James Hilton wrote his book. He based it on reports from early British expeditions to Qomolangma." Qomolangma—the Pinyin bastardization of the Tibetan Chomolungma. Mount Everest. "He has a pass, Shangri-La. We have a pass, Chengri La. He puts utopia in a very high Chinese monastery. We have this place. Rongbuk Monastery. Only now, not so utopia."

At the mention of a monastery, Abe remembered his epileptic monk and wondered where the poor boy had disappeared to. He made a mental note to ask Nima. He couldn't remember the boy's name, and that gave him a start. But then he couldn't remember Jamie's face either, and for some reason that evened out his losses.

"We can actually go there?" Carlos asked. It was easy to see that one did not visit the monastery with ease.

"It is my pleasure," Li said. "I am authorizing this for you."

"Can we bring cameras?" Stump asked.

"Of course," Li said. "Cameras. Video cameras. Everything. You will see archaeology of old Tibet. And something else. I have learned that tomorrow Tibetan nationals will perform an archaic ceremony. Very special. Very dark. Very educational." P. T. Barnum could not have done a better job. The climbers were hooked. Down at his end of the table, Carlos whispered the word *puja*. He was convinced they were about to get another blessing. Li smiled broadly at their enthusiasm.

As Abe and Kelly returned to her tent, he looked up at the ghostly white massif of Everest. Daniel and Gus were up there somewhere, probably holed up tonight in the cave at 8,000 meters. There was something vaguely mythical about that notion—a man and a woman in the mountain, their light mixing with the stars. "I hope they're okay up there," Abe murmured to Kelly as they were falling to sleep. He had his good arm around her shoulders and she was tucked close against him, each in their own bag. Chastity had little to do with their separation tonight. Abe was going to be in a lot of pain soon. The local anesthetic was wearing off and his arm was starting to throb.

"I wish they would come down with us," Abe said.

"Sleep, Abe." Kelly rolled her back to him. They slept.

Early next morning, in the spirit of a picnic, the climbers took off downvalley along the road that led out to the Pang La and out to the world. Bounding through the rich oxygen, they reached the monastery by ten and headed up a wide stone staircase that snaked around the mountainside.

The sun was huge and white in a sky that verged on black

outer space. Abe sweated, but the sweat evaporated the instant it hit the dry air. They carried rocks to throw at stray dogs, for there were Tibetan settlements nearby.

As they climbed the staircase, dust coated the sunblock on their faces. Some of them had elected to paint their noses with a bright green sun cream, their lips with blue, and that contributed to the festive spirit. Abe stuck with plain white. After an hour their faces were mostly just brown with layered dirt.

The staircase turned around a ridge and quite suddenly the fortress—or *dzong*—that had once protected the region, or what was left of it, unfolded before them. Acre after steep acre, the *dzong*'s remains lay in collapse, sprawled in terraces across the mountainside. Like a miniature Great Wall, a serpentine wall climbed straight up the incline. What buildings still stood were in pieces. Not one had a roof. The wind keened through gaps and across disintegrating walls as if this were a vast stone whistle.

The climbers were quick to unsheathe their cameras. Once before, on a trip to Inca ruins in Peru, Abe had observed how gothic settings were irresistible to the Western tourist. Decay and apocalypse made for excellent spice in home slide shows, and this *dzong* was saturated with both.

Childlike, the climbers fanned out. They scrambled into deserted rooms, proving for themselves that living people had once eaten and prayed and slept here. A narrow labyrinth turned into a series of cells with entrance holes barely the size of a rib cage. They decided these must be meditation chambers, where solitary monks had lived for months and years at a time. Faded paintings of Buddhas and pop-eyed demons decorated some of the leeward walls. Some of the listing walls showed traces of old orange and white wash, brilliant against the darker earth.

Here and there, they found caves in the hillside filled with big heaps of clay tablets, each stamped with Buddhist figures. Some caves held thousands of the little plaques. Abe knelt in front of one such pile. The tablets were made of worthless clay, but they sparkled like Spanish doubloons in the brilliant light.

"Souvenirs," said Li. "Yes, Doctor. Go ahead. Take some. These are not precious antiquities. It is permitted under the law."

"But they're religious, aren't they?" Abe was hesitant, even though his daypack was wide open. He wanted to bring some of these tablets home. How else could he ever prove that something so common could be so beautiful?

"Artifacts of a dead religion," Li said. "And anyway, they will turn to dust here."

The monastery and its fortress had apparently been dead for centuries. Abe contemplated aloud what sort of holocaust had been visited upon this civilization.

"I wonder what brought this all down," he said. "Drought? Or maybe famine? Or plague?" Immediately he felt like a gringo touring overgrown pyramids in the Yucatán.

Li didn't answer right away. Finally he said, "Earthquakes," with a sobriety that was almost mournful.

"Here?" Abe was surprised. The land had such an immovable quality, a look of infinite gravity and stasis.

"Oh yes," Li expanded. "The Himalaya is a very young mountain range. The Indian subcontinent is all the time pushing against the Chinese land mass. There are many earthquakes here."

Abe ventured that they must have struck a long time ago.

Again Li looked at him curiously. "Very long ago," he said.

"That's what it looks like. Centuries ago."

"Yes," said Li.

Like clockwork, the afternoon winds began at high noon, three o'clock Beijing time. Slapped by the wind, the climbers hastily regrouped and headed on higher.

As the group strung out along the trail, Abe walked with Carlos in the rear. Carlos's sprained ankle had worsened and he was crutching along with two ski poles. The hike was painful, but he was determined to keep up. Abe shared what he'd learned about this place.

"Earthquakes?" Carlos barked. "The L.O. said that?" He came to a halt and turned. Abe faced his own reflection in Carlos's sunglasses.

"Look around," Carlos said. He pointed at a building and then a section of the wall, then more structures. "See those holes? You ever heard of an earthquake that punches round holes in a building?"

Abe hadn't.

"Artillery," Carlos said. "Chinese artillery practice." Then he went on walking.

They reached the backside of the mountain and a whole system of hidden valleys opened magically in the distance. Their flat spacious floors were outlined with commune plots. Abe could just barely make out a line of tiny people working in rhythmic unison, an almost indiscernible ripple of labor upon the earth. The wind blew. The line of workers shifted like a slow tide.

Suddenly the smell of pines washed across them. The aroma was quite powerful, then it was gone.

There was not a tree in sight. Indeed, Abe hadn't seen a single tree on the whole Tibetan plateau. And yet, suddenly, for that brief moment, the air was thick and sweet with cedar. It was like spying a rainbow in a desert. A few moments later, the rich scent returned, then drifted away again.

"You smell it, too?" Carlos inhaled the breeze.

"Pine," Abe said. "Cedar pine."

They followed the corkscrewing trail around to a second shoulder of the mountain. Fifteen minutes higher, they reached a ridge where the others were drinking water, waiting for them, taking pictures. They had stopped beside a pile of mani stones. There were several hundred of them in the heap, each rounded by ancient rivers, each carved with prayers in beautiful Tibetan calligraphy.

Atop the pile lay an animal skull, carved and painted with prayers. The rocks were piled at random, but the skull was lodged in place with great care. The display sang of a people embedded in the land. Robby fired off some more Kodachrome, angling for the light.

"Folk art," Li said. "I am reminded of primitive cave paintings." For all his gab, The L.O. seemed to be getting nervous, as if they were straying into dangerous regions.

"You guys smell the pine smoke?" asked Carlos.

Stump pointed to the top of the mountain.

Now Abe saw white rags of smoke and smelled the smell again. The smoke was whipping down from a crumbling building which crowned the very summit.

"We are on time," Li said.

The trail led up to a breach in the crowning structure. The mountainside dropped away beneath the breach. Loose rocks spilled down from this gap, the leftovers from the old wall.

Using their hands, the climbers cautiously pulled up through the breach.

Nothing could have prepared Abe for what lay within the walls.

"Oh lord," breathed Jorgens.

It was a lost world in here.

A manmade forest of prayer flags surrounded them. It engulfed them, a dense breathtaking grove of red and yellow and blue and white squares of cotton. Each flag was block-printed with Tibetan prayers. Each fluttered rapidly upon a thin willow branch that was bunched with many dozens of others. More of these bunches were planted in haphazard piles of mani stones. Some were new and bright, others bleached and rotted by the sun.

The summit structure was barely eighty feet across and even less wide. But no cathedral in the world could ever compete with this holy place, broken, bare to the sky.

For a minute the climbers just stood where they'd surfaced through the breach, listening to the cotton stroking infinity. Kelly's mouth was wide open. Robby doffed his Dalton Hardware cap and a whole floodplain of dry wrinkles broke out across his broad forehead. Their archaeology had come to life.

Then the wind shifted, and there was that smell of cedar again.

This time the white smoke engulfed them, turning the ruins into a cupful of flags and wood fog.

Then Abe smelled something else, too. An unpleasant, saccharine odor. It took him a minute to place the smell. And then it came to him. Something had died.

Voices drifted in with the smoke. They came muffled, from a distant part of the ruins.

"This way," Li said with waning confidence. "But we must stay together. We must take care. There are dangers. There are bad stories."

Abe wended his way through the smoke. The summit structure was not very large, but they had to pick their way through so many clusters of prayer flags and *mani* stones that it seemed enormous and mazelike. Abe passed another horned animal skull embellished with paint and carved lettering, then another. The voices grew louder.

At the rear of the old structure, a collapsed doorway opened out onto a wide flat ledge on the outside. On every side of the ledge, the mountain dropped away, a thousand feet deep. Far in the distance, Everest was blowing her afternoon plume.

Abe stepped through the doorway. Then he stopped, frozen, for they had emerged into the middle of a funeral. At first Abe wasn't even sure of that. He had no idea at all what they were doing.

Three Tibetan men had stripped naked a dead woman.

One of the men was holding a knife.

The woman's clothing lay in a heap.

The scene struck directly at Abe's mind, unbuffered by language or thought. A big hand grasped his shoulder from behind, someone trying to come through the doorway, and Abe heard the person gasp sharply.

A cedar fire was smoking away on one end of the ledge. Back against the *dzong* wall, to Abe's left, sat what he took to be the woman's family, maybe eight people of different ages. For a moment, deceived by the thick white smoke, Abe thought he saw his monk seated on skins, droning his monotone into the empty blue. The smoke shifted. His monk disappeared.

For a moment, some of the family members didn't see the climbers and kept on muttering prayers. Then all was silence. They froze, as if ambushed.

The climbers stood paralyzed, too. The Tibetans considered them for another minute or so. They were not welcome, that was clear. But Abe and the others were too stupefied to be moved by the hostile glares.

"What's the traffic jam," Thomas groused, squeezing through the doorway. Then he saw the body and went still, too.

"Trespass." Carlos said it firmly. "This is trespass. We don't belong here."

But before they could retreat, Li squeezed through the bunched climbers. "Trespass?" he scoffed, and the fear was gone from his voice. He seemed oddly triumphant, pleased by the climbers' shock at this raw, strange sight.

"We are within the law," Li said with growing confidence. "We are not trespassing. You can take photographs. Yes, it is within the law."

The Tibetans didn't speak to one another. Each of them scrutinized the climbers and especially their Chinese guide.

Then as suddenly as they had stopped, the Tibetans started again. They began droning mantras without syncopation, almost without breath. The cedar smoke changed direction and fell into the valley.

"Come." With great firmness, almost as if he were disciplining them, Li ushered the climbers to one side. "Please, sit," he said, indicating the ground by the wall.

Abe was dumbly obedient.

"What is this?" Kelly asked, hunkering by the wall.

Stump spoke in a whisper. "I don't know."

Abe felt their fear and helplessness, too. That bare knife, the corpse, the wind and prayers: He wondered what they meant to do.

"I've heard of this," Carlos said, keeping his voice low. "Daniel told me about it. He has pictures. They call it sky burial."

Robby squirmed, horrified. "They push her off the edge, or what, man? What is this? What am I doing here?"

Before Carlos could answer, before Robby could leave, the man with the knife bent down and made a long cut. From just right of her lightly haired pubis down to the inside of the knee joint, the butcher drew his blade fast and hard.

Kelly groaned aloud.

Abe squinted in the cedar smoke. He tried not to flinch, though, telling himself this was the stuff of gross anatomy, nothing more. And they were travelers and this was culture. He took out his camera. Somehow, looking through the viewfinder made it easier to watch.

Quickly now, because they had begun, the corpse was tilted up on one hip. From the pelvic saddle down, the butcher sliced again and the quadriceps flopped loose onto the cold stone.

The knives were sharp and these men had obviously done this with human beings many times before. It took just minutes before the woman's leg bones were bare white sticks. Losing his revulsion, Abe marveled at how quickly a body could be undressed of its flesh.

"They throw their poor and their dead children into the rivers," said Li. He spoke aloud with a tour guide's voice. "Their monks are cremated or else buried in big hollow tree trunks. But for many, many centuries, this is how the common Tibetans have been. Cutting up their loved ones like chickens. Feeding each other to the animals."

Gigantic blue-and-white vultures that had been wheeling in the abyss came closer now and roosted, first one, then others, landing with ungainly hops.

Like a pack of grotesque schoolchildren, the birds gathered into a semicircle at one corner of the ledge. While they waited with eerie pique, they nipped and nudged each other and flexed their six-foot wings.

The birds began to unsettle Abe in a way that the butchers had not. The vultures looked like a parody of their little band lined against the *dzong* wall.

Yet even as Abe and the other climbers sorted through their guilt feelings, they kept on snapping photos. Robby was firing away with a little black Samurai. Its motor-driven telephoto lens pumped in and out with electronic frenzy. Abe's own camera was bulky and old, which kept his picture taking slow. It made him seem studied, even reluctant.

"Go closer," Li encouraged him. But Abe didn't.

One man finished stripping the woman's arm bones clean. The other two began working on the flesh already cut away. They sliced it into pieces and threw it to the vultures. As the birds shoved about for bits of meat, their big dry feathers rattled.

Li was grimly jubilant.

"Now you see," he said, "we have come to the edge of the world. And they are barbarians."

It Was Nearly June and summer was loosening the countryside. The moraine thawed a little more every morning, and
their separate islands of tundra grass turned spongy. Abe found
mud on his shoes. It was a sign. The earth itself was compromis-
ing. The separate elements—the mountain, the wind, the cold,
the ice, the sunlight—were reaching a sort of peace, mixing
together, melding. It was a season for changes and for the
Ultimate Summit the changes came swiftly.

First, Gus brought the word down to Base, catching them
at noon in the olive-green mess tent. They were all there, a few
hard at work rewiring the stubborn walkie-talkie sets, most just
swapping lies and snacking on popcorn and generally taking it
easy. From out of nowhere, Gus burst in upon them with her
pack on, the waistband still clipped.

They barely had time to recognize the windblown creature
before she had delivered her message. "He's done it," she
rasped. Corroded with bronchitis and strep, her voice cracked
through them like distant thunder. The words came out more
animal than human and Abe wasn't sure he'd understood her.

A length of parachute cord bound her red hair and she
had on a filthy cap over that. The smear of zinc oxide across
her cheeks and nose was flecked with old food and older scabs.

What made Gus most alien, though, was not the filth but her wildness. Something close to dementia burned in her green eyes—Abe recognized it as his own—and she looked menacing, a berserker fresh from the glory fields.

Robby was the first to recover from her entrance. "Sit down, Gus," he said.

Kelly was next. "Gus? Are you okay?"

Gus continued standing there with her craziness, weaving in place, drunk on the rich oxygen. She stared at them.

"Where's Daniel at?" Stump asked with a most casual interest. He had a Phillips-head in one hand and a welding gun in the other and amateur electronics on his mind. Having found the glitch, he had sworn to get their walkie-talkies up and running by tomorrow morning.

Gus stared at them, mute.

It suddenly hit Abe that Daniel might have fallen. Had he done it, then, sailed a day too far? But Abe was just guessing, and no one else seemed concerned.

"How about some herbal spice tea?" Kelly asked her. "It's great, sweet without sugar. Real cinnamony."

Abe goggled at Kelly's banality. Here was this ferocious woman with ropes of snot splayed across her face like a horse whipped too far. Then he realized the banality was Kelly's very point. Down here at Base, the status quo had its own rhythm and coziness, and before things got too incendiary, they were banking Gus's fire, and their own, too.

Gus would have none of their pacifism, though. She stood at the head of their table. "Daniel broke through."

"I knew it." Heads turned. It was Thomas, the blood drained out from his cheeks. "Are you saying Corder topped out?"

Gus heard his hostility, and chose to let him dangle. "I'm saying he found a way out of the Shoot. He placed Five. We're home free."

"Gus, would you take a chair, please," Robby said. "Sit down before you fall down and tell it in plain English."

She sat. She told them. While she stayed in the cave, Daniel had soloed out of the Shoot's lethal tube of rockfall. He had discovered a sprawling snow plateau at the base of the so-called Yellow Band—a thick sandwich of sulphur-colored limestone that girdled the mountain at 27,500 feet. Blazing his path with nine-mil rope, he'd spent an extra day humping a load of Kiwi gear up to the plateau and pitched their next camp. Then he had descended to ABC. A dozen questions swarmed to Abe's mind. Before he could ask even one, the others started interrogating Gus.

"So?" Thomas demanded. "Did he solo to the top?"

Gus ignored him.

"Five's not much," Gus said through the steam of her tea, "but we don't need much. There's wind up there, but no more rockfall. Daniel told me to tell you, from Five to the top it's a cruise."

"A cruise?" snorted Thomas. J.J. scowled at him. Thomas scowled back. On this north side, the hard yellow rock lay in tiles canted downward at a 30-degree pitch, with successive layers overlapping one another. The Yellow Band wasn't particularly dangerous or technical, but neither was it going to be a cruise. Thomas was probably right. The climb wasn't over yet.

Gus rolled right over Thomas's fatalism. For one thing he hadn't earned it; and for another his cynical tone cloyed. "Daniel says, Five's close enough, you can see the top."

"Yeah? Well I can go outside and see the top from down here, too," Thomas said. "That doesn't mean we're close."

Gus had the punchline ready. "Yeah, but you can't see the tripod. Not from down here."

It took them a minute to gather the significance of that. Then a light went on in Robby's eyes. "Daniel saw the tripod?" he breathed.

"Fantastic," Stump said.

Thomas looked slapped silly. Speechless, he blinked rapidly.

The news galvanized them like a shot of crude voltage. In 1972 a Chinese expedition had climbed via the easier North Col route and erected a five-foot-high metal survey tripod on the very summit. Ever since, it had become a feature as natural as the fossils and space shuttle vistas that awaited summiteers.

"I've never seen him so certain," Gus added. And that in itself—Daniel's confidence—spurred them even more than the other news, the camp, the Yellow Band, the tripod. They were close all right.

"And Corder? Is he coming soon?" Jorgens guessed. His beard was more salt than pepper now, his motions slower. He looked older and used up. But with this news, he perked up. This was good news, very good, tantamount to victory.

"I parked his butt at ABC," Gus said. "He's in no shape for a bunch of round-trips to Base." They understood. Everyone had seen the way Daniel limped around on the flats, and had heard the crepitation of bone on bone. It was harder on him to descend an easy trail than to climb a sheer face. Climbing, he could at least compensate with his arms for the kneecaps and cartilage a host of orthopods had cut out.

"One thing else," Gus related. They fell silent. "He made a promise. He said he'll wait for us."

She said it to remind them. Daniel could just as easily have continued on the last thousand feet to the tripod alone. Instead he had roped down to join hands with his teammates and take the Kore in a classic finish. Abe knew it was a gamble, Daniel turning his back on a solo flash that must have seemed a sure thing. But apparently it wasn't as much a gamble as lone wolfing through the rest of his life. Even now, several days later, Gus looked relieved by his decision. She really thought she could save him, Abe thought. Bravo, Gus.

The elated climbers bubbled out of the mess tent and into the sunshine, leaving Gus in the dark with her mug of tea. Abe lagged behind. Unfinished business.

"How's he doing?" Abe asked her. She was changed. At least she would look him in the eye now.

"He's whipped," she said. "He's in pain. His hands are like meat. His ribs are bad, busted I think. And he stayed high too long. You know, the thousand-mile stare, all that." A sternness flickered across her face. "But the nightmare's almost over. We're going to nail this bastard. And then he's free." She spoke it like a credo. She nodded to herself and Abe nodded, too. To control the mountain was to control the entire pyramid of obsessions that had led to it. None of them yearned for that power more than Daniel.

"Is he taking care of his hands?" Doctors were supposed to ask questions like that.

"Of course."

"How about you, how are the lungs holding up?" She had once developed double pneumonia deep in the Karakoram range in Pakistan, and it was again a doctor's kind of question.

In truth, he was stalling. He wanted to know if there was any room to negotiate on her dislike for him.

She was staring at him, deciding something. "Daniel wanted me to tell you something," she said.

Abe braced himself.

"He wants to summit with you, Abe."

Abe was dumbfounded. Then it occurred to him that Gus had gotten injured and couldn't climb anymore. It would be like her to hide an injury. That would explain Daniel's need for a new partner.

"Are you hurt?" Abe asked.

Gus reacted with scorn. "Hurt?" she said. "What the hell do you think?"

Now Abe saw his error. She was whole, but she was indeed hurt. "No," he said. "I meant injured."

Gus waved aside his clarification.

"Then what is this?" He knew better than to feel sorry for this woman, and yet Daniel had betrayed her. Alone and weary, she'd had to carry the news of it down ten miles and then deliver it to the man chosen to replace her.

"He wants you with him when he hits top," she said. "Same day. Same rope."

Abe was flattered. He hadn't expected anything like this, to reach the summit, to lay the past to rest once and for all. But could they? Forgiveness was something granted, not attained. It was not the same as reaching a mere mountaintop. Like that, Abe made his mind up.

"I'll tell him my answer when I see him," Abe said.

"Tell me," Gus demanded. She had a right.

"I already have a partner."

Now was Gus's turn to be surprised. She stared at him as if he'd stayed too high for too long as well. "Kelly?" she said. But her real contempt was for Abe. "You're not telling me you'd hang yourself up with her. Daniel's your one sure shot."

Abe shrugged. "It's me and Kelly."

Gus frowned, trying to turn with this latest about-face. Odd, Abe thought. He hadn't noticed until now that her red hair had turned nearly gold. The great stone crucible was changing them. To see her from behind, you might almost mistake Gus for Kelly.

"You're making a mistake," Gus said. But she wasn't really arguing. For all her muscular gruffness, she had a wonderful transparency, Abe realized. There was no hiding the ray of hope lighting her face. Nor, a moment later, hiding the suspicion that darkened it.

"I get it," she said to herself.

"Gus?"

Her green eyes glittered in the afternoon sunlight. She was angry now, once again with Abe. "See here," she said. "I don't know what's with you two. But if this is how Daniel wants to break his damn curse, great. It's worth the summit to have him done with Diana. So don't play noble with me."

"Nobility has nothing to do with it."

"Daniel needs this, Abe. Go bury your ghost. Together. Whatever it takes."

"Gus, you don't understand. I didn't come for an exorcism. I'm not ditching Kelly. And I can tell you, Daniel's not ditching you. He was being dramatic, that's all."

"Fuck off," she said. "If you want to patronize Kelly, be my guest. But not me, guy. I don't need your help. I don't need your permission. Got it?"

Suddenly Abe was tired of trying to soothe this woman. He had no desire to be her foil, but it was hard to turn his back on her. She was heartbroken. Something Kelly had said came back to him.

"Love has nothing to do with it, Gus." He kept it simple.

Gus was speechless, just as he'd hoped. Now they could both pretend ascent was built on colder realities. He started to walk off.

"By the way." Her voice caught him.

Abe heard the change in her tone. She had an ailment.

"Yes, Gus." He took a breath and made himself the healer once again.

"While I'm here, did you bring any of those home pregnancy tests?" The way she said it, the timing she used, even the fact that she said it at all, was meant to sandbag him. Of course they hadn't brought such a thing.

Abe groped for a reply. "You're late?" he finally asked.

"Three, four weeks." She was right to shrug. Everyone's rhythms were out of sync up here.

"What about other symptoms?"

"Besides nausea and loss of appetite and exhaustion? Last time I looked, everyone had those." Right again.

And yet there was the possibility. Abe pursued it. "Gus, if it's true, and if you want this baby . . ."

She held up a hand. "One, if it's true, I don't know if I want it. And two, either way, I don't need a lecture. You've already said your mouthful."

"But, Gus." He had a duty to warn her about the solar radiation, the bad food, the raised blood pressures, and all the myriad dangers of high altitude. He stopped himself. She'd had weeks to think it all through.

"Does Daniel know?"

"Nope. And it's not yours to say."

"Of course not." Another secret to hold. "But don't you think . . ."

"Tell him? Tell him what, Abe? There's a chance I might be carrying his child? You know what he'd do? He'd sack the climb, just on the very chance. And then what if it weren't true?"

"But what if it is?"

Now she handed it back to him. "I thought you said love has nothing to do with it."

"I didn't mean that."

She quit bantering. "We'll never be this close again," she said. "We can make it."

But on the eve of launching their final assault—on the very afternoon before they were going to trek back to ABC and inhabit the mountain all over again—a Land Cruiser arrived to kill the Ultimate Summit. It came roaring toward them like a small dinosaur, smoking out plumes of white dust, and at first Abe had trouble integrating the return of the twentieth century.

For nearly a hundred days now they had lived like the native denizens of this strange, lost nation called Tibet. They had lapsed into a pack of trolls, mountain beings who were ugly and twisted and hunchbacked beneath the sun. All their great works of music and literature had been shucked as incomprehensible. These days, instead of Proust and Milton, they applied themselves to Conan the Barbarian comic books, scrupulously reading and rereading key balloons. It could take a full evening to complete one issue.

The climbers gathered as if the white Land Cruiser were a

spaceship landing and watched three PLA soldiers dismount. The soldiers were marvelously clean, their hair cut, cheeks shaved, their pea-green uniforms unscathed by the weather or rockfall. None of them limped. The flesh on their faces was unblemished by the sun. Their rifles glinted in the light.

The oldest of the three, an officer, was perhaps Abe's age. The other two appeared to be in their late teens, and they couldn't pry their eyes away from the climbers. Abe wanted to believe their shock held some measure of homage or at least mutual respect, but all he saw in their look was a curious disdain.

Li came crisply dressed from his tent as if this visit were no surprise and their timing was precise. The homesickness was gone from his face. He had spring in his step. Still he was not prepared for what the officer told him in Mandarin, even less so for what he next read in a dispatch that was handed to him. He was visibly shaken and took another minute to read the dispatch again and ask the officer many questions.

The climbers kept their distance, even after Li spoke to them. "Mister Jorgens," he called.

"Hey, Lee," J.J. bellowed. "Those guys bring any mail for us?"

"Not bloody likely," Carlos muttered.

"Mister Jorgens," Li somberly repeated.

Jorgens detached himself from the climbers and walked over to Li and the soldiers. The conversation was one-sided, with Li doing all the talking. The climbers couldn't hear a word, but instinct told them something was off and wrong.

Jorgens leaned in to glean the softly spoken words. Li repeated himself. Jorgens swayed back.

"Not good, not good," Stump muttered.

Li turned his back on Jorgens then and led off toward the mess tent with the soldiers in tow. Jorgens didn't move. As a group, the climbers surrounded him by the Land Cruiser.

"Five days," Jorgens said. He looked pasty and ill. "We have five days."

The climbers glanced at each other, mystified. Finally Robby spoke. "*No comprendo,* Captain."

"They pulled the plug on us. In five days a convoy of trucks will arrive. We have to leave."

"Five days?" J.J. wailed. "We can't finish in five days. We can't even occupy our high camps in five days."

Jorgens was squinting. "No more climbing," he breathed. "We have to pack up and be ready to go. We're done."

The news stupefied them.

"But we have permission. We paid. It's ours." Carlos tripped out his argument.

"They pulled the plug on us," Jorgens said.

"I've never heard of such a thing . . ." Stump started. But they were too stunned to be angry. They were scrambling just to understand the implications.

"Five days?" Thomas said. "Even with yaks here right now, we couldn't start to strip the mountain. We'll lose everything. From ABC to Five, we'll lose it all."

Jorgens nodded slowly. "Yes."

"But they can't do that."

"We have five days," Jorgens said. "They want us to load the trucks and leave the same day. These soldiers will escort us to the Nepal border."

"What the fuck happened?" It was Gus, quiet, furious. Now they started finding their anger, too.

"What did I say," J.J. railed. "You can't trust gooks."

"There's been trouble in Lhasa," Jorgens said. "A Tibetan riot. A Chinese police station was burned. Several Chinese stores were destroyed. The army opened fire. That means bloodshed. They've declared martial law."

"These fucking Tibetans, man," J.J. shouted. "Now we're fucked."

"Say we stay. We climb," Gus said. "We make our way across the border when we're done. Li can go home right now." It was farfetched.

"The country's under martial law," Jorgens said. "They want all tourists out."

"But we're climbers." J.J. beat at his chest. "We're climbers."

Robby took care of that one. "We're tourists, J.J. That's exactly what we are. And keep your voice down."

"Li said he'll recommend us for a permit. For the very next season, whenever martial law gets lifted, whenever the mountain opens up again," Jorgens said. "He said this is unfortunate."

"So, carrot and stick." Gus spat. Her disgust washed over them, more than enough for them all. "Go along, get along. Shit."

But Stump considered the proposition. "It just could work, though. Next season, if it really was next season? The minute we leave the yakkies will plunder our stores here and at ABC. But they won't go onto the mountain itself. And at least some of our camps will survive the monsoon. We'd have a leg up, stock in place. It might just work."

"Yeah," said Robby. "A definite advantage."

"Two, three months," Carlos thought out loud. "Not so bad."

"Like a sequel climb," Robby added. "I like it."

It was Abe who popped their bubble. "Count me out," he said. "I can't come back next season. Med school starts in September." He wasn't sure why he shared this nugget of information. It presumed that he'd even be invited to return, and he'd barely been invited along on this one.

Nevertheless, it reminded the rest of them of the realities. They had girlfriends and wives, children and jobs. There were mortgages to pay, commitments that couldn't be broken. From many dinners and small moments and shared days and nights together, they remembered that Thomas was getting married in October and J.J.'s little girl was starting first grade, Gus was lined up for an all-woman's expedition to the Caucasus and Kelly was moving to Boise for a new teaching job.

The fantasy of a return to this climb—with these climbers in this perfect weather upon this route—fell to pieces. The instant they left Everest they were going to disperse into tales that would have nothing to do with their comrades'. Their joined dream, such as it was, could never be recaptured.

They spent another half hour trying out other solutions to this sudden collapse of their expedition, but the facts only weighed heavier. The Hill had won.

Then Kelly raised one final bittersweet thought. "If only Daniel had gone the little bit further," she said. It was true. When even one climber reached the top, the entire expedition did. But none had and time was out. In the end, Daniel's noble gesture of waiting for them had disserved them all.

"So close," Thomas said.

"And the radios," Stump said. "Just when I finally fixed the bastards."

Abe had his back turned to Everest. When he turned to look at their lost prize, the mountain attacked with a wave of raw white light. Unprepared, Abe gasped and bowed his head, clawing for the sunglasses in his pocket. Ordinarily the sight would have provoked a nod of admiration, but not this morning.

Even with the glasses covering his eyes, the mountain was too bright to look at for more than a few seconds. All definition was gone, washed away by the pure illumination. No lines or shadows, no stone or ice, no ridges or cols. Even the summit pyramid was illegible in the midst of all that radiance. The mountain simply fused into sunlight and sky, hiding itself in infinity. It made their ambitions seem fruitless and tiny.

Gus asked Jorgens to talk with Li again. It was hard for her to ask, because she didn't like or trust Jorgens. But the mountain was a higher priority worth more than her pride and she spoke the words. "One more try, Jorgens, please."

Jorgens didn't make her grovel. "It won't work," he said, "but if that's what you want, okay. I'll try."

He was back from the mess tent within ten minutes. "It's written in stone. Li said his orders come directly from the Public Security Bureau in Lhasa. The army is out of its cage. He wishes to ensure our safety."

"You can't get any safer than our dead end," Carlos pointed out, but of course that wasn't Li's consideration anyway.

"One other thing, people," Jorgens said. "I want you to steer clear of our military guests. No contact whatsoever. Is that understood?"

"Screw," said J.J.

"I'm not asking, J.J. I'm ordering. Things are already bad enough without hard words or more tension. Got it?"

J.J. didn't answer.

Jorgens put it bluntly. "They've got guns."

They spent the rest of the day cursing the Chinese and Tibet and the mountain, finally dropping into an exhausted silence as alpenglow lit Everest orange. As everywhere else in the world, bad news traveled quickly through the Rongbuk Valley. Before nightfall, a tiny contingent of herders showed up driving seven yaks. They were eager for work, and also eager to get a preview of the booty getting left behind.

At dinner that night, Carlos got the climbers drunk. He had stocked the expedition pantry with enough Star beer for one big blow, and this was it. "With victory in clear sight," he raised his toast, "here's to blind defeat."

It was not a happy drunk, but neither was it an ugly one.

Someone pointed out that at least they hadn't lost anyone on the climb. They hadn't lost so much as a toe or finger. They were quitting the mountain in one piece, and that was always something to be grateful for.

Finally Jorgens spoke. "Somebody needs to go tell Daniel and bring him down."

"I'll go," J.J. volunteered. He had pulled out pictures of his daughter and had tears in his eyes.

"Damned if I'm staying down here," Stump said. "I don't think I could put in five days without hitting one of Li's soldier boys."

"I've got cameras and film up there," Robby remembered. "And all my ice gear and double boots. I can make two, three round-trips down with full loads in the time we've got."

In that way, the whole group decided to go up to ABC. Their spirits lifted by ounces. En masse they would break the bad news to Daniel and strip the camp of their most valuable gear. Above all they would get to pay their respects to the enemy. Stump wanted to finish a watercolor of the North Face. Thomas declared a great urge to piss on the mountain once and for all. Carlos said he'd be happy just to sleep with the Mother Goddess one final night. Few if any of them were ever going to return to the Kore Wall, Abe could hear it in their voices.

Abe slept poorly that night. At daybreak he walked down to the water skull and sat there to clear his mind. Overhead, Everest was floating in a scoop of soft dawn light. With her manelike summit massif and outstretched ridges, the Hill had the aspect of a sphinx splashed with rainbows this morning.

They had come close to cracking her riddle, Daniel closest of all. Abe felt the closeness of it as a weight in his skull. He felt the frustration of having a perfect summarizing word on the tip of his tongue and knowing it was forever beyond his articulation. For the rest of his life he would have to carry around this freighted silence.

He was thinking these thoughts and generally feeling sorry for himself when the sound of a dislodged pebble interrupted him. An image—half man, half animal—took shape in the glacier pond. Abe glanced up at the rim. Standing there, if a sideways stoop upon ancient ski poles could be called standing, was the monk in old yak skins and Daniel's black and orange baseball cap.

Abe's mouth came open. The two of them observed each other until Abe began to wonder if this wasn't another one of his hallucinations. Then the monk teetered between the ski poles as if he were fixed atop stilts and more pebbles pattered down off the rim.

Abe didn't need Nima's translation to know he'd come to say good-bye. It was going to be a two-way *adios*, Abe realized. Good-bye to the expedition. Good-bye to the monk. The boy needed full-scale hospitalization. Yet four days from now he wouldn't have even Abe's quackery for a stopgap. Abe let his breath out slowly. That was the cold fact. This holy man was going to die.

The boy was in such bad condition that Abe wondered if he might have been hiding near Base Camp the whole time. That or one of the yakherders had brought him in overnight. One thing was certain, even if *tulkus* could fly, this one was anchored to the few inches of soil he currently occupied. As if to confirm Abe's pessimism, the boy sank his rump down upon a stone and stiffly lowered himself backward to rest. He was too weak to take his hands from the ski pole straps, so the poles lay attached to him, pitched askew.

"*Tashi-dili*," Abe said, approaching. Nima had taught him that much. The monk didn't return his greeting except to smile crookedly. He was wan and his eyes had a dull luster. Closer up, Abe saw saliva stringing loose from his mouth. Abe didn't need to open the boy's clothing to know the infection was back. He could smell the yellow and orange fluid staining what had once been a clean white expedition T-shirt.

Abe squatted and palmed the boy's forehead. There was fever, though not so bad as to account for this delirium and weakness. No, with this drooling, Abe's suspicion grew that the boy had suffered a closed head injury. Between that and his wounds and whatever damage lay beneath the abdominal bruises, the monk was in deep waters.

"What am I going to do with you?" Abe asked him in English.

The boy's eyes rounded onto him and he smiled at Abe.

"What *are* you going to do with him," another voice asked.

It was Gus over by the water skull. She had materialized as softly as the monk.

"Start over again," Abe said. "Patch him. Drug him. Pray."

Gus seemed frightened by the monk's presence in camp. "Why did he have to come back," she demanded.

"I don't know. But he did. Now we have to get him squirreled away. It's going to take me a few hours to clean him up and he can't be out in the open like this."

"He shouldn't have come back," Gus grumbled.

"It's okay," Abe reassured her. "The Chinese will never know about him. And in four days we'll all be gone, us and the Chinese, and he can have the whole valley to himself."

Once again they occupied the hut made of memorial stones, the Tomb with its ceiling of cannibalized tentage. The boy lapsed deeper into inertia and finally a twilight delirium that was close to the coma in which Abe had first found him. The word passed among the climbers that the monk had returned, and they conspired to keep his presence a secret. Lest the soldiers see people going in and out of the Tomb, everyone stayed away except for Krishna, who brought Abe and his patient food and drink. Abe slept in the hut that night, lying on the bare ground. The monk slept on Abe's air pad.

And then something strange happened. With three days to go before their forced departure from the mountain, Li came into the mess tent while the climbers were at breakfast to make an announcement.

"Now what?" Robby grumbled.

"I have decided," Li said. "You may have ten more days to climb the mountain. After that, I must obey my orders."

When no one replied, Li expanded. "There are things in life that require finishing. You have taken many courageous risks. Now it is my turn to take a risk also."

And still no one spoke, though Abe could see agitation blazing on every face. If Li was waiting for them to thank him, he was out of luck. So far as the climbers were concerned, the mountain had never been his to withhold. And this bizarre reversal only reminded them of a power they could not ignore. It didn't seem possible, but Li's generosity had made him even more unpopular.

"But why?" J.J. demanded.

"J.J.," Thomas warned him off. They had just been granted

a stay of execution, and as rankling as the principle was, the fact of it gave them a second life.

"Even in difficult times, it is wrong to punish the innocent," Li told them.

After Li had left, the climbers tried to fathom his sudden altruism. When Robby tried to credit Jorgens's last-ditch request, Jorgens rebuffed him. "It wasn't anything I said. Li didn't look at me once the whole time I was talking."

"What then?" Stump wondered.

"Does it matter?" Thomas asked. "Now we got no one else to blame. That's as clean as it gets in life."

They left within the hour. With his sprained ankle taped and iced with a bag of glacier chips, Carlos stayed down to man the Base Camp walkie-talkie. If necessary, he could try to talk Li into an eleventh-day extension. The rest of the climbers surged up the trail to finish off the Kore Wall.

Everest was a weather factory, so they said, but for a hundred days Abe had seen no weather, no change. Day in, day out, the sky had seduced their eyes with its blue-black constancy. What few clouds came had stayed in the distance, white feathers that scattered in the wind. Abe had begun to believe it never snowed in Tibet.

But on the afternoon they reentered ABC, the sky turned greasy silver. Daniel was there, looming on the boulders, gaunt, irresistible, arms wide to them, and he promised victory. But in the space of half an hour, the mountain wove a grimy cobweb of storm clouds into the sky. By sunset, the cloud cover stretched from east to north to west. The climbers took their meal early and scurried back to their tents just as the first of the corn snow rattled down.

Bolts of lightning began igniting among the snowflakes, something Abe had never witnessed before. He and Kelly zipped their door tight and crawled into their bags.

"What does this mean?" Abe asked. Kelly was lying beside him in the twilight, propped on her elbow. It was too light to turn on their headlamps, but too dark for much except talk. The wind loped through camp and their tent walls rhythmically popped in and pulled out.

"It's the monsoon," Kelly said. "It's late." She might have been talking about her period, she was so morose. Her eyebrows were dark dashes in the failing light and her golden hair black ink. Her nose was burned the cancerous red that only comes from repeated delaminations.

"So we're finished," Abe said.

"Not necessarily. It comes on in waves like this. There's usually breaks in between, especially on this north side. We're in a rain shadow here. Chances are, we'll see a window. The summit will open." But she didn't sound pleased.

Above the rattling of snow pellets on their dome, thunder blossomed in the distance. Without the lightning, Abe would have thought it was avalanches.

"I hope I can sleep tonight," Kelly said.

Abe said, "That thunder's loud."

But Kelly shook her head no, it wasn't that. She was agitated, and her worry was more complicated than thunder or a mere threat to her summit bid.

"Is something wrong, Kelly?"

Her white eyes flickered at him, then darted away, and she dropped her head. A moment later she looked at him again, weighing some enormous risk, judging him. "Yes," she started. "But I don't know how to tell you."

"Don't tell me."

"Just don't laugh."

Abe nodded his assent.

"To tell the truth . . ." She faltered, then found the words. "The other night I had this dream."

"Tell me," he said.

"It's not like me," Kelly quickly had him know. "I don't believe in dreams. I don't talk about them."

"But this one . . ." He opened the way for her.

She looked him straight in the eyes. "Something's going to happen up there."

Abe let her finish.

Her voice turned timid. "Abe. I think I'm going to die."

For a minute, the snow clattered against the drum-tight walls and the poles creaked under the wind's weight.

"There was a woman in a storm. She was trapped on the Hill, tangled in a rope, upside down. Her hair was long. It was blowing in the wind. Her eyes were wide open." She whispered the woman's identity as if telling a ghost story. "It was me, Abe."

Abe didn't know what to do, argue or agree or touch her or otherwise make it all right to have premonitions of death on the eve of danger. He suddenly seemed very young to himself and Kelly very much older.

"I know what that sounds like." Kelly grinned mournfully, and Abe sensed she was about to detour into a joke at her own expense. She didn't, though. She just quit talking.

In another setting, Abe might have tried snuffing Kelly's anxiety with some sort of label—cyanotic hysteria or rapture of the heights, something poetic or at least polysyllabic. But an unusual somberness had been afflicting the other climbers in the last two days, and now he realized that it was apprehension. Except for Daniel, who had been spared Li's vacillations, they had been plunged into their own futility and had resigned themselves to leaving the mountain. They returned to the mountain with all the joy of a chain gang off to hard labor.

"I want a child." Kelly spoke it with a certain grief. "I wasn't sure before. Now I am."

"It was just a dream," Abe tried to reassure her.

"I saw it." She was clear.

Then Abe had a bright idea. "Maybe you shouldn't go up," he ventured hopefully.

"Don't think I haven't thought about it."

Abe had no other solutions, so he pursued this one, even though it would not satisfy her. "It's okay to stay down, Kelly. You've pushed it. Nobody will say different."

"You know that's not true."

"It doesn't matter. Nobody has to know why. Just stay down."

"I can't. You know that."

Abe did. Maybe a man could have stayed down. Not Kelly. She was healthy and strong and proud. And blond. Eventually it would get out that she'd had a bad dream. The word would spread. The men would expect nothing less than for her to bail. She would hear the worst from Gus. Kelly swallowed hard.

"Damn it, Abe."

Abe heard the need. He laid aside his hesitation and slipped his arm under her shoulder and wormed closer to hold

her tight. Kelly came into his embrace with the familiarity of
a longtime lover. She settled into the crook of his arm and
placed one bare hand against his chest. It was one of the few
times on this mountain when two people could comfort each
other. Usually the bad times and fear came when you were
critically alone, at the far end of a rope. This embrace was a
luxury.

"Unzip your bag, Abe." They had learned, through someone's joke about them one night, that the expedition-style sleeping bags could be zipped together. Now they made a common
bed. It was the first time they had lain together, unhampered
by separate cocoons.

They didn't make love, that wasn't the point, and besides
it would have been ridiculous in this tent at this altitude, a cold,
short-winded fuck, hardly the way Abe wanted it. Maybe they
would make love someday, he thought. Maybe not. Tonight, at
any rate, they didn't even kiss because their lips were so shredded by the sun.

What they did do was more precious still. They just lay
there, Abe with Kelly in his arms. On the verge of sleep he was
full of wonder at what this virtual stranger was to him and
what he might be to her. She could have been practically any
woman—Jamie or Gus or some other—a softness against his
hard rib cage, a warm weight where her thigh dangled across
his. But she was Kelly, and he held the thought of her as he
held her long back and big shoulders. He tried to imagine what
he was to her just now beyond a heartbeat and whiskers like
sandpaper against the tip of her forehead. She could be thinking of anyone else. But Abe hoped it was him she thought of as
she drifted off to sleep.

"There's something I've wanted to say to you," he started
to confess.

But she stopped him. She knew. "Not now," she said. "Another time. Please. Another time."

There was only a trace of her coconut shampoo left. Her
hair smelled almost entirely of smoke and sweat and human
grease and Abe inhaled it. She smelled like an animal. Before
this, he'd never thought about how much mountain air smells
like a mountain, like snow and still rocks and ice sweating under
the stars. Nor had he ever craved human company so funda-

mentally. Up here it was the sight of blood or the smell of raw humanity or a simple embrace that married you to what you had become, an animal on a mountain.

Love reduced to this quiet possession, then, this touch and shared warmth.

By dawn, the squall had passed, leaving behind six inches of snow. The sky hung gray, but nothing was coming down out of it, and that was worth a day more of hope. Daniel was the first to strap into his crampons, of course. He alone seemed unaware that the mountain had entered a new configuration. Six inches of snow wasn't much in the way of armor, but another storm or two could sheathe the mountain with lethal defenses. Between Li's deadline and the invading monsoon, they were definitely running out of time.

Kelly's head appeared from the tent door and she smiled at Abe. Not once through the night had they disentangled from each other's arms. There had been no more mention of Kelly's bad dream and Abe had let it drop. It came to mind that maybe his embrace had exorcised her premonition, and he snorted at the notion. What a journey that would be, from ambulance cowboy to full-fledged physician to shaman and exorcist. At this rate he would end his days droning prayers in a Tibetan monastery cell. It was time to quit believing in his own magic.

Even as he watched her, Kelly gave Abe a surprise. Unfolding her long limbs from the tent door, she stretched to her full height wearing a skintight, powder blue Nordic ski racing uniform. It had bold white stripes up each leg to the armpit and down from her neck to her wrists. Lithe and streamlined, she was spectacular, which Abe already knew. What really puzzled him was where this outfit could have come from.

But then he looked around and saw that most of the other climbers were emerging dressed in the same powder blue uniforms. He remembered. It was product endorsement time and all through camp brand-name costumes were surfacing clean and new, saved especially for the camera and their summit bid. The uniform looked Olympian on some, silly on others. Bird legs and chicken breasts stood pronounced, and Abe was glad no one had remembered to issue him one of the suits. The uniform had its merit, however. For the first time since Li had undercut their morale, the climbers had the look of a team bent on tagging the earth's highest point. Shaking the snow off their equipment, they got to work peopling the Hill once again.

Over the next five days, the climbers took up their positions in the forward camps and prepared to rush the summit. It was a slow and orderly rush. Spaced a day apart, they moved up. The weather got no better, but at least it got no worse.

By the end of the fifth day, Abe found himself once more at the cave camp designated Four. To his delight, the foul weather seemed to have locked the mountain tight. Not so much as a single rock had bombed the Shooting Gallery all day long. He took that as a sign of good luck, and told Kelly so at each of their rest stances along the fixed ropes.

Abe was now as fully acclimatized as he was going to get, with the result that he actually felt strong as they entered the cave near three o'clock. His last time here with Daniel and Gus, he had been gasping and hurt, but his rest at lower elevations had restored him. He was hardly a superman—at 26,500 feet, there was no way not to gasp for air and his entire being hurt— but he was functioning quite well this time around, and the idea of going higher was not at all mind-boggling.

Two teams of two—Daniel and Gus, and Stump and J.J.— had stayed here the night before, then gone on to occupy Five. Someone, probably J.J. judging by the elementary school scrawl, had left them a note: "Big E or Bust."

The plan was for Abe and Kelly's team to spend the night here, then move up to Five in the morning. They would occupy Five while Daniel and his bunch made its push to the top and then descended as far as possible. On the day after tomorrow, if all went well, Abe and Kelly would repeat Daniel's success. Behind them by a day, the final team of Robby and Thomas waited at Three, poised for their turn to rotate up and have a crack at the summit. The two men were realistic. If the weather didn't scotch their summit bid, their sagging health probably would. Thomas had never fully recovered from his pneumonia, and Robby was suffering through his latest rampage of diarrhea. Thomas had dubbed Robby and himself the Lost Patrol, astounding them all. It seemed impossible that Thomas might have a sense of humor.

Jorgens was far below at One. He had "Four-F'd" himself, bowing out on medical grounds. In theory he was a support climber in case someone got in trouble above. But it was no secret that Jorgens was incapable of going much higher and his presence was strictly as a cheerleader to the rest of them.

And all the way down, with Li for a chess partner, Carlos was manning Base Camp. The expedition was spread thin over the huge mountain, but this time around they had the advantage of radio contact. Just being able to hear other voices had given the various teams more confidence.

The sky stayed dense and leaden. It was so uniformly overcast that no one could predict the next storm. They hadn't seen the sun in nearly a week, and that was a mixed blessing. They didn't have to fight the noonday heat, but for the last five days, everyone had been complaining of a chronic lassitude that made them feel heavy. Abe was starting to wonder if the change in barometric pressure might be responsible. Others in the team decided on a different scapegoat.

It was Li's fault, they said. The L.O. had shackled them. He had derailed their freight-train momentum. They muttered about him and there seemed no doubt in their minds that he had deliberately sabotaged their morale. Some went so far as to accuse him of setting them up for failure and humiliation, conjecturing that he must have hoped the team would just throw in the towel without this last effort. But they were wrong. Li wanted them up here. On the very eve of their summit assault, they learned why.

The six o'clock radio call opened routinely. Abe was sitting hunched in the tent with the cold walkie-talkie in his hands. Kelly was lying behind him in a sleeping bag, most of her face obscured by an oxygen mask. From here on they would be sleeping on oxygen, and anyone who wanted to could climb on it, too. His last time here in the cave with Daniel and Gus, Abe had been so weak and hurt that no amount of oxygen would have gotten him higher. This time, the oxygen was like a kiss.

In preparation for the radio call, Abe had taken his mask off and poked the antennae through an unzipped triangle at the top of the door. The cave's position was such that he could be relatively warm and comfortable inside the tent and receive transmissions from anywhere on the mountain.

"Five to all camps. It's time for the six o'clock news," Abe heard. It was Stump's voice. "Let's get a head count. Over."

Each of the teams checked in. Everyone was doing fine. Everyone sounded tired and excited, especially Stump. "It's going to be a long night," he said. "We got a crowd. Four people, one tent, over." His words came slowly, blurring on the edges from the extreme altitude.

"At least you're snug and warm. Over." Robby was handling the radio at Three. Count on him to find the silver lining.

"How's your wind up there, Five? Over." To his credit, Jorgens had set aside his wounded pride. He earnestly wanted Daniel and anyone else to reach the top. Abe was starting to like the man.

"The wind's stiff," Stump answered. "I hope something's not blowing in tonight. Over."

Protected by the cave, Four was unaffected. But Abe could hear the wind blasting the face. It sounded like Niagara Falls out there.

"How about the tripod?" Robby asked. "Did you see the top? Over."

"It's there," Stump answered. "We'll hang a flag from it. That's tomorrow, folks. ASAP. Over."

"Go team. Over."

Abe waited for a break in the chatter. "Any medical problems up or down? Over."

The climbers knew better than to complain about hangnails. No one was healthy, but no one was dying either.

Jorgens returned to the air. He wanted to clarify the assault plan and work out any bugs before the high team committed itself. "You guys are all synchronized? Over," he asked Stump.

Stump didn't mind the repetition. It was good to have some oversight, especially from someone at a lower altitude. "We're synced up," he said. "We'll wake at oh-one-hundred. I doubt anyone sleeps anyway. Over."

"And you'll be out the door by oh-three-hundred. Over." Jorgens was going to walk them through the whole thing.

"Roger that. Over." Radio time was one of the few occasions for the two ex-soldiers to trot out the patois without getting teased by the other climbers. Abe listened.

"Two ropes? Over." It was like an aviator's checklist.

"Two ropes. Two bottles per man. Over." There would be two teams of two, each linked by a fifty-meter rope of nine-mil. Each climber would start off with two bottles of oxygen. They would discard the twelve-pound cylinders, once emptied. According to their best calculations, two bottles would last a climber all the way to the top and partway down again.

"And if you haven't topped out by sixteen-hundred, you will turn around. Over." This one wasn't a question. By mutual agreement, they had decided that if the summiteers couldn't finish by four o'clock in the afternoon, then they had failed. By that time they would have been climbing for thirteen hours. To push any longer would only increase their risk of not getting back to the tent at Five. And a night outdoors above 28,000 feet—especially in a wind like this one—meant certain death. The windchill factor combined with their oxygen deficit would terminate their ambitions for good.

"Sixteen-hundred, turn around," Stump verified. "Over." Like bankers' clockwork, Abe thought. They were going to beat this extreme chaos with their extreme order.

Just then Base Camp broke in on the conversation. It was Carlos. He sounded very frightened, which was odd since he was on flat ground and the safest of any of them.

"Base to the mountain. To anybody. Can anybody hear me? Over."

"Five to Base, we read you. Over."

"Something's going on here. Something bad."

Stump answered. "Clarify yourself, Base. Over." He was annoyed that Carlos had forgotten to say "over," and it was clear he didn't appreciate the note of urgency. In just a few hours the summit team was going to head off into the night. They needed support, not last-minute problems from the abyss.

"It's the monk."

Abe's breath went out of him.

"They've got him."

"One to Five. What's going on up there, Stump? Over." Down at One, Jorgens was not in line of sight with Base Camp. Between him and Carlos lay the satellite peak Changtse, which cast a sonic shadow. The rest of the camps sat higher than Changtse's blunt summit and so their communications with Base were unrestricted. He couldn't hear Carlos. At best he could only deduce that Stump was talking to someone at Base.

Stump took a moment to respond. "Please hold, One. And Base, tell me more. Over."

"It happened this afternoon. Li comes up to me. He says we've been harboring a fugitive. But now they know and they've taken the prisoner into custody. And they have. I saw him."

"Damn it, Carlos. Say over. Over." Stump was upset, but Abe knew it wasn't by the breach in radio etiquette.

"They took him out to the Tomb. The soldiers and him. He's hog-tied, hand and foot." Carlos added, "Over."

"What do they plan on doing with him? Over."

"The soldiers are going to return him to Lhasa. Li said the monk is a state criminal. He said this is an internal affair of the People's Republic of China. Our interference is a serious breach of international law. Over."

Abe couldn't contain himself any longer. "Internal affair?" he barked into the radio. This was his patient, a boy, a holy man. And the last time the Chinese had him in their possession they'd tortured him half to death.

"Is that you, Doc?" Carlos asked.

"When are they taking him off to Lhasa?" Abe asked. He remembered to say, "Over."

"Li said maybe tomorrow, probably the day after tomorrow. He wants to finish making out his report."

"One, here," Jorgens interrupted. "What are you people jabbering about? It doesn't sound like mission talk. Over."

"Bad luck," Stump told him. "Li sniffed the kid out. Things are unwinding down at Base. Over."

Jorgens didn't sound surprised. His irritation was immediately replaced by a tone of calm succor. "I was afraid of something like this," he said quietly. "The way I saw it, nothing would happen until after we were finished and gone. But I missed my guess. Over."

The one person who didn't hear him was Carlos, who now asked the question Jorgens had just answered. "It's worse than bad luck," Carlos said to Stump. "Li said we got the green light to summit because somebody cooperated with him. The summit is our reward for turning the kid in."

The ugly charge hung in the air like the smell of sulphur after a lightning strike.

Robby came on. "I don't believe that."

"None of us would have done that," Stump declared.

"That's what Li told me," said Carlos. "But he wouldn't tell me who."

Abe looked over the shoulder of his blood red parka. Kelly's eyes were huge in the lamplight.

"Look," Jorgens exhorted the climbers in their precarious camps upon the mountain. He turned on his basso profundo, smooth and polished, the one he used to address the American Alpine Club. "These Chinese will say it's none of our business, they always do. And they're right. It's none of our business. The boy took his chances. He should never have come waltzing into camp when their soldiers were there. The important thing is for us to keep our eye on the ball. Over."

Everything about Jorgens repelled Abe. He was working them like some Texas politician, and he'd just betrayed them all.

"They'll kill the boy," Abe declared as flatly as he could. It was a fact, like the stone in this cave's walls. His anger would only make it seem negotiable, and it wasn't. "I've seen what they do."

"We can't stop that," Jorgens replied. "We're up here. They're down there. It was a matter of time before they found out. And besides, we're tourists. You people said so yourselves. Tourists and climbers. Not saviors. Over."

"Maybe not saviors," Robby said. "But not traitors, either."

"Pete," Stump said to Jorgens. If grimness had a voice, his was it. "Carlos tells us that Li didn't just find out. He was informed. Someone traded the kid for our summit." He didn't ask for a confession. He didn't have to. Jorgens knew what he meant.

Abe strained to hear Jorgens's answer. He couldn't distinguish between the blood roaring through his head and the wind outside.

"Damn you, Stump," Jorgens murmured. The two men had climbed many mountains together, never with trouble like this. Bitterly, Jorgens surrendered the transmission to their static.

"This is a serious matter, Pete. And you were the last to talk to Li. Over."

Jorgens let it dangle.

Robby broke in again. He was dependably their good-time man, the one who, with a word, could breach their deadly mood and finesse this disaster. "Motherfucker," was all he had to say, and there was no mistaking who it was aimed at.

Down at Base, Carlos pieced together their judgment. "You're not saying it was the captain, are you?"

The damnation of Jorgens could take all night, Abe thought. They were losing sight of the victim. Someone had to get this back on track and quickly.

"Carlos, can you talk to Li?" Abe asked. "Tonight. Before he sends the boy off. Over."

"Negative. I tried," said Carlos. He sounded more weary than they were, and he was two miles lower. "Li's got his hackles up. He's acting real funny, like we're in deep shit. He'll mention our cooperation in his report, but we're no longer being escorted to the border. We're getting deported, folks."

"But he can't do that," Robby said, shocked. "We didn't do anything."

"Who can't do what?" Jorgens demanded.

"Li's declared us persona non grata," Stump relayed. "The Chinese are deporting us. Over."

"For God's sake," Jorgens said. "What's going on down there at Base? Handle this thing, Stump. Over."

Stump thought it over. "Base, can you stall Li?" he asked. "Two or three more days. We can finish our business up here and come down and finish our business with him. Over."

"No chance." There was a long burst of static, then Carlos broke through again. He sounded defeated, as if the group had let him down. Obviously they had no solutions he hadn't already thought of and discarded. "Li knows us, guys. He told me it's very unfortunate. He's sad that we chose the wrong mascot. As far as he's concerned, this is kind of like putting the family pet down. You wait until the children take off for summer camp and when they come back, Rover's already gone to heaven. Li doesn't want any trouble. This way everybody gets what they want. We bag our summit. They bag their desperado. Just to show us what a stand-up guy he is, Li asked me to convey his best wishes for our climb. He said we've earned it."

Abe felt sick.

Finally Stump returned to the air.

"Well that's that, people. The kid's gone." His voice had grown weak. This was supposed to have been a quick radio call, a few last words to help levitate the high team to the top. Instead they had been handed this terrible news, and in the process had just whittled their battery power down to a splinter on a human rights debate. Worse, and once again, all their forward momentum had been sapped.

"I lost a friend on a big mountain once," Stump continued. "And when it happened, we quit the mountain. On the spot, right then and there. We just quit. It seemed like the right thing. We can do that here, I guess. Over." Abe took a moment to realize Stump was polling them. He wanted a vote.

No one spoke for a long time after that. Each camp listened to the radio plasma and Abe thought how the very stars were bombarding them with radiation, a steady crackling assault. Between the wind and the turning of cosmic machinery, their defeat seemed inevitable. Part of him accepted the end, theirs and the monk's. Part of him rebelled.

Then Gus came on the radio. Stump had relinquished the walkie-talkie to her, probably gladly.

"I've lost people in the mountains, too." In different circumstances she would have sounded monstrous with her throat infection and the raging static. But tonight, given the monk's certain fate, her hoarse grating seemed to ring with grief. "But we didn't quit. And *that* seemed like the right thing, too."

Suddenly Abe wished Daniel would take the radio and speak. He wanted to hear what the man was thinking as these people described their losses. But Abe couldn't make out his own thoughts. He'd probably seen more death in the hills than all of them combined. He'd become a virtual undertaker to the luckless and star-crossed. The Chinese weren't going to leave him a body to take under, though. There was nothing to scoop this time, nothing to carry out in the litter.

Gus gave the other camps a chance to register their opinions. When none did, she spoke into their silence. "I've lived my life in the mountains. It's a hard way to go. But I never quit, okay? Out here—Tibet, the Hill—there's nothing between us and our choices. No buffer. No excuses. That's just how it is. And the monk made his choice. And we made ours."

In the background, Stump told her to say Over. Gus didn't bother. No one else wanted air time anyway.

Their silence stretched on, though for no good reason. They had their minds made up, every one of them. Even Abe. They had spent major portions of their lives getting this close to the highest summit.

"It's settled then," Stump concluded. "We go. God speed us all. Over and out."

ABE WOKE To D day with Christmas morning zeal.

"Kelly," he croaked. His larynx was rusted shut with strep and he felt badly depleted. The oxygen had not proved to be a magic bullet after all. He recalled Robby's prescription for summiting. Quick penetration. Quick up, quick down. Abe cobbled together his resolve. Today was the day they toppled the Hill. First Daniel, then all the rest, a stream of barbarians, today they began crashing the breach. Abe palmed his oxygen mask away. "Kelly, are you awake?"

Her back was pressed tight against his, but her voice came from a great distance. "You slept?" she said. Vaguely, as if from a long time ago, Abe recalled her dream of death. It was a moot point. They were much too close to the summit for dreaming.

Abe sat up, still cocooned in his bag. His head brushed the tent wall and hoarfrost rained down. From inside his bag, he switched on his headlamp. The whole interior of the tent sparkled with their crystallized breath.

"The weather's let up," Abe said. "It's quiet. The wind's stopped." There was a peculiar humming sound, but Abe figured that was just high altitude tinnitus. He was learning you could hear illusions as well as see them.

"What time is it?" Kelly rasped. It was dark enough to be night.

Extricating his arm from the loose clothing and the radio and gas cartridges and headlamp batteries nested inside his sleeping bag to keep them warm, Abe poked his wrist from the neck of the bag. "Six-thirty."

That meant Daniel and Gus and Stump and J.J. had been climbing for over three hours. By now they should have punched through the Yellow Band, and judging by the silence outside, there was nothing more to keep them from the top. The Ultimate Summit was about to penetrate this purgatory all the way through to the sky.

Abe cooked them a hasty breakfast of last night's left-overs—Top Ramen boosted up with salami slices, raisins, and Tabasco sauce. While the icy block of food thawed over a flame, he made the seven o'clock radio call. It was very brief. The camps compared notes on the night's passage and the weather. The lower camps reported extremely high winds, but everyone took heart when Abe said the air was as still as June in Texas up at Four. The summit team didn't call in, and that was more good news. It meant they were too busy climbing. No one mentioned the monk.

Abe and Kelly geared up inside the tent, a clumsy process. Between the cramped space and the lines running from their oxygen bottles and headlamps and the dangling cookstove, their movements were knotted and cumbrous. They could have opened the tent door for more room, but that would have disheartened them. Though the mountain had gone silent, it was bitterly cold. The tent walls let them enjoy the appearance of cozy warmth for their final minutes at Four. At last they were ready to ascend to the high camp. And tomorrow, Abe thought with a pleasure too distant to be called joy, tomorrow the summit.

Kelly unzipped the tent door and the cold poured in. Like deep sea divers, they clambered to their feet and stood upright by the cave mouth. Abe was unsettled by the darkness outside the cave. By this hour there should have been more light, even with the sun buried in clouds. If conditions didn't improve, Daniel and his team would have to use a flash to take photos of their summit triumph projected for noon.

"It's so peaceful," Kelly marveled.

"The storm has passed," Abe said.

But he should have suspected otherwise when he placed one hand on the green-and-white checkered rope that led out of the cave and up the face. It was vibrating like a plucked guitar string and he realized that here was the source of the odd humming noise. Abe made nothing more of it and went ahead with his preparations. He clipped his jumars onto the rope and adjusted his goggles. Even in this darkness one could go snowblind. He stepped from the cave onto the face.

The world turned upside down.

Abe flew. He was swallowed into the air.

It was instantaneous. The thought flashed past that he was falling, but he wasn't. It was utterly impossible.

Far from disappearing, the wind had grown into a hurricane gale and with his very first step onto the face Abe was ripped from his front points and actually lifted ten or twelve feet *up* the mountain. If not for the rope, he would have sailed right off the face, a bit of dust swept into the jet stream.

Abe lay plastered against the wall, too astounded to move, not certain he even could. He wasn't hurt, but his confusion was almost painful. He had to fight back his shock just to register bits and pieces of what was happening.

The darkness was in fact a snowy whiteness so flat and dense his eyes could hardly see. Thunder had usurped the silence, indeed the silence was thunder, and the goggles were torn from his face. If not for the oxygen mask strapped across his mouth, the wind would have stripped the breath from his lungs. Loose pack straps lashed him where the skin of his face was exposed.

Sucking hard at the oxygen mask, Abe hoicked his body around. Hand over hand, he hauled himself down the rope and back to the cave entrance. There Kelly helped to pull him inside. "God, Abe. Are you all right?" She knelt beside him in the cave mouth, aghast.

"Not good," Abe said, crouching on one knee. The oxygen mask was dangling at his throat. "And it's got to be worse up high. Daniel and the others, they've got to be pinned down."

"I don't think so," Kelly said. "If they were pinned in Five they would have told us. They would have made the radio call this morning. I think they're climbing. They're on their way."

There were other explanations for Five's radio silence, of

course. Their radio batteries might have gotten used up in last evening's arguing or frozen overnight. Someone might have dropped the radio handset or they might just have slept in or forgotten to call. The other possibility, the worst one, was that Daniel and the others had set out in the early hours according to plan and the wind had exterminated them. Abe left it all unspoken.

He couldn't get over the preternatural power of the wind and stared fearfully at the mountainside. There were no benchmarks—no tree branches or tumbleweeds or flags or wind socks—to help him gauge the force, nothing to even suggest the wind was blowing. Any loose snow had been scoured away. But for all its peaceful appearance, the North Face was now a gigantic maelstrom.

"Do we stay here or go up?" Abe asked.

Kelly didn't pause. "We have to go up," she answered. "They'll need us up there."

Abe slipped an extra bottle of oxygen into his pack for ballast, then braced himself and stepped from the cave once again. This time, turning one of his jumars upside down on the rope and slipping both tight, he managed to keep his footing. Kelly did the same, and after the initial blast, they adapted.

He looked up and saw a ball of purplish Saint Elmo's fire fifty feet higher along the rope. He'd seen such a thing on a friend's sailboat once, but never in the mountains. The ball of glowing electric flame had been drawn to the metal of their next anchor, and despite the wind it didn't move. Beyond that an immense dark white halo was crowning the summit. Abe forced himself to breathe deeply. It was imperative that he ignore this world of beautiful images. He had to concentrate on the climbing. He felt very afraid.

The air was murderously cold and it shook and rattled their clothing. Even standing side by side at the rest stances, neither could hear the other over the din without shouting. But it gave them one advantage. It graced them with wings. Abe was carrying three bottles of oxygen plus his jump kit for medical emergencies, and even so his load felt lighter than empty. It was almost as if the mountain were sucking him higher and higher. He couldn't shake the feeling that he and Kelly were being drawn into an ambush.

Abe approached the first anchor cautiously. The blue ball

of flame was seeping up and down the rope around one of Daniel's titanium ice screws. Abe couldn't remember if the phenomenon carried a dangerous electrical charge. There was no way around it, however, and so he finally dipped his hand into the strange shimmering light to clip his jumar onto the next rope. His hand tingled, no more. He could smell ozone, but on second thought decided smell was impossible in such wind and through an oxygen mask to boot. One more illusion. He kept on climbing.

They seemed to be moving much faster than human beings physically can at such altitudes. They had no choice in the matter. Kelly had the worst of it. Despite a hundred days of lost bodyweight, Abe still outweighed her by fifty pounds, and it told now in their footing. A dozen times Kelly was rocked and buffeted off her feet. Each time she patiently righted herself and dug her crampon points into the snow and ice and started again. She didn't complain.

Abe positioned himself a few steps behind in an effort to cut the wind. He couldn't afford to lose Kelly. Things were getting stranger by the minute, and his sole comfort was in being able to watch over her. Love had nothing to do with it. This was altruism stripped bare. The only way he could identify his own welfare anymore was by looking after hers.

Kelly's pace began to falter. She took more rests and her rhythm was off, afflicted by missteps and occasional wobbling. Abe was slow to fault her performance, blaming the wind. Finally he realized Kelly was in trouble. Her coordination was melting away before his eyes. She kept lumbering off to her right, plainly disoriented.

Abe called her name, but she continued up. He called again, then plodded fast enough to catch her by one arm. "Kelly," he shouted. "Are you okay?"

"Cold," she mumbled through her mask.

The easy explanation was that she'd run out of oxygen. Abe hoped it was that. He stepped above her and fumbled for the cylinder tucked in her pack. The regulator showed three-quarters full. Next he checked her mask. It was a standard military issue for aviators, a diluter-demand system. It drew pure oxygen through a demand valve and mixed it with air drawn from outside the mask. It was a simple enough tool, but the exhaust valve and ports tended to freeze up. Abe had

practiced dismantling the assembly and putting it together
down at Base Camp, and prayed it wasn't the demand valve
that had iced up. Fortunately it was the exhaust ports. He
squeezed the rubber mask in his mitten and freed the ice. Then
he fitted the mask back over Kelly's helmet and cranked her
regulator up to two liters per minute.

"Try that," he yelled.

She gave him a weary thumbs-up. After a while her pace
improved.

At the head of two more pitches, the Shooting Gallery's
steep narrow cleavage opened wide and the angle of the slope
grew more and more manageable. They found themselves
breaking trail upon a snowy tilted plateau. Compared to the
vertical gauntlet of the last few days, the plateau felt almost
level. They left the abyss behind them, out of sight, almost out
of mind.

The rope ended. Daniel had decided it was safe enough up
here.

They continued on for another hour or so in the deafening
howl, then Kelly stopped and pointed. Not far in the distance,
perhaps two hundred yards away, stood a solitary orange tent.
Daniel had taken it from the cache of gear the New Zealanders
had left in the cave. For the time being anyway, it represented
the highest human habitation on earth. The camp was built on
snow, at the intersection of the plateau and what Abe knew
could only be the Yellow Band. Through his goggles the rock
was lime green and plated like lizard scales.

Kelly was pointing above the tent, though, and Abe moved
his attention higher. He saw a thick wide shelf of snow that had
accumulated three or four hundred feet above the camp. It
probably held a thousand tons of snow, a perfectly formed
avalanche ready to cut loose. Then Abe saw similar pockets
coiled all along on the downsloping tiles. The whole region was
primed for a catastrophe.

The sight was almost enough to make Abe turn tail and
descend as fast as possible. But one further sight held him
steady, a rather sorry sight. There, almost within reach, stood
the summit.

Abe was disappointed. For all its majesty and fury, Everest
didn't finish with a dramatic sculptured prow or a sharp pinna-

cle. Instead the mountain just rounded into a sorry little hump-back, a gray lump shrugging at the gray sky.

The top was perhaps a half-mile away and a thousand feet overhead, but it looked much closer and very easy, an afternoon romp. Just as Daniel had said, you could see the summit tripod from here, a tiny, sticklike protuberance. The tripod reminded Abe of an altarpiece for ants, ridiculous and not at all trium-phant.

Kelly pulled at Abe's arm and shouted something. She had taken her glacier glasses off. Abe bent his head closer. Their helmets knocked. "I can't see anyone," she shouted above the wind, and Abe thought she'd gone snowblind.

"Your glasses," Abe shouted back. He gestured to her to put them on.

Kelly didn't hear or else didn't care to. Either way she let the glasses dangle and whip about on the string at her throat. She pointed at the summit again.

Abe realized she was hunting for some evidence of climbers on the summit slopes. Now he looked, too. Their vantage point was ideal for spotting any movement up there. If they could see the summit tripod, there was no reason they couldn't see a moving figure wrapped in expedition colors.

In vain Abe tried tracing a route upward from the orange tent to the top. Then he tried working down from the top along five or six different paths. Kelly took out her camera and screwed on the telephoto, and they took turns scanning the top. They saw no one. The climbers had disappeared.

Kelly's eyes were streaming tears from the wind. She shouted something, but Abe shook his head, deaf in this hurri-cane. He tried replacing the glasses on her face, but his fingers had gone wooden with the cold. Besides that, he could see Kelly's tiredness and disorientation. He suspected her mask had packed in again with ice, and that would need more work still.

"The tent," he yelled.

Abe led off, plowing his knees through the snow crust. He left it to the wind to blow Kelly in his wake. As they slogged up toward the orange tent, Abe tried to arrange his thoughts for an orderly discussion. Matters of search and rescue or simple retreat had to be weighed quickly and clearly and ruthlessly. But with each step he only got more confused and tired.

It took them an hour to ascend the two hundred yards to camp. By the time they reached the orange tent, Abe's fingers wouldn't work and all Kelly could do was kneel and stare at the closed door. Finally he pried a flap open with his ice axe and slowly peeled it open. He was careful not to break the zipper, because if they couldn't close the door again the wind would surely kill them.

Abe pawed Kelly's pack off, then his own, and dumped them in the snow. Then he pushed her inside and crawled in behind. It took five minutes to worry the door zipper shut again.

"There's no one here," Kelly yelled over the wind. She, too, had been hoping the climbers would be inside.

Four sleeping bags lay heaped in the back of the tent. Daniel's team had broken the rule and entered the tent with their crampons on. Abe could tell by the ripped, punctured floor. Then he noticed that he had neglected to take off his own crampons. Kelly's were still on, too. He took them off.

The tent walls shook so fast they buzzed. Abe was thankful the tent hadn't blown away. Kelly sat in the corner, staring, mask off, mouth open. Her lips were bright blue. They stared at each other, exhausted. Abe felt asleep. Or dead.

Another thought came to him. "Oxygen," he said to Kelly. Her eyes had closed though. Abe set the mask back across her mouth. He checked the regulator on her oxygen bottle. It was a quarter full. He checked his own. It was empty. He'd been sucking on ambient air at 27,500 feet. For how long, he couldn't say.

Abe pulled the mask off Kelly's face and strapped it to his own face. It was like robbing a child of candy. She didn't protest or even notice. He cranked the flow rate up to four liters per minute and breathed as deep as one could up here, a modified pant. After five or ten minutes, he felt warmer and less stupe-fied. His few priorities marched into view. They had to breathe, drink and eat.

He unzipped the door. The wind blasted him and the tent bellied in the rear. As quickly as possible, Abe opened his pack and pulled in two more bottles of oxygen, then closed the door. It took awhile, but he finally got a second oxygen set assembled with a regulator showing full. He nestled the second mask over Kelly's mouth and turned it on. It would be good for four to six hours.

Kelly slept. Abe cooked. Rather than open and close the door each time the pot needed more snow, he simply ripped the floor apart and took snow from underneath.

Since Kelly was out of the loop, Abe talked to himself. "We're in trouble now," he said. He wondered if the regulator had lied. It seemed likely he was out of oxygen again, but it was too much effort to check. He wasn't scared. To the contrary, a host of old friends and half-familiar faces had come from nowhere to offer encouragement. They were friendly and anxious for him, mumbling kind, if incoherent, advice. The tent seemed much larger than it was. It filled with dozens of visitors. Abe kept at his stove. There were suddenly so many to give water to.

At one point, the tent shook harder than ever. More voices cried out, adding to the disembodied conversations Abe was enjoying. The tent door opened. More ghosts joined Abe's gathering of souls. He looked for Jamie among the new faces, but she was nowhere to be seen. Abe's father drifted through with his old oil-rig scars, and the Tibetan monk rested against one wall, smiling, bundled in yak skins, looking more boyish than ever. Daniel was there and Gus and all the others. The babble of voices sounded like the roar of the wind and the roar of the wind reminded Abe of one vast, unending prayer, a sort of high mass. And he was the priest. "Water," he offered one and all.

Abe sat jammed against Kelly, who curled fetuslike. He handed out cups of melted water and went on with his cooking, scooping snow through the hole in the floor. There was no room to work really—too many bodies in one tent—and he had to protect his hanging stove from their elbows and commotion. Finally someone volunteered to take over. It was Daniel. Pressed tight against Kelly and with someone sitting on one of his legs, Abe fell asleep.

He woke slowly, still sitting upright. He was breathing oxygen through his mask. The tent was full of people, but everything seemed different. The people had changed. The wind had stopped. The simplicity and friendliness were gone. Once again the tent was a small, shabby space. The walls had grown dark.

Daniel looked at him. He wasn't wearing an oxygen mask. "You okay, Abe?" he asked.

Abe nodded yes.

"You were singing," Daniel said. "We came in. You were out of oxygen. And you were singing."

Besides himself, Abe counted a total of three others in the tent, Kelly and Daniel and Gus. Gus and Kelly were dozing, crammed in one corner, zipped in bags. Daniel was minding the stove.

Abe started to decipher his long, bizarre afternoon. He must have run out of oxygen again. He'd been hallucinating, that was clear. Maybe he still was.

"We couldn't find you," Abe said. He lifted the mask off to speak. "We thought you were dead."

"So did I," Daniel said. "We had trouble getting through the Band. The wind trapped us. We were close. But we ran out of time. We had to come down."

"Where's Stump? Where's J.J.?" Abe asked. He accepted that Daniel had lost them.

Daniel squinted at Abe, perplexed. "They came in the tent for a while. You gave them tea and talked. Then they went down the ropes. They made it as far as Three before dark stopped them. I talked to them on the night call."

"I don't understand."

"It's nine o'clock, Abe."

Abe frowned. So many hours had passed. There was still a disembodied sheen to the people and things in the tent, and he realized his escape from the underworld was not yet complete.

"What else?" Abe asked. "Any news?"

"Robby and Thomas came up to Four. But Thomas is dog sick. Unless there's some improvement, they go down in the A.M."

"And Jorgens? He's still at One?" It helped for him to be locating the others. Already he felt more composed.

"Still in One. Tonight he went on the record. Not guilty."

"Not guilty?"

"Jorgens said it wasn't him who turned the kid in."

Abe hadn't forgotten the monk. But he had to remember if Jorgens's treachery really mattered to him. He couldn't say. It seemed to matter to Daniel, though.

"Jorgens hangs for this one," Daniel said. "Stump and I decided. He can explain this to his precious AAC."

Abe hadn't thought of that one. The American Alpine Club took itself very seriously, and Jorgens's presidency wouldn't last the first round of cocktails at their next meeting. That would hurt Jorgens where he lived, more than any curse or fist could.

But Abe's small pleasure vanished when he pictured the board members who would vote. Most were lawyers and professionals used to savoring all the grays between black and white. And besides, few climbers thought of ethics as anything but a set of rules governing how much chalk they put on their hands or how many bolts they hammered in the rock. Ten thousand miles and months or years from now, the notions of guilt and betrayal would strike them as absurd. They would say what Jorgens would say, that a climber has no duty except to climb. And so revenge didn't matter, especially not tonight at 28,000 feet with the ghosts crowding in.

"What about the boy?" Abe asked.

"Carlos said they take him off tomorrow. He hasn't seen the kid since the one time. Hog-tied in the Tomb."

Abe would have sighed if there was the extra air for it.

"Also, Li wants us down."

"I thought we had ten days."

"Two more days, Abe. Then our ten are up."

"I guess so." People, days, even reasons for being up here: It was so easy to lose count anymore.

"Carlos said one other thing. The yaks down at Base, they've run off."

"So?" For all Abe knew, yaks regularly ran off.

"Carlos said the herders are all freaked. The yaks were fine until today. Then they started getting nervous and running around. Then they bolted. They headed north. The herders say it's a bad omen. Something's about to happen. It's been a strange afternoon down there."

Right now Abe didn't have any room for premonitions and superstitious babble. "It was a strange afternoon up here."

"Welcome back." Daniel smiled. Abe liked that they could joke about their madness.

To Abe's side, Kelly whimpered. She mewled like a kitten inside her mask. Her eyes were closed and Abe thought she might be having her nightmare again.

"How'd that happen to her eyes?" Daniel asked.

Abe licked his lips and frowned. His headache was back and it was hard trying to keep up with Daniel.

"She's snow-blind," Daniel said. "I gave her a half tab of Valium for the pain."

"Valium? At this altitude?"

"Abe. I asked you. It was your idea."

Abe looked at his hands. He clenched and opened them. He wondered what else he'd said and done that afternoon.

"So what's the program?" he asked. Daniel's team had misfired on their summit assault. Kelly was blind. They were down for the count. There weren't going to be enough of them left to push it. The mountain had scored another defeat. Their only remaining mission was to get off the Hill in one piece. He only hoped Daniel didn't want them to descend right away, tonight, in the dark.

"I know the way now," Daniel said. "We cracked the Yellow Band. I thought it would be simple and it wasn't. But now I know the way."

Abe was sorry for Daniel. To have come so far and learned so much, and now to have to turn his back on it all. But Abe had no doubt Daniel would return. Someday he would complete his cycle upon this mountain. Carlos had told Abe about a mountain in western Tibet where pilgrims circled around and around. This was that mountain for Daniel, only the circles moved vertically, up and down.

"What do you say, Abe?"

"First thing in the morning," Abe said. "We can start at seven o'clock." That would give them a full day. They could descend most of the face in that time, maybe all the way to ABC.

"I was thinking more like six."

"Fine, six."

Daniel grinned. "Don't worry, Abe. This time, I know the way."

Abe grimaced. He was appalled. They were talking about two different directions. Daniel meant to go up.

"I thought you meant down."

"He meant up," a new voice intruded. It was Gus. She had been listening. She looked broken to pieces by the combat. The sun and wind and fatigue had cut her face into separate parts, and the parts were coming unglued. Everything was.

There was no possible way he could go farther. Now that the afternoon was over, now that he was learning how lucid he'd been in his craziness, Abe was frightened. He had to get out of this zone of illusions before it consumed him. But instead of risking his hard-won alliance with Daniel by telling him no, Abe pointed at Kelly. She lay asleep in a pile of down gear and gold hair.

"But Kelly's blind," he said. "I have to take her down." It was true, but also it was a way of cutting his losses. This way he could descend and still have Daniel's respect. But his gambit failed.

"Negative." Gus sounded a hundred years old. "I'll take care of Kelly tomorrow. You go up. I'll go down."

"But Gus," Daniel faltered.

"I'm whipped." She stated it categorically, with no pathos. "I can't go on. And I know it."

"Gus," Daniel protested. But they knew she was right. Once a climber turns her face from the mountain, there's nothing more to argue. Without faith, without obsession, a climber was no more than bait for disaster.

Abe watched the gravity steal into her eyes. It was like watching a person die, a terrible and private twilight. Yet Abe felt he'd earned this voyeurism and Gus didn't turn from his gaze nor clothe her pain. Watching over Daniel had exhausted her.

"I'm sorry, Gus," Daniel said. At the same time, Abe noticed, Daniel wasn't offering to retreat. He didn't propose to descend with her, hand in hand. They weren't going to stroll away from the mountain into a happy ending. This wasn't Hollywood. Nor was it pity. Daniel's words were a simple, dry-eyed acknowledgment of her loss.

Gus was not particularly touched. She shrugged. "I'm not sacrificing myself," she said. "I'm making way." Then she looked at Abe. "I had my run. Now you have yours. Get it over with."

It was remarkable how she managed to bring it off. Here she was setting him up and yet it sounded so benign. But the facts stood. Having exhausted herself trying to deliver Daniel his summit, Gus was simply making certain her lover had a replacement. Regardless of what had just been said, Gus was definitely sacrificing. She was giving away her second try with the calculation of a kingmaker, and she was giving away Abe's fear and maybe his life and, who knew, maybe even Kelly's life if it depended on his medical know-how. Gus was willing to sacrifice them all, herself included, in order to get Daniel to his salvation. And yet Abe could not resent her.

"Leave him alone," Daniel said to Gus. "You made your decision. He made his, too. I misunderstood, that's all."

Her eyes stayed locked on Abe's. "He talks like you're blood, the two of you," she said to Abe. "You act like it, too."

"Stop it, Gus." Daniel hissed at her.

She faced him. "If Abe goes down, will you?"

"That's beside the point."

"But it is the point," Gus said. "You can't do this alone." She turned to Abe. "And you can't either."

She quit talking. If she had said one false thing, Abe would have turned away. But he'd felt the night in his heart for too long, exactly as long as he'd known Daniel. It was time for them to escape, together. A thousand more feet of climbing and they would break through to the sun.

"You're right," Abe said.

"Damn it, Gus." Daniel's shoulders looked thin beneath his parka. He was at once angry and defeated.

"Shut up," Abe said to Daniel. It surprised them both. "I'm going. We're going."

"Listen," Gus said. "The wind. It stopped."

And it had. The tent walls were no longer buzzing. The thunder was gone. They were talking at a normal volume.

"We should sleep," Daniel said.

"It's so quiet," Abe noticed. It was more quiet than just the absence of the wind. Now he touched the still tent wall and found that it was solid and heavy, like cold wet concrete.

Daniel zipped open the top of the door and shined his light outside.

"It's snowing," he told him. "Snowing hard."

"It will stop," Gus said. "Like the wind, it will stop. Now you should sleep."

Long Ago, Drinking straight shots on flat land at the end of a sunny day of rock climbing, Abe had held forth that a mountain is nothing more than a pyramid of memories and dreams. He had insisted. No mountain exists without the climber to perceive it.

There was the opposite possibility, of course, that every climber is simply the invention of long geological slumber. Just as climbers can manipulate their dreams, a mountain can manipulate its own ascent. And when the mountain wakes, the dream ends and the climber evaporates.

But Abe hadn't thought of that one that sultry twilight in a Mexican restaurant, and now it was too late, for the Kore Wall came alive. It caught Abe, booted and spurred, in the very act of checking his watch.

None of them had slept a wink, not once Kelly's Valium wore off and she started begging for more. Abe had refused, saying she needed to be coherent for her descent. She had cursed him and wept, but the tears only hurt her burned eyes more.

At 3:30 in the morning, Abe and Daniel started arming for their final assault by headlamp. Gus and Kelly stayed in their bags to make room in the crowded tent. After the men were gone, they would gear up for their own departure.

For a hundred days, they had forgotten time, living like exiles. Yet this morning Abe couldn't remember it enough. Like a condemned man, he tracked every minute. His destiny seemed to have become a matter of seconds.

At 5:15 Abe started working into his boots and super-gaiters. He snapped shut the heel clips on his crampons at 5:40, strapped on his helmet eight minutes later, and five minutes after that double-checked both his and Daniel's oxygen regulators. The last thing Abe did before pulling on the wrist loop of his ice axe was check the time again: 5:57 A.M., 6/12.

That was the moment the earthquake struck.

It was subtle. Kelly felt the trembling first. She said, "What's that?" Then Abe felt it, too. Then they heard the snow.

Like a giant serpent loosening its coils, the first of the avalanches let go with a hiss. Each of them knew what it was with hair-trigger wisdom. Like the snow itself, their awareness of the danger had collected heavier and deeper overnight. The Yellow Band overhead was loaded with dry snow shingled with wet snow and they were in the cold white field of fire.

The first avalanche missed them.

Eyes wide above their oxygen masks, they listened to it empty down the limestone tiles and hit their plateau with a boom. Moments later the backdraft blasted their tent with a roar of air. Spindrift the texture of beach sand was pressure-injected through the closed zipper and the air turned white.

Daniel started to yell something. But the mountain had its range now.

The second avalanche did not miss them.

The door blew out—not in—and a tremendous suction dragged at Abe's lungs and heart and bowels, threatening to gut and empty him in one sweep.

An instant later the vacuum reversed. The tent walls collapsed. The fabric wrapped Abe's every contour tight. The whiteness went black. Sound turned to silence. All perception stopped.

Abe's first thought was that he'd died. He thought, I can live with this. It was so peaceful. He felt warm. Nothing hurt. Paradise was rest. He'd been laboring to find this calm since birth.

But then he drew a breath. It was a wracked, burning suck of air, and with it he plunged into hell. For half his lifetime, Abe suddenly knew, he had been dreading this moment, when he would face the fate of the lost girl Diana. Yet now, like a wasp capturing an insect alive for her young to feed upon, the Mother Goddess had enclosed him in her core. The mountain was going to feed upon him through eternity.

Abe tried to move his arms. He was not surprised by their capture. But the claustrophobia spasmed through him anyway. All his strength poured into thrashing and bucking and tearing a hole through this imprisonment.

He had to move, even if it was only a fraction of an inch. He yelled and shouted, but that only made it worse. He had the voice of a human being trapped inside a mountain. Finally he passed out.

When Abe returned to consciousness, his throat hurt. There was no telling how long he'd been out. Not long enough. He went mad again. Again he passed out.

When Abe came back this time, he tried to reason with his horror. But in trying to picture his position—up or down or flat or sitting—or his location upon the mountain, he lost control and consciousness again.

This time when he revived, Abe was too tired and ill to struggle. From a far distant place, he felt pain. It was the stitched laceration on his right arm, he knew. But it came to him simply as pain, without reference points. This was life then. Stripped of its compasses and timepieces and sun, life reduced to a mere sensation. Abe no longer wanted it.

Locked inside his coffin of snow, Abe felt inspired. If he couldn't control the directions and movement of his life, then at least he could end it. The simple fact of having a choice, no matter how final it was, calmed him. He didn't debate the issue. One way or another he was going to gain his freedom.

Suicide was easier said than done. Abe slipped toward panic as he realized how helpless he really was. It occurred to him that he could pack his mouth full of snow and drown, however slowly. But upon opening his jaws for a bite he learned that the oxygen mask was still on his face. He couldn't even honestly suffocate, it seemed. He was doomed. Just before the avalanche hit, his oxygen regulator had showed a full tank, and he hadn't yet cranked the flow rate from a half-liter per minute—his sleep rate—to two liters per minute for climbing. A quick calculation told him another eight to nine hours of air remained, and he couldn't even move his head to push the mask off.

Abe's last hope was to go mad, then. But he no sooner invited the awful claustrophobia to take him off into madness than it completely vanished. He was left feeling calm and horrified at the same time. He remembered someone telling him that Tibetan *tulkus* could select their moment to die. Through meditation they could depart this plane of existence. He remembered the tiny cells in the monastery where monks would have themselves buried for six and twelve months at a time. He stared into the blackness.

Abe may have slept. At any rate another thought entered his mind like the sweet arrival of dawn. It was less a thought than a whisper. It beckoned to him. It drew him. Right through the snow and ice and rock and years, it drew him down through the planet and connected him with his own past. It was like dreaming. Sensations were traveling through the mass of his imagination like earthquake tremors. I have become the mountain, thought Abe. He was pleased. It was the ultimate union, the mountaineer with his mountain. He felt saved.

And then he was saved. Impossibly, he was saved.

Hands, voices, light—he was wrenched from the tomb and brought back to the world. No one asked if he wanted to come out to face it all over again. They simply hauled him kicking and bawling into the blistering gray light and cold wind.

It started with his face. Someone's hand scooped away the snow from his eyes and cheeks and hair. Abe looked up from the bowels of his tomb and saw a woman looking the way angels must, torn by the elements, with her long blond hair torn loose of its braid and guttering through the jet stream. The storm raged all around her.

"Abe," Kelly screamed in the wind and snow. "Abe." How she had survived, he did not know. She rocked back upon her heels, blind and spent.

Abe's head was trapped in the snow, but even so he could see the summit, or where it had been. The sky had atomized, blue to gray. The color had leached out, the border between earth and heaven was erased. The summit was gone forever.

Above and behind her a dark shape loomed. Daniel came

into view fully equipped, from his helmet to his crampons to the axe in his hand. As Abe squinted up at him in the driving snow, he noticed the black figure-eight brake dangling from Daniel's harness. The brake was for descent. Abe did not need to ask. They had been on the verge of leaving him buried.

"Is he still alive?" Daniel yelled in the wind. He had shucked his mask, and Kelly's, too. There was no more bottled oxygen up here.

Weeping as if Abe had been lost, not found, Kelly reached down into the pit. She fumbled blindly and pulled off his mask and the smell of freshly mined rock poured into his lungs, raw and pungent.

"Are you alive?" Kelly shouted at him.

Abe tried to speak, but the lining of his throat felt flayed. He tried to nod his head but it was lodged in place. With her glove upon his mouth, he managed to move his jaw.

"He's alive," Kelly shouted.

Daniel seemed disoriented by her answer. He looked almost shattered by the news.

"We've got to hurry," Daniel shouted. "There's more coming."

Dear God, thought Abe, more avalanches. His serenity crumbled. He tried to yell and beg and pray, but his vocal cords had done all they could. All over again he fought his lost battle with the snow binding his limbs. Snowflakes fell from the sky and bit at his eyes.

"Please," Abe hissed at Daniel. By whispering, he got the word out.

"Keep it together. We've got you now." Daniel was talking at him, not to him. It was rescue rap, the kind of chatter you used to keep a bleeder from going under. Abe didn't feel any wounds. But Daniel seemed repulsed by him, and for the first time Abe wondered how badly injured he might be.

Daniel dropped to his knees beside Kelly, practically knocking her to one side. Without a word, he grabbed her ice axe and began chopping and scraping at the snow with the adze. He worked desperately.

"How long was I gone?" Abe whispered.

Daniel pawed at his sleeve and mitten. "It's nine-fifteen,"

he said, and went back to work. Abe had been under for more than three hours. Avalanche victims rarely lasted over thirty minutes. After an hour you quit digging. But these people had not quit.

"Thank you," Abe whispered.

"Don't thank me," Daniel said, and kept digging. He was angry.

"I'm sorry," Abe said.

Daniel paused, panting for air. His mood seemed closer to guilt than anger now. It was guilt, of course. He had nearly left another partner to die. Daniel resumed the task of resurrection. His pace was furious.

For the most part, Kelly lay hunched against a pile of snow. Now and then she summoned the strength to crawl forward on her knees and scoop away snow, but her efforts were feeble and only put her in range of Daniel's axe strokes. "Move away," Daniel ordered her and she obeyed.

Daniel freed Abe's head first. That let Abe look around at the devastation. The avalanche had scythed across the slope and chunks of slab snow and raw limestone lay everywhere. It was a miracle any of them had managed to claw their way from the jumbled debris. Their tent had ruptured like a balloon and been churned under by the slide. Orange tatters flashed in the air.

Overhead, the band of yellow limestone was fat with snow. Even the portions that had emptied onto them were rapidly accumulating a new white covering. A long, heavy bosom of snow hung immediately above, menacing them. Daniel was right to work with such desperation. They had to leave this area or stay forever.

Daniel widened the pit, unearthing more of Abe's body. Abe's ice axe turned up, then Daniel found the radio, but it was broken. Grimly he placed these relics to one side and went on digging. Abe understood that they were in grave danger, but he could not understand Daniel's severity and gloom. The man didn't speak. He didn't smile. In Daniel's place, Abe would have been rejoicing to discover a friend alive. Abe felt strangely unwelcome.

Then the screaming started. It was a keening almost too high to hear. Abe decided it couldn't be screaming. The wind must have found a sharp stone to whistle on. But it came again.

This time he caught the animal note in it and there was only one kind of animal up here. It was human. It was a woman.

"Gus," Abe whispered. No one answered.

Again the banshee squealing laced the wind.

Eyes squeezed shut against the gray light, Kelly bared her teeth. She clenched her jaw and aimed her head away from the sound. Daniel was equally callous. He didn't say anything, just kept chopping and slashing at the snow. The axe hit chunks of limestone. Sparks flew among the falling snowflakes.

Daniel freed Abe's right arm all the way to the shoulder. "Lift it," he told Abe. "Bend it. Move it." Then he worked lower to excavate a leg.

"What's wrong with Gus?" Abe demanded.

"You better be whole," Daniel stated. "We can't afford more broken bones."

Now Abe saw the blood on their cherry red parkas. It smeared pink on the white avalanche debris.

Abe grew alarmed. "What happened?"

But Daniel wouldn't say any more. Kelly seemed close to hysteria.

It wasn't hard to answer his own question. The avalanche had mauled Gus badly. Judging by the blood and Daniel's remark, she had sustained at least one compound fracture. They had found her and then packaged her for the descent. And just as Daniel was preparing to go, Kelly had discovered Abe. Daniel had been forced to leave Gus screaming in the snow and dig Abe out. *Don't thank me.*

Abe waited for one of Daniel's downstrokes and caught at the axe shaft with his free hand. Daniel tried to pull away, but Abe hung on. "Start down," Abe whispered up at him from the bottom of the pit. "I can do this alone."

"I wasn't leaving you," Daniel exploded at him. But he had been leaving, that was plain to see. Until this moment Abe hadn't known how utterly wrecked the man was. Gus had been right. Daniel could not afford his own memories.

"Daniel," Abe whispered. He pulled the axe closer. Daniel resisted. Abe didn't know what to say until he said it. "I am saved," he hissed.

Daniel froze.

Abe wasn't sure Daniel had understood him. And so he added, "I don't need you anymore."

Still Daniel didn't move. He could have been listening to a ghost.

"I'll bring Kelly down with me," Abe clarified. "Go as far as you can go."

Daniel exhaled with a groan and released the axe. He straightened from the pit and stared down at Abe, then climbed to his feet.

"She wouldn't give up." Daniel pointed at Kelly. He was visibly shaken by her faith and intuition. For the first time it struck Abe that a blind woman had found him. "Take care of her," Daniel shouted.

"I will," Abe promised.

Daniel picked up the walkie-talkie and stuffed it into his parka. Then he staggered off into the storm, half bent from his cracked ribs and bad back and other old injuries.

A minute later, Abe heard terrible screaming and knew that Gus was being lifted and moved. It was going to be an ugly, brutal evacuation. There was no help for that. The four of them had been lucky to survive the avalanche. Abe didn't pretend to himself that their luck could hold.

Kelly had fallen asleep in the snow. Even as Abe chopped at the shroud covering him, a thin layer of powder started to bury her. With his one free arm, Abe shoved and cut at the snow. It was slow going. Another hour passed before he managed to sit. Like a B-movie corpse wrestling up from the soil, he bulled his chest through the snow.

Abe was exhausted. He wanted to rest, just for a minute or two, just to breathe, to close his eyes and take a catnap, no more. It was the wrong thing to do, but he would have done it anyway, if not for Kelly.

She was gone. The powder had drifted over her like a dune. "Kelly," Abe rasped. He sat there, piled with debris, and called her name again. Fear won out over his fatigue.

Now that they were in full rout, the mountain was reclaiming its territory with a vengeance. There were no prisoners up here. Those who lagged, died. If he hadn't seen Kelly lie down, Abe would never have believed she was there. To the naked eye, she had never existed.

Abe bucked at the snow and yanked at his legs. At last he was able to worm loose from the pit. Panting, he rolled onto the surface and lay there. Snowflakes lit down with astonishing weight. Abe knew he was under attack, yet the snow warmed and coddled him. The snowflakes crashed into his face and melted and ran past his ears. Abe commanded himself to get up.

"Kelly," Abe whispered. He didn't suppose it would rouse her, but he needed the reminder. Every muscle and joint ached from his subterranean struggles. He made the pain work for him. It too was a reminder.

Teetering in the wind, Abe stepped toward the dune hiding Kelly. He plowed his hands through the powder and grabbed her arms and lifted her into the storm light.

He brushed the snow from Kelly's face. She was mumbling and she turned her head from the light. Saliva had frozen into her golden hair. Abe couldn't get over the fact that, even blind, this woman had saved him. Abe bent to her. He kissed her.

It wasn't much of a kiss. His lips were scabbed and filthy and grown over with beard. But some part of Kelly responded. She looped one arm around Abe's shoulder and spoke his name.

"Help me," Abe whispered.

"Rest," Kelly invited him.

Abe shook her hard. When she wouldn't cooperate, he simply dragged her across the snow.

There was nothing to fetch or bring down. They had lost everything in the avalanche. Abe eyed the Yellow Band overhead. There was enough snow gathered up there to wipe the face clean. Most of it would funnel straight down the Shoot. Anyone caught out would get washed to the base of the mountain. He tried to hurry.

Before they could start down the rope, Abe had to find it. And before he could find it, they had to cross the plateau. The whiteout was in full blow, though, and the snow had piled hip deep. Daniel had slugged a path through, but that was hours ago. Fresh snow had filled in behind him.

Abe wondered if he and Kelly were trapped after all. Every step cost him five or six breaths. The snow gave way like quicksand. Gusts of whiteout cut visibility to a few inches, only to be replaced by light so flat it killed all perspective. The closer they got to the edge of the plateau, the greater their danger of walking right off the North Face.

Abe didn't give in. He dragged Kelly after him, keeping a sharp eye for the first rope. The wind howled.

At last he reached the plateau's edge. It dropped away six

thousand vertical feet. He couldn't see the abyss—it was just more whiteness—but he did sense a change in the wind. This new wind tasted different from the monsoon curling over the summit. It was a Tibetan wind, blowing in from the north and sweeping straight up the immense Kore Wall.

Abe had found the edge then, but there was no rope. For an hour, he hunted back and forth along the lip of the wall. Without the rope they were marooned. Without the rope there was nothing to do but go to sleep in each other's arms. Abe was just getting used to that idea when the rope appeared.

It was checkered green and white. All Abe could see were the green dots, a long chain of them. He grappled the line to the top of the snow, then went off to find Kelly. She didn't want to wake up, but he bullied her. Then he lost the rope again. Finally he located the chain of green dots and they could start down.

Their torturous descent reminded Abe of the childhood riddle about the cannibals and the missionaries trying to cross a river. They had one rope, one blind climber and one climber on the verge of surrender. He tried the various configurations, going down first to check the anchor, going down last to make sure she descended and going down side by side to describe what she could not see. At her best, Kelly ran the drill like a sleepwalker, eyes closed, limbs wooden. She was at her best for only twenty or thirty feet at a time.

Over and over, Abe reached the bottom of the rope to find Kelly hanging limp in the wind. She had neither the hand coordination nor the vision to clip into the anchors, which complicated Abe's own descent. After several hundred feet, he rigged a separate line to lower Kelly himself. Like a sack of rocks, she knocked against the wall, sometimes whimpering protests, mostly just dangling mute. The method bloodied her nose and scraped holes in her clothing. But it was far quicker than waiting for a blind woman to feel her way down the steepening ice and rock.

They were halfway to Four when the mountain tried for them again. Abe's feet were planted square against the face, and there was no mistaking the earthquake this time. The tremors traveled up the long bones of Abe's legs. His crampon teeth scratched across the bare rock like a stylus gone wild.

Abe felt sick all the way into the core of his heart. He looked up the Shoot's narrow walls for the avalanche that had to come. It came.

Abe grappled with the rope and got a handful of Kelly's jacket. He shoved her beneath an outcrop.

The main mass of the avalanche sluiced past in a tube of thunder and rubble. The bulk of it struck the face several hundred feet lower.

Abe and Kelly clung to one another and kept their faces to the wall, breathing inside their parkas to keep from suffocating in the cloud of fine spindrift. The aftershock beat them against the rock and ice, but their rope held.

Kelly hung on to Abe. He hung on to her. He felt more tremors shaking them through the wall. Then he realized the tremors were actually from a person sobbing. But when he looked at Kelly's face, she wasn't the one doing the crying.

All day long, Abe pressed to catch up with Daniel and Gus. Teamed together, he and Daniel could speed the descent and pool their precautions. At the top of each rope, he felt the line for human vibrations. He peered into the depths, but didn't see a soul.

They landed at the cave just as darkness tinged the white storm. Abe had hoped to reach Two or One or even ABC before nightfall. But he was getting used to dashed hopes. At this hour it would have been foolhardy to try for a lower camp.

Abe unzipped both tents at Four, sure Daniel and Gus would be inside one of them. But the tents were empty. It looked like Daniel had stopped here just long enough to melt some water and root around for an oxygen bottle. Then he'd gone on. Abe wondered if the two had survived the afternoon's avalanche.

Abe led Kelly inside and zipped her into a bag. With rest and care, her sight would return. But it wasn't likely they would get such a respite until ABC or lower.

He started some snow on the stove, then assembled the last two bottles of the Kiwis' oxygen supply and fit an extra mask over Kelly's mouth and took the other for himself. They got a single pot of water from the remaining butane. It would be their first and last water on the descent.

In the morning, Kelly's eyes were no better, but at least they were no worse. Abe's whisper had upgraded to a hiss. Outside, the storm continued. Since they had slept fully clothed, not removing even their boots, they were able to leave first thing.

They reached Three at noon. The tent walls had been perforated by falling rock. One of the platforms had taken a direct hit, knocking its legs out. The camp looked desolate. Daniel and Gus had spent the night here. Frozen blood and dirty dressings lay everywhere. There was no butane for melting water, no food, no oxygen. No reason for Abe and Kelly to pause a minute longer.

Camp Two no longer existed. It had been scoured away by avalanches. Abe followed Daniel's makeshift string of ropes across a blank stretch, then picked up the line as four expeditions had laid it out over the years.

Minutes after traversing a gully, another avalanche scrubbed away the route behind them. Once the billowing powder settled, Abe saw that the ropes leading up to Three had been erased once and for all.

The terrain below Two eased considerably. Ironically, the easier angles made descent more difficult. In the Shoot, where the wall was pitched at 70 to 80 degrees, gravity had done most of Kelly's work. But as they approached One, Abe had to cajole and push and lift Kelly across sections that defied simple lowering. It exhausted them both.

Just before dark they reached the yellow tents at One. The wind had flattened one of the tents and one was missing altogether. Abe scavenged for anything of use. Except for some rock-hard nutrition bars—useless because of their loose teeth— the camp was barren of food. There was no gas to melt water, no oxygen for Kelly, no sleeping bags, no medicine, not so much as an aspirin. He wondered what had happened to Jorgens and Thomas and Stump. It was entirely conceivable the mountain had stalked and caught them.

Abe considered spending the night here. They could haul the collapsed tent inside the one still standing and wrap themselves in it and probably survive the night. On the other hand, there was still a little more light left.

While he was trying to decide what to do, Abe spied the third tent. It looked alive as it wiggled slowly down the slope beneath them. At first he thought it was just blowing downhill. Then he saw a tiny figure—Daniel—fishing it into the depths with a rope. He had bundled Gus inside and made it into a crude sled.

Abe put his lips near Kelly's ear. "I see them."

"They've found us?" she cried.

"No. It's Daniel and Gus."

Kelly tried to put a good face on it, but she was crushed. Abe had to pull her to standing and then herd her down the slope. He didn't waste time trying to attract Daniel's attention. The two teams of climbers joined together a thousand feet lower at the bergschrund, the deep crack dividing the mountain and its glacier. It was a border of sorts. And they needed to escape across it. It was so dark Abe and Daniel could barely see each other. Across its gaping four-foot-wide split, the Rongbuk Glacier awaited them with all its crevasses and obstacles.

No sooner did Abe reach the schrund than he realized they were going to get caught out tonight. It would have been suicidal to try crossing a mile of open glacier at this hour. The past several days of snowfall would have collapsed all their markers and new crevasses would have opened during the earthquake. So there was no alternative. They would have to wait until morning.

"I thought you were lost," Daniel greeted Abe. He seemed oblivious to their danger. It was night. The wind was extreme. None of them had eaten or slept or drunk much for two days and nights.

"Daniel, we've got to get out of this wind."

"I don't think we're going to make it," Daniel replied. His voice creaked. His blue eyes were rheumy. The bones of his face declared famine.

"We'll make it," Abe said. "But we need shelter." A blast of wind knocked him back against the snow. Daniel nodded his agreement, but he had no solution.

"Here," Abe pointed. He was standing on the upper lip of the gaping crack. "Maybe we could go down in there."

Abe knew that climbers sometimes bivouaced in crevasses. But the thought of descending into the crystalline underworld had long been his waking nightmare. It was their only hope, though.

"Maybe," Daniel shouted into his ear. Daniel had scrounged a headlamp from one of the deserted camps. He shined it into the black depths. To Abe's surprise, there seemed to be a distinct bottom some fifty or sixty feet down. Avalanches had apparently filled in some of the hole.

Together, Abe and Daniel cut a long section of rope loose and lowered Gus into the crevasse. She made soft noises when they knocked her against the walls. Kelly was next, then Daniel. Abe went last, checking to make sure the rope was firmly anchored for their exit. He dreaded descending into the opening, almost preferring the darkness of night to the possibility of another earthquake sealing the crevasse's lips above them. But Daniel's little light beckoned to him, and he went toward it.

The crevasse walls were spaced ten feet apart and had the slick feel of glass. Closer to the light, he could see the glass was dark green and turquoise. It terrified him.

Abe touched beside the others. Instantly he sensed that the snow they were standing upon was a false floor. It could go at any moment. The illusion of security was better than none at all, though, so he gingerly settled his boots onto the surface. At least they were out of the wind and driving snow down here.

After a while the climbers were settled enough so that Abe could take a look at Gus. He untied the ropes that bound the yellow tentage around her. With Daniel holding the light, he opened pieces of her clothing, one at a time to preserve her warmth.

Gus had broken her left femur, possibly snapping the ball off her hip joint. Abe couldn't be sure of that without an X ray. The blood had come from a compound fracture of both her tibia and fibula.

"Her foot was turned backward," Daniel explained. "I twisted it around." Then he added, "I just hope I twisted it the proper direction." It was a worthy hope. If Daniel had rotated her foot the wrong way, this leg would have been set 360 degrees out of alignment. It would have been the same as tying a tourniquet around her leg.

Despite Daniel's makeshift splinting with an ice axe and a tent pole, the broken leg was grotesque. He had controlled the bleeding, it seemed, but that wasn't good enough. The fractures—probably the splints, too—had cut off the blood supply to her foot. It was swollen and black with frostbite. If she lived, Gus was going to lose the foot, at least. Abe didn't see how she could possibly live through the night. It was amazing that clots and blood loss and shock and exposure hadn't finished her off already.

There was little Abe could do to improve on Daniel's handiwork. The splints and bandaging were as good as they could be. He tried without luck to get a pulse at the ankle of Gus's shattered leg. His fingers were too cold to feel much, but he knew that wasn't the real problem. The leg was dying. Abe was helpless. Without his trauma kit and oxygen, Abe couldn't even begin to work on her.

"Are there any other injuries?" Abe asked.

Daniel mumbled, "What?," less punch-drunk than distracted. Abe had never seen him like this. The fire in his eyes had burned to common ash. Daniel looked downright mortal for a change, as if pain and defeat and exhaustion were things that could happen to him, too.

"Just hold the light," Abe told him.

Gus's teeth showed yellow in a ghastly grimace under the lamplight. Kelly lay hibernating in a ball in the snow. Daniel said, "It's done now."

"1 know," Abe said. It was so done, there was no sense even remarking on it. In Abe's mind, the climb no longer even existed.

"Gus talked," Daniel said. "On the way down, she talked."

"That's good," Abe said.

"No." Daniel touched her forehead. "It's not so good."

Daniel had checked out. He was delirious. Abe found himself resenting that. He had counted on Daniel, they all had. They had hitchhiked on his composure and talents and depended on him to be sane and wily and dominant. Abe felt betrayed by this new frailty. He had counted on Daniel to defend them from this awful catastrophe with plans and reassurance and energy. But this shipwrecked creature kneeling in Abe's light was too lost to find his own way, much less lead others through to safety.

"Tomorrow will be hard," Abe said. "You should rest." They had several thousand feet to drop, plus the glacier to cross. The snowfall would have wiped out their marker flags at the crevasses, and the earthquake might have opened new ones. They would have to rig a sled and drag Gus, and Kelly would have to be led by the hand.

"Gus said this happened because of her," Daniel went on. "But I don't know. What do you think?"

Abe knew better than to talk to delirium. Hadn't they both heard that kind of final confession before? Abe went ahead and talked, though. If he could find just a spark of lucidness in Daniel, maybe he could fan it to sanity. Otherwise Abe was going to have three invalids to shepherd in the morning, and that was more than he could bear.

"Of course it's not Gus's fault," Abe said. "There was an earthquake."

"I told her that. An act of God. She said, no, we should blame her."

"She's out of her head."

"In a way she's right, you know."

"That's crazy. You're giving Gus credit for an earthquake?"

"No." Daniel swung his eyes up in the yellow light. "For our presence."

"And you listened to that?"

"We weren't supposed to go up this last time, remember?" Daniel said.

"Each of us chose," Abe pointed out. "It was my choice."

"But it wasn't your choice," Daniel said.

"No one forced me."

"No. But someone allowed you."

"I'm tired, Daniel. Say it straight."

"Li said we couldn't climb. Then he said we could. I wasn't there. But you were."

"Ah, that." Abe had pushed it from his mind.

"It's my fault, really." Daniel lost him once again. Abe waited. "She gave me the mountain. That makes it my fault."

Abe shook his head. Daniel had cracked after all. "Daniel," he said, "that's nuts. Nobody gave you the mountain."

"Not the mountain," Daniel conceded, "but the way. You know?"

"Daniel, I'm tired."

Daniel leaned toward Abe and the light gouged his face with shadows. "Abe," he said. "She told me. It wasn't Jorgens, Abe."

Abe closed his eyes. He felt stabbed. If not Jorgens, then. . . . He turned his head one way, then the other, but there was no way not to hear.

"It was Gus. She told me. She traded the kid."

"No," Abe said. But he knew it was true. It should have been Jorgens. But it had been Gus. She had sacrificed a child to this mountain. Worse, she had done it for love.

"She thought we could finish the mountain and still have time to descend and save him," Daniel said.

Abe stared at the mangled, suffering woman. He was dumbfounded. How could she have thought such a thing?

"She was wrong," Daniel said.

Abe was quick with it. "Yes," he said.

"I've lived with this for two days and nights now." Daniel was mournful. What an awful truth to carry, Abe thought, and through such destruction. And here Gus lay near death and the monk was gone and all for nothing. At least they had not climbed the mountain. That would have been obscene.

"Do one thing for me," Daniel said. "It's the only thing I'll ever ask from you."

"What is it?"

"Don't hate her."

There hadn't been time for Abe to think of that yet. But now that Daniel had mentioned it, of course he would hate her. If they made it through this—if Gus didn't die and the crevasses permitted passage and the Chinese ever let them leave—of course he would hate her.

"I don't know, Daniel."

"Please," said Daniel. "She did it for me. Now it's mine to deal with."

That night they curled against one another and lay against Gus to keep her warm. Snowflakes settled through the lips of the bergschrund and lighted down on them as gently as dust at the bottom of the sea. The glacier creaked like a huge armada of empty ships.

Gus survived the night. In the morning, they hauled her up from the glacial pit and started off for ABC. Abe kept expecting someone to see them from camp and come up to guide them across the dangerous plains. No one came. At the end of the day they learned why.

The storm quit around three in the afternoon. They entered ABC at five. The camp was absolutely deserted except for a surprised yakherder. He was an old man who had brought three yaks up to plunder what remained.

"Help us," Abe rasped to the man in English. But the herder refused to come any closer.

"He thinks we're ghosts," said Daniel. "They think we died."

Sunset brought the last avalanche, the largest yet. A bolt of roseate light had just lanced through the cloud cover when they heard the mountain crack high overhead. The slide started all the way up at the Yellow Band and it took fully three minutes for the mushrooming whiteness to devour the north wall.

ABC was a mile away from the base, but the aftershock still shook the climbers and the spindrift stung Abe's face. When the avalanche hit the Kore's base, its rubble fanned long and wide. The apron of debris barreled closer and closer to camp. The yaks snorted and tore away from the horrified herder and he ran after them.

Abe didn't move, though. He didn't flinch. He was too tired, but also he knew it would be futile to dodge. He had learned that much here.

For the rest of his life, Abe would be glad he stood and watched, because a rainbow sprang up in the white powder. Its colors were almost not colors, they were so close to white themselves.

Then the slide came to a halt and the rainbow settled back to earth and there was silence.

It Took Five days for Abe and his rabble to plow their way through the sea of snow from ABC to Base Camp. Somewhere in the middle of that tempest of piled drifts and missed turns and sudden storms, one of the yaks died.

They were a sorry sight. Blind and seasick, Kelly rode one of the yaks. Comatose, or nearly so, Gus had to be carried by hand on a litter made of tent poles. Even the old yakherder had to be taken care of. Along with his goiter and some species of lung disease he had senile dementia. He was more lost than they were.

As for Daniel, he was in ruins. He performed the tasks Abe gave him. Otherwise he seemed puzzled and uncertain. He never strayed out of eye contact with Gus's body, and at night he guarded over her.

Abe did not sleep during their entire exodus. Without warning the earth would start trembling, and even when it wasn't, he imagined it was. At night Kelly had him hold her tight, though in truth it was he who needed the holding. While she dreamed of demons stirring deep inside the earth, Abe stared up at the iron-cold stars, wide awake.

He was changed. They all were. What they suffered was worse than defeat. They had been believers—richly pagan in

their devotion to the mountain—but the earthquakes had exposed their foolishness. They had lost their faith. Abe could see his despair in the others.

On the fifth morning, Abe went ahead for help. The snows had gotten deeper and bogged them down. Weak and slow, he feared the group wouldn't last another night out.

Alone, he ripped a path through the frozen desert.

After many hours, Base came into view on the flat valley floor. The camp may as well have been avalanched, for the blizzards had buried it under five feet of snow. Fully half the tents had collapsed. Those remaining were connected by a network of deep trenches.

Abe found the other climbers gathered for dinner in the big khaki mess tent. It was dark and cold inside. A kerosene lantern hung from the bamboo roof support, though it leaked less light than inky black smoke.

Abe took a minute to adjust to the dim light. The smell of food dazed him.

They didn't see him at first.

"Abe?" someone asked. "Is that you?" The voice became a face. Stump had survived the descent.

It looked like a bomb shelter in there. Part of one wall was lined with the remains of their gear and food. At one time the expedition pantry had lacked for nothing. Now they were ransacking the last of their stock.

Abe searched around for others. Through J.J.'s parka, he saw white tape binding his rib cage. Thomas was slumped over the table behind a curtain of derelict hair, eyes bloodshot. Robby lay propped in one corner with huge frostbite blisters bubbling across his fingers. An ancient man leaned forward from the shadows. It was Jorgens, emaciated. In the space of a week, he had aged a quarter-century.

"Impossible," Jorgens protested. He was stunned the way men are upon learning they've forsaken a companion.

"We called and we called," he stammered. "But the radio was dead. We waited for you. We watched the Hill. But you were lost."

"No one could have lived through those avalanches," Thomas added. "We got mangled ourselves. And the snow was getting deeper. We had imperatives. . . ."

None of them moved. Abe scarcely listened to them. He felt disembodied. The climbers seemed less real than hallucinations.

"Are you the only one?" Stump asked.

Abe shook his head. The ice in his beard rattled like beads.

Thomas posed a different type of question. "You made it down. But did you make it up? Did you guys top out?"

Stump frowned at Thomas. The question of victory sounded mercenary. All the same, Stump didn't tell Thomas to shut up. Like the others, he waited for Abe's answer.

Abe looked from one pair of eyes to the next. His answer was obviously of great importance to them, but he was suddenly unsure what the answer really was. For some reason the summit tripod loomed large in his memory. It seemed close enough to put his hands on, to tie his red *puja* string to the wire. He felt for the string at his throat, but it was gone. He wondered where it could have disappeared to.

Abe tried putting it into words. At last someone led him to a chair. It was Krishna. He placed a cup of hot tea on the table before him.

"Where are the rest of your people, Abe?" Stump gently asked. Abe heard his pity and saw the doubt in his eyes. Stump didn't think there were any other survivors. It took an effort for Abe himself to believe that his band of refugees was not a phantom.

"They're there all right," Abe finally croaked.

"But where, Abe?"

"In the snow. On the trail." That was the best he could do. He searched for something more relevant. "Hot tea," Abe recommended. "They would like that."

Stump and Nima and three Sherpas set off to rescue whoever was left. At midnight, by the light of their headlamps, they found the refugees. The night sky had clouded over and so, fearing a new storm, they immediately started back down the trail. It was nearly dawn before they reached camp.

They laid Gus on the wicker table in the mess tent because Abe's hospital had caved in beneath the snow. At his request, the hospital had been partially excavated overnight, and so he had access to all the medicines and oxygen and other supplies. Steeped in caffeine and braced with hot food, Abe went to work on her.

The sun was just creeping over the east shoulder of the
Rongbuk Valley, and the tent wall lit up as he cut away Gus's
bloody clothing and exposed her injuries to full view. The
months had taken their toll on Gus. Her beautiful athlete's body
was gone, replaced by a construction of sinew and bones. Every
rib showed and her carefully wrought muscles had vanished.
Her moon-round breasts had withered.

"What's that stink?" Robby asked. From experience, Abe
knew. Daniel would know, too. Clostridia: gas gangrene. Abe
dreaded what was coming. But first things first.

Because Daniel refused to leave, Abe gave him a Betadine
scrub to wash Gus's upper body. That let Abe consider the
destruction below her waist.

With a pair of kitchen scissors, he finished cutting away her
windpants and the layered underclothing. Every snip of the
scissors revealed more injury, more atrophy, more loss. Between her legs, cupped in her panties, Abe found Gus's most
secret loss. She had been pregnant with Daniel's child, after all.

The remains were a week old, dating back to the avalanche.
The mountain had killed it. Quickly, so Daniel wouldn't know,
Abe balled the desiccated sac inside her panties and laid it in
the pile of rags. Its disposal would have to wait.

Abe turned his attention to the injured right leg. He cut
away Daniel's makeshift splint and exhaled.

The leg was so damaged that the broken bones were almost
secondary. Only now did Abe verify that Daniel had rotated the
leg properly. Daniel had done the best he could under deadly
conditions, but even so Gus's knee joint was completely devas-
tated.

"Daniel," Abe said. Daniel paused in his tender cleansing
of her bony arms. "You need to go away, Daniel."

"I can't do that," Daniel said.

"Okay," Abe said. "But look away."

With Jorgens's help, Abe began to reorganize the leg.
Bones popped and grated. Abe kept one hand on the knee and
felt its parts leap and dip. Jorgens—the ex-marine—had to
leave the tent to vomit. At the sound of the gruesome noises,
Daniel crouched by Gus's ear and whispered, though she could
hear nothing.

That was just the beginning. Next Abe tried to determine
the extent of her fractures. The limb was so swollen he could

barely trace the bones, much less find any "override" of broken ends. There were at least three major breaks, possibly four, and traction would have been his choice of treatment. But any sort of splints, even a soft plastic air splint, would cut the blood supply to her mottled foot even more. He couldn't afford that.

The frostbite had spread above her ankle. Every toe had turned black with necrosis. They would have looked like mummified claws in a freak show, except the blackness wasn't dry. It was draining and the unbroken blisters were inflated with gas. Death was creeping into Gus through her toes.

"I'm sorry," Daniel whispered to Gus. "Forgive me." The sight of her toes had set him off.

"J.J.," Abe said. "Take him out of here."

"I'm okay," Daniel said.

Robby saw the toes and guessed what was coming. "I'll help J.J.," he volunteered, and the two of them led Daniel out.

"Don't do too much," Daniel pleaded with Abe from the tent door.

Abe opened the kit he'd never imagined using. He didn't dwell on the instruments, barely knowing how to use them anyway. He wished now that it were a real physician standing here in his place. Stump choked back his repulsion enough to disinfect the toes by pouring a bottle of purple Betadine solution over them. Abe selected what looked like a pair of stainless steel garden shears and Stump dumped Betadine over them, too.

Abe was surprised by the shears' leverage and sharpness. The bones parted with a snip. He stayed as distal as possible on each toe, figuring he could always trim them more aggressively as the gangrene advanced. As it was, he had to prune most of the joints anyway.

Stump poured more Betadine over what was left and Abe lay cotton dressings on top and taped it lightly. The two of them finished washing Gus's thin body, then dressed her in clean clothing and put her on oxygen. Finally they laid her in the eight-foot-long plastic Gamow bag and pumped it tight with a foot pump. Each time Abe peered through the clear face panel, Gus looked a little more at ease.

"That was an ugly job," Stump told Abe. "You did it well."

"Now she has her chance," Abe said.

"I guess," Stump allowed.

"I need to take these rags to the garbage pit," Abe said.

"I'll do it," Stump said.

"It's okay," Abe insisted.

The trench to the pit was still frozen and slick. He dumped the rags on top of other camp refuse, then headed off toward the stone hut. No one had approached the Tomb since the storm. It took Abe ten minutes to plow his way up the little hill.

Inside, the fabric ceiling bulged down under the weight of snow. Abe pried a stone out of the floor and laid the tiny fetus underneath. Then he tamped the stone tight again and left. No one would ever know—not Daniel, not Gus. Conceived here, this one secret, anyway, would stay here.

The sun came hot that day. It blazed away at their cirque, triggering avalanches on distant slopes and melting nearly half the snow in camp. By midday, the trenches between tents had become waterways. Everest glistened to the south, once again untouchable.

Every hour or so Abe peered through the face panel on the Gamow bag to check on Gus. The big plastic tube lay in one corner of the mess tent like a piece of furniture no one wanted to talk about. They ate lunch and dinner in there, but scrupulously avoided mentioning it.

Abe slept beside the Gamow bag that night. He wanted to be close for any emergencies, and it was up to him to know what an emergency looked like. Periodically he opened the chamber to check on Gus's oxygen supply and take her pulse and respiration, then closed it up and pumped it full again. At one point, he woke and the beam of his headlamp caught Daniel's gleaming eyes. He was crouched on the far side of Gus's chamber.

"Can we take her out of there?" he asked Abe. "I want to hold her. Just for a minute."

"If you do that, she'll die," said Abe.

"But it looks like a coffin," Daniel said.

"Not yet it's not."

Daniel placed one hand on the chamber. "Before it's too late," he begged. "One more time."

"Not yet," Abe said.

"I have to tell her something."

Abe knew what Daniel had to tell her, he'd been hearing Daniel whispering to the comatose woman for days now. He loved her. He forgave her. If she loved him, she should forgive him. And she had to fight and live because they had a life to share.

"Maybe later," Abe said.

"Later . . . it might be too late. She needs to know."

"Maybe she hears you."

"But if she doesn't. . . ." His desolation was breathtaking. Daniel was in mourning. No one believed in Gus's capacity to survive anymore. How terrible, thought Abe. One more terrible thing.

"I'm afraid, Abe."

"The trucks will come," Abe said. "They'll take us out of here. Gus will go to a hospital."

"The trucks won't come. I know."

Abe dropped it. "Go to sleep, Daniel. We need to sleep."

The issue of their evacuation was on everybody's minds. In the beginning, they had waited for yaks to move them onto the mountain. Now they waited for trucks to move them away from it. Their helplessness seemed never ending.

The alternative to waiting was also on everybody's minds. Daniel knew the way out of here. They had followed him up the Hill. If need be, they could follow him across one of the high passes into Nepal. But no one favored such extremes. For one thing they knew from Daniel's experience the awful price they were likely to pay for crossing the range in the monsoon. His Lepers' Parade was not something anyone wanted to join, especially after the spectacle of Gus's blackened foot.

The blackness spread. When he ran his fingertips along her ankle and shin, the flesh crackled with subcutaneous crepitus. By evening it was clear Gus would have to lose the leg to her knee or else die. Abe informed the others and asked for volunteers. Never having done this, he had no idea how many people the operation might take. Then he went off by himself to read in his medical books about amputation.

At the appointed hour, people came into the mess tent, even Kelly who still hadn't recovered her vision. They took Gus out of the plastic chamber and laid her on top of the wicker table that had served as their dining table a thousand years ago when times still allowed for good jokes and big plans and long rap sessions. Abe steeled himself. He emptied himself of emotion.

Under Abe's direction, they took up various assignments.

Someone had to look after her oxygen supply. Someone had to take her pulse periodically. Someone had to be in charge of the blood pressure cuff Abe had fitted around her upper thigh for a tourniquet. Someone else had to sterilize their scalpels and knives over a gas stove. The Sherpas were instructed to take care of the kerosene lanterns and keep them bright. And J.J. was charged with finding Daniel if he could, and even if he couldn't to keep the man out of the tent at all costs.

Stump and Abe tied a piece of nine-millimeter climbing rope around Gus's black ankle, then tossed the end over the roof support and hoisted her leg straight into the air. Most of Abe's work was going to be on the underside of the leg. There were no ripsaws or hacksaws in camp, much less a surgical saw, and so the leg had to be separated at the knee joint itself. The front of the knee would be simple, all bone. It was the back of the leg with its hamstring attachments and the veins and, most important, the big popliteal artery, that would require all the unriddling.

Abe made his first cuts several inches down around the calf. Carefully he skinned the flesh over the joint for flaps to later sew over the stump. The bone and muscles stood exposed now in an eight-inch band at her knee. Abe wanted this to take fifteen minutes, tops. Longer than that, and they'd have to loosen the tourniquet. Things could start going wrong when that happened.

He found the big artery and fished enough into the open to clamp it with a hemostat. Below the clamp, he sewed the artery tightly shut with suture, then cut the artery to the lower leg.

"Fifteen minutes," Carlos said.

The words startled Abe. He hadn't realized how silent the tent was. "But I just began," he protested.

They loosened the tourniquet and there was some blood, but not as much as Abe had feared. "Let's keep going," he said. "Pump it tight again."

Next he sliced the hamstrings, parting the meat from its white tendons. "Thirty minutes," Carlos sang out. Abe exhaled. He was going too slowly.

"You're doing fine, Doc," Stump told him. Frost coated the inner wall of the tent, but sweat was gleaming on Stump's face.

Abe took a deep breath and bent to the task again and

again. He cut through vessels and nerves, only stopping long enough to cauterize the ends with heated knife blades. The smell overpowered several people. Abe didn't know who they were, only that they left. He could feel the cold air rush in each time someone went out or came in. He could hear the night wind suck and slap at the tent canvas.

A blast of cold air blew in. "Gus?"

Abe lifted his head. It was Daniel, eyes enormous in the kerosene light. A moment later J.J. wrestled in through the door, bested again. "I tried to stop him," he said.

"For God's sake, get him out," Jorgens said.

"Gus?" Daniel cried.

Her leg was cinched to the roof like an elk carcass. Most of the tissue had been debrided. The bone was white and bare. The sight unhinged J.J. He just stood there.

"Get him out, damn it," Jorgens yelled again.

"Daniel," came a woman's voice. It was Kelly, blind in the corner.

Daniel was weeping.

"Daniel," she said. "Come with me now. Take my hand." She was reaching from the shadows. "Lead me out."

It worked. Daniel took her hand and they left.

Abe returned to the leg. Three hours passed. When he cut the final ligament, Gus's thigh slapped onto the table. The lower leg dangled overhead while Abe raced to finish.

At midnight they laid her back in the chamber and pumped it full of air. For another hour afterward, five of them sat around like tornado victims, speechless.

"Poor Gus," someone finally pronounced. It was Jorgens. "She's climbed her last mountain."

On the next afternoon, beneath another boiling white sun, they heard the sound of an engine gunning through the snow. "The trucks," someone shouted, and everyone poured into the blinding light to see their rescuers. The old herder's two yaks stood nearby, grazing on the last of some dried grass scattered on top of the snow.

In the far distance a vehicle was cutting straight toward them from the north. All they could make out was the glare of its windshield between two brilliant roostertails of slush, a ship of pure light.

"Home! We're going home!" It could have been anyone's voice. It was everyone's sentiment.

They gathered to watch the vehicle approach. Even Li emerged from his tent to join in their excited babble. This was the first Abe had seen him since their retreat from the face.

"Wait a minute," J.J. said, shading his eyes with a piece of cardboard. "That's no truck. It's a Land Cruiser."

"Makes sense," Stump reasoned. "You send in your ice-breaker first. It's got four-wheel drive and good mobility. The rest will come behind."

"Come to papa," Robby shouted at the Land Cruiser.

"Mr. Burns," Jorgens said to Abe. "Would you please ready your patient for transport. Gus goes first." For a moment, anyway, some of the timber returned to his bearing. "I'll see to it that Mr. Li agrees."

Li was glassing the distance with a pair of binoculars, too busy to answer.

Jorgens went right on laying the groundwork. "With the Gamow bag on the back floor, that will leave room for two. Burns goes, obviously. And it's either Kelly with her eyes or Corder or . . ."

Abe was standing close enough to hear when Thomas muttered, "What the hell." Abe glanced at him, but the man was staring off into the north intently.

Slowly, as if disbelieving his own eyes, Li lowered the binoculars. His smile had faded.

"Pete," Stump said. Sober looks were suddenly epidemic. Abe wondered what was wrong.

"I'm going out with Gus," Daniel was insisting. "We'll make room for Kelly. But I go with Gus." There were no two ways about it.

"I don't think so," Stump said.

"It's okay," Jorgens said to Stump. "Corder should go with her."

"No," Stump said.

Jorgens stopped.

"We're not going anywhere."

Engine whining, the Land Cruiser closed on them. It hit a wet drift with an explosion of diamonds and the vehicle slung left, then right. The spray of slush reached for them, sparkling in the sun. The yaks spooked and bounded into the snow, but were too famished to run very far.

The Land Cruiser breasted another drift. Thirty feet from the front of the mess tent, it braked.

"Tell those guys to keep the engine running," Daniel said. "Let's load Gus on."

No one moved. Daniel plucked at Abe's sweater. "Come on, Abe. Let's move. We can make Shekar by dark."

The engine cut off. Abe's heart sank.

"Tell that driver to fire it up. We're taking Gus out of here."

Daniel walked between them as between statuary. The climbers were motionless and silent.

He was the only one among them who had not seen this same Land Cruiser before. He did not recognize the three soldiers who now emerged.

"What are you guys waiting for? Stump, give me a hand."

The soldiers' pea-green uniforms were filthy. They looked ravenous and tired. The two younger soldiers seemed very happy to be here again. The officer did not.

Taking the initiative, Li approached them. He highstepped through the snow. Li and the officer stood by the Land Cruiser and conferred for several minutes, casting nervous glances at the climbers. Jorgens started to join them, but Li held up his open palm to stay in place. After some more words, Li came over to the climbers.

"Not good," he said with mechanical bravado. "Pang La is closed. Earthquake, snow, not good."

"The hell," snarled Daniel. "If they got in, we can get out."

Daniel's ignorance confused Li and he goggled at the climber.

Stump stepped forward. "They didn't get in, Daniel," he said.

"The hell," Daniel said again and he started to wave at the Land Cruiser. Then it sank in. His hand dropped back to his side.

"Where have these men been for the last week?" Jorgens asked.

"Rongbuk Monastery," Li said.

It was simple to see. The soldiers had set off with their prisoner. Then the earthquake had trapped them on this side

of the pass. They had started back toward Base Camp, only to be
caught by deep snows. Without food or sleeping bags, probably
without fire even, they had taken refuge in the ruined monastery for the last seven days. Now they had completed their
fateful circle.

"These men require food," Li said. "They require shelter.
They require medical attention. They require . . ."

Daniel cut him off. "Where's the kid at?" he demanded.

"What you say?" Li was outraged, though Abe perceived
more bluff than anger. The man had to be just as disappointed
as they were at being trapped, but with one significant differ-
ence: He was now trapped with them, and they were the enemy.

"What did they do with the boy?"

"I forbid . . ."

Daniel's black eyes dismissed the L.O. and without another
word he bulled past him toward the Land Cruiser.

"You," Li shouted. "You stay away."

Daniel didn't highstep through the snow, he simply slugged
his shins through it and tore a path. The officer saw Daniel
coming and he ordered the two younger soldiers to intercept
him. But the week without food and warmth had depleted
them. Daniel pushed between them.

The officer barked a high reedy command in Chinese.
When Daniel kept coming, he unsnapped a leather holster cover
at his hip. Abe watched the man perform his motions, and they
seemed perfectly natural. Of course he would draw his gun. It
was as inevitable as Daniel's advance.

With ritual determination, the officer pulled his automatic
pistol and gestured Daniel away. That didn't work, of course.
There was too much forward momentum. But when the officer
extended his arm its full length and aimed the pistol at Daniel's
face, things stopped, or at least paused. Daniel came to a halt.

Abe wanted to shout. This was a mistake. They were climbers and their climb was over. They had finished with this place.
It had finished with them. There was nothing more to do here.
This was unfair. They had tried to free Daniel. Now was his
turn to free them. He should let them go home.

All the climbers could see of Daniel's head was the greasy
mane that hung to his shoulder blades, black against his once
white sweater. Over his shoulder, the officer's face was in full
view, cold eyes in partial eclipse.

For a full minute, the two men remained frozen and con-
templative. Their impasse was physically painful. Abe ached
from it. The heat and whiteness lodged them in their footsteps,
all of them. The silence was immovable, larger than a mountain.

And then something happened. Bored by the human
drama, one of the yaks moved its head away. The small bell
around its neck rang. A single note shivered through the air. It
was enough.

The silence broke. Daniel moved, skirting around the officer. The black pistol stayed upraised, pointing at the climbers
for a moment, then drifting downward. The officer looked
straight through them, and by that Abe knew he had come very
close to pulling the trigger.

Daniel circled to the back of the Land Cruiser. He pressed
the door handle and pulled. Everyone was watching as the
Tibetan boy slowly spilled out upon the snow. Even the soldiers
seemed surprised by the power of their prisoner's appearance.

The boy was tied—with expedition rope—hand and foot.
He was unconscious and dirty in yak skins, exactly as Abe had
first encountered him. He lay in a heap, jaw slack upon the
melting tire tracks.

Daniel bent to him. "He's alive," he said to them all.

"Ah, Jesus," Stump muttered, and it was not a hallelujah
Jesus. Abe felt the same way. So did the others, he heard them.

"Why didn't the bastards just finish him?" someone said.

All the simplicity they had earned, all their separation from
the world outside, was ruined by this boy's reappearance. They
were haunted, not by his death, but by his life. It was a mean
sentiment, Abe knew, but an honest one. No one, from the
climbers to Li to the weary soldiers, wanted to deal with this
anymore. The monk would not let go, though.

Abe started through the snow, following Daniel's track. He
was the doctor and there was suffering and misery lying piled
before him. They all had their roles to play, and this was his.

"Stop," Li commanded. "This Tibetan minority is a criminal of the state. This matter is our internal affair. You have no
right." His words sounded rote, straight from a government
primer.

Abe pressed forward. Li spoke something in Chinese to the
officer, who instructed his two subordinates to step into Abe's
path.

"Mr. Jones and Mr. Corder," Jorgens interjected. "Our liaison officer has stated a position. And I remind you, we are guests in this country."

"So are they," Carlos said. "These Chinese don't belong here any more than we do." His words were bold, but he didn't move to join Abe and Daniel.

"Screw your politics," Thomas retorted. He'd had his fill of this country. "I came to climb. Period."

They were all performing their designated parts, no more or less. Abe could not do any differently than he next did. Like Daniel, he went around the soldiers.

"Repeat," Li declared. "Stop. Now."

Abe knelt beside Daniel in the snow. He put his head close to the boy's mouth. The respiration was delicate and fast. Even before taking the pulse, Abe knew it would be rapid and thready. The boy's hands were bare and blistered with frostbite. His feet would be black. His condition had been terminal enough without getting trussed and frozen and starved for a week. They had just saved his executioner the price of a bullet.

"Untie these ropes," Abe said.

Daniel worked at the ankle knots, Abe at the wrists.

"You," shouted Li. "This criminal is property of the People's Republic of China."

Abe held up a handful of loose rope. "This is not your property. This belongs to us." He was talking about more than the rope. This child's captivity belonged to them, too. Even without the betrayal, they had acted as if silence were enough.

"Let's take him to the mess," Abe said.

"You, stop," Li shouted. He issued a string of words to the officer. Abe and Daniel went ahead.

When they lifted him, the boy weighed less on Abe's end than some of the pack loads he'd carried on the mountain. They had taken scarcely one step when the gunshot barked. The body twitched in Abe's hands. It may have been Abe twitching, he wasn't sure.

A cry of anguish wailed out.

Terrified, Abe spun his head toward the officer. A thin signature of smoke bled from his gun barrel. But the gun was pointing away. It had been more than a warning shot, however.

Ten feet away, the yak that had carried Kelly down from ABC lay crumpled in the snow. A geyser of blood pumped into

the air from its head. The old herder was struggling through
the snow to his animal.

Now the officer pointed his gun at the boy dangling from
Abe and Daniel's hands. This time, Abe thought, it was check-
mate. They couldn't push it any farther. There came a point
when you had to turn away from the summit and admit defeat.

"Damn it," Abe whispered.

"It's not done," Daniel said to him across the limp body.

"It is, Daniel. They'll kill him."

"They'll kill him anyway."

"Daniel, it's done," said Abe. "It is."

"We can't leave him," Daniel protested.

"We must," he said. And with that a faraway darkness
sealed itself off.

"Please," Daniel said.

But before they could lay the boy on the ground or return
him to the Land Cruiser, the standoff ended. A slight snap
sounded from among the climbers, an ounce of noise.

All eyes shifted from the officer and his black gun aimed
point-blank at the body between Abe and Daniel. They saw
Kelly. She was holding a camera.

The Chinese didn't know she was blind. Abe didn't know
if there was even any film in the camera. But she had it pointed
in the right direction. She triggered the shutter again. With a
single finger she stopped the violence.

Carlos was next. He groped for the camera dangling
around his neck and took a picture, then three, then twenty on
autodrive. Robby aimed his own camera.

The officer's face darkened. Li winced. Even if they confis-
cated every camera and strip-searched every climber, there
were still witnesses.

Abe made the most of their pause. He spoke directly to Li.

"I'm a doctor," he said. "I must treat him. It's my responsibility. It's my duty." He left the boy's future unspoken. There
was no future. He could feel the soul ready to spring free of
this poor body.

Li considered this opening. "Yes," he finally declared. "You
must treat the prisoner. It is your responsibility. Your duty.
You are our doctor."

They laid the boy in a sleeping bag beside Gus's red and
yellow chamber. He balanced the benefits of rotating his pa-

tients in the Gamow bag. But Gus seemed to be stabilized inside the pressurized atmosphere, and the monk was unlikely to recover anyway.

The Chinese soldiers set up camp in the stone Tomb a hundred yards from the rest of the tent city. Li had several of the Sherpas move his tent up onto the hillside beside the hut.

Both camps dug in. It suddenly seemed likely they would be trapped here until the end of the monsoon in late August or September. Stump and Thomas butchered the dead yak and hung the meat in a tent. Some of the others took an inventory of their remaining supplies. There was enough food to last until August. Kerosene for the stoves would run out by July.

A day passed with little change. A distinct boundary sprang up between the Western and Chinese camps. Only Krishna crossed it, to deliver hot meals up the little hill to the soldiers and liaison officer.

That night Abe was lying curled and shivering on the frozen earth, breathing his own hot animal breath inside his sleeping bag. He couldn't sleep without drugging himself, and that wasn't an option, not with two unconscious patients bracketing him like bookends.

"Abe," he heard. Abe flipped on his headlamp and Daniel's gaunt face hung in the glare. It gave him a start. *Godforsaken:* The word assembled in his mind. Some of the others had been remarking on Daniel's crash ever since the descent. The amputation seemed to have broken him altogether. They said he slept in some rocks by day. At night you could hear him stalking through the camp, plodding through the snow, ceaseless.

"Aren't you cold, Daniel?"

Frost was guttering from Daniel's filthy beard and he was trembling. But he denied the cold.

"Will she be okay?" Daniel asked.

"Her pulse is stronger. The wound seems clean. I've got her jacked full of every antibiotic we have. We nailed the gangrene cold. There's no reason she can't recover, Daniel." He paused. "Now there's an extra bag in the corner. Why don't you bring it over and get warm and sleep. You can sleep beside her."

"What about him?" Daniel was staring at the Tibetan boy.

"I don't know."

Daniel knelt beside the still body and pulled the corners of the sleeping bag back to see the boy's face. "He deserves better than this," Daniel said. "He deserved better from us."

Certainly the boy had deserved better from them. In a sense they had been the final guardians of his passage from Tibet, and they had failed him. Abe no longer blamed Gus alone. The others did. Daniel had told Kelly about what she had done. At his request, Kelly had told the others. He wanted them to know why she'd done it. He wanted them to blame him, not her. But even blaming her was beside the point.

For the boy had been in danger since the moment he appeared in their camp. He had come to them bleeding and in rags, and they had done nothing but give him a clean expedition T-shirt and a baseball cap and stick Band-Aids on his torture wounds. That and their silence was supposed to have screened this frail, lone child from the Chinese wind. What had they been thinking?

"You're right," Abe said. "He deserved better. But the truth is, I just don't think it's going to get any better for him."

"I've been thinking," Daniel said.

"You should rest," Abe said, trying to head him off.

"We owe him," Daniel declared. "We do. And there's nothing more I can do to help Gus. You'll watch over her. I know you will."

Abe listened to the tent poles creaking under the weight of the wind.

"He can't stay here," Daniel said. "They'll kill him."

"Forget it," Abe said.

"Three days, maybe five," Daniel continued. "From here it's a day to the Chengri La. I know the way. We can meet you guys in Kathmandu."

"No," Abe said.

"No one gets hurt. And we save the day."

"I'm needed here."

"You're not invited." Daniel smiled. His teeth glittered white in the crack within his beard. "It's my deal."

"They would punish us," Abe said. "Gus would suffer."

"No." Daniel didn't really have to deny it. Abe didn't believe the Chinese would punish an injured Westerner, either. The only punishment would be immediate expulsion, and at this juncture that was no punishment at all.

"Do what you want," Abe said. "But do it without him. It's

not his deal either." It was obvious what Daniel was after, but transcendence was no longer an option, if it ever had been. He placed one hand upon the Tibetan boy's chest. He could feel the respiration, the terrible struggle in these bones.

"They'll kill him," Daniel repeated.

"And so would you. He's had enough pain for one lifetime."

And so have you, Abe thought, watching Daniel's face.

Then Daniel did something remarkable. He winked. It wasn't conspiratorial. It wasn't defiant. He just winked. Then he stood up in stages, carefully, slowly, his knee joints cracking.

"Try to get some sleep, Abe," he counseled. "You look like shit."

Abe said, "I didn't want it this way, you know."

"Want?" Daniel said, backing toward the door. The tent flap dropped shut behind him.

The sun cooked camp through another day, rendering the snow in camp to a mere ten inches or so. Gus developed a fever. It alarmed Abe. His medical ignorance left him virtually helpless before her. A fever was like an avalanche, something to be waited out. He waited. The fever abated.

Over dinner, the group discussed sending a small party of climbers on foot over the Pang La. If they could climb a vertical wall to five and a half miles high, surely they could surmount a road pass. They could try to arrange for a helicopter to pick up Gus. At the very least there would be four fewer mouths to feed.

Wasting no time, Stump and Carlos and J.J. and Thomas set off first thing next morning. Those staying behind said good-bye and wished them well. Breakfast was a glum affair.

"I wonder if we'll ever see them again," Robby said. They got their answer sooner than later. Shortly before sunset, J.J. was back, alone and out of breath.

"The trucks are coming," he joyfully trumpeted. "We saw them through the binoculars, five big trucks. They'll get here in the morning."

That was good news for everyone but the Tibetan boy. It meant the pass was open. They were saved from a summer beneath Everest. They could all get on with their lives. They could get on with their forgetting.

The Tibetan boy's breathing grew labored at midnight.
Despite a continuous flow of oxygen and a drip feed of glucose,
he died at two. It was a soft passage. Abe was catnapping. He
was dreaming of horses. When he searched for a pulse, the
boy's carotid was silent. Abe listened through his stethoscope,
but the heart was still.

Abe's light and motion woke Daniel, who had chosen at last
to sleep beside Gus's plastic chamber. "The boy's gone," Abe
told him.

"All he wanted was to get over the mountain," Daniel said.

"We did what we could do."

"You know that's not so," Daniel said.

"It's done now."

"I keep thinking, what if we'd just got him over the mountain?"

"Daniel, it was too late."

"I mean before it got too late. I mean instead of working
the summit. We could have got this one poor bastard out of
hell. We could have, you know."

Abe covered the boy's face. "He got close. As close as we
did."

With Daniel's help, Abe carried the boy outside. The stars
were glittering, no clouds. The North Face of Everest was milky
with the quarter moon's light. They set the body in a small,
tattered equipment tent, and gave it a moment's vigil.

"We can bury him in the morning," Abe said.

"There won't be any burial," Daniel said.

"But we can't just leave him."

"He won't be left, don't worry. He's a reactionary and trai-
tor, remember? The Chinese still have uses for him. They still
need to complete their records. They'll photograph him. Then
they'll sell him back to his family, if he has one."

"No," Abe said. "We'll bury him."

The world rushed in at dawn. Abe opened his eyes to the
distant sound of engines. It was six o'clock. Daniel was already
gone. Abe paused to check on Gus before charging outside to
confirm their rescue.

At the north throat of the valley, five military trucks were
crawling out onto the floor. Slowly they lurched across the ice
and frozen mud. The climbers crawled from their tents. They
waved and shouted hysterically like castaways upon a sinking

raft. Li's soldiers were more dignified, emerging from the Tomb to button their uniform jackets and arrange themselves.

"Let's system it, people," Jorgens yelled to the climbers. "I guarantee they will want to load and leave inside the hour. Let's see some system."

The climbers and Sherpas began rushing around the camp, packing the few items worth salvaging. Abe took the opportunity to root through the folds of his collapsed hospital to see what was left. That was where Li found him.

"Now I will take custody of the prisoner." The sun had not yet reached into the valley, and Li's words appeared as blue smoke.

Abe let go of the torn tentage. He'd meant to avenge the boy by condemning Li and his government's abuses, or perhaps demanding some paperwork, before revealing the death. Instead, Abe just told him.

"He died," Abe said.

"What? What you say?"

"Last night."

"Impossible," Li said. "I give him to you. Now you give him to me."

"He died," Abe repeated very softly.

"No." Li's voice rose. "He is alive when you take him from official custody. He is alive."

It occurred to Abe that Li needed a prisoner to justify himself. He had disobeyed orders from martial authorities to close down the climb. Toward apprehending an escapee, he had, on his own, permitted the expedition to continue. He had then given a group of Westerners custody of the prisoner. Without a living, breathing fugitive to show for his insubordination, there was no telling what the personal consequences might be. Abe felt sorry for him.

"We should bury him here," Abe said.

"Impossible." Daniel had been right. There would be no burial after all. In the distance, the officer was watching Li's upset. "You show me. Now."

Abe led him to the little equipment tent behind the mess tent. They passed people furiously jamming gear into packs and burlap bags.

The first truck was almost upon them. Abe could hear its

big tires crackling over the icy tundra. Standing in the bed of the truck, Carlos and Thomas and Stump were hooting and punching their fists into the sky.

Abe unzipped the door to the equipment tent. At least the boy had died in the middle of the night. He would not have gotten his moment of silence otherwise, not from the celebrants swarming through the camp. He was already forgotten.

That was when he found the body was gone.

The cherry red sleeping bag that Abe had zipped closed around his head was empty.

"He was there," Abe pointed.

Li's eyes were furious. "You make him escape," he said, and bolted from the tent.

It took another hour for them to determine that Daniel was missing from camp. Not without good reason, the Chinese refused to believe Abe's story. The climbers didn't buy it either. It made no sense that Daniel would lead a corpse to freedom.

Ten o'clock came, with no resolution.

Abe's concern was for Gus. She needed medical attention as quickly as possible, but the Chinese showed no hurry to depart. Already half the morning was gone. They could have been partway up the Pang La by now, that much closer to Kathmandu and home.

Jorgens and Thomas were almost as outraged as the Chinese by the escape attempt. They had suffered Daniel's conduct for months on end, and this latest stunt was going to cost them. Li threatened to haul them all off to Lhasa for an inquiry. He had declared that Jorgens's permit for another attempt at the Kore Wall next year was already a dead issue.

"Screw Corder," Thomas growled. "He ditched us."

"The man deserted," Jorgens agreed. "You don't save deserters. You arrest them. Or shoot them."

"We have to find him," Abe argued. "He'll die out there."

"He laid a death sentence on himself a long time ago," Thomas said. "And now he's taken that kid down with him."

"The boy died last night," Abe said. He'd already told them. Only Kelly believed it, though.

"He's made it over the passes before," Stump said, but that was just to counter the harshness.

Even the climbers who at first cheered Daniel's bid to free

the boy grew disgruntled. Earthquakes and slides had closed the Pang La once, they could close it again. Daniel had gambled with their well-being.

At noon Li summoned Abe to the Tomb. The stone hut was circled by trucks and looked formidable. Li was sitting inside the hut with the officer plus several men who had arrived with the convoy. Five of the six wore military uniforms.

Abe knew what they would want.

"Mr. Corder is taking the prisoner to cross our international border." Li was almost too angry to speak. "We have found footprints. You must lead our soldiers to find him."

"I have a very sick patient," Abe said. "She needs to go to a hospital."

"The Chinese government is humanitarian," Li reminded Abe.

"Then send Gus out."

"This is a serious matter," Li said. "Internal affairs of the Chinese people, you see."

"Help Gus," Abe said. "And I will help you."

Li reversed the proposal. "Help us," he said. "Then we will help you."

Abe said, "All right." To save Gus, he had to risk sacrificing Daniel. That seemed to be how it was written.

Though Thomas volunteered to track Daniel all the way to hell for them, the Chinese would only take Abe to guide the patrol. They trusted him because he had proved himself untrustworthy. They preferred to use the enemy they knew.

Abe set out at the head of the soldiers. There were six of them, including Li. Two had rifles.

The footprints—amorphous in the sunny slush—led south up the trail to Everest. At the giant stone arrow where the expedition had gone right, Abe turned left. He had never been this way but knew where the tracks would lead, toward the Chengri La, out from this utopia.

The high altitude punished the soldiers and Li. Abe watched their gasping and nausea with detachment. He considered leading them on a wild goose chase up a subsidiary valley, but there was no need to. If they actually caught up with Daniel, they would simply find the truth. Their fugitive was dead.

Abe stayed alert for places where Daniel might have buried the body beside the trail. He was convinced Daniel was alone by this point. For all he knew, Daniel had tucked the body under some rocks back at camp and then dived uptrail to mislead them. One thing was certain. Presented with the corpse, the Chinese would cancel this hunt and they could all leave the mountain for good. Mile after mile, there was no body. The tracks led on, huge footprints deformed by the sun.

"We should return to camp now," Abe said at three o'clock.

The sun had warmed the air and beautiful veils of white spindrift curled on the mountainside. Underfoot the glacier groaned and snapped. Deep underneath rocks exploded into powder. On either side of the trail, little sunballs rolled down the banks.

"No," Li said. "Walk more. More slowly."

Shortly afterward, two of the soldiers became very ill. They sat on rocks, holding their heads, with vomit on their pants and boots. The officer shouted at them, then sent them back to camp.

Li and the remaining soldiers grew more and more uncoordinated. Hopping across a glacier stream, one fell into the water. Farther on, another twisted his knee. It was painful to see them groping onward. Each wore the grimacing mask of altitude sickness. Abe wondered if Daniel had meant to punish the Chinese so badly. Probably not, he decided. This wasn't about revenge.

Abe tried again at four o'clock. "We have to go down."

Li was weaving in place. Everybody else was sitting. "They will escape," he said.

Abe didn't argue. They could believe what they wanted.

Li consulted the others. He came over to Abe and pointed at a ruddy young soldier. "You go more with this soldier," he told Abe. "We will go down now. You have the responsibility."

The Chinese boy, perhaps eighteen years old, climbed to his feet with an automatic rifle slung across his back. He smiled at Abe with the solidarity of top athletes, and Abe nodded to him with faraway recognition. He had been roped to gung ho kids like this on a hundred different mountains. Once upon a time he had been this boy. Under different circumstances, they might have been heading off for the summit together. Abe started up with the soldier in tow.

He felt strong and lithe and fast, and was grateful for the hair on his face and hanging down over his eyes. They had reached 20,000 feet, but the air felt rich and smooth to him. He bounded from stone to stone, almost playful. I belong here, Abe thought with surprise. Not so long ago, he had been convinced this wasteland was unfit for any animal.

The Chinese boy was soon struggling for breath, but Abe didn't slow down. He wanted to exhaust the boy. If possible, he wanted to make him ill. Abe knew it was imperative that he return with the soldier boy. It was one thing to supposedly abet a supposed escape attempt. It would be an altogether different issue if Abe showed up in camp alone. Regardless of whether the soldier had fallen off a cliff or slipped into a crevasse or even decided to defect to Nepal, Li and the officer would cry foul. The entire expedition would suffer then, Gus worst of all. Abe gave the soldier some water and received some words he took to be thanks.

The irony was that only by pursuing Daniel faster could Abe hope to slow the pursuit. The faster they went, the more likely he could wear this boy down. But no matter how fast they went, the soldier didn't sicken or quit. Somehow he kept up.

At the end of another half-hour, Abe tapped his watch face and pointed at the sinking sun. He gestured downward. As it was, they would be descending to camp in darkness, probably hampered by the rest of the sick and tired patrol. He had a single headlamp and no bivouac gear.

The young soldier chewed at his lower lip, trying to decide. Their valley had plunged into twilight. The air turned cold and as blue as cornflowers. Abe took off his glacier glasses and replaced them with his spare wirerims. Underfoot, the wet snow was already crystallizing.

Up ahead, a butt of green ice formed yet another twist in the trail. Abe could just make out a cast of penitentes at the turn, their sharp icy spires tilted toward the summit. Five minutes more and they turned the corner to come upon a high, wide glacial basin. They had entered what Robby, the photographer, called the magic hour, that space before sunset when the light painted every shape with color.

The basin unfolded like vast, iridescent wings, as if a gigantic angel had quickfrozen in flight and crashed here between two mountains. The sides of the basin swept upward in long, simple curves, resting to the right upon the steep slopes of Everest and to the left upon some darker nameless satellite peak. Not much higher from where Abe and the soldier now stood, the wings joined at their neck. The basin pinched together forming a ridge. That was the passageway. They were looking at the Chengri La.

There, in a wildfire of gold and red alpenglow, they found Daniel.

He was not alone. The monk was strapped to his back with climbing rope. When Daniel turned to look at them—the soldier had shouted something in Chinese—the monk's head turned with him, lifelike, grinning.

The fugitives were very close, perhaps a hundred yards ahead, but it might as well have been a hundred miles. The snowy trail was blown to bits on this open expanse and the plateau was pure wind-polished ice.

Daniel turned back to his trek. He had crampons, of course. He had been here before and knew what was needed. His progress was slow, hobbled by the weight on his back and the pain in his joints. Very old men moved this way, one foot after the other, stirring up the dust of old dreams.

The soldier boy paced back and forth along the edge of the icy plateau. He shouted Chinese words at Daniel without effect. Then, like an overeager hound, the young soldier raced off to apprehend his prey.

He got three steps and promptly slipped, hitting the glassy ice hard. Though it looked level, the ice had a slight pitch to it and the soldier began sliding. He tried to scramble back to his feet, but dropped his rifle, then dove for it. His slide accelerated.

Eventually, hundreds of yards lower, perhaps a mile down the valley, the soldier would pick up enough speed to brain himself against a jutting rock. If that would have finished their problem, Abe might have let the bewildered, scrabbling soldier disappear down the sheet of ice.

The boy scraped and clawed at the ice, increasingly desperate. Abe jogged along beside the ice on a bank of glacial pebbles and sand. "Throw down your gun," he yelled.

"Huk," the boy grunted. He held on to the rifle.

After another minute, Abe saw his chance. A bank of pebbles was reaching out onto the glistening ice like a jetty. Beyond that point, the glacier turned wide and deep and the soldier would vanish into the abyss. Abe galloped out onto the jetty.

Throwing himself partway onto the ice, he stretched long

and snatched a handful of the boy's quilted pantleg. He hauled the soldier back to safety.

Instantly the soldier scampered off, back up the pebble bank to where he'd fallen. Daniel was not much farther off now, but it was clear to the soldier he didn't have a chance of physically apprehending the climber and the monk. He would have to force their surrender. Or end their escape.

Even before the soldier unslung his rifle, Abe knew he was going to use it.

"Daniel," Abe yelled. His voice ricocheted across the ice. "Just show him the body."

Daniel twisted at the waist and the monk's head bobbed alertly. "We're going to make it just fine," Daniel said. His words bounced off the glass. "I know the way now."

A gust of wind tugged curtains of rose light between them. Then the curtains receded. Daniel hefted his burden. The monk seemed to look around.

"He has a gun," Abe warned. "Just show him the dead."

"He wants a little peace," Daniel said. "It's not so much higher, really. I'll bury him where he can rest out there. I have a knife." A sky burial, Abe realized. Daniel was going to give the monk up to the birds and the wind.

"Daniel," Abe yelled. But he had nothing more to say. There was no more warning to offer nor forgiveness to give and take nor times to speak of. They'd said it all.

"Tell Gus to meet me at the . . ." But the wind swept his destination away. Curtains of spindrift bloomed like moving wheat, then disintegrated, then rose again.

Daniel plodded on, storming the vapors. The crystalline basin swept upward. Where the pass crested, snow dervishes spun and raced about, pierced by the crimson sunlight. Daniel climbed into their midst and the monk's flapping arms seemed to wave the dervishes to one side. If Daniel could just gain the next hundred yards, Abe saw, he would be looking out into Nepal.

A precise metal clatter sounded. Abe turned. The soldier had chambered a round. He was lying on his belly and his rifle was balanced on a rock. He was taking careful aim.

Daniel's crampons flashed in the light. It was getting harder to see as they mounted the swell. From Abe's stance, it looked as though the monk were pointing out new routes on the North

Face above. Indeed, the monk and the climber seemed to have merged into one.

"No," Abe said to the soldier. "Don't." He was too far away to dive at the boy. Besides, it was far too late for heroics.

The bullet cracked. The back of the monk's yakskin jacket twitched. It could almost have been a puff of breeze: The soldier had aimed well. His bullet struck the monk high between the shoulder blades, a killing shot.

Daniel never quit moving. Waves of spindrift surged across the ice. The upper mountain was burning bright now. The light seemed to be spawning deep inside the towering walls.

The soldier chambered a second round. He nestled his cheek against the rifle stock.

"Please," Abe begged the soldier. The boy lifted his face from the rifle and looked at Abe. They didn't have a word in common.

"Please," Abe repeated. Somehow he needed to ask this young man if a single death more could ever begin to fill the vastness around them.

But they had no words in common. Abe lifted his hands in entreaty. He watched the boy watch him.

For whatever reason, the boy changed his mind. He lifted the barrel of his rifle up and away, off toward Everest. He pulled the trigger to empty the rifle. The shot banged hard. It echoed in sharp cracks across the basin.

Abe lowered his hands. The boy got to his feet.

That was when the third and final crack resounded.

Abe ducked because it was so loud and crashed through the entire basin. Both he and the soldier whirled around to see who had followed them up and what huge weapon they had fired. But downvalley the shadows were empty. There was no one there. The soldier's face mirrored Abe's confusion. Then Abe thought to look up.

From high upon the summit band, a vast white rose blossomed. It seemed a mile wide up there, absolutely beautiful. The soldier uttered his astonishment. Head craned back, mouth open, he was mesmerized by the thing. Ever so slowly the great white flower lost its petals and the snow came tumbling down.

"Daniel," Abe bellowed. But Daniel was already looking up at the avalanche. The mountain wall funneled directly into this basin. It would strike Daniel first, then flood the basin.

The sound of thunder reached them. Abe pulled the soldier by one arm, dragging him from his trance. He shoved the boy toward the trail and away from the basin's expanse. They could never hope to outrun the beast. But with luck they could turn the corner of the ridgeline and get down the valley far enough to dodge the slide's direct onslaught.

The soldier dropped his gun. Instinctively, he stopped to grope for it, but Abe pushed him on. They were close to the ridgeline. He looked up.

The avalanche had consumed the entire mountain nearly to its root now. Nothing showed but the front curtain of snow and, behind it, a tempest of billowing whiteness. The thunder encased them. It rocked and deafened them.

Abe threw one final desperate glance up the pass, and there he discovered Daniel in search of him. Daniel knew better than to run. He looked calm up there, with only one thing on his mind, this glance from Abe.

And so it was. The last thing Abe saw of Daniel was the same thing Daniel saw of him, two upraised arms, hands reaching.